MODERN GREEK WRITERS

Iconostasis of Anonymous Saints

The translation costs of this book have been covered
by the Greek Ministry of Culture

Typeset in Greece
by Photokyttaro Ltd.
14, Armodiou St., Athens 105 52
Tel. 32.44.111
and printed by
M. Monteverdis & P. Alexopoulos
Metamorphosis, Athens
For
Kedros Publishers, S.A.,
3, G. Gennadiou St., Athens 106 78,
Tel. 38.09.712 – Fax 38.31.981
June 1996
2ηd reprind July 1998
Title in Greek: Iconostasio Anonymon Aghion
Cover photo: Kostas Fines
Cover design by Dimitris Kalokyris

© *1996 by Kedros Publishers, S.A.*
Athens, Greece

ISBN 960-04-1202-2

YANNIS RITSOS

Iconostasis of Anonymous Saints

Ariostos the Observant Recounts Moments of His Life and Sleep
Such Strange Things
With a Nudge of the Elbow

Translation
AMY MIMS

KEDROS

Iconostasis of Anonymous Saints is a general title for a series of nine books. The first three are included in this volume. All nine titles are as follows:

Book One:	*Ariostos the Observant Recounts Moments of His Life and Sleep*
Book Two:	*Such Strange Things*
Book Three:	*With a Nudge of the Elbow*
Book Four:	*Maybe So*
Book Five:	*The Old Man with the Kites*
Book Six:	*Not for You Only*
Book Seven:	*Sealed with a Smile*
Book Eight:	*Less and Less Questions*
Book Nine:	*Ariostos Refuses to Become a Saint*

Acknowledgments

Preliminary work on the translation was done at the British Centre for Literary Translation, with special thanks to Dr. Terry Hale and Ms. L. Anagnostopoulou-Banaka.

NOTES

The reader will find certain essential notes at the back of the book.

BOOK ONE

*Ariostos the Observant
Recounts Moments of His Life and Sleep*

Waking up

I'm Ariostos. That's how I've christened myself. I don't know how and why I chose this name. Now I see that by one small anagram – in other words, by transposing one of the omikrons – I become *Aóristos*.* This pleases me. I'm in the habit of folding my newspaper in four sections, so it fits into the inner pocket of my jacket. Nobody realises I have a newspaper there. But *I* know and it makes me smile. In the evening, I try to solve a crossword puzzle. Never manage to though. I leave my pencil and smudged newspaper on the table and fall asleep, with some difficulty. Next morning, I am awakened by a square sun, which is like the back of a porter lugging a huge wooden crate to our house. He throws it noisily on the floor and mutters something through his teeth about its being sent from Uruguay or Paraguay or Paranoiay. I feel slightly disturbed, embarrassed and weak. I don't know what can be inside. Perhaps that fake crown made of shiny gold paper and an army tunic with lots of buttons. Perhaps some glasses wrapped in newspapers and packed in straw. I don't know. Do you think an uncle of mine has died and made me his sole

---

* "Aóristos" in Greek means indefinite or vague.

heir? But how do you go about arranging the funeral announcements? Why bother to look? What's the good of legacies anyway? I flap my arms to make sure I'm awake. Get to my feet. Approach table. Place letter in envelope. This way, I think, I'll find my own line of continuity. How old my slippers are. I douse my head in plenty of water.

Innocent

I remember when flowers climb a staircase, they shake their heads back and forth, like birds bathing in a small water-basin in a courtyard. I sense this with great clarity and ease. Like the time they were measuring the next-door plot of land, I felt quite certain they would build a house with a garden and the garden would have iron railings exactly opposite the ramshackle house; there on the balcony, three blankets were spread (one of them yellow), which became so hot that tufts of wool fell out and the nettles down below were full of fluff. I even knew how the honeysuckle would twist around the wrought-iron gate. Like a servant girl, so to speak, with a green apron, climbing up the winding iron staircase at the back of a four-storey house. I have my secrets too and smile about the naive persons who suspect nothing. Today in Constitution Square, for example, I noticed somebody with his right ear slightly eaten away. This made a huge impression on me. Imagine that, said I. Do you think a rat ate his ear, while he was asleep in the pantry, with his mouth wide open – after the burglary? I went up to some policemen and pointed the man out to them. But they didn't have a clue. Then, one at a time, I pulled various scraps of paper out of my pockets, with

my notes scribbled on them, also one or two toothpicks,
a pack of cigarettes, keys to the cupboard, to the house,
to the drawers, to the suitcase – actually, I forgot to
answer my friend's letter. Over there, there must be
plenty of greenery and it won't be necessary to suffer a
whole hour before you wake up, and here you are. Aha.
What's this? Instead of my newspaper, something
smooth and soft as velvet. A wallet with the gold initial
of Prince Hopekeio. Who stuck this in my pocket? I
mean to throw it out cautiously next to that lamp-post.
But what if they see me? I'd better hold on to it. Who
knows what it can possibly contain? Perhaps photographs at the spa. Then, a hand lands on my shoulder.
We are moving among houses and more houses, and the
houses are absolutely white. My eyes sting from the
whiteness. I keep silent. Thinking of that slit ear and
the houses. Never have the houses been so white and
their interiors so dark with hot and dusty furniture.
Well now, why is this hand gripping me? Since it knows
– it must know – I'm not the one; and since it knows I
will never ever slip away?

Passage

The other day I asked a man with a grindstone to sharpen my knife. Now that does it. I can cut my bread so easily and pleasantly, it's as though I'm cutting off a head. One, two, five slices. My appetite is whetted. Five heads, ten. My hands feel blood-stained. I am proud. I think I'll have my portrait painted with my fingers spread out on my knees – yes, spread out just as the photographer spreads the hands of newly-weds from the province, there, at the corner near the Municipal Theatre. Just so the blood will show. I'll wear patent-leather boots. And in the midst of all those severed heads, I'll look like a fierce, but handsome African hunter surrounded by the carcasses of the lions and tigers he has killed. But I'll be extremely tolerant and modest. I'll call to a child and buy him some candy. As a matter of fact, I'll hand him a head to play ball with. After this, I'll visit the neighbourhood of Kesarianí and hand out free tickets for the performance of a juggler, who will play with ten rubber balls and at the same time, dance the Charleston. How beautiful the faces of the poor are when they're watching some extraordinary game with an anxious smile. Even more so, when they laugh. At such times I can forgive even the Director of my office, who summoned me the other day to lecture me on my inexcuseable carelessness (so he said) in mixing up various documents; also, because once when I was in pain from a callous, I took off one of my shoes under the desk, and because once, I stuck a big chrysanthemum in my lapel. In the process of chiding me, he charily pushed his glove (lying there on the brightly polished black desk) and flung it on the floor to test me. The glove must have been lined with the skin of an animal – perhaps lamb or rabbit-fur; not lion-skin. And naturally, I was supposed to pick it up and hand it back to him politely. But no. That could never be. Just at this point, a regular right-angled triangle was formed out of sharp, glittering metal and its three angles were the Director's gaze, the glove and my own gaze. Henceforth, our conversation continued inside this triangle and I was perfectly aware of what tossing the glove meant for rivals. I was given the privilege of choosing the weapons. My heavens, what weapons. Here, a pile of swords. Further on, a pile of pistols. How do you hold them? How cold the metal is. Who will be my witnesses when we find ourselves in some dry deserted place full of yellow weeds, out beyond Goudhi? I can see the muzzle opposite me, growing out of bounds, till it turns into a cavern filled with magnetic force, about to swallow me up. Now I burrow my way inside, crawling through the muzzle on my belly. I am aware that only my feet are still outside, shaking in the air. My head hits something which is sticking out. A little "click" is heard and then, nothing. Hushed discussions above me. The noise of a carriage rolling along on anonymous ground. The clop-clopping of the horses' hooves on the stones. How calm everything is. And the light, which is lost inside its own self. And I am totally inside myself, like a person returning home after an exhausting journey. Slowly I open my eyelids. Next to me, there's a lady in a covered carriage with the curtains drawn. Her hand is on my brow. A delicate hand full of silence. In a voice I cannot hear, I ask: "Is it raining?" An inaudible voice answers: "The sun has just come out. Just come out. Go to sleep." I close my eyes again and listen to the distant rattling of the carriage, like the buzzing of a fly against the window-panes of an afternoon room, where a child is convalescing.

Snapshot

For a moment, only for a moment, I stare silence straight in the eye. Afterwards, I close my eyes and go walking among human beings. Stumbling against their elbows, even though I fumble my way close to the walls. Elbows are harder than the corners of a table in the dark, when you get up at night, because you're thirsty, and the kitchen has moved towards an unfamiliar direction. A child points his finger at me. "Here comes the blind man," he cries. I pretend not to understand. In haste, I halt a man who is selling lottery-tickets and choose a ticket with a number I like. "Maybe you know when they'll announce the results?" I ask. He grabs my money and turns his back on me, without giving me my change. Then, I realise I've forgotten to close my eyes. So I close them.

Far down the road

Perhaps the clouds are to blame for my bad mood today. Anyway, I'm not really worried about learning what's to blame. I strike my hands against each other, as though flicking off bread-crumbs and say: "Whatever it may be, so be it." When I board the tram, there are lots of people. Luckily, someone gets up and I'm just in time to find a seat near the window. Now I intend to avoid paying the fare. In such a crowd, the conductor will never notice me. I'll stare out the windows in a nonchalant manner, so he'll think I've paid for a ticket. No, no. Everyone plays the same trick. He'll realise what I'm up to. So I'd better look at him in a natural, straightforward way. But my eyes can't stand the strong glare from the sun. I start fiddling with a small chain. "Your ticket, Mister," says the conductor. I give him a disapproving, rather angry look, as much as to say: "Do you want a second ticket?" But he isn't at all convinced by my expression. He persists. Then I point to a gentleman wearing a black tie. "The gentleman paid for mine," say I. That imbecile becomes flustered and protests: "But I don't even know this man," says he. The conductor clangs the bell three times. The tram stops. They make me get off. Behind me, I feel the uproar of thousands of gazes crowding in on my back, as though I've turned into a piece of magnetic iron, attracting a whole pile of pins and needles. But I hardly feel any prickling sensation. I go straight to the first kiosk and buy three cheap "roll-up" cigarettes. As I watch the tram go on its way, I light one. My cigarette changes into a long slender cane, which I twirl through my fingers with ease and unexpected dexterity. Then I walk on. And all of a sudden, I sense that my shoes have grown inordinately large and are pointing outwards. Far down the road, I discern a circle of light, which becomes smaller and smaller until it closes, as it reveals the shrinking silhouette of Charlie Chaplin, who disappears in the distance, walking with his back to me.

Ordeal

I am sitting outside the Royal Gardens, staring at the strollers. Staring them straight in the eye, till they are forced to lower their gaze. Even this Colonel with the boots and this lad who is selling sesame-buns. My eyes feel as dry as two small coffee-cups which have just been wiped. At some point, the lids grow heavy and then, I make a move as though to prop them up with a broken toothpick, or as though I'm wearing a monocle. Finally, I get tired and begin staring at the feet of the passers-by. I count their footsteps. One, two, ten, ninety-three. Strange. When they step on one foot, they raise their other foot, as though pondering the weight of their shoe in the air. I also attempt to walk in this same plain, casual way, but don't manage to. For *I* am aware that they are weighing their shoes in this way. If they were aware of it too, maybe they wouldn't walk like this. At the very most, they'd go to the grocer's, put their shoes on the scale, learn the weight once and for good and then, forget about the shoes, the weighing and the weight, and go on walking perfectly well, as though they were barefoot or had no feet at all. But they never stop to think that their shoes are wearing out in the meantime and the weight keeps changing. The inner layers get full of holes; water and mud seep in; their feet freeze. Between the toes, black clots of dirt coagulate. With the fingers of their right hand, they rub these clots before going to sleep and close their eyes. "You fools," I say. Somebody nudges me angrily. "Me?" I ask. "Yes, you," he answers. "I'm Ariostos," I tell him. And I'm sure he doesn't understand that I am Ariostos. Then I can hear my eyelids dropping like the lid of a trunk on top of heaps of useless things: an old waistcoat of Father's full of stripes, a Carnival fez, a lace dress which is torn, a half-finished yellow sock with the stitches still on the knitting needles. The person doesn't understand anything. But he did see me lower my eyes. In order to forget, I take the needles out of the sock and rip out all the stitches, leaving the crooked yellow thread dragging along behind me. The person glances down now, careful not to step on it.

Dispositions

The window looks out on the garden. Today two winter roses have budded. For some time now, I've been meaning to prune this rosebush and collect some cigarette-butts to scatter on its roots. Suddenly, the light has become cool and pink, like the frocks of young girls running through the meadows in the summertime. Under their armpits, a perspiration stain is made – a broad stain. In that place, the material turns yellow and stiff like a withered leaf from a plane tree. This ruins my mood. In front of me, I catch sight of my boss from the office. I feel angry and pick up a stone to throw right at his face. This stone is the brick my mother used to heat whenever I had a stomach-ache. So this is how I'll throw it at him. His whole mug will turn black and blue. He smiles, just looks at me and smiles. "You'll never throw it," says he. I turn red, all over. I know that when I blush, lots of freckles appear on my face, from the pimples I used to have as a boy. This cuts down my anger. Then I become twice as angry. "I am *so* going to throw it at you," I tell him. "I am *so* going to throw it at you," he repeats, mimicking my voice. The stone drops out of my hands. He smiles. I grab the gardener's shears and start pruning the rosebush. Then I put on my hat and leave.

But I'm not sure whether I've locked the door. So I go back. It *is* locked. Glancing at my key, I think to myself that the paving-stones are not regular. Not at all regular.

Replacements

Mother had a wicker basket filled with balls of thread, thimbles, needles, buttons, hooks, buckles. This was a genuine small garden, where Mother's dreams could roam. A blue thread opened a tiny gate to the sky. Atop a green thread, treading like tightrope walkers, leaves and parakeets, young peacocks and a bird with a red umbrella and an inexplicable afternoon sadness paraded with successive little leaps, until they reached Mother's round embroidery frame of taut satin. Every day I removed a piece from the trees, the light, the air and added it to Mother's embroidery. Till little by little, a mystical exchange took place between our home and the open air. Our furniture gave way to birds, founts, bushes. Gradually, the outdoor area was emptied of its greenness and filled with couches, cupboards, mirrors and curtains. Apparently, Father didn't even notice the change, for he continued to flick his cigarette-ashes into a lily – in other words, precisely where the ashtray used to be. Mother and I used to steal a glance at each other and nod our heads with a smile. Then I began to smoke too, in an attempt to hide my eyes behind the smoke. Years later, a boy with a similar basket was selling cherries. Immediately I was full of love. "Mother's basket," I told him. He looked at me, took out two cherries and handed them to me. Mother is no longer here for us to nod our heads in unison, with a smile. "Thanks," I said to him and gave him two ha'pennies. "That was a gift from me," he retorted. "I don't want payment." And he threw the pennies at my feet. I picked them up. In my left hand, I am still holding the cherries. I think now I'll plant the pips inside two thimbles in Mother's basket. And surely, two small cherry-trees will grow in the place where her hands used to embroider. And they'll have the same benevolently tolerant expression she had. "Thank you," I said to him once more. For I loved him very much and could not feel angry.

One evening

Tonight I feel cold. Folding my arms under my armpits, I calculate the day's expenses. Arrange the words I spoke this morning, noon and early evening. My previous gestures I place like freshly ironed napkins far back in the drawer. Everything is good, correct, empty. I read my thoughts out loud, one by one, as though from a badly printed menu. Nothing worthwhile. You see, I'm also just getting over my sickness. But I still insist on selecting something beyond these commonplace foods. I'll need some kind of flavour when I get back home. Particularly at the moment I unlock my door, I must feel happy about something or, at least, justified. For this is the hardest moment for me, the very worst of all, when I hang my hat on the hallway rack. Like a spider, this rack collects my hat, my cane, my jacket, my braces, and delivers me denuded to the cross-examining mirror, covered in dust and unshaven. Until I even imagine that one morning I'll get up and find nothing on the rack to wear. The spider will have devoured everything, just as it devours flies, leaving behind only the flimsy paper shape of their empty carcass. Then, of course, I'll have to stay in my room for ever, wrapped up in old newspapers. I stare at the waiter and ask: "Isn't there anything else except what's listed on the menu?" "No, Mister," he answers. "Ariostos," I add. "No, Mr. Ariostos," says he. "What a pity," say I, getting up to go. But just at this point, I catch sight of something gleaming in his eyes like the backbone of a fish. He must surely have a pistol in his back pocket. Which is why he's thrown such a long napkin over his shoulder. So I sit back down on the chair. "Eh, in that case, bring me whatever you like," I tell him, as I gaze at the glass door swinging open and shut, distributing the reflection of the electric lights first to the one wall, then to the other. How distressing for a lady when she's obliged to loosen her corset after a soirée. The only thing she's left with is a sparkle from all sorts of glasses. And what about the girls who perspire and their powder cakes on their forehead, while the boys chat all by themselves in quite another corner. By the time the waiter comes back, I'll have made my getaway. He'll set my plate on the table and wait, thinking I've gone to the toilet. The food will get ice-cold. It's chilly weather. The street is deserted and the trains make all the more noise – but a rather forlorn noise, tiptoeing along with the smoke and the dust raised by the policemen's motorcycles that afternoon. I peek through the opening between the houses. High up there, a tiny star is coughing, all shrivelled up next to a cloud. I think of the children, who weren't given their favourite toy from the Christmas tree. Why so much repentance in the air, prior to the sin?

Illicit springtime

Summer's on its way. This is perfectly clear from the peculiar noise made by the trams. The conductors wear their caps at a slightly more tilted angle. The shoeblacks and all the roving pedlars train their voices every morning, now and then, adding something like a red bead. People's clothes smell of resin and the girls have curlier hair. Large posters on the walls announce the opening of the open-air cinemas. In the evening, I sit on a small bench and meditate under the trees. Reflecting on certain curious, extremely risky dice-games and the gamblers' knees under the table. How come everyone is a loser? Even the young people. Above all, the young people. Across the way, the Museum is all lit up. Through a large window, the stone head of Zeus appears without a beard. Do you suppose there's a barbershop for statues? Maybe at the back of the yard behind the piles of excavated earth and the wooden shacks. I wonder what the sightseers are doing in the Museum at such a late hour. I approach. Climb the marble stairs. They're taking photos of the statues, with magnesium light. Down the corridor, I notice my boss from the office, ensconced in a leather armchair. Strange. What's he doing here? He's smiling again. Barely moving his little finger, he beckons to me. I just stand there and greet him. He sticks a scrap of paper in my hand. Under the electric light-bulb I read: "Those who fear brothels pay visits to Museums." I become rabid. Right in front of him, I unbutton my trousers and piss between the limbs of Hermes. Our genitals touch. I get excited. A spasm. Then another spasm. And the sudden flash of magnesium. I start to run. Race down the staircase. Slip into the shade of the little park. And this sensation that my face and hands are full of soapy lather – didn't I rinse myself after the shave? It's damp. I shiver. Tomorrow, all the newspapers will have my photograph with Hermes in such a pose. And that touch of summer. I straighten my clothes and look up at the sky. Small yellow daisies are tossing about in the air. I whisper the Lord's Prayer to myself. The trees shield me. Well then, is it so sweet to die? Nevertheless, I should have wiped off the razor. It's going to rust.

Circumscribing a stone

Secret encounter with a stone. Face of the stone is deep, nude, abandoned to this – whatsoever – point of indfference. Calmly, without resistance, I have a premonition of death. The stone imposes a positive silence on me, like all things which do not make humble efforts to justify themselves, like all those dignified passive things, which do not at all costs seek a purpose. Circumscribing this stone I concentrate, like eyebrows circumscribing a thought. I sense this and once again begin to be besieged by time. I twist and turn, lying in wait near the stone like a rat near its trap. Then I hear the voice of the newspaper-vendor out on the street and leap up. A door closes suddenly in front of me, before I manage to see the hall with the speechless guests and the big grand piano. Then, I pay particular attention to the objects in my own room – above all, the table, for it has preserved such a simple square certainty. I speak their names one by one, tenderly, almost emotionally. Chair, bed, ashtray, glass. I tell them my own name as well, as though entrusting something terribly important to them. "Ariostos," I say. But I can see my shadow gesticulating on the wall, as though it is taking a fencing-lesson. Then, once again, I try to come to a standstill withir the meaning of the stone. In the opposite house, I notice a noise made by the knives and forks. What time is it? They must be eating, of course. I am aware of the movement of a hand lifting a small silver spoon to a girl's mouth. Stewed prunes, I say to myself. Yes, stewed prunes. The pretty mouth spits the moist brown pips onto the plate. There is a seascape hanging on the wall. I smile and appear content, although I know I have deceived a secret mirror, the stone and time.

Evening-star

To whom does the first evening-star smile, as it dangles solitary in space? Perhaps to me? Or is it the torch of a sad angel falling on all the wayfarers' faces, one by one, in search of the faithful? It feels like a cool, little spotlight on my face. I don't lower my eyes. Or blush. I move on in that same direction. The road is peaceful. I am alone. I know that my whole face is glowing. Someone points me out to two other men and to a woman. "Look how he emits light, like a lantern," says he, approaching me. "Why are you a-glow?" he asks. I lift my finger to show him the star. But the star has vanished. And now, he and the other two men and the woman will think I've painted my face with that cheap gold paint used for frames and suspended lamps and cast-iron beds. Under the dining-room lamp, on the table laid there, were a plate of apples and an illustrated book.

A young flower-vendor

From time to time, I feel I've become a little girl in a black dress, who must sell her basketful of tiny bunches of jasmine intertwined with pine-needles. Nobody shows any respect to this girl. She is shoved into the corridors of restaurants. The waiters chide her; the customers dismiss her; the owner of the restaurant bawls her out. She doesn't say a word as she leaves her jasmines on each table, where sweat-stained, hungry people bend over their plates, as though they have no eyes or are angry about something, and just go on chewing. She waits a second or two. Then picks up her flowers and rearranges them in her basket. Nobody buys them. Only a faint scent and an imperceptible smile remain above the hurried trays of the waiters, I no longer know what to do with these tiny bunches. Then I recall a dog's grave. I can remember the dog's name. Jack was his name in the voice of our childhood. So I visit Jack's grave and leave my basket of jasmines. "Jack," I tell him, "my good friend, I've brought you a few flowers. But I don't want to cheat you, Jack. I'm giving them to you, because nobody else will buy them; nobody wants them. Forgive me, Jack." I look around in all directions. Nobody. Neither Jack nor anything. Nobody sees my devout offering and my tear about to drop. I decide not to weep, reflecting that I should have sold the flowers at a bargain price and sent the money to the Charity Fund for Poor Children. At least that way, they'd have put my name in the newspapers, in those elegant Columns in honour of Donors. So I pick up my basket from Jack's grave and roam the streets, calling out in the uncouth voice of an apprentice newspaper-vendor: "Jasmines, lovely jasmines here. Two drachmas for each little bunch." But when I hear my own voice – and above all, that diminutive "little bunch" – I feel like weeping again. So I stuff the jasmines into my bosom and sell my basket to a greengrocer. Then I count my money and think about getting something to eat. At last, I've been able to sell something. And I feel joyful, overjoyed, so joyful that this time, I let my eyes overflow in a rather lovely way, as when I have a head-cold. In any case, the pine-needles in my bosom are prickling me.

Nocturnal encounter

At sunset, offices shut. I just have time to see the last patterns of dusk on the upper part of the walls, preferably rose and purplish. The weather seems to have a slight headache. People keep taking off their hats and greeting something invisible among the first shadows. The evening unties the ribbons under her chin, also removing her hat, which is full of small black shiny flowers. She holds her hat in her hands. Then, my head feels suddenly cool and light. Astonished, I lift my hand to see if I've been shaved with a fine-bladed razor. This is the road. I am walking. At each step, an extremely slight delay is like a premonition of freedom. Any moment now, all the lights will go on. Because the light which vanished is now a glass polyhedral globe on a long table in a science lab. On all sides, persons wearing white smocks and white masks are conducting chemical experiments. I know they want to resurrect somebody in the next room, who is lying on a marble slab covered with a sheet. I urge them to take off their masks and go out on the street and relax. "What's the need of resurrection," say I, "since there is no death?" They don't hear me. I go out by myself. Little by little the streets are getting empty. The noise ends up in the sewers. Inside me, I can hear the footsteps of a labourer coming back from work for supper. The light in the shop-window is orange. Two girls are sitting near a window. So time is indivisible. No, no. I don't want to think. I recall the vase of flowers on young Maria's piano. There was some water in it. No flowers. "Maria," said I, "will you come with me to the forest to pick cyclamens? First thing in the morning. I won't be late." I'd be wearing a hunting-costume. I'd also have a horn and we could listen to the echoes. Above the closed workshop of the carpenter, three stars appear. Someone is passing by my side: "Good evening," he calls back. "Thank you," I answer, then. In astonishment, he stops short. I give him my visiting-card. He can't see clearly enough to read. So I light a match for him. "Ariostos Observant." He still doesn't recognize me. But what then? Is it so difficult to recognize a human being, who says "good evening" and "thank you"? Is it so difficult, since the evening has so many stars? Then, I tear up my card and tell him: "I'm an unknown person, sir. Now that you've learned who I am, good night."

Oath

All day long I glued my hours side by side, meticulously, just as we glue newspaper-clippings in a notebook containing unfavourable reviews of our most recent book. But this twilight hour is a fresh multi-coloured stamp you must bring to your lips, lick with spittle and stick on the envelope of a love letter. I feel I'm becoming agreeable, but not self-sufficient. I go into my kitchen. Prepare my afternoon tea. Serve it in two cups. For of course, someone must come. That's indispensable. A beautiful, sad woman, rather weary. She'll have travelled a great deal and she'll utter unfamiliar names of cities, harbours, rivers, boats, mountain-ranges. And all of them friendly, thanks to the way her lips are shaped. I take the tray into the big room. I want to share with her the colours of the twilight still shining through the open window. If she takes off her shoes, her toes will have a roseish sheen. This is just what I want. We'll sit on the same couch, drinking our tea and chatting about gardens and equestrian statues. Afterwards, a dove will fly in through the window, one of those stray doves from the neighbourhood, and sit there between us. Then, as my hand moves this way to caress the dove, it will encounter her hand. And our hands will remain on the back of the dove, as on a small white altar, taking an eternal oath. "Áristos,"* she'd say (not Aríostos or Aóristos). "Áristos." Nothing else. And our bodies merged in the mauve velvet evening, while the tiny half-slice of lemon went on floating in my half-drunk cup of tea, like the new moon in an Athenian sky. And I knew it.

---

* "Áristos" in Greek means best.

Hats

I am enormously fond of hats, because they eliminate the repulsive shape of the skull from a man's head. Inside its own hat, a face becomes complete. Becomes like a house under its own roof, like a light-bulb inside its own lampshade. At this point, the light falls gentler on a person's nose and corners of his lips, ash-grey and blue, intermingled with shadow and safety. Inside my own hat, I feel the pleasant comfort of a familar environment and just the right temperature for my brain to brood. That's why I fall into a bad mood every time I'm obliged to take off my hat to greet someone or to enter an office or a doctor's office. But I am not aware of the same difficulty when I am bare-headed in my own room, merely because in that case, my whole room turns into a hat. Or again, when I'm out in the country under the trees, for at such times, the entire sky turns into a big blue hat protecting me from all resentment. At these moments, I hang my felt homburg on a branch and wait for a butterfly or a bird to perch on it. Often I stand around idly gazing into milliners' shop-windows. Many of the hats, though no one has worn them yet, have a finger mark in front and are turned so as to conceal a lovely, invisible face. Some are terribly serious, as though made of evening smoke from a train or boat. Others are pure revery. I pity the hats retired from active combat, tossed on top of the cupboard, all crumpled, dusty, moth-eaten. Down below them, the large full-length mirror insinuatingly reveals a bedside table opposite them, with a brush on its marble top and little phials full of the dead man's medicine. Actually, the dead never wear hats. That's why when the long glass carriage passes by with its eight plumed horses, we take off our hat and hold it in both hands, in all humility – not humiliation. At such moments, what sort of humiliation could be appropriate? Oh surely, I must buy a new hat in order not to look like a dead man. What would be the good of all the salutations, then? On my way up Stadium Street, I stroll along, softly whistling an improvised little ditty about straw hats at the seaside. High up above the houses, the Parthenon stands out, like an elegant rose-coloured hat on the crepuscular head of Athens.

Settlement of debts

"Ariostos, old boy," say I. "What's all this?" Almost tenderly I say it, feeling loved. My body and my face are extremely malleable. They reflect manners and attitudes from trees, houses, carriages, iron-grille gates, birds, balconies, animals, human beings. Yes, I know. They reflect lights, shadows, musical sounds. Everything. So, they say about me that in my gait I resemble so-and-so, in my gaze so-and-so, in my attitude I am like that column, in my gestures like this man, in my laugh like that man, in my voice like such-and-such a singer, in my hair like the statue of Antinoüs, in my legs like the athlete Aghias. Oh indeed. My entire property consists of my debts. In my entirety, I am one big debt. So who am I? Does this suffice for me to *be*? Once and for all, I decide to settle my debts, to find a way of getting rich and to start lending – more likely, giving – in order to gain my own self. I count my money. It isn't even enough for my evening meal in the small neighbourhood taverna. At this point, I say: "My good people," (the Hall is almost full; a child in the front row gazes at me in a sky-blue way and he believes me), "I owe money everywhere, but I cannot settle my debts, because I'm poor." Ah yes, I know now: I am something I do not owe to anyone – I am poor.

(Suddenly I recall that years ago, I wrote in my secret diary: *"I have nothing. All things are mine."*) I smile. This smile is all mine. Yes, I know: I resemble all the world, but even more, the world resembles me. (The Hall is empty now.) I go out the door alone. In my left fist, I am clutching a gold coin. Where did it come from? I stare at it. A beautiful sculpted head of Apollo. Can it be counterfeit? I examine it and take a bite. No. And there now, on the street, that child from the Hall, who was looking at me in a sky-blue way, believing me. I stuff the coin into his fist. "Take it," I tell him, "go buy some roasted chick-peas." "All this?" he asks. "All of it," I answer. Then he smiles. I smile too. Our two smiles intersect. The street is shining. And I am as rich as the one who gave everything away and can contemplate the entire heaven. Behold, I remove my last garment. I am naked. Am my own statue. And I must take my last stand under the palm trees in the large public Park, near the fountain. I want to listen to the water and want the drops to come rolling down my face and shoulders.

Exhilaration

Today I observed the little curtains on the window jesting with the light and breeze. They are two petite, very coquettish dancers with short lace dresses, every so often looking at themselves in their mirrors – namely, the window-panes. They keep pretending to tug at their dresses, supposedly to hide their legs; but as a result of all that tugging, they are left stark-naked and their rosy plump little buttocks shine like four small full moons in the early morning (for you see, there are two other buttocks on the window-panes). I really relish my little curtains; they're clever and extremely sly; they've caught on that I'm observing them and in order to deceive me, they start changing shapes. Now, dancers; now, Pierrot clowns; now, children's sailboats; now, busy, busy little housewives lifting a corner of their apron and tying it to their waist-band. But I am amused and it is precisely from these metamorphoses that I can discern their character more clearly (for as everybody knows, metamorphoses reveal what basically they're seeking to conceal). Ariostos knows all these tricks backwards and forwards – and from personal experience as well. Beyond their ordinary use, all objects have their secrets and their private lives: chairs, beds, glasses, knives and forks, sheets, towels, toothbrushes, combs. How very many objects made of cloth, wood, metal, stone, clay, bone, plaster and (why not?) air. How unconnected and yet, how connected with each other and with me. And beyond their ordinary use, beyond their voluntary or involuntary shapes (pressed by alien factors or their own wish for disguise, whereby they avoid both certain and uncertain dangers), I can observe their dramatically unchangeable nature, as well as their inevitable decay. But I am discreet. I keep silent about their bitter unchangeability and praise the virtuosity of their transformations, their will for survival and this miracle of indefatigable quest (or even conquest) for a bit of immortality. A genuine miracle. Because my two window curtains do not exist for the purpose of hiding me from the neighbours when I return from work, drenched in sweat, and when I strip myself to re-discover that I am Ariostos – not someone else – and that I have a body of my own, which needs another body. Not for this purpose. The curtains have their own story, their own love-affairs, peculiarities, sins hieroglyphically inscribed on their innocent strips of lace. When you climb a high mountain, surely your shoes get full of holes. And I returned barefoot to Missus Demetra's little house in the country, with the chickens cackling enthusiastically in her courtyard, at golden high noon. I cut a lettuce from her garden, washed it very, very carefully at the tap, went into her house (the door was open, there was no one inside), sat down on a chair and began chewing my lettuce. Just then, outside, a horse stuck its head through the low window and began staring at me. The horse was white. I got up and cut a lettuce leaf and put it in the horse's mouth. We both chewed away in the same rhythm, staring at each other. I've always wanted to tell you about this miracle.

Affinity with silence

Evening has fallen. I watch the shadows climbing the walls of the houses across the way, holding a basket of roses high up on their heads. A peaceful, humble neighbourhood with its small balconies dangling in the evening like children's swings dangling from the trees. The balconies sway lightly to and fro, airing freshly laundered dresses of young girls, striped shorts and white sports vests. A scent of jasmine together with an orange. A woman's voice is heard inside a room, where the lamp has not been lit yet. This voice suits me so well, it dresses me, fitting me like a fine mended sock on a freshly washed foot. Again, the woman's voice and I – together – are so well suited in the evening, like a sock and a foot – together – in a freshly polished shoe, which is not too narrow and not too wide, without any thought of pressure, without any feeling of wideness – a neutral feeling devoid of feeling. Pure freedom. The sky, the woman's voice (which is silent now), me. A star has come out. My own. My very own. Eh, Ariostos' own star. Tonight I'll have to brush my teeth very quietly to keep the burglars from hearing me. I'd better not brush them at all. I'm fed up. There's only me and the star.

Sunday morning

Until yesterday, I had a name in my absolute possession. It belonged to me. If anyone shouted "Ariostos" on the street, I knew that among thousands of other persons, I was the one being called and even before turning my head to look, I straightened my tie. I held my name in proud esteem. When I introduced myself, I used to repeat it twice: "Ariostos, my dear sir. Ariostos." And I was sure of the fine impression. Now, one Sunday, who the hell impelled me to open that old Encyclopedia, not yet bound. At one fell swoop, I lost my property (the only property I had) as well as my personality. It was as though my money had been stolen and I had none left to pay my rent. As though I'd been stranded in the middle of the road, stripped of my trousers. Let me read: "Ludovico Ariosto, one of the most celebrated of Italian poets (1474-1533). He was a diplomatic envoy of Cardinal Ippolito d'Este. As a poet, he gained immortality thanks to his epic *Orlando Furioso*. Furthermore, he also wrote comedies, satires, sonnets and Latin poems." This was my calamity. I became alienated from the thing I loved most – namely, that which defined me in a unique and irrefutable way. Now – without being invited – this gentleman intruded between me and my own name, with his Latin letters, trampling on my land and usurping my allotted place in the sun and the air. If it weren't for this Furious Orlando, at least. I imagine him as a black bull with huge horns. This is a barrier to all communication between us. Two horns intrude before each and every attempt at reconciliation. But I want to be blasé and calm. So I decide to forget my name. To offer the other one my place at the window along with my chair. But no. I'd better take my revenge on him. I'll refuse to pay my rent. (I've got it there in the corner of my drawer, already.) Then we'll see how this gentleman with his fine sonnets will succeed in finding a roof over his head. Somebody's knocking on my door. "Mr. Ariostos. Mr. Ariostos." It's my landlady. I don't answer. Since I don't know – maybe she's calling the other one. Let *him* go pay the rent. "Mr. Ariostos, are you there? I'm bringing you a bit of cake – I've just brought it from the baker's." "For me or for the other one?" I ask. "For you, of course. Who's the other one?" I open the door for her. "Take your rent," I tell her. "I was just about to bring it to you. And take this useless Encyclopedia, to kindle your fire. Thank you for the cake." "Thank you too, Mr. Ariostos." I grab hold of the "thank you", the "Mister" and my own name. And take my place in the Sunday sun near the window. Ultimately scornful of the libraries of the world at large. The cake is still hot. How delicious it smells. I raise it to my mouth. No, no. I won't eat it. The black raisins in the cake are like the mischievous eyes of children. They are staring at me. So there are still Luna Parks in the morning, filled with girls and boys riding little wooden horses, going round in circles, circles, circles, – I too have a horse – a golden horse. Circles, circles, circles, I write above the violet city – circles, the light, light, light. Can't you see? I, Ariostos (or if you wish, Aóristos), the Observant. Light.

I'm not nosey

Many people gathering at the tram intersection. And other people crowding in, on their way down from the four roads. This reminds me somehow of rivers descending to the sea, dragging a huge tree-trunk. What's going on? Everybody asks, running along. An accident, you said? I keep going. Asking nobody. Heading straight for my job, staring at my own feet as they tread the damp road. I move on, without turning my head. But my left ear slows down. Stands still. Refuses to budge an inch. The more I move forward, the more it moves in the opposite direction. I can feel it shifting from my side and sitting on my back, just below my neck. It cuts loose. Rushes towards the tram intersection. It has turned into a telephone receiver connected to me by a long cord. I can hear the cord dragging along the paving-stones. This makes an aggravating noise and prevents me from hearing. Nevertheless, I continue on my way. Except that I make a gesture to pull the cord and relocate my ear in the right place. At this point, I seem to be pulling the leash of a stubborn little dog, who doesn't want to follow me and constantly delays at all the corners and lamp-posts. "Madam," I ask her, "can this be your little dog? I found it on the road." "Oh sir, I'm much obliged," she answers me. "I lost it in the scramble." I hand her her little dog, white and fluffy as feathery down and glance furtively at the palm of my hand. Its leather leash has left a red line engraved there. Suddenly I look at my watch. And rush off. I'm about ten minutes late for my job. And the man wasn't killed. He merely fainted. He was wearing red socks, actually.

Theatre ticket

Any man capable of going into a shop all on his own to buy vests or underpants seems to me to be a real hero; also, any man capable of entering a new restaurant all on his own, for the first time, and going to the unfamiliar lavatory to wash his hands and wipe them on tons of paper. I feel the same way about any man who fearlessly, buys fruit or fish from the market. Above all, any man who stands with his back turned to the box-office of a theatre, then gets a ticket, picks up his change and actually counts it under the big electric light. Then coolly saunters past the inland revenue official and the other official at the door, who check the tickets. The ticket isn't forged and does not drop out of his hand. So I imagine the man is going past the door of the Ministry of Defence at a forbidden hour, between two boorish guards with their bayonets bared. I truly admire these people. Even the way their hands are made is different (I've observed this). Particularly, the thumb – which is very coarse with a very broad fingernail pared down all the way to the flesh. For hours on end, I wander around outside the Theatre. In my right hand, I have exactly the right amount for the ticket. After stealing a glance at the prices listed near the box-office. Now I stand on the pavement admiring the elongated motor-cars gleaming under the multi-coloured neon sign. I also admire the two gold-framed photographs of the leading lady, though I'm surprised the flies have left no marks on the frames. When she undresses, her arm must be extremely long – it must reach the very ceiling. At long last, I approach the person in the box-office. "One ticket, please," I say to him extremely politely, so as not to annoy him. "The performance is over, sir," he tells me. That's just how he says it: "Sir." "Over, sir?" I ask him? "Bah, over." (I didn't like that "Bah" of mine one little bit.) I make a correction. "Ah, indeed – it's over. Thank you." How nice the person in the box-office was. Not at all nervous. Not at all irascible. But what about me? I glance at my thumb. The nail is in actual fact broader. As I turn the corner, I buy some roasted chestnuts with the ticket money. Calmly I remove their shells and feel certain that I love the entire world. My hands look black and I like them. Now I glance upwards. The sky is crystal-clear. A few sniffling clouds lift the lapels of their overcoat and move slowly westwards, bowed down above the city. I do not lift my lapels.

Etude

In the mornings I enjoy roaming the streets of the province. All night it has been raining. The soaked tiles sparkle in the faint sunshine. I particularly love the roofs. They bend their shoulders so the childish chimneys can leap over them. And they have a scent of fallen mulberry tree leaves. The local priest can't decide whether to go out on the road, lest his shoes get muddy. All things want to confide some secret to you – nothing very urgent. So do the voices from door to door or from that window behind the naked trees. The stones curve their backs like cats asking you to caress them. One old lady complains to the other old lady: "Poverty," says she. "Rheumatism," says she. The plates break, one by one. Also the glasses. After the noise, the silence is greater – and you are aware of it. Especially, when a mirror breaks. The paper on the dish-rack needs changing. Not white paper, because that gets dirty too easily and shows the fly-specks. On the other hand, dark paper – green or blue – fades when the sun enters the kitchen every afternoon at the start of springtime. One cuts the edge of the paper in a lacey pattern and then, lots of holes in the shape of tiny daisies. Of course, a flute also has holes, but every evening, it resounds from the room of the young student, who hasn't changed his sheets for three whole months. I know this very well. Which is why I go straight to the public library. I greet nobody. Anyway, who's there for me to greet? Only one old man sitting at a table full of scratches. A malevolent old man with eyeglasses and thin hands, so thin they seem eager to strangle you. I open my book and stay there. In the next room, the mice are scampering back and forth. The door is nailed shut with long rusty spikes. No one can get in. But I know about it – it's big, totally empty, full of dust. It used to be a dining-room. But not totally empty. Far back in a corner, in the shadow, is a plaster statue. Because of the dark and the dust, you can't discern what it depicts. I pick up a dust-cloth and climb on a chair. But behind the statue's back, a guard is standing and he stares at me, as he rolls his cigarette. I'm barely in time to dust the statue's face. I recognize it. It's me when I'm dead. But my book says nothing about all this. Suddenly down on the street, outside the library, the sound of triangles is heard, played by children singing carols. A fragrant scent of hot bread buffets my face. I glance through the oblong window. Clouds, clouds, frozen and sick with the flu. And other clouds more cloudlike. Clouds cannot become statues. But then again, who knows?

Hands

I prefer hands to faces. Faces are puffed up with present time; they are foolish, false, and their memory is unreliable. But hands have long-term experience, replete with almost hieratic solemnity. And incorruptible sincerity. The proof: They never look at themselves in the mirror. They don't premeditate their expression and their pose. By following the shape and movement of the hands, I can create the missing face, unalterable in time, made of iron or stone or glass. Sometimes, I offer people their true face, sticking it on their shoulders as though placing a vase on the kitchen-table between the small bottles of olive-oil and vinegar, the forks and spoons and the salt-cellar. From gestures and from the smell of food as it is wafted through the windows out to the street, I can recognize faces, as well as the houses where they live and the arrangement of the furniture. I often sit outside houses, just as evening starts to fall and the supper lamps light up, not in order to learn, but to corroborate. With three fingers, a faintly lit hand is holding a glass. This is someone who has loved but little. That other hand stirring sadly above its own shadow, is a mother's hand. Her child is certainly ill and is covered with a brown blanket on that big bed in the inner room. She is feeding him chicken broth with a silver teaspoon. Next to him sits a doll with a broken arm. The doll eats nothing. On the bedside table is a cup of lemonade half-full. A dog from the yard across the way barks at me. I don't know which dog, because as everyone knows, dogs don't have hands, only paws. I am compelled to leave. All night I plan to carve a little wooden boat to bring the sick child tomorrow. "Madam is not here," the servant girl tells me. She keeps her own hands in her apron pockets and she's angry. Eh, then there's no reason for the child to have the little boat. Nor is there any reason for him to be sick. "He ought to put his hands under the blanket," I say to her. "So he won't catch cold." And I too put my hands in my pockets. Perhaps the servant girl also understands about hands and will stick on my shoulders a similar silly vase with a lettuce inside, or else the wickerwork demijohn of wine, or the copper pestle, or even that glass jar of pickles soaking in salty water.

Concerning sleep

When I'm asleep, I'm uniquely sincere. When I talk about my sleep, I destroy my sincerity. I realise this immediately. Thereafter it is impossible for me to conceive the preceding plan of sincerity. This error intervenes in a sovereign manner, imposing its own reality on me with a terrible barrier. After this, I grope my way haphazardly. It is no longer possible for me, as previously, to climb a dangling staircase or to cross from one roof to the opposite roof, without even catching hold of the telegraph wires, or to copulate in a real way with the loveliest aethereal body. I can no longer be inside all of time and outside time. Nevertheless, in order to resemble my own sincerity (even in retrospect), I veer around skillfully and assume the pose of a sculptor chiselling a statue according to his lost plan; precisely in this embarrassing situation caused by the loss of the plan, he strives to make the lost plan tally with his own work. This subterfuge is what later adds a tone of sincerity to the whole factitious work. From this point onwards, I observe the artifice in its successive retractions and realisations. For sleep knows no obstacles of space and time and morality. It needs no means of transport for any distances, needs no confined consequences and continuations. In spite of being changeable, quick, volatile, sleep is not divisible. It is like light, which illuminates things from within, fusing them from within. As soon as the sun comes out, that light vanishes, and things are no longer clouds and crystals, but simply things with multitudes of names and colours, which get detached from their correct place, like cubes from a mosaic depicting the "love-affairs of fish and angels" – in the words of a late-lamented versifier. At this point, I rub my eyes, with a grave feeling, as though for many days I've had an urgent letter in my pocket, which I should have sent at all costs, but I've left it till it's soiled and crumpled. Now, I keep saying I must change the envelope and post it, but I constantly postpone. With my finger, I touch this wrinkled letter as though touching a toothless mouth disfigured by a stroke. It stutters. I comprehend the original imperfection and irresponsibility. This is not enough of an excuse for me. I won't stand for any excuse. I must acknowledge and be acknowledged. I search the corners of my face. My jaw makes an effort to become square. But does not succeed.

Glasses and other matters

I always get into bed as though I'm climbing onto a bus. I don't know where it's going to take me. I count my money beforehand, but forget to calculate the return ticket. "Life," remarks the gentleman next to me – and he's wearing a large ring on the index finger of his right hand – "is not only life per se. It is resistance to death. Wherever resistance succeeds, resistance is forgotten; some kind of victory is won; the fine pristine life returns, which knows not or has forgotten the battle." Without looking at him, I listen. He isn't addressing me. I notice his ring. "Art," says the gentleman near his side (the one who is wearing a little ring on the little finger of his left hand), "Art is the act which resists the act, justifying life without needing to know, although it does know. In particular, Poetry is resistance per se, tending to abolish resistance in order to exist as life. It is the act of incapacity for the act." This person speaks in a shrill, but strong and clear voice. Obviously he wants me to hear him. I pretend not to hear. Not even glancing at his little ring. "Criticism," the same person resumes now in an affectedly officious tone of voice, "is the fear of personal death and the resistance to fear, or rather the forgetting and converting of fear. When the critic is less afraid, he comes closer to Poetry. When he succeeds in resisting the fear of himself as well as the fear of the work being judged (which reveals all his own fear) and the fear of someone else's glory, he creates criticism. He lives the function of the Artist himself: he consumes himself and constructs. He founds his glory on the death of his own personality. This is a terrifying encounter with all of death." This phrase "terrifying encounter" he uttered in such a droll tone that I couldn't stand it. "Balderdash, gentlemen," I retorted. "What death, gentlemen? What life, what poet, what critic? When you wash glasses, you leave them upside down on the marble ledge of the sink, to drain dry. When you pick them up, there are some wreathes of water left on the marble ledge, but these by no means signify the previous presence of upside-down glasses. They are merely wreathes of water. However, in the air, the shape and transparency of the glasses are left precisely. So if you just move your little finger like this (without a ring), the whole air reverberates with a tinkling sound. In a poem, this is what we mean by 'I hear it'. But gentlemen, how could the critic possibly hear – even if he has a shiny button in his ear attached to a wire apparatus in his waistcoat pocket?" That's just how I spoke, at first angrily, but afterwards, not. I went down the three steps from my bed, gently nudged the sleeping conductor, and climbed up to the roof. I could see the bus going on its way and the two gentlemen with the rings gaping at me like imbeciles from behind the window-panes.

While smoking

I am incapable of portraying that which is, because it *is* and has no need of portrayal or somebody else's voice. It doesn't think about being. This is why each time I want to portray it, I transfer it to another level, relating it to something else, which is either relevant or totally irrelevant, and I put an "as" in front of it. Thus I destroy it in order to preserve it in a richer form and to offer a proof of life to myself, to other persons, to life itself, to whatever seeks no proof from me. I mirror the most natural flux, flux to the point of immobility, flux with a spasmodic utterly refracted quality, where straws and lemons and dead birds float on the surface. And yet, a little while ago, how calm everything was, how well arranged in the right place – the bottle on the table, the clock which had stopped, the brush on the chair, the iron posts of the bed and the battered slippers under the bed. And the air in the room unperturbed, disinterested, immoveable. Now I wind the clock and try to find a rather serious answer to this foolish (here you are, I'm already using adjectives) tick-tock. If somebody suddenly taps me on the shoulder, I'll become like a cigarette, which has been lit and forgotten on the edge of a table; it burns away all alone and its ashes will fall noiselessly on the floor. Then I'll say: "The room is full of smoke. Let's open the windows now." And I'm certain that if I'd forgotten this lighted cigarette in my mouth, it would have burned my lips. This man understands nothing. I'll give him the broken chair to sit on and he'll collapse on the floor, with his legs sticking up in the air absurdly. But I won't laugh then. I'll offer him my arm and help him stand up and I'll carefully dust off his whole body with that brush. If only he collapses on the floor.

Autumn

The clouds are gathering. Swarms and swarms of birds are returning to sunnier motherlands. The poets are returning to their papers. The light is becoming more and more pensive, but also more secretive. I've been told this gentleman is an expert at evaluating works of art. A splendid art critic, so it seems. With a single word of his, he has rescued many persons from obscurity and others he has sunk with two words. From the very outset, I pitied critics. I could sense their embarrassment in the presence of something new, their humiliation, their obstinance and their ambition. No writer has ever been such a faithful mirror of the reverse image of human beings as the critic. I want to test him. So I scribble a poem on my knees:

> *The light-bulbs are sleeping with their faces turned*
> *towards the dark part of the corridor.*
> *Two young men try their keys in the door of the night.*
> *They cannot open their own home. They remain out*
> >*on the street,*
> *staring now at their useless keys, now at the stars.*
> *Whose fault was this? Whose fault is it? Tell me.*
> *Three flags from some past fête flap sluggishly*

hanging loose on the balcony of the Town Hall. Nightfall.
I have no matches to light my cigarette. This cigarette is the white remorse for an entire day of idleness.

Afterwards, I add two silly pseudo-lyrical verses underneath, from an old poem of mine scratched out:

White flowers return sorrowful from the funeral of a canary wearing a wire bracelet on its right ankle.

Ready. Bravo. Modestly I hand it to the critic. "Your opinion?" I ask him. Good heavens, his eyes become two discs of a scale bobbing up and down. He weighs my words. He weighs his own words too. How I pity him. Bilious, squint-eyed, sullen. "What a lovely colour your complexion has," I tell him. "Yes, yes, I won't deny it," he says in a pompous and distrustful manner. "And of course, your verses are lovely too – that juxtaposition: keys and stars; yes, *but*..." This *but* is spoken in a peculiar tone. Herein lies all his power. He must make prudent use of it, between two half-hearted eulogies. Sometimes he omits the "but", as though it is self-understood. He fears I may play some trick on him and he may fall into the trap. He fears I may be a genius and he may ignore me. He fears I *am* a genius. However, he also fears to ignore me, for if (in spite of all this) my work is triumphant, he will be the one whom people will ignore. His name won't show up alongside mine as sponsor. Just in the nick of time, that salutary "but" saves the day. Everything is resolved in a very nice way, ambiguously, amicably, warily. I go on writing my verses and he his criticism. Occasionally we meet on the street and greet one another, but both of us are in a hurry. And we turn down the very first side-street, clenching our fists and gritting our teeth. And if I happen to encounter a friend just then, I tell him: "I've just run into that fool of a critic." And the critic tells his own friend: "I've just run into that fool of a poet." But we are also separated and linked by many other benefits, interests, ulterior motives. There is no end to this story. And what story does have an end? The window-panes of the houses have become miniature square mirrors of the clouds. Later on, the evening will stuff her black sack with these little mirrors she has purchased from the pedlars' baskets on Athenas Street, in back of the old railway station. Oh, I must write something about this station. I believe it used to have wooden benches. A silent old woman used to sit in a corner there, holding a basket on her knees, as though she possessed nothing else in this world. Suddenly I remember that in the same poem, at close range, the word "white" occurs twice. "White remorse," "white flowers." I'll have to change this. No, no. It's better like this. It will appear to have been put there on purpose. It suggests a feeling of balanced sorrow – the feeling of the snow-white colour. Besides, the wall of the Town Hall will by all means be whitewashed – a third *unuttered* white colour. Splendid. And I'm sure that no scruffy critic will notice or pinpoint this finest, fortuitous detail. But so what? Do we write only for the critics? This they understand and they put on airs. But what will become of them if we refuse to go on writing? They'll disappear. They hang on our very lips. I think I'll declare a General Strike of Poetry. We'll go out on the streets with huge placards: "Down with the negative." "Long live the positive" – and not only for criticism, but for everything, for life as a whole. But what are the coppers and the fire engines looking for? Is it raining? I hide away inside the Arsakion Arcade. Yes, it *is* raining. Good heavens, what vile weather. Those white flowers have been swept away by the rain. Go to the devil, Mr. Ariostos, say I. You've glutted us with your whites and your critics. Just listen to the *unutteredness* of the rain on the glass roof of the Arsakion Arcade, with all its shops selling shirts and the one and only music store of Konstandinides. There are various scores exhibited in the shop-window: the Waltzes and Nocturnes of Chopin, the "Well Tempered Clavier" of Bach, and the "Old Mazurka in the Rhythm of the Rain", by I don't know which composer. But I can clearly hear its *unutteredness*. Do you hear it?

In the dynasty of the mosquitoes

The light is near the bedside-table. Before switching it off, I examine my hands. Finding them very natural, very present. I feel calm. I close my eyes. A mosquito keeps whirring above me like a ventilator, blowing on my face annoyingly. Little by little I get on familiar terms with it. I pay attention to the whirring of the ventilator, which sets all the particles of the shadow in circular motion. I'm a labourer in grease-stained overalls and I'm installing some plumbing equipment in a very deep damp basement; or an electrician setting up a radio antenna on the top floor of a tall house, high up on a rope-ladder in the night hours, dangling above the telegraph wires and the neon signs. How simple and how complicated is the aerial view of a city. The persistent rumble of machines in a factory working the night shift deprives me of the ability to observe and traps me at the centre of the hubbub. That old man had a cane too – or maybe an umbrella? I make one last effort not to collide with the glass fragments of sound, in order to comprehend the mechanism of sound and become free of vertigo. My other foot slips off the ladder. I grab hold of the railing on the balcony. Am just in time to see the airplane passing by next to me. The pilot is wearing a leather jacket and big goggles. The suitcases in the net keep shifting about. The railing falls off. There is nothing left for me except to let go. I fall with terrifying gravity, but also clarity, into the atmosphere of the mosquitoes. Suddenly I turn into a mosquito. A mosquito whistling stubbornly above my own ear, while at the same time, thinking to myself: Tomorrow morning, as soon as I wake up, I'll write a poem. And I must find someone to read it to immediately. Even if it's only my landlady, when she brings me my coffee. Whenever she laughs, her rotten teeth show.

Training course on avoiding plans

I don't want to have any plans. Confronted with my plans, I always feel I'm taking exams. This robs me of my inclination for work, makes me aware of time, takes control of me. Nothing worthwhile is possible like this. A sense of duty forces me to work, exactly at the point when I refuse to acknowledge duty. So I tear up my plans, accepting the triviality of all things and I move freely in the void. But I am still pursued by fear: that I will always move within the negation of my plan or each new plan. This is also a plan, more confining, more oppressive. It imposes a duty so arid that it destroys all my naturalness. So I curse plans and counter-plans and decide to keep quiet and one way or another, to die. I stretch out flat on two chairs in the sunshine and unfold my newspaper. I don't read. I toss it over my head. That's fine. The green table in the coffee-house, the waiter bringing me my coffee, the rattle of backgammon, the ant walking on my hand. They don't even suspect how beautiful they are, how innocent. And the foreignness of the air and the contemptuous compassion of the air for their innocence? I love them. And rather envy them. I, who have my pockets crammed with old bank notes devoid of purchasing value or any bank security in gold. My jacket weighs me down. I'd take it off and hang it on the back of a chair, if my shirt with the faded embroidered initials weren't so torn. You see, I'm a little prince in exile, sixteen years old, with blond hair and very delicate hands. I know I was not to blame for anything. I have no people; I have no power. In the shoeshine-parlour where I work, my hands get full of polish. Impossible to wash them clean with soap. So I rub them with a pumice-stone. Occasionally when I go to the theatre, I wear patched gloves to hide my grimey fingernails. A little seamstress whom I sleep with in the iron bed tells me: "There's something princely about you." I stretch my hands up to the moon, which is streaming in through the dormer window of the attic. I begin to weep. She bends over me as though I'm an orphan. I open the door and hurl her down below the winding staircase. Did she hurt her hands? No, no. There's only a tiny mark on her upper lip. "Did it hurt very much?" I ask her. "Not much," she answers. I take off her other stocking and kiss her poor foot. "I forgive you," I tell her. "Truly, I forgive you." She looks at me and stuffs her knickers under the pillow.

What time can it be?

Peaceful evening full of secret kindness. Speaking in a soft voice and walking smoothly without moving its arms, like a distant relative of my mother, dressed in black, who used to visit our home once or twice a year, usually in the late afternoon before the lamps were lit (indeed I recall that at such hours, the big mirror in the drawing room took on a particularly transparent blurriness, like a vertical strip of sea water removed from the deep sea). Well, Aunt Anna (that's how we used to call her) used to bring us children bonbons in little sacks made of flimsy green paper – always green, a pale sad green, maybe because Aunt Anna was poor. That's what people said. I don't know. I am overwhelmed by a delicious premonition of past grief. I gaze at the stars just as seafaring men gaze at them aboard their ship on Easter Eve. And suddenly, for no reason, I feel I've become a small green light-bulb in the corridor of a cheap hotel, when the sleepy night-porter writes in a thick registry, jotting down the names of a young student and a girl in a calico flowered frock. Holding each other by the hand, they climb the inner wooden staircase, half in the dark. But a bit later, there's a Police raid. They bang on the doors. The boards creak. "Get dressed," the girl cries.

"Just a moment," the boy answers. He still has an erection. Once again, they knock at the door. "Open up –", the voice is imperative. Who? Behind the closed door, hurried muddled snatches of conversation. Violent footsteps in the corridor. Suddenly a tremendous noise. What is it? What's happening? All the doors open. Nothing at all. The plaster bust of Kanaris has leaned back and gotten smashed on the staircase. Now the doors gape open in front of the empty corridor where they've hung two framed portraits of the persons who founded the hotel. The residents, dishevelled, go back to their own rooms, disappointed and indignant, with their hair dishevelled. "What a pity," says the fat cleaning-woman. "I imagined someone must have committed suicide – maybe the gentleman in number 5, the one who plays the violin." The doors slam shut again. No sign either of the Police or that couple. Only the unfinished sleep of the hotel-residents remains in the corridor, staring at the two frames. I stare at the headlights of the last bus scheduled between Akademias Street and Vouliagmeni. Well now, behind each star do you suppose there's a child sitting with some glass marbles in his fist? And what can possibly have become of Kanaris? They'll toss the bits and pieces of plaster into a big barrel of rubbish, along with orange peels and green paper sacks. A young man walks by next to me. On the brim of his hat there's a hole from a cigarette burn. If I had some money, I'd buy him a cap. The cap would suit him nicer, because he's swarthy and casual. "I've brought you a little gift," I'd say to him, "just a trifle." But what about his address? How can I take him the cap now? At the corner, a copper lights a match and glances at his wristwatch. "What time is it, please?" I ask. "A quarter past twelve," he answers gently. His face looks pleasant in the bright light from the match. The flame goes out. Yes, a policeman with a gentle voice. I want to become reconciled with the whole wide world. Want to go back to my own room, get undressed, lie down on my bed and stare at my toes, one by one, again and again. And want to like them.

Twilight stroll

Houses have their own secrets. They beckon to one another with colours, carved motifs, windows, anthemium patterns, chimneys in the most unbelievable and suggestive positions. As soon as I go out my door, I catch them red-handed, chatting in low tones of voice. All at once they are silent and their facades grow serious, as though a stranger has intruded into their friendly gathering. They have the vexed expression of a person who'd been drinking his tea until some outsiders bothered him so much that his hand along with the cup froze stiff under his chin. Streets are the same. As soon as they catch sight of me, they hastily lock up their secrets, sometimes under the street-lamp at the corner, sometimes under the very few pepper trees, sometimes in the shadow of a parked lorry. So they are like that huge locked cabinet in our old house. Behind its chiselled crystal panes, which reflected the luminous squares of the window in miniature, I could surmise the delicate *raki*-glasses, the tiny silver spoons used only when we received formal visits, an enormous fork for serving garfish, chinaware, jars full of bitter-orange preserve, and something else (I can't remember, since I never saw it) on the topmost shelf; I was too small and couldn't reach high enough to see, though I did bring a chair and climb up there one afternoon when Mother was away and she'd forgotten to lock the cupboard. "Good evening, Ariostos. How are you getting on?" I hear a strangely sweet voice. A colleague of mine from the office. His voice pities me. In his eyes, I can see that I am sad and unshaven. The sunset flares up on the iron-grille rails of balconies and windows, utterly glorious and mournful. And I am like a man abandoned by his wife just yesterday and now, as he walks the streets, he knows his house is locked, the rooms are empty with a bit of dust on the back of the furniture, and only on the edge of the couch, there still remain her brown threadbare gloves, which she forgot at the last minute before going out. Nevertheless, the twilight overflows with colours – rose, violet, yellow, indigo blue, emerald green, porphyry and a golden goblet filled with lukewarm water. There, I moisten the tips of my fingers. Wipe them on a white towel. Raise the goblet. I can perform the ritual, all alone in the world.

The rosebush and I

Now that it's springtime, I go out to the small square patch of earth in the space between the open houses. This serves as my garden. I sit in my chair and have a chat with my rosebush. All things seem to have become more beautiful – myself, my shoes, the chair, the walls, the sky. We can hear the post-office coach setting off for the province, along the upper road. We know its two horses are white. We realise this not so much from the noise of the hooves as from the sound of the bells. We both know this – I mean, me and the rosebush. Suddenly, a very light breeze starts to blow. Shadows from the branches gesticulate on the ground, as though they are locking little drawers. Then, they toss the key in their bosom and remain calm and still, feigning ignorance, as though nothing has happened. So even the rosebush is concealing something from me. Of course, so am I. From the window across the way, someone queries. The other man from that other window across the way also queries. No answer. Then they both go back inside and their hands play with the keys of those closed drawers. I can hear the metallic sound. So, is there no answer? The shadow of the wall has moved. The entire rosebush is in the shade now. It has no shadow of its own. Nor do I. I pick up my chair and go inside.

After the end

Well now, will the day truly come when this handsome boy will no longer exist in the house opposite me, in this humble room, where every morning (trusting that nobody can see him) he undresses and does Swedish gymnastics? (I stand behind the shutters, holding my breath.) Futhermore, will the little girl with the grey jumper no longer exist, the one who's been passing by at daybreak for three months now, holding an empty basket? And is it true that this earth of ours will die some day like an old woman in an empty pitch-dark room, without any fire, as she folds her bony hands over her wrinkled belly? And will these square patches of light, which are slanted onto the suspended oval mirrors, no longer exist; and the poor people with their saddle-bags; and the rich people with their coloured neckties; and the windows, the glory, the small aluminum pan, the words, or a garter? Only by thinking about all this, I become so calm, so indulgent and carefree I decide not to go to the office. I open the iron box where I keep all sorts of buttons and I start to count them. Then I roll up my shirt-sleeves and wait for somebody to cut my veins, so that I can say "thanks" to him and make him believe me. He *must* believe me, because I won't have anything else. And this "thanks" must remain somewhere, like my dead brother's little sword, which never killed anything and remains hanging on the coat-rack in the hall; or like that rainy umbrella which sheltered the kiss of two young people on their way back one night from a three-hour class in Latin, or in numismatics, and the traffic police had removed their stools from the intersections and gone away.

Noon dream

Hot bright summer noon. I am sleeping. At the same time, upright in front of my bed, I watch my self sleeping. I kiss him once more – not on the lips now, but on the forehead – and I cover him with a sheet up to his throat. (I've changed the sheets and actually put a rose in a glass.) "My good Ariostos," I remark, "you are not my image in the water. You are here in this solid bed with the four large brass knobs. How shiney they are up above your closed eyelids. Well, we won't drown. Go to sleep." And as he dozes on his back, stark-naked under the sheet, he is a cold statue exuding warmth. I observe the reflections from the knobs of the bed on his face, the proportions of his legs and arms, the curve of his chest, the hollow of his waist, the bulge on the upper part of his thighs; and I detach myself from time. With eyes devoid of pupils – like statue's eyes – I observe. With unique plenitude, I comprehend the void. I am the statue, which needs no other statues, or any observation of its own immobility. Is this self-sufficiency perhaps? Perhaps death? However, a slight undulation of the breast breaks the stable equilibrium between the white of the sheet, the light of the window and the human body. This breathing is an incontestable *present*, which is a continuation of transciency and is reminiscent of it. I find the missing element and try to restore the statue to the order of an abstract theorem. If I lift the sheet now, there won't be any statue at all. Just at this moment, I notice last week's dirty socks sticking out from under the bed. Furtively, I push them back and noiselessly head for the window. I no longer remember the pose assumed by statues. Here, is only a man who is sleeping and actually, snoring a little. I close the shutters to keep the glare of the sun from waking me up. For even in my sleep, I can hear my snoring with pleasure – it reassures me that I am sleeping, that I exist, that I am Ariostos with the big blueish green eyes, which even through sleep, know how to see the indefinite and the invisible, the brightly-lit and the shadowy, and these few withered narcissus buds in between the pages of Porphyras' poems. I'll have to throw away these narcissus buds. They'll stain my book. Besides, I don't like them, because they have the same name as Narcissus. Do you understand, Ariostos? You do understand.

A fortnight's paid leave

Springtime in full sway. Heat. I come back from the market. After buying some fruit. I dump it on my table. My room is full of its fragrance. The light is almost blue, like a doubly large sheet bleached in indigo. On the rough paper where the fruit was wrapped, with a blue pencil I draw bewildered lines, words, verses, birds, huts, a bridge, four small paper flags, the profile of a billy-goat, and again words, as though I'm sitting under the trees out in the country. In any case, springtime has something to hand out to everybody, to the children and the old people, and above all to the women – though the women try to conceal it. Nevertheless, the roses are conspicuous on their bust – roses with a hundred or a thousand petals. Besides, the fragrance betrays them. And the sun is always punctual. Arriving just on time above the wooden benches in the gardens, above the humble chimneys, through my window. Ah, how lovely. Now the children will be playing around the well and old Barba-Stathis will be climbing the hill of olive-trees (just as in the old days), a serene, good-tempered old man, like a blind man leaning upon his staff as though upon the shoulder of Antigone. He can hear the tiny bells on the tails of the cicadas. He can see the tiny fires sparkling in the dewdrops on the leaves. "Where are you going?" I ask him. Where is he going? He smiles and doesn't know. Nor do I. I know only that I'm thirsty. I'd like a glass of very chilled water. For of course the water in the soldiers' canteens will have become hot from the blazing sun. I peel a pear. Chew it very, very slowly. It has the taste of a kiss. A bit of a breeze slips in through the window. The wrapping-paper makes a grating sound. Something like a *sandouri*-instrument played at the tradesmen's Fair of Aï-Yóryis, with the horses and cows and brightly coloured blankets. And here's a bee. Where did it come from? It just buzzed in and perched on the pear peel. And all at once, I understood how honey comes to be, and the poem.

The challenge of the day

As soon as I go outside and close my door, the road opens its own door. The day is an immense chamber – white, utterly white, utterly clean. A waiting-room in a doctor's office with wide-open windows. Sun everywhere. My eyes smart from the light. But I insist on not closing my eyes, for the sake of my own self-confidence. Here, the chairs are also utterly white, as well as the little tables with the ashtrays and magazines. Why do they have these medical magazines since they too are utterly white, devoid of print, and they don't write about how to cure death? Two ladies opposite me hold their x-rays rolled up on their lap. Off to one side, a young man politely scrapes his tooth with a toothpick. (Surely, the toothpick must have been in his pocket for many days and it must be almost black; that's why he puts his other hand in front of it, in order to conceal it.) Then I realise my own collar is also dirty. I haven't changed my shirt for two weeks now. I can see them scrutinising me in silence. Suddenly my head is detached from my neck. It vanishes. I become like one of those thick headless dummies in the old neighbourhood tailor-shops (the dummies are made of black satin and stuffed full of straw or bran), where people try on their altered overcoats or jackets. Now I feel at ease. Since I have no head, they can no longer make out whose dirty collar it is. Once again the room becomes utterly white. But little by little, my eyes get used to all this light and I start to notice a bit of dust here under a chair, a cigarette-butt in the corner, a ladder in a lady's stocking. At long last, I feel relieved. "Ariostos, old boy," I say, patting myself on the shoulder in a friendly way. I walk faster. Further on, I meet a man who has rickets. Then I do my utmost to stretch my backbone and I grow tall, tremendously tall, so tall I can no longer fit into the neighbourhood tailorshop, where I'm supposed to try on my new jacket.

Winter evening

What can you do about this snowy weather? Especially when you haven't got any heat. I withdraw into my own room at an early hour, light my lamp and read a book. Books are a good thing, even if I curse them occasionally. Friends. Faithful friends. They never abandon you. Philology, philosophy, sociology, political economy, history, mythology, psychology, novel, poetry – above all, poetry. Sometimes, of course, my brain feels overburdened, as though I'm holding a number of jugs on top of my head, piled up on each other, and I'm afraid they may fall and break. This is why I have to stand still, erect, gazing straight ahead of me into the distance, in order to keep my balance. But the waiter in the restaurant can hold a tray full of more than ten plates stuffed with all sorts of food; and he moves among all those tables and chairs with unimaginable ease and flexibility and indeed, with the grace of a dancer. I try to move my head in front of the mirror. All right. Nothing is broken. Again, at certain times, I feel embarrassed, stranded among the pages of a book (especially books on philosophy or aesthetics), like that poor wretch Fernandel amidst his own long disjointed arms and his broad breeches with the pockets gaping open as they stare at his own confusion. Suddenly the rain starts pouring down. He gets thoroughly soaked and starts to slobber. But he stretches out his clumsy hand and with hilarious coquettery fixes the crease in his trousers. He laughs to himself. Somebody calls: "Fernandel, Fernandel." Fernandel turns his dilapidated body. Nobody there. So he's free to remain himself – comically charming, naive, ungainly, satisfying to his own self and self-satisfied in his own ignorance – an ignorance so pure and agreeable that he is impelled once again to fix the crease in his trousers (with even greater tenderness now). And the rain continues pelting down on the zinc roof of the shed, like masses of typewriters being pounded by poor typists, who are writing the claims of the unemployed for a feeble Christmas bonus. Nevertheless, books are indeed unique company for the winter. Except that literary books are rather monotonous. Behind their ending, they all say approximately the same thing: That nothing is worth anything except the paper and the ink. And that everything happens in order for writers to be able to write books (*since all this happens only in order to give your verse a pretext* – in the words of a certain poet). I have no objection. But what makes me uncomfortable is the fact that some days ago a button fell off my coat. I've been keeping it in the top left-hand pocket of my waistcoat. The other two buttons are about to fall off too. Every morning I remember this and I twist the thread to fasten them somehow or other and I say that by nightfall, I'll sew them on at all costs. But tonight, there's no more postponing. It's good I remembered. I leave my book open on the table, thread a needle and prepare for the assault, like a warrior, ready to conquer an awesome foe and rest on my laurels ever after. But I can't find the button. I turn all my pockets inside out, curse, ransack all my drawers, throw the spools of thread on the floor, in the end, I lose the needle as well. Then I abandon everything and leave my room in a mess. I cut off the remaining buttons and rush out to the street, in the fierce cold, with my overcoat wide open. If someone were to ask me now why I'm traipsing around without any buttons, I'd tell him that's the way I like it, that I'm not cold and I'd start laughing loudly so he wouldn't hear my teeth chattering. Further on, I'd actually take off my coat and my jacket too and hold them over my arm (real bravado, you see), though I'd know for sure that tomorrow I would collapse in bed with bronchitis. Who'll look after me then? Who'll boil some milk for me? Who'll shake the thermometer when the mercury soars up to 107 degrees? And each morning, the unwashed glass on the bedside-table will glisten like the glass coffin of a bird. And only one thin strip of light, slipping in through the crack of the door, will slowly shift its position along the dusty floor, like the long minute-hand of some invisible clock tracing my last cycle. My God, I feel deeply moved. My nose starts running. But see here, old man – here's the button. On the table. And here's the needle with the thread. Right next to it. I sew the button in place. Also fix the other two buttons. Good heavens, how nice. I button myself up (for even inside the room, I'm wearing my coat). I feel warm and worthy. Ah, yes. The greatest misery in the whole world is to postpone. I close my lovely book, as though I am buttoning the three buttons on my friend's jacket, to keep his body-heat from escaping. Now let the rain rattle as hard as it likes on the zinc roof. These are no typewriters. No, no. They are tiny drums accompanying a song from our childhood, high upon the watch-towers of Monovasia, out towards the never-ending Myrtoa Sea. Oï, oï, bitter motherland never to be forgotten.

Mealtime

Noontime. Cold weather. The roads muddy. A dull sun like a rubber ice-pack on a sick woman's bosom. I come back from my office and set about warming up a plate of broad beans left over from yesterday. Maybe they're rancid. The spirit-stove is rusty. Will there be enough alcohol for me to make a cup of coffee? I go for a walk and think about my room with the unmade iron bed. In front of me, walks a barefoot man in ragged clothes. Behind him a swarm of children burst out laughing, throwing stones at him and jabbing him with their wooden swords. He laughs an unintelligible laugh, enveloped in his long arms and long legs, as though enveloped in an excessively wide coat and baggy socks. How enormous his eyes are. In the act of walking, he seems to be striving to channel the movement of his oblong body to the very end of his disjointed legs. So all his strength is spent in the effort and when he tries to move, he remains totally motionless and so ridiculous in the circle of his awkwardness that he feels dazed under his own laughter, as though under an umbrella which has turned inside out. When he stoops, his laughter falls, splashing in the mud. A soft drizzle starts. In the middle of the road, he stretches out his huge arm – like

Karaghiozi's arm – as though to catch an invisible bird. And to tell the truth, there is a bird sitting in the palm of his hand. The children around him are making a rumpus. Suddenly from the opposite direction, a blond boy with severe blue eyes arrives on the scene. He stands there, staring. Nothing more. At once the children hush up. Laying down their wooden swords. The rain stops. A bit of sunlight turns his hair golden. Could this be the twelve-year-old child who chased the merchants from his father's house? And could the other man be his father? Here he is, stepping forward with a smile. My hands feel warm. In the puddles full of rainwater, the clouds appear to float by serenely; and here and there, is a patch of very blue sky. I'm hungry. A bit of hot food will be grand on a table laid with a clean, white and blue-chequered tablecloth, and two sets of knives and forks facing each other.

Deprived of company

These days when the sky is crystal-clear and the horizon becomes a frame of tautly stretched satin, where beautiful silent women embroider lots of flowers out of rose-coloured threads, I've been longing to pay a visit somewhere, to some friendly family residing in a tiny white house among the trees, nearby, in a suburb of Athens. Out in the open air, they'll offer me cool water from the well and a spoonful of *masticha*-sweet. I can already see the sun sparkling in the glass of water and through the open door I observe the tidiness and cleanliness of the house and the big mirror, which reveals a small bright piece of the countryside, isolated and pinpointed in the shady calm of the large room; meanwhile, outdoors the birds are singing at the top of their lungs, in raptures. Through the open door, I so enjoy watching this same landscape, transposed into the silence of the mirror like a work of art I've been the first person to see; or rather, I myself have created it, but haven't yet presented it to the public. Then, in a soft voice and with little pauses, I'll begin to tell them about how a flower grows, or how a prematurely awakened rose-petal opens and unfolds and yawns. After this, I'll become very silent and place the palm of my hand on my eyes. But in a little while again, I'll remember that I am Ariostos and I'll take a large wrinkled handkerchief out of my pocket and blow my nose loudly so they won't take me for a romantic nitwit. That's how it is, Ariostos old boy. That's how you can always reverse beautiful things. That's how you can also reverse unhappy things. And let the other people laugh. Isn't this what you want? It *is*. And you consider this a trifle? A mere trifle?

The bell in the empty house

Here you are, the next-door house is deserted. They're off for their summer vacation. Through my window, I saw the suitcases and trunks being loaded into a big car. There was a copper pan gleaming on the sidewalk. The children were in a hurry. The lady rather pale and nervous. The maid vivacious, wearing a red dress and her hair fixed with a fine comb. A smell of severed bits of string and hastily made coffee. Afterwards, nothing. Now the house is all mine. This evening, I think I'll go ring the door-bell. The sound of the bell will roam through the empty hallway, where a dusty hat and an ash-grey jacket are hanging. It will ring more persistently over the small kitchen-door. In the old mirror, the sound appears like a round button on a coat. In the room facing the north, there is an unmade bed and a rat under the bed. The last room, in the back, is completely bare and there are two women sleeping there on the wooden benches. They don't budge an inch when they hear the bell. On their forehead, a spider is meticulously weaving its web in the space between the eyebrows and the nose. Of course, the persons who are on holiday now, haven't got the slightest notion of what's going on in here. I ring the bell once more and prepare to leave. Just then, the door opens. An ageing gentleman appears in dark pyjamas. "What do you want, sir?" he asks me. He is holding a salt-cellar in his left hand. With his right hand, he sprinkles a few pinches of salt on the two steps. "I just wanted a bit of salt," I answer. He shuts the door.

Insomnia

I've also been chosen to be a member of the Committee for claiming an eight-hour work-day and increased wages; the meeting with the Minister will take place tomorrow. They've actually made me responsible for the palavering. "Ariostos," they told me, "you're so wise, you'll explain everything nice and clear." So how could I refuse? All night long I've been torturing myself to formulate a single decent phrase. "Mr. Minister," say I. Nothing else. As a matter of fact, just how do you address a Minister? Sir? Your Excellency? Your Majesty? Very Reverend So-and-So? I've never even seen a Minister, except in newspaper-photos. But they're retouched. Anyway, they must have a fat wide snout and eyeglasses. In the glasses I can see the window, a corner of the table and the inkwell reflected in miniature. Gradually, the face disappears. Only the eyeglasses remain, suspended in mid-air. Involuntarily, with a clumsy move of my hand, supposed to emphasize the phrase: "Obstinately frugal", I upset the inkstand and stain various documents with ink; the ink trickles onto the floor, soiling one of the Minister's shoes and the whistle. I leap through the window. A big bird catches me in its beak, clutching me by the back of my jacket. I grow heavy. My buttons pop off. Now, my jacket is empty of me. I drop onto the sidewalk. I can see the bird flying high, high up, still clutching my jacket. Well, I'm not dead. Just cold. "Very Reverend Mr. Minister, even blankets get worn out. And certain big birds come and snatch them off the bed; indeed, one of these blankets got caught on the hook of a window and was torn to shreds. Therefore, venerable sir, the eight-hour workday is indispensable..." Ah, that damned word "wise". Suddenly, someone enters my room. A colleague. "Ariostos," says he, "our demands have been accepted. There's no reason for us to be presented to the Minister now." I wrap myself up very carefully in my blankets, close my eyes and find a speech which is so diplomatic, so strong and so beautiful and has so many arguments and splendid expressions. Where will I deliver my speech now? What a pity that our demands were accepted.

Acceptance

The evening cringes and is mute, like a young girl in black, sitting on a wooden bench at the chemist's shop, which is open all night, and she tries to hide her feet in the holey shoes underneath the bench. In silence, she waits for her little brother's medicine to be prepared. Her eyes look around at the shelves, which are full of all sorts of bottles. All these bottles are tightly sealed like mouths, which are unwilling to answer – like mouths which have nothing to say, like mouths which conceal something terribly serious in their unknown chemical substance. This is why I remembered that a colleague from the office (not one of the worst ones) spoke to me curtly the other day and for no reason at all, remarked: "Ariostos, you're a pseudo-progressive intellectual and nothing more." Pseudo-progressive? At first, I was furious. But I said nothing. Then, gradually, I was able to stomach it. I'm not angry any more. Not even sad. What else could I be? I pat myself on the shoulder and say: "Ariostos, you're a poor pseudo-progressive intellectual. Of course, that word '*pseudo*' will have to be erased..." I smile my own smile – my very own smile. But where is this light coming from? From inside me? Ah, if only I could offer it. I'd want nothing more. I lock my door from inside and crumple up in my nook. I think of a very wide road with a great deal of sun, where I will never walk. That doesn't matter. As long as I'm in time to offer this light. As long as I am able to.

Return

What is a lamp in the night other than a glass cage with a canary meditating inside? So when I turn off the light-switch, it's as though I'm opening the tiny door of a cage and I have the feeling that a yellow bird is flying out the window towards the open air. Then the pieces of furniture in my room, imprisoned by the light in their own shape, become free and without making any noise, walk like tame animals. As for me, once I am free of objects, I open the door of the glass cage, entering inside (me) and turning into light. I receive light. I give off light. I give shape to *other* things – clouds, shadows, winds, sounds, water, a nod, the void. A thimble becomes a lake, where pine-cones and leaves float. A tortoise becomes a train laden with chairs and statuettes from the Cyclades. A girl in a yellow dress sits in the lighted frame of a window and beckons to me. But I myself do not come out of my glass cage. I only start to warble. And I can hear this. Perhaps that girl can also hear me. If you too could hear me, the sack of stones on your shoulders would become much lighter. Indeed, maybe two wings would sprout for you. Who knows?

A summer evening in town

To be sure, other summers must have passed like this, but I never noticed. What we used to say in the old days I neither know nor care to know. Trudging up and down the staircases of the Ministries, your briefcase constantly under your arm, dust and grease in your hair, crumbs in your pockets, women buying talcum-powder for their skin-sores and polish for their fingernails, crowding into lifts full of persons drenched in sweat and smoke, statistics, logarithms, and sometimes a pause, and an opening and an old, long-forgotten song of the sea. Tonight when I left the office, I suddenly reflected that it was summertime; and absent-minded in the mute jollity of Saturday evening, I headed for the working-class district where I live. I didn't take the tram. Strolling slowly, pensively with myself for company. Here and there a geranium on a window-sill, a bit of basil and the motherly interior of humble rooms with oil-lamps. All of a sudden, I remembered my cat locked up in my room, waiting for me behind the door. I quickened my pace. Went into a little taverna and asked them to wrap a few fish-bones in some paper. But then, I recalled that my cat died at least four months ago. So I laid the small packet on a ledge and silently shuffled off with a guilty manner, but also with infinite tenderness for my own grief. Maybe another cat will rip open the newspaper and enjoy the fish-bones like my own cat. So when I reach home, I head straight for my tiny garden, cut two roses and put them in a glass vase on top of my papers. Just then, a cat rubs up against my legs. I bend down and pet it. It doesn't leave. It is white and soft as silky down. I pick it up in my arms together with the roses and go into my own room. Tonight I'll have somebody to share my meagre supper with. And it's summertime. Now, I'm sure it is summer and there's a moon as well.

One number and another number

I'm attending a matinee performance in an open-air folk theatre. The stage-lights become intermingled with the afternoon light, lending a dim yellow colour to the air. Something smells like past sickness and lemon. Outside the theatre-enclosure, a motorcycle is heard disappearing into the distance of the old neighbourhood, along a dusty road. On stage, they're performing a satirical number. A huge tall man is dressed up like a woman and he puts on mincing airs. The spectators are tremendously amused. So am I. Every gesture of this mime turns into a glistening glass, which falls from a tray and goes rolling along the floor. We observe this glass intently. We ourselves turn into a glass, which rolls along the floor with a tinkling sound. It's going to break. Going to break. Here it comes. No. It didn't break. There's an even louder outburst of laughter. The glass did not break. We did not break. Glass creatures, we roll along the ground. By my side somebody laughs so noisily that I start to suspect him. I observe him. Then I understand. He's laughing in order to punish the feminine part of himself, while stimulating the other part: the male. His physiognomy is masculine, strictly masculine. But his hand, as it flicks the cigarette-ash – a hand with long slender fingers – delineates the profile of a woman in the smoke. Now he starts to applaud louder than his own hands permit. His laughter grows louder. I start to laugh too. I listen. Yes. I too am laughing loudly. Suspiciously, I glance around me. What can I do? Not laugh? The people surrounding me will hear. Shall I laugh? Maybe someone next to me is observing me and accusing me of all the things I accused the aforementioned man. I stare at my fingers. They are long and more slender than the other man's. I stand up, ready to run away. Behind my back, the crowd's laughter bursts out very noisily. Can they be laughing at me? "Ariostos," I say, "remain cool-headed. Look serious. Wrinkle your eyebrows very hard and turn your head to make sure." In the end, I manage to turn my head. Everybody is laughing, but turned towards the stage. So nobody has even noticed me. I sit down again on a seat in the last row. No longer in the mood to laugh. I can't even see. I think of Old Teiresias, after his death, in the midst of those merry unfair gods. I can hear the sound of a glass slipping from a tray and breaking. I'm the one who falls off the tray and simultaneously, the one who collects the broken pieces of glass from the floor, so that nobody else will step on them. I, Ariostos the Observant.

Awakening after the conflagration

Was it a dream? An earthquake? A conflagration? The entire city was burning. Doors and windows bursting into flames. People leaping from terraces like parachutists, screams teetering like acrobats on tightropes made of fire. Pitch-black burnt out walls, arches of bridges looming up above the flames and collapsing in great chunks or crumbling, stone by stone. Porphyry, mauve, orange colours in all their glory behind the charred doorways of palaces, banks, theatres. The sooty smog lifted blazing awnings and suspended them high in mid-air for a while until the flames died out. A dog with singed fur passed by on the road. There was a black bird perched on its back with closed eyes and the dog didn't even know it. Only one ash-grey factory is still standing, with its huge smokestack raised high amidst the exploding flashes of light, as though it wants to compare something. All the neighbours are out on the road. Nobody's come to any harm. Since we're still alive, who cares about the houses, the furniture and the blankets. All of us, both enemies and friends, chat away in harmony. No, there aren't any enemies. A truly beautiful spectacle. A little girl passes by holding a small bundle in her hand. An infant whimpers pleasantly. We can breathe. I even make friends with that Ludovico Ariosto. Calmly, I share my name with him, like a slice of hot bread. In a friendly way, I even shake hands with my boss. This unfortunate man must have lost the most (just two days ago actually, he'd purchased some splendid lace curtains; I imagine the conflagration must have looked magnificent behind these curtains – like a porphyry-gold arabesque; and of course, they must have blazed away still more magnificently, dancing de Falla's "Fire Dance" with aethereal grace). After clambering up some tall, tall ladders and spraying gold and rose-coloured jets of water, the firemen are taking off their helmets now and with the back of their hands, they wipe off their sweat-stained brow. Further on, the big vehicles of the Fire Brigade stand securely above their own square shadow traced on the asphalt, which is still bright. Two strong-armed, hefty firemen spread their legs apart and piss, entirely absorbed by their own strength. Of course, the children who are going to be born tomorrow will not resemble us or remember us. The nocturnal vapours begin turning blueish. Daybreak. I've woken up. Abundant light streams in through the window, inundating my room. Like another fireman, the sun rests its golden helmet on my low window-sill.

My ticket

I'm overcome by immense shyness every springtime. A joyful tremour and fear. Yes, fear. I enter the light as though entering a stranger's house and carefully wipe off my shoes so as not to soil the polished floor, which two cheerful sturdy girls have just waxed – the one girl in red and the other in a yellow dress. The corridors are very big, with oblong windows, marble columns, panes of glass and mirrors everywhere. In a corner, an old brown velvet armchair, with a small open book on top of it. I pretend not to see it. Maybe that's why I hesitate. Maybe because the trees, which are extremely green, were not planted by me. But I was expecting the greenery. Even more than other people, actually. I began observing some little notes which had crept into the birds' song and also, the paint on the shutter cracking and peeling. To be sure, I never knew how to plant trees. But no. I too have planted a rosebush. I pick a rose and show it to the conductor on the rural train. "May I come aboard?" I ask him. He – I mean, the conductor – nods his solid, good-natured head. "Do come aboard," he answers. I get off at the seaside. Looking people straight in the eye. A bit further on, a group of demonstrating workers passes by. I plunge into their midst and shout:

"Hurrah." Someone next to me, very handsome and very serious, wearing a workingman's cap, looks at me rather strangely. I lower my eyes. His hands are tremendously broad, like a twofold Peloponnese. Slowly I raise my eyes again, at the same time as my right hand. I show the man my rose. He seems to be convinced at that point. He acquiesces. Perhaps with a touch of indulgence. And he becomes still more handsome. We walk on together, under the sun – I know not where. It is hot. I take off my jacket.

My photographer

There you are. This photographer is trailing after me again. At first, it was rather amusing. I was actually flattered to have a person dogging my steps and recording my every movement and gesture. Especially, such a discreet and agreeable and politely observant person. But soon enough, he started to annoy me. There were certain things I had to do which no one should ever see. And there he was, just at the moment I assumed a not so modest pose – click, and my photo was ready. This deprived me of all freedom and still worse, all naturalness. I began to calculate my footsteps, the way I opened my mouth, the way I unbuttoned each button. Furthermore, he was becoming less and less discreet. He started to interfere in a brash way, according to his own taste, suggesting this or that pose to me – supposedly at a more aesthetic angle. For example, at the moment I drank my coffee after a sleepless night, or at the moment I lay down to sleep, worn out by this all-day posing, there he was again: "Ariostos," he'd say, (no: "Mr. Ariostos", as at first) "tilt your head a bit more; lift your right leg a bit higher"; etc. He considered me some grand personality travelling incognito and he had no intention of letting a single act of mine go by without immortalizing it. Of course, it was also my fault for corroborating this notion of his; now and then I would drop a newspaper clipping about Ludovico Ariosto (that diplomatic agent of Cardinal Ippolito d'Este) and his epic *Orlando Furioso*; or I would remove from my innermost pocket (with feigned tact) a multi-coloured plume I'd plucked from the peacocks in the Royal Garden. But now he's become insufferable. I can't go on living constantly exposed to his lens, as though I'm under the huge, hideous eye of some god, painted on the dome of a modern church. At all costs, I must get rid of him. So I start assuming outrageous poses: I strip naked in front of him, behave indecently, commit blunder after blunder, in hopes he will finally drop me. But he just carries on clicking his camera. Today I gave him the opportunity to photograph me – I simply can't admit how. And I'm sure the idiot must have entitled this photo: "How the Hindi of Agra-Oudh do their praying". And what if he prints it some day? All night long I haven't been able to sleep a wink. Eleven o'clock. Midnight. One o'clock. Two. Do you think they'll stone me? Two-thirty a.m. Three. Three-fifteen. I stand up. Head straight for his studio. It's dark. I remove my shoes. Creep up the staircase. All's quiet. He must be asleep. I enter his studio. The glass roof lets in just enough light. It's deserted. Not a soul, not a sound. Only there in the middle, the big camera is entirely covered by a black cloth. At long last. Here are my photographs scattered over the table and the floor. I reach out my hand. Click. An enormous click, as though the world is tumbling down on my back. Inside the black cloth, it's he. And I am a thief, who is about to rob and kill his own self. I collapse. A hand lifts my head. I am offered a glass of water. He kisses me on the forehead. I throw my arms around his legs and start to weep: "Is that you?" I whisper. "Yes, it's me," he answers. He caresses my hands. "You're my only friend," I say to him. "So are you," he answers. He sets me down on the little couch and switches on the light. We look at the photographs together. "They're beautiful," I say. "Yes," he says. "Shall we burn them?" I ask. "Let's burn them," he answers. "Thank you," I say. We fall silent. Staring at the photos. And other photos too. From the first to the last of the great robbery. "They are beautiful though," I say to him. "Truly beautiful," he repeats. "Let's keep them, but not print them." "Let's not print them." We fall silent again. A small mouse scuttles past, close to the wall. "But they're so beautiful," I repeat. "Will no one see them?" "No one must see them," he answers. I feel really tired from the sleepless night and the effort. I close my eyes. Can hear him picking up the photographs. And suddenly, the crackling sound of a match. I spring up. "Don't, don't," I shout. Seizing hold of his hands. I get tangled up in the legs of the camera. The black cloth engulfs me. Opposite me, the mirror. I can see. A handsome monk in a long cassock. "Right now," I tell him, "like this." My photographer has vanished. I take his place. I photograph the mirror. The mirror is empty.

NOTE

Ariostos the Observant was written in October 1942, in Athens, in the midst of the German Occupation. In 1971, during the Colonels' Junta, the poet went through the text again, making a few minor changes. The book was published for the first time in 1981.

BOOK TWO

Such Strange Things

These and other things

Strange things, without any meaning at all, completely insignificant, call them foolish; but there you are, I don't know how and why, for me they have a certain (not only a certain), they have great, unique significance – perhaps because of being insignificant (and strange), they do not compel me to look for concepts, ideas, purposes, explanations, excuses, prevarications, obligations, limitations, prohibitions. I merely dally with them. And they help me rest. As though I'm asleep, and these things happen of their own accord, without my interfering, even when they do concern me and my legs get entangled with ropes, crates, stones, water, a snare, an old parrot-cage, a hard white ancestral collar full of rust stains, a chicken's chopped-off leg, moving its claws in a funny way; in those days, in the countryside, at noon, in the big vineyard (such light, such cicadas, and a partridge and a small brook smothered in osiers and brambles), well in those days, from the tip of the chicken's chopped-off leg, we used to pull the nerves (or the tendons – I don't know how they're called) through the tough skin, and they moved in a very funny way, yes, the chicken's claws, hooked and long – some movements like those of an old woman crossing herself – no, no, like comical imitations of an old woman crossing herself; or as if they were chasing a fly from the forehead of a sick, paralysed old woman 123-and-a-half years old; or as if they were tickling drunken old Uncle Lambis behind his ear, and it really suited old Uncle Lambis to be drunk at high noon, and his name (meaning bright) especially suited him in that drunken brightness of our childhood noontime; meanwhile the chicken itself, inside Aunt Evanghelia's pot, in the company of pan-browned okra and onions, wafted its fragrance through the door and open windows, five, ten metres away, out in the open air where we were playing, and the other chickens were feeding on the dry weeds, feeling not the slightest twinge of pity for their missing sister or mother, because in the strong, ear-splitting glare of the sun no suspicion of slaughter or whiff of death could fit; and the downy feathers of that chicken turned iridescent, reddish-golden, blackish-golden, greenish-golden atop the tall yellow thistles, which were well aware that further down was the small brook, where the children (with their knees and elbows covered in a thousand scratches), were picking blackberries, and they munched them just like that, all dusty; their jaws and cheeks were stained red, there by the side of the brook, where the somewhat older boys were masturbating and their sperm kept falling, "tsap ... tsap ..." into the brook, and there were frogs too, croaking, now and then, at rare intervals, because they were saving their voices for the evening. And by the time we went into Aunt Evanghelia's house – they'd been calling us for quite a while – how inviting they sounded: "Come on, dinner's ready, it's all ready, come now" – our eyes were full of sparks from all that sun, the room inundated with long yellow shadows and the long, wood-planked table laid with a chequered tablecloth and the plates were also yellow and it didn't smell of chicken cooked with okra, but there was a strange smell of brand-new Sunday shoes. Inside the cool shade of the house, I became more intensely aware of how big was the light outside, how big the world with its rivers, seas, streets, trees, mountains, country chapels, windows and an extremely large tree, all in the sky, and instead of fruits, it had tiny angels playing tiny mandolins (as I noticed later on, in the coloured etchings by Demetres), but they may also have been those minuscule ancient cupids with the puffed-up little cheeks; and all things ran, quivered, stirred unstirringly and were immeasureably and infinitely radiant. And I told Aunt Evanghelia: "I don't want any chicken at all, just okra." At that very moment, through the open window, in flew a large, very large butterfly, blue with orange splotches, and it settled on the salt-cellar (which all at once had grown a metre taller, into a crystal column) with her wings unfurled, one wing covering the salt and the other the red pepper, so that even if I wanted to sleep that evening, I wouldn't be able to close my eyelids.

Athens, February 26th, 1983

Climbing the stairs

Well now, as I was climbing up the indoor stairs, as slowly as slow could be, all the while restraining my desire to leap up the steps five at a time and reach the landing, all out-of-breath and laughing in the manner of a champion who had no opponent or competition, comparison or rating, I found time to smile to myself and make sure there were 18 steps (it would have been a silly victory, that of the gasping ascent, almost flight, without the wings of a bird or an angel) – anyway, I could still remember my failure with those cardboard wings I'd made out of beer-boxes (luckily, without any witnesses), at the far end of the garden where the daisies were, and afterwards, I said I'd slipped and fallen on the rocks, and in two weeks there was no mark left on my ribs, legs, cheeks (those cardboard wings I hid behind the gate; one rainy night, they got soaked, warped; I cut them into strips and made a Karaghiozi, a Kollitiri, and an enormous Barba-Yorghos out of one whole wing); and here I go now at the top of the staircase, slowly, seriously, solemnly, with the number 18, and here I am exactly opposite the second storey window with the 6 panes, and behind the window-panes was the sea and it resounded "phsout ... phsout ...", not 18 plus 6, but one thousand "phsout ... phsout ..." sounds, and then another thousand kept continuing and another, my fingers and toes would not suffice, combined with the fingers and toes of my schoolmates in my primary school and in all the grown-up schools throughout the whole wide world, they wouldn't be enough to count these "phsout ... phsout ..." sounds; and I was so entranced (and indeed, secretly proud) that I, only I alone, had heard and tasted the uncountable, and of course I wouldn't tell anybody, lest they punish me by standing me against the wall, or refuse to play with me; then I drew closer to the window, and there, on the third pane to the left, was a small spider, and exactly behind the spider, a small caique with sails, motionless and smaller than the spider. Oh certainly, that spider, like myself, was listening to the "pshout ... phsout ..." sounds of the sea, and must, like myself, have sensed the uncountable. And I was jealous and angry that I wasn't the only uncountable. At that point, I took a toothpick out of my pocket and put it under the spider. And it caught hold of the toothpick and I drew it out. And it hung there dangling from its own saliva and tried to creep down. But apparently it changed its mind and like an acrobat, climbed back up the thread of its saliva, slowly, seriously, solemnly, till it stopped, deep in thought (and perhaps, entranced) on my toothpick. That's why I felt sympathy for it and left it on the window-pane again, so that we could both listen to the "phsout ... phsout ..." sounds together, fellow-athletes and comrades, fraternally sharing the unshareable, in equal (though whole) parts. Thus, our secret alliance was sealed. I went into the next room and stood in front of the mirror to see if I was the same. Yes, the same, but stripped of my clothes, naked, stark-naked, and on my shoulders, back there, two big blue wings, bigger than the gold frame of the mirror and almost touching the ceiling. Where is my shirt? Where are my trousers? And that toothpick? And what if I tried, suppose I'd be able to fly? To fly? The afternoon was advancing. The room was lit by the glow from the sea. It looked blueish. I turned my back to the mirror, stuck my hands in my pockets and grabbed the toothpick. On my way into the first room, I stopped at the window a moment. The spider had gone and I went down the stairs quickly. In front of the entrance-door stood Chrysanthi cleaning the glass top of the oil-lamp. Just then the whistle of the steamship was heard and tiny pieces of crystal filled the dining-room, and a rose fell onto the chair.

Athens, February 26th, 1983

Shoes

I have such an obsession with shoes. Ever since I was a little boy. Not that I collect them the way philatelists collect stamps or some people collect match-boxes, others worry-beads or pipes made of wood, bone, clay. Nothing like that. And when I say shoes I do not mean only different styles of shoes, men's, women's, children's shoes, boots, army boots, rustic shoes, sandals, court shoes with flat or higher heels, etc.; but at the same time (even more so, actually), I mean the feet and the toe-nails, and the path they take at night along the damp, brightly lit avenue next to the big patisseries; or in the morning upon the hill where fallen pine-needles crackle; or in the field on the soft grass where a few drops of dew are left on an ankle-boot, shining diabolically bright; or on the seacoast and as they tread, some tiny white pebbles or shingles spring up behind the heel with secretive noises, full of many meanings, and you wonder: "Is this the answer?"; "The answer to what?"; "And what is the question?"; and there are also the other noises, lingering or abrupt, e.g. when it rains and the mud gets stuck on the shoes and the soles become heavy and whoever arrives outside the house wipes his feet on the little iron shoe-scraper off to the side, and you're inside waiting quietly: "Will he wipe his shoes again? Will he bang the knocker again? Will he persist?"; and what if his socks are wet? and no callouses on his toes? – back last summer, in the course of our swims, Telis had said: "How beautiful your feet are, mate; by any chance, have you stolen them off the statues?" and Goghos had blushed, as though we'd caught sight of his cock and hastily, he'd put on his socks, with his feet still soaking wet, and immediately his shoes as well, beautiful white linen trainers with grey-blue, diagonal, leather stripes. But this is not the issue now; we're talking about some other completely unknown people – from the cut of their jib, they appeared to be peasants, whose boots had sunk into the snow up to the knees and one man had stuck his crook into the snow and left it over there, alone and coal-black; and when they finally reached the railway station, they went into the stationmaster's house and the stationmaster was smoking his pipe and said: "Sit down by the fireplace; take off all your clothes; my wife's away; there's hot milk in the pot; no train will be passing by"; and the house smelled of homeyness and oakwood smoke and a hot, shaggy wool rug. And they all took off their duffle-coats, boots and socks, like ancient shepherds, and the two older ones also took off their breeches and were left in their calico buttoned-up underpants; but the three younger ones, twenty-year-olds, left their trousers on and rolled them up to their shanks covered in coarse hairs; and all of them together stretched their legs, still tanned a reddish colour from last summer, spreading them out in front of the fire, and their feet dried and were steaming-hot, and these lumpish lubbers didn't even realise their feet had traversed the sacred ritual of eternity and had left indelible tracks upon the belly of the earth, deeper than the tracks of wolves or elephants; and surely, some beautiful humble woman kneeling in front of them, ought to measure the length and width of their soles, by a wax-covered string, just as people measure a plot of land near the seaside for the purpose of building a big church, while their boots, all lined up near the door, also warmed themselves; and the snow was melting, and I was sure that a little later on, when the oil-lamps would go out and they would all close their eyelids, as they sprawled on their backs upon the same straw mat, just then, the minuscule ancient cupids, bereft of their quivers, would burrow into the boots, and with only their heads sticking out, they would giggle in high-pitched tones or cackle in a fake manner, like hens laying eggs. But these things are self-evident and don't need many words and frills, just as horses are white with a black spot between their noble, upright ears. Therefore, my boy, I'm telling you, you'd better take off your shoes and hang them over your shoulder when you're on your way to the city at daybreak, in springtime. So, in your bare feet (and you're "left-footed", to boot), you could nicely kick the golden ball, at the very moment the sun comes out. As for the rest – play it by ear, my dear.

Athens, February 26th, 1983

Sequel to the previous installment

Self-evident things, as I was telling you. Self-evident and inexplicable. No need for words and explanations. No words at all. What the devil are shoes anyway? Just shoes. Gloves, as it were, for the feet. Except that they're permanent – winter, summer, on the street, at home, in hospital, in that long corridor, or at the Luna Park, or on the Funicular (isn't that how it's called?), and even in the sea, those long plastic flippers, green, yellow, blue flippers, and in the background the dolphins frisking about and a motorboat with 100 nude girls whizzing past near the seashore, and Telis, tall and sunburnt saying: "Won't you take those masks off your feet, so your toes can breathe?" (that's just how he said it: "masks"; this is something I'll have to remember; do feet also have masks?); and Alekos "platsch ... platsch ..." in the sand with his flippers, "platsch ... platsch ...", receding like a big bird as though incapable of flying, or like a drunken captain balancing on the bridge of a big white ship, sailing away without emitting a wisp of smoke, and it did actually sail away. In this way, by remaining three-quarters of their lives encased in shoes, feet have no practice in hypocrisy (they don't need it for the sake of protection or deception); that's why when feet remain bare, they appear adorably clumsy, boorishly unaffected, sincere, innocent, rather shy; precisely for this reason, more erotic and rapacious. And then again, when we say "footgear", we don't mean only the soles and the toes, but also the knees and thighs and navel and breasts and the armpits with a bit of sweat on the shaggy part and the neck and the hair and the face, the eyes, nose, ears, lips – in a word, the entire body with its movements, vibrations and shudders, like that acrobat in his pink tights which covered his whole body though he looked totally nude, as he arched his body backwards extremely slowly and with both hands grasped his ankles and stuck his head out in between his soft pink shoes and smiled celestially at the spectators, with his jawbone resting on the floor – a perfect, eternal circle, so perfect that the crowd forgot to applaud, as though all of them, women and men alike, had ejaculated and they were all floating in an enormously sad state of bliss. And perhaps, precisely because of this, by way of reaction, I recalled that fat woman of the island (they called her crazy: "Lock her up," they shouted) and stripped nude, with her big broad breasts, she laughed to herself; and wearing the forest-ranger's high boots on her arms up to her armpits, and crawling along on her knees, she crept under the iron bed, leaving her fat white bottom sticking out like an August full moon in Monovasia, with nocturnal fishermen, acetylene lamps and seals; and her slit was clearly showing, brownish-pink, full of thin, thin little puckers, without any hairs at all; and down under the bed, she started pounding dap-dap ... dap-dap ... the forest-ranger's boots on the floor, dap-dap ..., the nearby tam-tam, the far-away tam-tam ... dap-dap ..., night in the forest, black men, black women and three leopards, and a bear, that's what I call dancing, heels up in the air tam-tam ... tam-tam ...; "catch her," they shouted, "lock her up," they shouted, "crazy, crazy, crazy" dap-doup-dap ..., and moon and leaves; and my boy, when I tell you all this, I don't mean the patent-leather shoes of the dead, or, God forbid, the senile slippers of the philosophers, or even those dainty ladies' slippers which are open at the back, however lovely, however lovely, all satiny and garnished with pearls or little tufts of yellow fluff; because trains do depart and there's a smell of spilt petrol and closed pork-butcher-shops; and when a woman lies on her back, the only things protruding are her nose and the tips of her breasts and her toes with those polished toenails, while her shoes near the bed inhale and exhale loudly, phsui ... phsui ..., blowing away – why are you rushing? – and again, when you enter a woman, her legs press tightly against your ribs or link themselves around your waist or your neck or remain in mid-air under your chin, and at the very moment your sperm comes pouring out, you bite her heels and they turn into wings smeared with spittle, and you have wings and my word, you fly, and goddam the wings – what are they anyway? – nor do you care; ah, night, tam-tam, stars and pine-cones falling, the waters roaring hurrah in the void, cascades flicking off drops of water, laundry clothes-pegs, white sheets, underclothes, petticoats, bras, knickers, underpants, undershirts, an undulating scarf five metres long, birds with their feathers slightly damp, cherry-tree branches always in a hurry, not in time to display their diaphanous colours, and stockings, stockings, stockings worn by beautiful feet of women, socks by adolescents, grown men, labourers, farmers – a storm of stockings, and the poem ends up more or less like this: *"Then, we lit the great bonfires; we placed the old man on the rock; / we removed our army boots and thus, sitting down upon the ground / in pairs, facing one another, we measured the soles of our feet. / Constandis, the youngest one, with the largest feet, was the first to dance on top of the dried carobs."*

Athens, February 27th, 1983

Shadowy space

The room seemed endless, extremely dimly lit. You didn't know if it was the reception-hall of a palace, of a luxurious hotel or of a Maritime Bank. Endless, yes, but separated into many sections, with a black satin screen embroidered with Chinese sprigs of flowers, probably, most likely cherry-trees or chrysanthemums and slender-stalked rice or barley – you couldn't very clearly discern in this half-lit obscurity. Only one dark red light-bulb, somewhere on a wall or on the ceiling, glimmered faintly without diffusing its light, like a large drop of blood, which has stopped and congealed in mid-air and has turned black. Anyway, there was no furniture, no tables, couches, vases at all, except for one armchair, also dark red, and two pianos – the one rather nearby, not a grand piano, and the other one over there, a big grand piano. Indeed, on the polished surface of the pianos, a moribund, pale rose reflection crept now and then, perhaps from that same light-bulb. Shadowy figures kept flitting past and you couldn't tell if they were butlers, waiters, clients, merchant-marine captains, adjutants, shipowners, or ballerinas dancing on their points with inexplicable embarrassment. Just at this point, a labourer enters through a revolving crystal door; with broad strides he advances and in front of the dark red armchair, *not* underneath the chair, he deposits something wrapped up in newspapers and tied with bits of string – maybe an aluminium mess-tin full of boiled chick-peas from some concentration-camp for political prisoners; in any case, obviously, dynamite and fuses are out of the question. No. No. And there he is now, on his way out. His shirt flapping outside his trousers. A nebulous waiter (this time, he *is* a waiter, even though he does have a white bird in his back pocket – probably a small goose) approaches, picks up the package, pulls off the strings, tears the newspaper. On the newspaper, written with a thick black felt-tipped pen, is the word COMPASS. Just then, as if from a concealed loudspeaker, a peremptory male voice is heard: "Leave it where it belongs. Leave it there, I said." The man places it in front of the armchair again. A lady, also shadowy, in a long violet-coloured gown, steps forward, through barely audible sounds of plates, glasses and silver cutlery, forward towards the piano. Simultaneously, I (utterly indefinite, although elegant and terribly pale – I'm intensely aware of this) step forward towards the second, the grand piano, having in my mind the notes of the "Caprices d'Amour", in A-minor, and the melody in my mouth mixed with my own saliva, like a few wedding candies. I can almost hear it. I can almost sing it. La si do si, la sol fa mi, mi-i, re-e. Four semi-quavers and another four, two quavers, a crochet rest; yes, A-minor, without any flats or sharps in the key-signature; si do re fa, mi re do si, si-i, la-a. Nevertheless, I hesitate. The lady comes first. It would be thoroughly unfitting for me to start playing, for two different melodies to get tangled up, maybe also tones and rhythms – what an asinine fugue – what if Bach were listening to us from behind a screen. Besides, the lady is wearing a necklace; from time to time, it sparkles barely visibly – probably pearls, not rhinestones; and what about that labourer with that shirt of his? – he has vanished. So I still hesitate. The lady is already standing in front of the piano. I am five steps further on. I turn my head slightly, with a sideways, discreet glance. I don't wish to appear to be observing. With her left hand, the lady, standing upright, slowly opens the lid of the piano. Her hand grows longer. It is yellow. From somewhere, the light grows stronger. The lid opens. The piano gapes wide open. Empty. Nothing in the place where the keyboard should be. No keys, no little hammers, no strings. An extremely shallow old trunk. And in there, some cardboard cartons of dirt-cheap "knock-out" cigarettes from the days of the Nazi Occupation; the cartons were filled with hair-clips, hairpins, hair-rollers, melted lipsticks, a belt-clasp, a few little wheels and springs from dilapidated old alarm-clocks and the silver handle of an antiquated umbrella. Music can be heard now. From over there? No. From the other piano? No, no. Anyway, from somewhere. I have the sensation I am evaporating, I am absent, and yet, I exist and I can see. It must have been raining somewhere else, out in the country, with abandoned millstones and fallen columns. The light dims again. Twelve waiters, lined up in a row, are holding at arm's length, big silver trays, empty. Almost no light at all. Only the trays gleam. And suddenly, down on the floor a brigade of turtles parades. On their damp carapace, silvery-ashen reflections vibrate from some unknown source of light. The lady retreats from the piano, with both her hands devoutly holding a cardboard cigarette-carton filled with those hair-rollers; she is careful not to step on the turtles, while at the back of the hall, a stark-naked man with muscular arms appears in a dim light – maybe that same labourer? or maybe Petros? – and somebody can be heard singing (maybe me?) that same melody – la si do si, la sol fa mi, mi-i, re-e, míre, míre, moira, destiny; si, do, re, fa, mi, re, do, si, si, la, a, a. Ah, oh boy, such buoyantly beautiful strange things. (This I can halfway hear myself saying.) And suddenly, a vast, utterly white light pours out everywhere, along with an utterly white chill, as if someone has opened the door of a gigantic electric fridge and all at once, everything has dissolved, pianos, screens, waiters, trays, turtles, ladies, the whole space has dissolved into an infinite whiteness, without a single stigma. Maybe it's daybreak. I rub my eyes. Nothing. Absolutely nothing. Only this providential light, which prevents you from despairing and imbues you with dulcet indifference full of love for the nothingness, for everything, and for yourself. But maybe somewhere there must be many fountains, because the sound of water can be clearly heard, laudatory, lofty aqueous curvatures, transparent spirals rising – arches of triumph – which triumph? Such strange things. Just try to disentangle these transcendental, so to speak, emotions, this stunned musical apathy, and furthermore, why and how? Where do you suppose that old book, *The Key to Our Dreams*, belonging to my dear-departed grandmother can be, with those drops of wax on the cover and the sprigs of marjoram between the pages?

Athens, February 27th, 1983

From without or from within

I often come back to this. I just don't understand. And the harder I try to understand, the less I do understand. Apparently, it's the effort which prevents me. Apparently, these "hows", "whats", "whys" of ours are not at all ways of penetrating and opening paths towards the interior of the incomprehensible; on the contrary, these imbecilic questions become bronze breast-plates of the incomprehensible and henceforth, it becomes inaccessible and you cannot even touch it with your little finger. But you still harp on the same theme – why this? why that? why the other? Maybe you are quite right. E.g. why, especially in springtime, do a butterfly's wings form a diptych, miniature town with select colours and tiny, tiny half-moon windows? You can't be serious. And why are flowers like multifarious butterflies, unable to fly and pinioned to the ground by delicate long green nails? And when it rains, why do lots and lots of lines of water trickle down the window-panes and in back of the panes, the apartment buildings appear and the school and the church, etched more or less diagonally with a crystal ruler? And in the entrance, near the staircase, why have they left a crutch, which has a brown imprint from a cigarette burn on the curved wooden top (the part which goes under the cripple's armpit)? And why does the minute-hand on my wristwatch walk in circles at a regular pace, but at the same time, seems to be slyly indecisive, smiling inside itself about something lovely, which is totally its own and contrary to me? And why, when you make love, do you remove your wristwatch and put it on the nearby chair and a button falls onto the floor from your jacket, which is hanging on a peg on the wall, "tak", just one "tak", and all things are at the right hour and almost uncontested? And last summer, when a grape-harvester, stark-naked, was washing the remains of the grape-must off his horse, at Platanákia, in the shallow waters near the seashore, I found an egg on top of his clothes tossed there in the sand, not a hen's egg, a small round egg, probably from a wild duck or a seagull, and suddenly, I recalled the Apocalypse of Saint John (not the Theológos), that Other Saint John, who with his own eyes, had seen *God shelling a boiled egg*. You can't really make heads or tails of this. To hell with it, said I, and I made up my mind *not* to understand, not even to want to understand, but to make up with the incomprehensible, to enter it and feel cosy inside it; and all at once, I felt calm and was actually happy and I really liked that white spot on the wall, which grew wider and wider till it covered three-quarters of the painting with the seascape, and I noticed that the coffee in the big cup looked tremendously natural, genuinely natural, like the whistle of a boat or a train, or children's voices in a schoolyard, or tangerines in the fruit-vendor's crate; and almost no shootings were heard; and the snow had settled gently on Mount Párnitha, so gently you could say "thank you" and just light another cigarette. And we did indeed light our cigarettes, with the same lighter, Alekos, Goghos, and I; at which point, Telis entered: "Hey there, my brave lads, have you turned monks or what?" said he, setting a half-kilo loaf of hot bread on the table and a toilet-roll, which Alekos picked up and started unwinding; and as he sat there with his knees apart, the toilet-paper fell onto the floor with a soft swishing sound, and in between Alekos' legs, an exquisite frothy mound was growing higher and higher – marvel, marvel, marvel – and we stared speechless, Telis standing up, Goghos sitting on the couch, me on a chair near the table – till all the toilet-paper was unwound and the only thing left was the inner cardboard tube, and Alekos placed it in his mouth and went *ouoúouou – ouoú, ouoú,* like a shepherd, *ouoúouou* – marvel, marvel – and could be heard as far as the kitchen; and Eleni rushed in and stopped in the doorway: "Have you gone bonkers?" said she, laughing loudly although she had a white napkin slung over her shoulder; but Telis just stood there, looking angry about some past vexation or perhaps some present one; and Goghos was extremely sad; and I was the most unhappy of all, because I was so very joyful deep inside me, ready to burst from so much light and air; I was actually embarrassed not to be able to say it and yet, also embarrassed to say and confess it; marvel and birds and a closed white and another infinitely open and absolutely white – and whatever you say, Eleni does have two taut little breasts, you touch them like this and your hand sticks to them, all rubbery, and can't get unstuck, and your mouth sticks too; for this very reason, but also for the aforementioned – namely, that frothy little mound – I cut off a corner of the loaf and started munching it and the crumbs fell on this notebook where I write and then

I rolled up the paper and threw the crumbs into the ashtray; and what do you think, Mr. Telis? – it was my turn to get angry: "Yes, well now, a real marvel," I yelled.

Athens, February 28th, 1983

Petros' return

We weren't expecting him at all. It had been a while. Not that we'd forgotten him. Impossible to forget Petros. He always makes the rounds in our nights, our dreams, our gestures (in some ways copied from his own); he is a unit for comparison, a measure for judging refusal, acceptance, acclamation and loud applause. Even Telis patterned after him in some respects – resembling him, though in a rather sloppy style. Approximately two years must have gone by and Petros had vanished. No letters, no phone-calls. Nothing. Could he be dead? No way. Killed? No way. Maybe he was working on one of the shipping-lines (he was crazy about the sea and good God, how he could swim; the girls used to scream: "ah, ah, ah – a dolphin, a shark, ah"). On a boat. Deck-boy? Cabin-boy? (no); engineer? down in the boiler room or at the printer's? Now what would a printing-press be doing on the boat? But perhaps a clandestine mimeograph-machine (like back during the Nazi Occupation) to print some leaflets "against nuclear disaster" and "those murderous military bases", for the purpose of disseminating them in various ports – and you really believed that under his shirt (always impeccable), there'd be smudged fingerprints on his shoulder and chest and maybe on his belly and thighs. And these smudged finger-marks did not remind you of fingerprints at police stations or Security Headquarters, not at all: on the contrary, they brought to mind underground passageways in the coal-mines of Ostrava and those mystical lamps, which search the bowels of the earth as well as our very guts. The name of Petros always hovered like such a lamp, within or up above our dark conversations and perhaps a thick hair from his moustache was still there on Anna's shoulder – for one afternoon, Anna herself had confessed to Maria that after *it*, the following morning when Petros left, she had collected the curly hairs of his body from the bed (still warm) and she kept them in a small pink bonbonnière from someone else's wedding (with a gold band round the box); and when she was completely on her own, she used to open it and look at these little hairs (which she actually wanted to call "big hairs", as she herself said) and she would smell them, though they had no smell, but they seemed to be calling more or less: "come here, come, come" and they were like soft hooks which you could throw into the sea to catch goldfish; yes indeed, soft hooks, which didn't tear the lips of the goldfish or make their tongues bleed. "Good heavens," said Maria (maybe she was jealous) and I don't really know if fish have tongues – in any case, soft, and for a moment, you catch the fish in your fist, stroke their fins and throw them back into the sea while they're still absolutely alive and for half a second they turn their "nose" and stare at you with a big, round and thoroughly fishy eye, and the sea kept growing further beyond than the beyond; and I didn't know (now it's me talking, not Anna), I didn't know a lot of things – everything was unknown; but I could *remember* them, almost with precision, all those unknown things, such as the interior of a barge anchored in a harbour at confidential midnight, or the spinning-mill of a star two inches above a forest full of fir-trees, or the iris in a slaughtered horse's eye directly after the battle and the soldier lads (those who survived) coming down to the ravine and drinking water from the river and filling their flasks and pissing buckets of pee and drinking more water and in bewilderment, lifting their heads towards the sky (not the way birds do, in order to show their gratitude for the existence of water), in bewilderment, knowing in an abstract way that they can no longer remember Orion, Berenice's Hair, the Lyre, Scorpio, the Big and the Little Dipper. And speaking of the devil, here he was in our old haunt, Petros, Petros, Petros. And I don't deny it, I was quite afraid he might have changed, our friendship might have faded, perhaps at the moment of shaking hands, there might be a delicate, rather chilly celluloid layer of distance or condescension or secret acceptance of the inevitable or the futile, in between the palms of our hands. So here was Petros at the door, the spitting image of himself, like our recollection of him, like us; the same uncreased trousers, the same shoes which looked a thousand times worn out and yet brand-new, and that face of his, good God, above the smoke-rings from our cigarettes, above our conversations, our objections, our silences, here he was straight, intimate, dogmatic, physically absolute. As for Telis, he wasn't competitive; his lips conveyed a sense of justified generosity: "Chicks? – plenty of them; take your pick." Goghos was in the lavatory and hadn't caught wind of anything. Alekos – he'd certainly be glad to tear up his own poems, which he kept in the right-hand pocket of his jacket on yellowed paper, folded in quarters, and the poems were so old that the corners were frayed and if you tried to unfold them, each page would crumble into four tattered pieces and at these points, the verses would be illegible – but it was better like this, because as some other poet remarked: "*A poem sparkles thanks to the verses erased*"; and still better, *he* would have torn up all the verses; and through the window, a square patch of crimson sunset was reflected on the wall – here's Petros, 'Hello, hello, hello'.

Athens, March 1st, 1983

Reminiscenses

Here and now, I am sitting on an old couch exactly opposite the large glass door which leads out to my balcony and the curtain is completely open so the light can pour in and I can see the snowy mountains facing me just above the apartment buildings covered in multi-coloured awnings, which go on fading with the years – the maroon-coloured turn brown, the green turn off-yellow, the sky-blue turn grey – and the jungle of television antennae keeps spreading. So I am sitting on this old couch, remembering and recollecting the unrecollectable; and tell me now, what can you remember first, see, touch, speak from all the complicated and infinite, tyrannical and marvellous things of the outer and the inner world? As I gaze at the faded awnings across the way, I also glance at the watercolour here on the wall of my room – the dreamy cow in the twilight and a peasant in the background and that smoke on the roof of the hut, slow, silent – this watercolour hasn't faded a bit throughout these past thirty years, not to mention the other oil-paintings: Saint Sebastian, the Artist's Family, the Nude Youth, the Caique-boats of Hydra, Erotocritus and Aretousa, Photinoula, the bronze sculpture by Apartis – oh, all this – nothing, no mark of time, no

shadow; well, this is why I sit here and in this visible
and invisible transparency, I recall and recollect human
beings, places, the depths of the sea, shadows and fleeting clouds and waters full of reflections from willow-
trees and floating pine-cones and erotic flings under the
linden trees or in miserable rooms lime-washed in pista-
chio-green paint, or in third-class hotels with cigarette-
butts tossed on the staircases and in the wash-basins;
and demonstrations and banners and placards along the
avenues and in the public Squares; and loud voices, bat-
tle-cries of revolution of an intense peculiar quality,
above any predetermination and command and premedi-
tation; but also that erect yellow thorn (I don't know its
name), with its round fluffy head, which you blow until
lots and lots of fluff – three times as much fluff – fly
away aerily and some of it settles on the hair of a woman
washing her feet in the river. But evening is falling and I
can no longer see clearly; I stand up and switch on the
light (no more oil-lamps nowadays) – what a weary light
inside the room, just like then, inside the funeral parlour, the one open all night on Acharnón Street, almost
opposite the Church of Saint Meletios, next to a shop
which sold bathroom equipment and was dazzlingly
white and brightly lit; but the light in the funeral parlour was greenish and sickly and a young girl (not even
seventeen years old), with a long pale face and two black
plaits, was sitting on a tall stool, sleepy from her all-
night vigil – she wore small grey boots, which were also
very sleepy and her eyes were about to close, and you
felt sorry for her; and perhaps she even envied the dead
who could stay there day and night lying in their wooden
crates, able to sleep to their heart's content – it's all
right for *them* – nothing compels them to get up and

wash themselves and comb their hair with those combs all full of broken teeth, or rush out for the daily bread, rain or shine, blow or snow, with the traffic cops all covered up in hoods; or other times again with the big heat waves, when the cicadas are busting a gut and red tongues start leaping out of the asphalt pavement and thousands of horns and fire-engine sirens seem to be fiendishly blaring; what a bore to have to go shopping with those little bags or plastic nets, running around to the butcher's (how clumsily those slaughtered lambs and pigs and oxen hang there on the hooks) or the baker's or the greengrocer's for the odd lettuce and a couple of apples – fucking hell, where can you find the money – so to speak; the dead take their own good time and laze about; for them there's no eating, no shitting, no shishkebab, no retsina, no changing their underpants or socks, no screwing (that's bad – said Telis), no setting their alarm-clock for some wild hour of the night, with a dead cat thrown out on the sidewalk along with a bunch of dried flowers tied with thread; *they* don't need a black umbrella or overcoat or tickets for the bus and train, the sort people throw away at bus-stops, where they flap around, not like butterflies but big, fat, senile flies – the dead don't need clocks to measure time, they have no time, they are outside time, all time is theirs in the midst of nowhereness, nothingness, alwaysness: which is why you'd feel sorry for that sleepy girl in her all-night vigil in that greenish light; and I thought of trying to take her place: "Come on now, lass, go get some sleep; I'll take your shift, and anything I earn all night I'll hand over to your cranky boss, down to the very last penny." – but her small boots won't fit me and how can I stay up all night? Besides, I know for sure that if I did stay up all night, nobody would die; so of course, I wouldn't sell a single coffin; and if anybody were to die and his relatives were to come whining and haggling about the funeral expenses, wreathes, purple ribbons, quality of hearse, I'd just resurrect the dead man and tell him we should spend the funeral money on a Saturday night binge, boozing with some women in Plaka – I would really resurrect him, as I resurrected Lazarus year-before-last, together with his bed; and last year, the barber of Sálamis and the only reward I accepted after his manifold entreaties was to be shaved and have my hair cut by him for one year. Naturally, because of all this, the owner of the funeral parlour considered me the most awful employee and first thing next morning, he sacked me, literally kicked me out the door; and outside on Acharnón Street, I began whistling an old *rebétiko* song; after staying awake all night, I felt slothful and filthy, but utterly cool from the dew of the dawn, out there, whistling away in front of that bright white shop full of bathroom equipment, I gaped at the glistening toilet-bowls and bidets and bathtub tiles, lusting after the beautiful naked bodies which will sit on them, what stalwart laughing waters (like Petros' laugh) will splash and flagellate those beautiful, stark-naked bodies – because my friend, there are some white things, sun-bleached whiter than the whitest whitewash, which leave not even the tiniest shadow (like half an inch of dream) under a chair, and do not even leave the shadow of one of your lashes under your eye, when you close your eyelids and fall asleep in the blissful ignorance and knowledge of this world.

Athens, March 1st, 1983

Brush-strokes, brush-strokes

"It's about time we drop this childish drivel," said Kyparissis (that's how we always called him, by his surname). "We must talk seriously about serious matters, like e.g. diplomats; with serious words – each word in its own absolute state, not interrelated with other words next to it, intransigeant, independent, above and beyond its own meaning or any idea whatsoever or image or emotion; and above all, bear in mind you must never ever use words like bird, rose, revolution, chimney, factory, winch, washtub-water; – some such words are coldly academic, others are romantic, others are for political parties or neighbourhood folklore; above all, let us avoid (occasionally, he used the first person plural, including himself, but obviously condescending to us), we must avoid anything small and insignificant and dandified, like e.g. the word 'butterfly' (and Kyparissis glanced in my direction). Mosquito or cockroach: a thousand times better – of course, they too are undersized, but at least, they are liberated from the sinful past of poeticising. So pay attention, no butterflies. Better let out a fart in a drawing-room than a butterfly in your conversation." (And he uttered the word 'fart' showing off a high-minded, blasé je-m'en-fichism. And oh my

God, this frank common word was so ill-suited to his litterati lips). And all of a sudden, amidst the ennui of that "Kyparissian" intellectualism, I recalled for myself the stentorian fart of Aunt Alexandra. Ah, Aunt Alexandra, how lovely she was, tall, imposing – with her French, her German, her piano-playing; but more than anything else, her enormous hats – an entire aviary: peacocks, pheasants, ostriches – only their feathers, no heads or claws. Whenever she visited my mother of an afternoon, the whole drawing-room became full of Aunt Alexandra's hat and indeed, an ostrich plume slipped out through the French window all on its own, almost having no connection with Aunt Alexandra's hat. And this exquisitely lacy, foresty, birdy shadow of her hat flooded the rooms, the hallway, the staircase, enveloping all of Aunt Alexandra as well; only her nose, which was caked with powder from Zante (she used to say, this was the only powder which contained no mercury and did not ruin the skin), only her nose stuck out like a white brush-stroke in a dark painting; it was eager to escape or vanish in the depths of the large mirror, where every so often, Aunt Alexandra cast a sideways glance; and whatever you might say, she did have a big nose. Well now, one afternoon, Aunt Alexandra (earlier on, she'd sent one of her maids to ask Mother "whether Madam will be at home, for her Mistress to pay a visit?" and Mother had answered: "With pleasure, I'll be expecting her"); well, one spring afternoon, Aunt Alexandra turned up again, perhaps in her very largest hat of all; they sat in the drawing-room; the maid brought in a tray with the sweetmeats (a miniature aubergine stuffed with almond flakes, in syrup), and the fine glasses and the tiny silver spoons; they ate their sweet very slowly, with their mouth almost closed and contracted (in those days, very small mouths were in fashion, which looked ready to whistle, except that they didn't know how to whistle); by now, the spoons were in the water-glasses; I stayed as close as possible (I must have been around six years old), in hopes of over-hearing some of the grown-ups' conversation, which was just as fine as Aunt Alexandra's hats and also took up a great deal of space; I'd been shoved almost into the corner, as though I were being punished. "Ion, won't you play something for us on the piano," said Mother. "Yes, yes, how lovely," Aunt chimed in. And I opened the piano and began playing the love-song "Night Revellers", which I'd been taught by my Cousin Rita, when I visited Athens for two months; how beautiful their house was with plaster-of-Paris statues decorating the façade and flowered anthemia and garlands, at the corner of Piraeus Avenue and Koumoundoúrou Square; and the interior staircase was quite exquisite with its thick embossed iron bars; my cousin was a splendid pianist (she could play all the Sonatinas of Weber and Diabelli by heart); she taught me how to play the "Night Revellers", with the indispensable accompaniments, although my fingers couldn't stretch enough to reach an octave; well, I performed the "Night Revellers" really beautifully: *"Why are you pining? Don't pine for me. / I'm not a goldfish, no gold treasure for thee."* But I played very softly, since I was longing to hear what they were actually saying. At which point, the stentorian fart of Aunt Alexandra resounded and Mama exclaimed: "Ion, for shame. Out with you." And I rose from the piano and said: "It wasn't me, Mama. It was Aunt Alexandra." And then for the very first time, Mama slapped me so hard that I could see the two tiny silver spoons flickering as they bobbed up and down inside the glasses and I rushed down the staircase, pursued by all the ravens on Aunt Alexandra's hat, and I hid between two trunks in the servants' room and wept and wanted to die and wept still harder and I very much enjoyed the weeping and the fact that I would die "just to show you: *'I'm not a goldfish, no gold treasure for thee'*"; and when I grow up, my fingers will play all those octaves properly. But why didn't Our Lady the Mother of God wear a hat? All fine ladies wore a hat; only very poor wives of fishermen and very old women who wove birds and fish and flowers all pell-mell on their looms, did not wear hats. Which is why next day, when I'd quite forgotten I was dead and was actually very relieved by all the weeping – as though I'd just stepped out of my bath with my hair neatly combed – I asked Mother: "Mama, won't you tell me – was Our Lady as poor as old Missus Stathoula?" "Not at all poor –" said Mother. "Her husband was an excellent carpenter and easily earned enough for their daily bread and clothes." "Then why didn't she wear a big hat full of feathers? In all the icons, Our Lady hasn't got a hat." Mama laughed and said: "Hats weren't fashionable in those days." "Better like this," said I. "The halo suits her better. You too, Mama – you're prettier without a hat." And Mama smiled just like Our Lady; and as we sat there in our courtyard, which was sparkling from the sea, the springtime sunset glowed around her golden hair. And I wanted to say: "You have a halo too, Mama." But I didn't say this, because that slap yesterday had taught me we must not say the whole truth, whether it be ugly or beautiful. Now, what was this conceited Kyparissis babbling on about (with all his stupendous studies in

Europe, not at all self-educated, you know): "Words must not smile," said he, "and no butterflies whatsoever"; whereas myriads of white butterflies were quivering above their own images in the sea, here on the seashore of Poros, where we'd gone for a Sunday excursion; and I didn't say the word "butterflies", only I stretched out my finger and pointed at them, and lo and behold, a butterfly landed on Kyparissis' nose, as though on purpose and started fluttering its wings and mocking him, and we all burst out laughing, Petros, Telis, Goghos, Alekos, Eleni, Anna, Maria, Martha, Persephone, Eurydice. And Alekos said: "Not only must words smile, but they must actually laugh with their mouths wide open. And the more butterflies the merrier." And a long narrow white boat was passing by and the laughter of the rowers could be heard crystal-clear above the shining sea of Poros.

Athens, March 2nd, 1983

Passageways through the present

Sometimes the present holds you in its grip. And at those times, you make an effort to leap over the fence (whether wooden or stone) to some nearby or distant past, now perfected. Which has nothing unforeseen in store for you – no impasses, no anxieties, no refutations, no changes of lighting, no shipwrecks, no light-house watchmen – a permanent mild autumn, accepted by all seasons, the sweetest meditation and all-pervasive concentration in your own self, without any gap between the inner and the outer – a host of yellow leaves, and how serenely curious it is that you can walk on them without their crumbling or crackling – intact gold, soft gold and the footsteps of the peripatetic philosophers (who are silent now) enveloped in the profound belief in immortality – although the heavily decorative elements of pottery (except for the white lecythus-vases of Attica) did betray, rather generally and vaguely, some kind of doubt; and the Agora statues, bored and blasé because of their everlasting immobility and their being such a spectacle, half-concealed amidst the fragrant scents of the orange-trees and their own apathetic (really?) nakedness; and on full-moon or starlit nights, do statues really copulate with one another, or even with us? – for on many an early morning, we used to find the laurel-leaf brooms of the fishmongers moist as though full of sperm and on top of the thick log stand (near the door of the butcher-shop), where they split the flayed lambs' heads with one fell blow of their special axe, there was a small ring fit for a child's finger, with a pale-blue stone. Again, at other times, you leap (this of course is undeniably in your dreams), you leap the fence towards a propitious future, difficult to conquer, where all problems, financial, moral or aesthetic – problems of housing, heating, education, pensions at the age of 35, medical care, traffic, poetry, publishing – have been solved irreversibly and words (although presiding over all things) have found their pure material essence and have become *precisely word*, without the humble inclination for communication, notification, exhortation, mutual understanding, and the word, just floats like a beautiful balloon, neither rising high into the sky, nor settling on the ground; and this is why architecture has also changed and once again people prefer one-storey houses – indeed, houses made of hand-carved wood, with a small garden on all sides, even though huge lunar laboratories still existed and in the middle of one of these, an enormous apple-tree had grown, laden with big red apples and during the noon break, the electricians cut them and sank their teeth into the thick flesh and all the red apples they were munching made a festive crunching sound, all in unison. Petros, however, was full of the present, and it was not too tight for him, like the jacket of a younger brother, nor did he want to leap over the fence, because, for him, friend, there was no fence; and as for Telis, fast as lightning, he traversed the here, the there, the beyond, never taking the kilometres into consideration or noticing the street-signs – he just kept changing streets, women, motorbikes, shirts; and Goghos was ambivalent, you never knew where he stood – his one leg on the sidewalk, his other leg on the staircase, with his jacket-pocket torn, even when he was at the café drinking his coffee and smoking, he was utterly absorbed in his own smile; Eleni, Maria, Anna (I don't know where); Persephone, Eurydice – they were different; – and Martha – oh, she was a genuinely modern, active, revolutionary woman garbed (virtually inside as well as outside) in freshly printed political leaflets, she was lovely God bless her, though she herself didn't care. As for Alekos – a very sensitive man this Alekos – he was like me – at times, the two of us chatted in the garden; he roved his childhood past, now ecstatically, now hilariously: in the old days, there were no *"bains mixtes"* and the bathing-compartments were made of boards in the sea, and all the men had to leave, and actually remove themselves completely before the women would come, mothers and aunts and grown-up cousins – what a lovely sight – with their big straw hats all full of imitation cherries and daisies and little ears of barley and poppies, even small birds, thrushes, nightingales, humming-birds (*"colibris"* they were called, or something like this) – joyful fields and flower-gardens – it was as though bucolic poems were taking a stroll at the golden hour of high noon; and as if the hats were not enough, to top them off, there were rainbow-coloured, exultant parasols, pink and mauve and silvery blue and violet; and not even these parasols were quite enough: attached to the hats were long diaphanous muslin scarves (to keep the glaring sun from tanning their faces: in those days, exceptionally white skin was the model) and when the mistral or the meltemi-winds began to blow, those scarves really blew, dancing cloudlike dances; and the ladies would take us children with them, girls and boys alike, up to the age of seven, eight at most, (we always had to be accompanied by a grown-up; the women used to worry, they never left us on our own; as for Aryiroula, well, one day a crab bit her foot – not to mention the sea-urchins); but they never took the big boys along; the big boys (how we envied them) mucked about all day long in the sea, in their own nooks, and crannies, stark-naked; occasionally in Portelo as well, down where the bathing-compartments were, just to spite the ladies (or to make the ladies look at them), especially that Kavouras (the "Crab"), he was so dark from the blazing sun, he was pitch-black – you couldn't even see the features on his mug, what with all that blackness, only the gleaming flash of his teeth and the whites of his eyes; they called him Kavouras the Crab, because he was always unkempt and his wild tough locks of hair looked like the legs and claws of a crab. Well, as we were saying, one day, Kavouras (at the very moment when the Ladies were heading for Portélo, looking out from Mikrí Dápia towards the sparkling sea and the precipitous rocks, to make sure there were no men still around), well, there he was – Kavouras the Crab, swimming away – the scamp, the rogue – on his back, with his cock sticking right up out of the water; and Evanthia, the servant girl (for the Ladies always had their entourage of servant girls to hold their parasols when they stepped out of the water and to wrap them quickly in big embroidered sheets of white linen), well, Evanthia shouted in a loud voice over the rampart: "Hey, you, Kavouras – come out now; we've had a good look at your prick"; and the

Ladies bit their lips and pretended they hadn't heard and the eighteen-year-old girl cousins concealed their titters behind their scarves and pretended not to peek in that direction. And the servant girls did indeed cover the Ladies and the older girls with those white sheets, as soon as they emerged from the sea and the sheets clung to their bodies, their wet breasts, their shoulder-blades, and the big furrow in their bottoms could be seen clearly between the two plump hemispheres of the earth – so large was the world – all these things we used to talk about with Alekos in the evenings near the garden well – so large that damn it all, even if it were possible to live two and three and a thousand lives, it would still not be enough.

Athens, March 3rd, 1983

Our childhood swims: a sequel

Well then, I was really fond of Alekos; in many ways, we were similar. And whenever the present became too confining, we would go back to a nearby warm childhood such as this, not to the mythological, historical or philosophical past of Greece (now and then, in secret, I slipped away from Alekos and headed in that direction); and I forgot to say that in those days, women did not wear swimming-suits at the baths, but long white nightgowns full of embroidered patterns and lace frills – how lovely they looked with the sheets clinging to their soaked bodies, like statues and even more lovely (in their wildest imagination, they'd never have dreamt of our modern bikinis – their hair would have stood on end, a full ell above their head; the false coils for their chignons would have broken loose and the girls' plaits would have swung up and down their shoulders like the legs of grand *tsámiko* dancers). But alas, in those days, mothers were terribly fond-and-caring and simply wouldn't allow us children to go swimming by ourselves, in case a sudden squall started up and we got drowned in the open sea (for true enough, we did go out to the very deep waters, and one chance in a thousand, a shark might appear); or in case an octopus were to snatch us by the leg and drag us down to the bottom of the sea; or a lobster might give us a scare; or some moustachioed rascal might seduce us; or the Nereids of the sea (not like Odysseus') might bewitch us, these other Nereids who do actually exist in the blazing noonday sun, and they're all nude but at the same time, covered in spangles and in the midst of the spangles, their nipples glitter like Turkish florins on their breasts; and you wouldn't call them fake phantoms like those described by grandmothers who are for ever dressed in black, the phantoms who blow through conch-shells among the arches of the Byzantine ruins, where the older boys took refuge on scorching-hot noons – Stavros, Mitsos, Pandelis, Botis, Kokovios the "Ninny" – and they used to measure their cocks and masturbate. By no means, fake phantoms, they were true women, good-tempered and inviting. Alekos and I had seen them more than 102 times, standing erect as they fanned the air half-an-inch above the high-noon sea, so vividly that you couldn't fall asleep at night and you'd keep rubbing the tip of one of your ears, and you'd squeeze your knees tight, and it's all right, you see, not to be able to make a hole in a stone, but in the air? Well now, on one such burning noon, Mother announced: "Ion, we won't be going for a swim today." "Why not, Mummy?" "I have to stay in the kitchen and tend to your favourite sponge-cake." "But Mummy –" "Unless your Cousin Fonie is willing to accompany you." So I raced fast as a whirlwind straight for Fonie's house, with my bath-towel under one arm. Fonie, you know, was the oldest daughter of Aunt Evanghelia. The second daughter was Thekla; I didn't like her name at all, because it rhymes with *karékla* and

* *Karékla* is the Greek word for chair.

though I like chairs very much and the older I get, the more I like them, still – well, Thekla seemed to me a forgery, a distortion, a false-sounding imitation (though I never told her so, because as we've already mentioned, we must never tell the whole truth) – I only called her Thekláki – (so, thanks to this diminutive, the "kla" suffix became slightly softer and sounded like a joke, concealing displeasure or mockery quite well; anyway, thus the name Thekla became generalised and lost its uglylooking particularity, since all names and words easily accept the diminutive ending "aki" or "itsa". Of course, I could always call her Theklítsa. No – Thekláki is better). The third daughter – the youngest and merriest one – was Maria. She was really something. When she laughed, two dainty little dimples appeared on her little pink cheeks. But Fonie had a strange vice: in order to do us the favour of taking us for a swim, I first had to sing her two (not one, but two) songs, because she insisted I had a very fine voice and some day, I'd become a great dramatic (not operatic, but dramatic) tenor. "Fonie, Fonie, Mama has agreed to let us go for a swim with you." And Fonie: "On that one condition." "Again?" Fonie: "As always." "Only one song." "Two." "Which ones?" "You know." And wretch that I was, panting for breath, I started off: *"Behold, all round us Nature / doth adorn the Earth with beauty / and the Springtime doth comply / with blossoms, colours, fragrant scents / oh, do not e'er forget me / for I simply can't live far from thee."* (And truly plaintively, I translated this to myself as: "Darn you, Fonie, *I* simply can't live far from my swim, with such a sea as this – darn it all, Fonie.") I'd finished the first song. "That's enough," said I. "We'll have the other one too," Fonie insisted. What could I do? *"Moon in thy kingdom / mayhap Angels do dwell / thou art my Angel / thou my golden love swell / thou my own sweetest mate –"* (or fate – I can't quite recall). "More slowly," cried Fonie. "This is a nocturnal serenade and you've changed it into a Germanic march. Once more." "Impossible," said I. "It's better we don't go for a swim." said I. "Just the refrain," she compromised. "All right, but quickly." And these were supposed to be the verses of a great poet – Rangavis or Paraschos; and it was such a smooth sea, like shiny glass the sea sparkled through both windows in the dining-room and you couldn't wait to plunge into the cold water, but you were forced to go on singing (bloody hell – fishermen are quite right to swear – but never you mind, I'll learn how to swear too), imagine having to sing (how frightfully out of place) all about pale moons in this bright sunshine blinding your eyes; well, thank God, we finished up with all this and out we rushed, a whole pack of us children: Thekláki, Maria, me, and other children joined us in the Square – Stavrakis, Mimis, Aryiroula, girls and little boys and here was Fonie with her parasol and not with that melancholy serenade and we all plunged platsch-platsch into the sea, this green, blue sea, this sea-born sea – But I forgot to tell you: Aunt Evanghelia had a brother, who, so they said, was Greek Ambassador to Egypt and each time he visited Monovásia on his vacation, he brought a pile of suitcases full of objects which could drive you crazy and we used to gape and gawp at them for hours: such finely-chiselled glassware, such finely decorated cups, such crystal vases and little lanterns, such grand pieces of chinaware and mirrors and cuckoo-clocks and clocks with chimes – paradise, I'm telling you; but above all else, pictures, oil-painting (not painted with crayons and watercolours), genuine oil-painting, soldiers on a snow-covered hill, and a very amorous horse, just massacred, and more: exquisite peasant-girls standing like make-believe dolls near a spring of water, with jugs on their heads; and still more: chrysanthemums in all sorts of colours: golden, purple, burgundy-red and very effectively painted lacey green leaves on pale yellow satin – how did such a world of things fit inside those suitcases? But after all, who *was* this Mr. Solon? We never actually set eyes on him. He always stayed on Aunt Evanghelia's second floor. And we children weren't allowed on the second floor all the while Mr. Solon was there. Only the grown-ups were permitted to visit him, dressed up in their best clothes, and a few ladies in their largest hats. One day though, the maids took Mr. Solon's shoes out to the little terrace to polish them. Good heavens, more than forty pairs of shoes. But for the love of God, how many feet did Mr. Solon have? And each time he departed, on a boat which never blew its whistle, no one even saw him, long past midnight, he disappeared into thin air. And when he'd actually gone (farewell, Mr. Solon), we were allowed to go up to the second floor again and it smelled entirely of invisible Mr. Solon, and we stood there idly staring at the other things as well – I was mainly interested in the pictures, the pictures, the pictures: I left no wall or notebook (particularly, my maths notebook, by way of revenge) without scribbling on it, using coloured pencils to draw chickens, suns, houses, trees, poppies; and in my evening prayer, the very first thing I asked God, before asking that Mama and Papa and Loula and Nina and Mimis be well, before all other things, I used to pray: "Dear sweet God, grant that I may paint ever so beautifully, like the pictures of

Aunt Evanghelia"; and I really did paint in my sleep, no longer with pencils, but real oil-paints, bigger and a thousand times more beautiful pictures than those of Mr. Solon: chrysanthemums and roses and butterflies and soldiers washing themselves in the river and Nereids of the sea (they too held jugs on their heads) and many, many horses, amorous, but not just massacred, racing joyfully through the grassy plain, they were snow-white or red (I also painted a green horse near the rim, but – I don't know why – this one I didn't really like and I changed it back to snow-white), and they ran through the plain with indescribable elegance, superior to that of the horses on the metopes of ancient temples, and it wasn't only the horses themselves I painted, but also the way they could run; and the world kept growing and growing, shining bright, and it was not merely growing, but I was making it grow and making it shine and I galloped along astride the whitest horse of all, and I was flying, yes, flying, not astride the horse, I myself had big snow-white wings, and I could fly high in the sky, higher than the kites, far higher, and I did not fall. And Mother came quietly at midnight and placed her hand gently on my forehead to see if I had a fever and next morning, she would ask me: "Ion, what were you dreaming that made you smile at me like a cherub?" And I couldn't remember (or maybe I didn't want to say?) – I only smiled and hugged her legs and kissed her, kissing her over and over again, on her utterly white dress and the world was utterly white and utterly warm.

Athens, March 3rd, 1983

More childhood prayers

We used to chat with Alekos – not about everything. We both knew this for certain: not everything and not with precision. There, in the garden of the small house, near the old bus-terminal on Acharnón Street, and the noise of the city hardly reached as far as here – the trams and lorries and only from time to time, the rumble and whistle of the train from Lárissa and the voices of the itinerant pedlars calling out: "Milk, fresh milk." (*Ghála, frésko ghála*) and the "la" ending sounded softer than the "gha", like a musical note at the end of a Largo pianissimo, in La-minore (or A-minor). But all these things quickly faded, as though absorbed by the foliage in the garden or as though sinking into the well, only the silence remained and the slugs crawling along the pail down inside the well and also down among the sprigs of mint; and our conversation – Alekos' and mine; and the odd night-bird flying by; and what did Petros dream about as a child, I wonder? Ships? Anchors, wet and crimson in the sunset? Fires? newspapers? flags? firecrackers on Easter Saturday night? tree-trunks from the Dodóni forest on a large quay with lots of lamp-posts in the nights, windlasses, stevedores and stowaways? And how about Telis? Perhaps he dreamt about all the various sorts of bicycles, including a monocycle like the one we'd seen at an open-air circus, mounted by a terrific acrobat who performed a thousand-and-one tricks, standing on one leg, with rubber balls and Indian clubs and hoops; and maybe about women with breasts as firm as the inner tubes of well-pumped tires – he himself had mentioned this once – and we knew that ever since his high school days, Telis had been a splendid cyclist; all the high school girls admired him and his classmates envied him, for when the afternoon lessons were done, in the evening he'd pass by outside the Park, where the jujube-trees were fragrant with eau de Cologne and make-up powder and blusher, smelling like the rooms of those particular women who never went out in the daytime (their shopping was done by an old woman, who was so heavily made up you'd think it was purple paint she'd used); well, Telis would ride past outside the Park with the jujube-trees, where the French teacher (by now, it was springtime, just before school closed) was drinking his lemonade, made of genuine lemons, and a very cultured person he was, so they said, and he knew all about painting and at home, he had big books of *"réprodoctions"* (that's more or less how he pronounced it) of works by great painters of the Renaissance and actually, he'd invited Telis home one afternoon to look at these reproductions, but Telis hadn't gone; and the French teacher was lame in one leg – indeed, according to rumour, he had a wooden leg with an iron joint behind his knee; as long as he was sitting down, you couldn't tell; it was only the way he walked; nevertheless (according to another rumour), he used to pinch the pretty girls on their bottom, given the opportunity; and they didn't squeal on him to their parents for fear he might given them a bad mark, and then they'd have to re-sit their exams – Well then, this daredevil Telis used to ride past outside the Park, out towards the edge of the Gýthion quay, right next to the sea, at top speed, pedalling away like a maniac right through the middle of the evening strollers, hands off the handlebars – op-op, with his arms in mid-air – and there he was, standing up on the seat and again, heave-ho the pedals, "that looney fool of a boy will get himself killed", till one day he was knocked down for good, "he's done for now, crippled, shattered," everyone said; young and old alike rushed in (and most of all, the girls) and my word, sweety-pie, he just stood up with the blood pouring down and got back on his bicycle and headed straight for the chemist's all on his own; they removed his torn trousers, cleaned his wound with hydrogen peroxide (it was a slash high up on his right thigh), put some yellow powder on it, tied on a broad white bandage, rolls and rolls of it; and there was Telis, as good as new – with his torn trousers under his arm – back on his bicycle, in his underpants now, heading straight for his home that spring evening with the big evening-star. It was nothing at all. In a week, Telis was fit as a fiddle. Except that in summertime, when he went swimming, a long pinkish-white scar showed on his thigh; "and it suited him," said Matina, "it was as though you could see inside him through that slash." Perhaps it was this story of Telis, which we'd known for years, that made Alekos confess to me (in a soft tone of voice, of course) in the small garden near the Acharnón bus-terminal, his three great (so to speak) weaknesses: first, he was unable to whistle, either by sticking two fingers in his mouth, the way shepherds do, or by just plain pursing his lips; second, he couldn't

twist his fingers and make his joints crack, or snap his
fingers the way men who can dance the *zeibékiko* do;
third (and most important of all, he said) he didn't know
how to ride a bicycle; his mother's sister, a sour old
maiden aunt, who'd taken charge of him as an orphan,
never allowed him to do sports, for fear he might become
consumptive, and never gave him any money to rent a
bicycle; she was always nagging him and always worry-
ing and she gradually infected him with her own pho-
bias, and afterwards, even if he could afford it, he didn't
want to learn how to ride a bicycle; and always in his
sleep: "When I was a child, you know, I used to dream I
was riding a very tall bicycle, racing along the terraces
and rooftops of terribly tall houses and I was endlessly
being hurtled into a bottomless dark abyss and just
before cracking my skull on the rocky bottom, I would
wake up, shaking in terror." Which is why in his own
evening prayer, Alekos used to pray: "Dear God, let
there be no bicycles, no guns, no sling-shots and let me
be a very good student and let my aunt stop wearing
those false teeth – the ones she puts in a glass before she
goes to sleep – and let her grow new teeth, the way
babies do." And there were multitudes of other childhood prayers. And in order for God to hear you and
believe you, you had to pray not only before going to
sleep, but also every time you passed a church. But
Monovasia was full of churches – every other step, yet
another church. In Byzantine times, people say, there
were 140 churches and how could you say so many
prayers? Luckily, in the course of time and after all
those sieges, quite a few of them had collapsed. But
there were still bevies of them: the Church of Elkomenos
Christ, Saint Nikolas, Saint Giorghis, Saint Onoufrios,

Our Lady of the Myrtles (Panayía Myrtidiótissa), Our Lady of Crete (Panayía Kretikiá), Our Lady the All-Golden (Panayía Chrysaphítissa), and other churches and others. Impossible to make a go of it. Not only because there were so many of them, but my own prayers were not so brief as Alekos' – they were very long indeed – that maths be abolished, that I be the best pupil without studying at all (except for reading Mama's books), that I be able to paint better than Mr. Solon's pictures – this we'd already talked about and I repeated it before all the rest, before going to sleep and every time I went past a church; and if anybody happened to speak to me, I pretended not to hear or see; and one day, the greengrocer, old Manthos, with his donkey, asked Mother: "Good Lord, Madam, since when has your little son gone deaf and dumb?" And Mama laughed wholeheartedly and answered: "He's neither deaf nor dumb – Ion's a fine healthy child." And I continued my prayer outside the long wall of Elkomenos Church, rather helter-skelter: snow-white horses and red horses and that re-painted green horse, and bigger white wings and I also prayed that I'd be able to swim better than Kavouras the Crab, that *mine* would grow even bigger than Kavouras', that my little cousin Maria would take off her knickers, that Papa would stop gambling and playing baccarat, that Mama would not grow old and never die, that Nina's mirror might be bigger so that Nina herself could become still more beautiful, that Loula's long plaits would grow still longer till they reached her very heels, and that Mimis could wear the grand uniform of Captain and not be killed like the other Captain – Uncle Nikos, in Chios – and that he would give me his little sword (the kind cadets wear) and that I might have a pocket-watch with a chain, like Uncle Thodoros', and an umbrella and a cane with a gold knob and a striped yellow-and-grey waistcoat, to put the watch in its pocket, and a very big kite with a thick ball of twine, and thousands of folds of string so it could fly higher than all – even higher than the real kites and seagulls – and so many, many, many other things that I lost the right order and got them all confused; and all this, each and every evening before going to sleep, but also each and every time I passed each and every church, and sometimes when I wasn't in a hurry, I made whole detours in order to avoid one of them (the churches, I mean), till I was late for school; until one winter night, when it was dreadfully cold and a fiendish west-wind was blowing and the floors were creaking inside our house, as well as the ceilings, the staircase, the tables, the side-board, the cupboards, the dish-racks, the photographs of our ancestors, and our nanny took me up to my room and dressed me in my nightgown and by now, the braziers had gone out and my feet were frozen and Nanny said: "Before you lie down, say your prayer standing up, like all the rest of us, just the way Mama wants you to"; at that point, I used a cunning ruse and abridged my prayer: "Dear God, you are omniscient and know everything all by yourself – and anyway, I've already said it all to you millions of times. Furthermore, as Grandma always says, even God Himself gets sick and tired of hearing too many Pater Nosters"; and quickly I jumped into bed, till I was warm and fell fast asleep, lulled by the whoosh-whoosh-oosh-oosh of the wind and the creaking sounds of the furniture, and I saw the loveliest dream of my whole life, though I forgot it. Thenceforth, both before I went to sleep and when I passed the churches, this was all there was to my prayer – indeed, I cut several more words, as superfluous. Thanks to this abridged version, God, sleep, dreams, the whole world became broader. Later on, of course, we grew up and had no god at all to pray to and to ask for this, that and the other; and we were left without any support except our work and our own hands; and the older we grew, the narrower home and the mirror and sleep and Monovásia became; Mother is gone, so are Father and Mimis and Nina; the whole place is filled with the smell of camphor and iodine, filled with barbed wire. But again, some evening, like that evening in the garden with Alekos, or some other evening, with a wee slip of a moon, with the scent of a rose, a song from a boat, the touch of a comradely hand, or with your own hand resting in the tender hollow between the neck and the shoulder of a woman, human beings began to grow broader again; free of boundaries the world went on growing in the totally unknowing maternal and erotic infinitude.

Athens, March 3rd, 1983

Concerning history

We had no love for history; we studied just to get a passing mark in the course; during the exam period, we knocked ourselves out all night long, writing chronological dates in tiny letters on tiny scraps of paper, ready for copying (oh those dates, what a predicament, what a torture – how can you ever learn them by heart? – they kept getting mixed up, changing positions; the numbers kept multiplying, arranging numerical patterns with five digits, ten digits, a hundred digits – what a bore to have to learn them by rote, put them in order, pin them down in your brain like flies on a strip of cardboard); so we had no love for history, it seemed to cut a span of time into small squares numbered as far as the end of the horizon and you had to hop over them as when you play hopscotch, without stepping on the lines, and you kept losing all your glass marbles and glass panes and those other marbles called stars, which we no longer have time to look at, being so swamped in the midst of so many numbers. It was as though you wanted to divide the sea, piece by piece, and learn the sea by heart. Well now, my friend, can this be done? And *how* can it be done? Let that be a headache for the historians. We couldn't care less. We immediately forgot whatever we read (especially the dates); we unbuttoned our shirts and liberated ourselves – and maybe this is why in olden times, let's say, in really ancient times, at those lovely Oracles, all covered in laurel and marble, along with the cicadas and the wells and the silences and the vestments, the initiates (the ones who wanted to elevate the Pythagorean maxims or the Eleusinian distorting mirrors made of bronze) first passed by the Seat of Oblivion and afterwards, the Seat of Mnemosyne (or Memory), as though oblivion were the antechamber of total memory. It seems this is why when we too forgot everything, we suddenly remained naked with the *whole* wide sea, or we climbed up the cobblestone lanes to the upper Fortress, to Ghoúlas, with those grand famous ruins like demolished history itself, with its dried up wells, its hiding places, lizards, nettles, thorns and ferns, the kind which flourish in the desert. Only on the very rim, upon the highest vertical of the Rock, the Church of Saint Sophia (white beehive), solitary but not at all supercilious, as she contemplates the *whole* sea – and the fiery sun blazing away, and other shades taking refuge inside the dark arcades of the gateway, faces, aethereal shapes, soundless footsteps – shades devoid of chronology, gold-embroidered garments dangling in mid-air, bronze breast-plates, knee-pieces, three helmets, names, straps, sandals, boots, banners, reins, beads, signet seals, sceptres embellished with diamonds, bishops' mitres and staves, rubies, emeralds, sapphires, Bibles, scarlet rubrics, a bat and then another bat, the old-time magpies, the big snake biting the apple and the other serpent biting its own tail, Eve, Artemis, Achilles, Odysseus, Chrysothemis, Justinian, Mauricius, the Andronici (both the Comnenes and the Palaeologues) and the echoing sounds: the tak-tak-tak of Master Manuel's amber worry-beads and the carding-comb of Missus Veneta's loom; Demetrios Daniel, the local priest Vovos, and the gasket ropes of Thodorís Korónis echoing on the night-blackened sea near the ill-omened dead seagull, and the squeaky sound from the warped shoes of the unburied dead mingling with the faintest of waves; and Licinius Andreas leafing through his Chronicles, the Patriarch Jeremias the Second, Job, the Elkomenos Christ and the liturgical *"He who suspended the earth in the midst of the waters, is suspended today on the Cross,"* and the lampion-lighter holding his long pole tipped with a tiny tin cone, for even inside the dark arches, many sparks dart upwards (undated, as well); and up above the arches, the one almighty sun and blue, blue, white incandescent furnace melting stones, ruins, marble, numbers, the horseshoes and the small gold crucifixes around the young girls' necks, and at the very top, white Saint Sophia pointing her white finger at the endless whiteness, revealing the white sea with five utterly motionless sailboats. And somewhere nearby, among the rocks, I caught sight of that wild-haired rascal, Kavouras the Crab, lying prostrate on top of little Sophoula, the youngest maid of Aunt Hyacinth; he was wriggling away, yes, wriggling, and writhing like an epileptic – ah, ah, little Sophoula. And he was the only thing wriggling in the sun-soaked, snow-white, un-wriggling stillness of the deserted city with its burning hot stones, its lethargic lizards, its noisily silent cicadas pinioned there – and it was as though you could see and hear the pulse-beat of incalculable and indivisible History. I pretended not to have seen. Stealthily slipping away with a few hot pebbles in my pocket.

Athens, March 4th, 1983

Those confessions

Those confessions of Alekos next to the well, in his humble, soft voice (and my own, yes, my own confessions to Alekos) had left a deep warmth inside me, as though *confession* is a human being's most sacred act, which conquers and abolishes all our weaknesses; and indeed, these (I mean, the weaknesses once confessed) are the supportive foundation for the power of life itself, as well as for the most beautiful poems. Even if certain persons deplore poets for their confessional, emotional, sentimental bent and all the rest of it. Let them talk, my brave lad, those bastards, those jealous, chicken-hearted, lily-livered fools. Let them talk. *"Life strives uphill, with banners and with drums."* That's just why I loved my Alekos, for those three weaknesses of his and for other weak points he told me about, little by little, other times. This is also exactly why I came to love Lefteris, later on – when we were political exiles, though not on Makrónissos (there was no time or inclination for confessions there, among all those stones and crows and whips and swear-words). Afterwards, on the island of Aï-Stráti, one Sunday when they allowed us to leave our tents and go down to the seaside "cafeneíon" (the one and only in the village) to listen to the Sunday morning concert on the radio (also the one and only in the village) and we happened to swig down a couple of jiggers of cheap brandy, one on top of the other, along with the music – ah, Lefteris (they don't make lads like him any more) talking and talking away, confessing in his spirited, swashbuckling, guileless way – what incomparable confessions – here's to you, you old rogue – and not only about prisons, exile-islands, tortures and the shadows of crows on collapsed tents, but also his own personal, ideological and sexual crises – his never-ending hunger and thirst for female flesh, the way he bit and tore and sucked his hard straw pillow, as well as his fantasies, paranoiac quirks, nocturnal visions, fucks, priapic erections, masturbations on the mattress, in the toilet, in the bushes, as well as piss, excrement, saliva, rounds of licking, tufts of hair in the mouth, intertangled with the tongue (20 years before Pasolini's "Sodom"); and with vapours pouring out through the holes in the rocks – visions both in a sleeping and a waking state (how he enjoyed calling things by their actual name), as with that naked woman who'd been hanged and her cunt was showing half-open (this too he called by its actual name) and when they took her down from where she was hanging, right there – in front of the crowd and in front of her mother, who was pulling her own hair and howling away – he jumped at her once, twice, thrice and the officer in charge (who also had a hard-on) pulled him by the shoulders, with both hands, to get him away from her, ripping his shirt to boot; but the dead woman had a black wart on her left breast, which Lefteris knew he wasn't actually seeing; and he woke up dripping with sweat, drank some water from his flask and immediately went back to sleep and in his sleep, he could hear himself snoring, and he saw the same dream again and woke up again still more drenched, and once again drank some water, but did not go back to sleep; daybreak was about to crack; only on top of his blanket, a black stain was left, like that wart on the breast of the hanged woman (though he hadn't actually seen it), but this stain grew wider and wider and then gradually, began to evaporate in the yellow light trickling through the slits of the tent. Lefteris also talked about other things, both imaginary and real (he didn't take the trouble to present the real things as though they were imaginary), Lefteris called a spade a spade, bluntly, naturally, absolutely purely (how could anybody else utter such things? – impossible for me to repeat them or even write them), desires which had been realised, as well as unfulfilled desires (but always complete, and with details – shape, size, intensity, quantity) – ah, our Lefteris – how I admired and loved the lecherous rogue and I said to myself: if Lefteris were to write poems and learn the technique of writing, he could make dwarves of Rimbaud and Lautréamont and fit them into the smallest pocket of his jacket. We drank two more jiggers of brandy, there at the far corner table of the "cafeneíon". And Berlioz' "Symphonie Fantastique" was coming to an end on the radio and the last notes were roaring stunningly inside my head; I felt dizzy; and low down on the four legs of my chair (maybe on Lefteris' chair too and on all the other chairs), I sensed small white wings sprouting like the wings on Hermes' ankles. However, that same night, I saw Lefteris in my sleep and he seemed very handsome and more fierce and rather sky-blueish. He smiled at me in a virginal way through his fierceness. And the mightiest hatred in the world welled up inside me – hatred against Lefteris, mightier than my hatred for the dictators (perhaps because in his sleep, Lefteris had lived far more complicated and mysterious visions; perhaps because his confessions were more daring, more unequivocal, more unabashed, more magnificent and promiscuous than my own; and on top of everything, he had closely-knit eyebrows). God Almighty, what hatred. I could not contain myself. And headed straight for him. "You son-of-a-bitch," I yelled at him. He just smiled. I flew into a rage. "You bloody son-of-a-bitch," I yelled at him again, under his very nose. At this point, he lowered his head like a bull (he even had horns) and started coming on with slow, ponderous strides, straight at me, snout to snout, and I started retreating, walking backwards, constantly retreating, until two invisible sinister policemen slipped handcuffs on my wrists, behind my back: and – "Hey there, comrade, are you still asleep? Get a move on, mate, you're a real lazy-bones, Ion – the sun's up." And it was Lefteris in the opening of the tent, in a bright white tranquil light of convalescence, handsome, with his eyebrows closely-knit and his stance gallant as Saint Giorghis himself, or Saint Eleftherios. And I didn't hate him at all. On the contrary, I loved him more and more. We made some coffee with a bit of sugar on camp-gas and we lit a cigarette and I felt sad in such a bright white joyful way, I did not confess my dream to him, as *he* would surely have done; and yet, he was really a handsome bull and through the smoke-rings of our cigarettes, to the right and to the left, sticking out of his thick black hair, two gleaming curved horns could be seen. Oh, our confessions, Alekos' and mine – were different, they were childish, belonging to another time and place: and some of them never actually happened and will never happen – and the day became more and more bleached and our comrades started coming out of the tents and some of them washed their clothes in a wooden tub; others swept the yards with brooms made out of twigs and others shaved with rusty razors and had small mirrors propped up on a ledge of the outer wall and the mirrors sparkled and cast something facetious into the air, and all things were beautiful and oblivious and white.

Athens, March 4th, 1983

Birds

I've loved birds dearly (ever since childhood) – all kinds of birds, small, big, humble, or haughty – white, red, yellow, green, rainbow-plumaged, grey, brown, silver, and almost sky-blue – beautiful or ugly – no bird is ugly – even jackdaws have a special charm and a wistful air in the autumn when they perch on the bare branches, like black fruits burnt by some mystical conflagration without being melted – they sit there staring at the clouds and thinking about the strong winds which will soon be on their way to pierce through to their armpits, separating their feathers one by one, for there are always unhappy women dressed in black, as well as black chimneys and black nights, and with their own black the jackdaws match the ashen clouds as if painted with a black pen in a maths notebook, sketched over the bad numbers (but not over 9), I'm talking about the bad ones, which don't know how to measure anything: 2, 4, 6, 8, 0 – my eye, 0 – this is what they erase first of all, and the numbers fade out, and things are left free of the noose of a number around their throat, in a word, they remain countless; and if you enter an empty house, and it's dark, there are countless things stirring: dust, shadows, lizards, a piece of string (oh, how I love pieces of string, they too are like the birds – but I'll tell you all about them later on) – where was I? – ah yes, a filter; a bicycle-wheel; a doll's arm; a repentant smell from the kitchen; long, barley-shaped, little mouse-turds; the empty cage of a parrot which used to say: "Good morning, children"; a ring of light on the ceiling made by an old oil-lampion; the breath of a big dog and a small one (Azor was his name); the half-open cupboard on the wall; the place where the missing, diminutive statue belongs: "The Grieving Girl" – that's how they called it – such a faint tenderness emerged from inside her – countless things, I'm telling you. Well then, I loved birds dearly – chickens, eagles, hawks (and bits of string and cats – even though they weren't birds), thrushes, seals (they weren't birds either), turtledoves, blackbirds, canaries (these were like oblong pointed oranges or like tiny wind-up suns, which sing and light up the house, even in the depths of winter), storks, oracular geese, partridges (the partridge our godmother brought me from Veliés as a name-day gift, and it was a lovely plump partridge, reminding me of some doggerel verses: *"Robust thighs like partridges enclosed in trousers"* – it died in a wide basket; and how Mama and I sobbed; and we buried it in the courtyard, alongside the grave of our little dog Azor – how we sobbed then too); (I forgot to mention that we called our own canary "Blond Prince"; he had a little bracelet on his right leg, and he was a frisky little thing, the rogue, and whenever we put a female canary in his cage, there he was right on top of her all the time, and he wouldn't dream of eating or drinking or even singing, he just kept shaking his wings, scattering the hempseed, draining the water from his little cup, drop by drop, tiny lumps of bright crystal); well

then, canaries, partridges, nightingales (oh, those
nightingales in the big olive-tree at Ayii Apostoli, ouside
Tassos' and Miranda's window, in summertime; or those
other ones at night in the drizzle up on Martyrs' Hill,
and Francesca told us about all this – everybody was
killed, men, old people, and children; the houses were
burnt down, the church was burnt down too and the
women inside the church, and it kept drizzling and
whatever Francesca could not remember was uttered by
the nightingales in sobs) – many nightingales on bitter
or erotic nights with young couples on green garden
benches, but also the smaller flying creatures: butterflies, insects with diaphanous wings, dragonflies (a
dream, like the dragonflies on Lake Mogosoaya with the
waterlilies – more diaphanous than diaphanous itself –
vague reminiscences of the absolute, piniored on a
golden or red leaf), or even locusts with their angular
legs and round eyes, apparently the poor things suffer
from protrusion of the eyeballs or else, underneath their
disease, the sly creatures are concealing their greed –
and one of them was sitting on a glass, rubbing one leg
against the other, as if it had scabies, and it kept rolling
one eye and leering at me: "I'm gonna tickle you and
scratch you." – or those white moths fluttering around
the light-bulb in the dining-rooom and the poor little
creatures kept falling on the table and often, even into
the dinner dishes; and once Father got furious and
threw his napkin into the soup and strode out into the
hallway and started smoking, puff-puff, and cursing
away, and Mama started to weep; gingerly, she picked
up the napkin and laid it on the tray, and though she
was still mutely weeping, she used her little finger to
remove the moth soaking wet from the soup, and the

salt-cellar looked sad, crammed between the weeping and cursing; but in general, everything that evening was terribly, terribly sad, so sad you might die that very moment, though you'd be resurrected in two hours, at most three; and the other moths, white as white can be even in the night, the kind which wriggle into women's long hair, and the women scratch themselves with their lovely hands (but extremely discreetly and politely, since they don't want anyone to think they have fleas), and when they comb their hair before going to bed, 9 or even 12 moths are left on the comb; but strange to say, neither the moths nor the women are sad – perhaps because it's summertime in Kálamos and there's sea and ships and fishing-boats and strings of lighted lanterns and glistening fish leaping out of the water and for an instant, nibbling at your heart and "ploutsch", diving back into the water, that's done it. And I said to myself: when I grow up and become (by all means) a great poet, I'll put many birds in my verses, even owls (not Athena's owls, of course – they're for the philosophers), even magpies, and many, many butterflies (and just let Mr. Kyparissis say whatever he takes into his head, and probably Mr. Solon too – except for his framed pictures), even pigeons, the white ones and the grey and the speckled ones, as well as the carrier-pigeons (and non-carrier too), especially the carrier-pigeons holding a child's letter in their beaks to post to God, or a letter from a soldier, carried by these pigeons unscathed high above the fires and the bullets, all the way to his mother or his sweetheart; or those other pigeon-doves with an olive-branch in their beak, or the doves which have moulted because of all those traps, until Picasso rescued them and they grew all downy again; or these flirtatious pigeons, which come and leave their droppings here on my terrace and I can see them through the large glass door of my balcony and I smile at them as they kiss one another on the mouth, I, a 75-year-old child, here on my couch, smiling still more smilingly, as I watch these pigeons on my terrace kissing, beak to beak.

Athens, March 5th, 1983

Sequel to the birds

But I've forgotten the sparrows. No, I haven't forgotten them. I've just left them till last; my favourites, the slightly cunning, frugal, scoffing, tenacious, obstinate sparrows – a thousand times their nests are shattered on those iron fixtures which raise or lower awnings on country-house verandahs; their eggs or even their babies crack on the tiles; and they just start the same old story all over again. But what do I mean by the sparrows being last? I still have the bats and the hoot-owls and the usual owls and the frogs – but no, frogs fly in rivers, in lakes, in the filthy black waters of leather-tanneries, though they do sing like birds, in a rather deeper tone of course and more monotonously, when *"moonless night has fallen"* – yes, frogs always fly in the water and not in the air, like flying-fish or kingfishers or herons (the latter I've never seen), or Greek-style seagulls – these mobile pediments by Phidias *of* seaside temples *of* evenings or *of* mornings (as someone used to say and I was annoyed by all these genitive plurals, though secretly, I really liked them). But for now, I'm talking about sparrows. (Besides, I haven't even finished up with the pigeons yet, nor have I said anything about the owls and the hoot-owls and the turtledoves; and how about the swallows? oh, how many,

many swallows, you'd say there's no end of them, in Veliés, in Aï-Demétres or in Hatzálaga; and the swans of the Royal Garden: high noon, wooden benches for students from the provinces, half-asleep, half-roused – three of them together in one rented room out in the poorer suburbs – and the Great Swan-Zeus? and Falitsa's seagulls – we'll talk about this again. Well now, the sparrows also come to my terrace, like the pigeons, flapping their wings a bit, above and around the railings, and then, in perpetual motion, flitting down to the mosaic floor of the terrace, where they walk about – walking in a regular way, like very coquettish little girls who don't want to grow up, pecking endlessly at whatever they find, with their heads bowed down full of sly modesty, though they keep shaking their tails; occasionally, they cast a glance in my direction through the glass door (because it's winter and my balcony-door is closed); one sparrow actually winked at me (this one was a boy), in a conspiratorial manner with the air of a jovial accomplice, he said: "You know, just as well as I do, but let's not tell anybody." And at other times, the sparrows are just like the girls, only they're poor and always wear the same brown apron, summer and winter, poor neighbourhood girls, who can't go to school and have to do the housework in bare feet or mother the other younger children in the family, babies and the plump, almost rose-coloured piglet; and the cheese-grater is rusty and has thousands of eyes, all prickly and bleary from that disease called *"con–"* or *"conjunctivity"*, which is why these poor neighbourhood girls dressed in brown (there's lots of mud on the streets – in Thymarákia or Koupónia) never want to weep, in case they catch conjunctivitis; and when all the grown-ups are off at their jobs, in the factories, or on the building-sites, or in the rubbish-dumps, they begin to sing (even if their ill-starred babies are bawling their heads off, up to their ears in shit), sparrows sing so very beautifully, tri-i-i-i, trou-i, trou-trou (just trou-trou, because they don't know the words – nor do they need any words). And strangely enough, these sparrows here never grow up, never grow old at all, not at all (perhaps because they keep singing); and of course, they don't die, since they never grow old, and they don't get sick, every so often, at the drop of a hat, like Myrto, bless her and Aliki, who is always into something – homeopathy, acupuncture, special breathing exercises, to relax her nerves, so she says, and her muscles, so she says. I used to tell them off and give them a piece of my mind, both straight to their faces and over the telephone. I've been through every sickness in the world and a heap of operations, smoking away in the operating-room (with only a local anaesthetic), blowing the smoke into the nostrils of my polite and tolerant surgeon (and he didn't take a bit of my money; and later on, I made him a gift of a large porcelain seagull, which he still has in his office); and outside the door of the operating-room, Falitsa and Phyllitsa were weeping away; and here I was, on the stretcher, fit as a fiddle, smoking again, and telling the male-nurse out in front of my stretcher: "Now take care, don't skin my elbow against the door." Fit as a fiddle; no joking; and modestly, naturally, without any swaggering; except that it seemed rather like a taunt, for the others and for me – mainly for me. And as they carried me along on the stretcher to my room, I glanced in the mirror above the sink, and *it was true*. So I used to tell Myrto and Aliki off: "For God's sake, you little dears, you whimpering cows, get going, set your asses down and get to work; you there, Myrto, write eighteen novels like your 'Angels of Metaxouryío'; and you there, Aliki, drop your psychiatrists, your whiskies, your tranquillizers; it's about time you finish your English-language doctorate: 'Ritsos and the Birds in His Poetry' (and not those structuralist or psychoanalytical themes filled with libidos, Oedipus complexes, plexus complexes, wirey plexi-glass complexes; just with your own warm touch and your own warm heart, which knows more than Freud and Adler and Jung); and you'll see, you little sweeties, that it's nothing, nothing at all: no sickness, neither kidneys nor spleen, or liver and thyroid or thighride, or neuralgia, headaches, hoarse coughs and green horses (that one and only green horse I'd painted in my sleep and I repainted it snow-white). A pox upon your grumbling; you'll make my white horse turn black-and-blue." That's just how I told them off. Well now, sparrows never get sick. No, from time to time, they *do* get sick – a light case of flu, a sniffle (and they don't mind rushing a few steps to the kiosk to buy some tissues) or a bruise from a stone hurled by a sling and their one leg dangles; and when they walk along the ground they start joking about, playing hopscotch, as we used to play on the hallway tiles, jumping from white square to black square, taking care not to step on the lines (when we did step on them, we lost and had to pay our playmate with a glass marble which had multi-coloured, twisted little snakes inside). Whereas when injured sparrows played hopscotch, they didn't raise their one leg back, bending their knee, but their leg dragged along. From this fact, it was perfectly clear they were in pain. (And I also noticed that, contrary to ours, birds' knees bent from back to front.) That's why Stavrakis, Kaloulis and I, during our school breaks, or on a summer afternoon, on the ramparts of Megáli Dápia, under the wild lilac-bush, after the stone-throwing fight, we used to talk of founding a hospital for birds, equipped with tiny bottles of surgical spirit, peroxide, iodine, cough-medicines, small bandages, strips of gauze, and crutches made out of toothpicks and match-sticks (not half-burnt ones like the matches grown-ups throw on the staircase after lighting their cigarettes), whole matches, we actually bought three boxes of matches (pretending they were for Papa – to keep the grocer from thinking we'd started to smoke). Indeed (although Kaloulis had some objections), we discussed asking Marina to use her doll's clothes (but without breathing a word of it to anybody else) to make some small white smocks for bird-nurses. Perhaps we might even start that Hospital for Birds. Something like this was written in a big book, pages and pages and pages and even more pages (*On the Foothills of Silence*, it was called) – I can't remember (maybe Andreas remembers better). Anyway, even if occasionally, sparrows do get slightly off colour, still they never grow old and never have a single wrinkle between their eyebrows. They are the same, absolutely the same, unaltered, as back then in Monovásia, 63, 65, or even 69 years ago, absolutely the same. They used to come in wintertime, when it rained hard and the wind blew incessantly and large iron barrels rolled up on the tiled roofs and the sea went wild with shaggy waves, standing erect on their hind legs; the sparrows used to come and their beaks would tap our misted-up windowpanes, where we could be seen drawing with our fingers houses and suns and a hare (which also looked like a cat) and a donkey with enormous ears like the horns of the Foul Fiend and a daisy twice as big as the donkey; the sparrows would tap away on the window, we would open it quickly for them, but close it immediately to prevent the wind from ripping the curtains and blowing down the light-bulb suspended in the dining-room; they would fly in, shake the drops from their wings and particularly from their necks, the little bastards, with indescribable coquetry, despite the wind and the rain; they would pounce upon the crumbs on the table, the gluttonous little things (unlike those frugal *"fowl of the fields and the lilies"*) were always nibbling and when they'd had their fill, they used to go berserk to escape through the window we'd opened for them; only one of them stopped short for a moment, only a moment, on Mother's shoulder, and then flew out, rushing away for dear life. And I thought of painting Mother like this with the sparrow perched on her shoulder right below her smile; but my oil-paints were used up (because at long last, I had some oil-paints, Uncle Leonidas had sent them to me from Liverpool – but that's also another story; perhaps I'll tell you about it some other time); so my oil-paints were all used up, all the colours, only the tube of white was left; but how could I paint Mama and the sparrow with just the white? – they wouldn't be seen at all on white canvas; and perhaps it is better like this; more correct; invisible. Can the most beautiful things we have inside us be seen? Can what we call immortality or eternity or love or poetry be seen? Better like this, white on white. And even though brown, the sparrows knew the secret of time-span and of white; and perhaps this is actually why they dressed themselves in brown, in order not to be invisible or in order not to appear extremely proud, just as poems also do.

Athens, March 6th, 1983

Telephones and Petros' dream

We manage fine with the telephone (despite the problem of its costing such a pile of shekels every two months and where to find the money). Just fine. You're sitting at the far end of the city and "dring ... dring ...", seven times with your finger, and you find yourself right in the heart of Omónia or Sýndagma Square, or Ambelókipi, or Milan, Paris, Teheran, Birmingham, Leningrad (of course, for those places, it's more than seven times, even 10 and 12 and 15 "dring ... drings ...", your finger keeps dialing whole circles and semi-circles), and here they are, at the very centre of the world, above seas, mountains, forests, statues, squares, factories, above museums, libraries, trains, airplanes, water-wagons, ambulances, troopships, ocean-liners; and here you are: Martha, Eurydice, Chryssa, Nana, Ninetta, Maro, Amphitriti, Persephone and Myrto and Aliki; and here you are: Alekos, Panos, Telis, Ariostos, Goghos, Lefteris, comrades and lesser comrades, in prisons, on exile-islands; here too are Fereydoun and Özdemir and Mahmout and Gassem and Volodya and Yuri and Gérard and Jacob, Tassos, Miranda, Fotis, Crocetti, Sangiglio, Lena, Selene and Niobe – from one solitude to the other solitude, two by two, good company, almost on the same couch, or even in the same bed; and in the background, from time to time, a faint noise from a radio or a record-player or a television-set; or for a few seconds, the warbling of the canary in its cage near the window, and the bawling of a child, and the conversations of the rest of the family having tea in the next room, with the door open and the steam from the hot tea penetrating your receiver, miles away, pelting your nostril – Ceylon tea; "What did you say? I can't hear you." "I love you, I said." "I can't hear you. Another voice is coming through on our line; leave it; I'll ring you when I'm alone." "I can't hear you any more either." "When I'm alone," (and who's not alone and when?); "I can't hear you," (and who *can* hear the other person?); you see there are ordinary distances and internal distances – because the voice – soft, tender, sad or angry, restrained or expansive, has a glass face, and everything is clearly visible in it, more so than your actual face; and however much static you add, it can still be discerned; even if the distance grows and the cable is cut; of course, you call in an electrician, he repairs something, we help him too, insofar as we are able to; the cable is reconnected – ah my fine telephone, my hand, my very own hand, stretching out beyond, far out, to shake hands, and yet, maybe the other hands are asleep, or caught in the gears of an urgent machine, or are holding a trowel or even a hammer, or broad during the lunch break; or maybe they're sucking their thumb as a result of permanent embarrassment; or maybe they remain open, entreatingly, and always empty, like the hands of beggars in the underground station and there's noise from the railway tracks and the cries of the *koulouri*-vendors and the itinerant greengrocers with their wheelbarrows sitting here full of oranges and apples, and the old women-vendors of dandelion greens, and the old women selling eggs – whole baskets of eggs straight from the hen and not from the fridge, and the lottery-ticket-vendors with their crutches; but personally, I prefer oranges to apples, because oranges glow and do not remind you at all (as apples do) of original sin; you see them on the wheelbarrows, percussive and bright like little mounds of miniature suns; but hands are either always pre-occupied or sunk in oblivion and they do not respond to your handshake. And at that point, your telephone-receiver becomes an inert curved shape resting on the apparatus, like the hand of a one-armed man resting on his hollow knee. And here we are again, "dring ... dring ..."; I rush out of the bathroom: "Hello, Ion," "Hello there, Alekos." "Shall I come tonight for a chat?" "Come right now." "Tonight, tonight." And how about Petros? – he never ever uses the telephone. Suddenly, you see him there in front of you, just when you're not expecting him. "I've missed you, man," says he. "Me too." And I was curious to know what dreams Petros might have seen as a child, or even now. Once I actually asked him. "I don't dream at all," he answered. "And even if I do, I forget them. What dreams and such rot are you talking about now; can't you see what's happening in Vietnam?" He fell silent. And then: "No, I *do* dream occasionally; seldom, but there is one dream I can actually remember. I was walking on snow, as it were, all alone; I'd lost the others; I was just walking and walking, till I saw a bear (not like the bear in your *Moonlight Sonata*, you read to us the other day and Alekos was thrilled with it, but I didn't find it sufficiently revolutionary), a white bear, walking upright, and I wasn't at all afraid of it, because it was white, and on my word, it was smiling; well, it came up to me and linked arms with me, to my right, just like a woman, and we went on walking in silence, over the snow, but without sinking into it, without knowing where we were going; and there was not a single black mark, absolutely nothing, no stake for instance from an old army camp-site, or a chimney, or some rusty spear stuck in the ground from the Thebans' battle with the Argive invaders – not a single thing, I tell you; and suddenly, for no reason, we halted simultaneously; simultaneously, we turned our heads and looked at one another as if by mutual agreement; and we were both completely white (all very well for the bear, but what about me, my clothes, my hands, my shoes, maybe even my face – I couldn't see my face – were completely white); and all at once, we burst out laughing and laughing, laughing and laughing; and as it were, we could see our laughter flying out of our mouths, and it was white too, whiter than the snow; and only for an instant, the bear's tongue looked red like a blazing torch and immediately, it sputtered out; and we laughed and laughed, we laughed completely whitely, and all things – as far as beyond, as far as for ever – were completely white; and our loud laughter woke me up, laughing; and the blanket had slid off my back." "Let me kiss you," I said to him. And I kissed him on the mouth. "Have you gone gaga?" asked Petros, slapping me on the nape of my neck. Just then, Alekos came in. But I didn't say anything to him. Maybe I wanted to keep all that white laughter of the bear and Petros to myself. And for the very first time, Petros seemed to feel ashamed of something.

Athens, March 7th, 1983

Dissonant harmony

How do all things become pell-mell – trees, towers, vineyards, trams, butcher-shops, soldiers, women of the night, bar-stools, lights, glasses, Sarafis' funeral with the military beret of ELAS placed on top of his hands, concentration-camps, a large oak-tree with an acetylene-lamp and underneath it five drunken men dancing, a sailor pissing in the sea; there are anchors, stars and green salad at the old taverna, while a shoeshine-man picks up his little box from the sidewalk of Ayios Konstandínos Street and disappears into the early evening down towards Pelopónnisos Railway Station. And in comes Lefteris with a paper-bag full of grapes and some *féta* cheese in wet wrapping-paper; but Telis had dropped bicycles and he had a little scooter, and then he'd sold the scooter and bought a Vespa, and then he'd sold the Vespa, and he now had a huge motorbike, I don't know how many c.c.'s it was; no silencer, but all the other paraphernalia, a lot of foreign-sounding names; and as we were saying, in came Telis with his thick helmet and that plexi-glass portcullis dangling over his eyes, changing the shape of his head and hiding his handsome face; but we who are familiar with his face, are able to see it as it is, even with his helmet and pilot's goggles, and we find it attractive, like a diver or a frogman, or still more, it's as though he's wearing the Aeschylean casque of Darius' Ghost, before the Messenger and Atossa appear – but it's more appropriate to say frogman and not Darius (*he* was a Persian), well then, a frogman grabbing a shark or a whale by the tail, or even you yourself while you're asleep, holding you stiff in mid-air with one hand pressed hard around your ankle, so hard that Alekos (who as a child, used to pray that "there be no more bicycles") got up and stood there in front of Telis, staring at him stupidly behind the mini plexi-glass portcullis, as though bewitched and with the comical clumsiness of a young girl, he removed the helmet and Telis just stood there, perkily, like a bridegroom getting dressed up, and he was wreathed in smiles; and then, Alekos sat down again on the chair with Telis' helmet on his lap, and he laid the palms of both his hands limply on the curved surface of the helmet as if it were the school globe of the world; and although it was winter, it was summer and cicadas could be heard in the hair of the statues, and Alekos became silent, completely lost in thought, and it was obvious he no longer knew anything, and for this very reason, he was like the Pythian Oracle, who used to chew bay-seeds, and if Alekos were to speak, he'd spit the bay-seeds out of his mouth, into his handkerchief, in a secretive manner, and he'd utter only one long, slow, soundless "yes indeed", a gratuitous (not a clement) *yes indeed,* and probably a grateful (not a commiserating) *yes indeed*; because all things were enchanting and enchanted and all pell-mell; "Put some order," they say, "order, order". "How can you put order?"; and where and when and how and what and why? – which order in this eternal, beginningless, dissonant harmony of disorder? Oh well, in that case, just put your thingummybob inside her thingummybob and everything will be unleashed, belts and Gordian knots and bridles and stirrups, with your eyes closed. "Come on, boys," called Phryni, as she started to undress; "I want to take all of you, one by one, and the others can watch; better this way." And she stripped completely nude, and we were dumbfounded, and there were mirrors all around, mirrors reflecting a thousand-and-one Phrynies, and yet there was only one Phryni, and she raised her arms upwards and lifted up her hair as if lifting up bright spurts of water (though we knew – this was the only thing we did know – that water does not flow upwards, only downwards); and in her armpits, the curly hairs seemed to be in a tumult; and on her breast the nipples were stretched taut like jubilant bows arched to kill five lions and seven tigers; "Come on now, all of you." And hesitantly, we brought our hand up to our loins, not to unbutton our pants, but to make certain that we were safely buttoned up and – how mysterious – what we touched was something hard as a rod – maybe that's why mad Kavouras the Crab, blind drunk from the blazing sun and salty brine, used to sing away in the central Byzantine arcade of Monovásia: *"I've got a fucking pistol / it's got every single tool / its cock is made of steel / its red head you can feel. / Phew, fuck all fucking hell / its nose drips yoghurt as well."* – and that Phaedon, who'd made up his mind to depart for the Other World – he was actually holding the copper coin in three fingers and keeping his hand concealed in the left pocket of his trousers – apparently he changed his mind, and he dropped the hot coin and squeezed his phallus, bellowing: *"Ay, ay, you bastard, bitchy, recluse life, how gorgeous is your smell / this brothel of a world reeks of brine, bayleaf, sperm and cunt."* And in actual fact, a neighbour's kitchen did smell of bayleaf and vinegar from an onion-stew; and suddenly, all of us, Telis, Goghos, Petros, Lefteris, me, all of us stark-naked, lined up in a row: army recruits with crew cuts at their first medical, each of us had an erection; and Maria, Marina, Eleni, Anna, Martha, Eurydice, all the girls all in the nude; and Phryni on the couch, her legs up, "Come, come"; and suddenly, an enormous thud: – Telis' helmet had fallen from Alekos' lap and all the mirrors had shattered.

Athens, March 8th, 1983

Mr. Kyparissis

Certain persons like Mr. Kyparissis make me absolutely furious, and I insist on calling him "Mister", always keeping the quotation marks in my tone of voice. Anyway, none of us calls him by his first name: Aristoboulos (fancy that, Aristoboulos-Benissovolent); we'd quite forgotten it. But now that I've recalled it, I think it suits him: this too, of course, in double quotation marks, which clearly suggest and emphasize the malevolence of Benissovolent. Just like that, out of the blue, he wormed his way into our clan one night, when we were discussing our own affairs, in plain warm tones, in the neighbourhood café; he stuck to us like a leech, extremely polite, still more negative and always supercilious. He approached everything from the ugly side (and what doesn't have something ugly inside or outside it?); so he would magnify the ugly side, magnifying it with feigned composure, dispassionate objectivity (which nevertheless could not conceal his permanent malice and envy, because he had never been able to create anything, either in life or in art – sheer intellectual sourness – and girls didn't like him either), and nothing was left but ugliness, ugliness, triviality, and Mr. Kyparissis' cogitation hanging above us like a garland of paper flowers (from some past national holiday) flapping ostentatiously. God forbid. And yet, it was good for us. Yes. Since he left nothing and nobody with a leg to stand on, everyone was against him. And this common aversion of ours united our clan more tightly, our ideas, our convictions (even when we had our doubts), our preferences, and this made us (perhaps in spite of him) see the good in all things, the beautiful, the luminous; and the rancourless smile of a general thanks-giving grew within us – yes, free of rancour even for Aristoboulos-Benissovolent. And to give the devil his due, occasionally, the rascal did unfold some complicated plausible arguments (with a certain depth, actually), where you might even agree with him if the man were not, by nature, so disagreeable, and everything about him, down to his cuff-links, so terribly sarcastic, even the name Aristoboulos and Kyparissis, because whatever you might say, for us the cypress-tree is the symbol of gallantry, or at least of mourning, replete with nestling owls; so nothing suited Mr. Kyparissis, not even his names. Nevertheless, they *did* suit him just fine, but by saying the opposite – as if we were to say Cacoboulos-Malevolissent or A-kyparissoglou – A-cypress-tree-son – and we all burst out laughing in unison, as if we were all thinking and feeling the same thing and in truth, we *were* thinking the same thing and our laughter grew louder, like the laughter of the white boar and of Potros (and Potros was with us), as we saw Mr. Kyparissis and his paper garland striving not to get angry and blushing red as a beet, this yellow-faced creature; and Martha laughed loudest of all; and the lights of the café flickered over Mr. Kyparissis' cheeks, as though mocking him and rather as though they felt sorry for him (and this was worst of all – this was something Mr. Kyparissis couldn't stand); and suddenly, just at this point, as though on purpose, a big strapping fellow dressed up as a woman entered the café (although it was not Carnival – or perhaps it was?) a strapping big fellow with army boots and moustachioes and an enormously wide pink dress of Rosa (that fat Rosa who'd been written up in the cheap magazines); and he had thickly padded boobs and a red wig and a huge hat with lots of feathers, just like the hat of Aunt Alexandra; and in his right hand, he held a few brightly coloured streamers he'd unfurled and a paper garland, which he waved above all the tables like a thurible filled with incense, and he kept making gestures as if blessing people, very elegant gestures, and our whole clan and all the other clans, as well as the neighbourhood youngsters and the café proprietor himself, we were all convulsed with laughter, all of us except Mr. Kyparissis – ah, yes indeed, with our laughter we cornered him once and for all into his own freezing solitude – "so, just to teach you a lesson, you want to freeze the whole planet with your crankiness" – whereupon the Great Masquerader stood in front of the one and only Glum-One, very coyly, perhaps imperceptibly imitating the pose of Mr. Kyparissis' hands (which he'd just then hidden inside his jacket pockets, with immense dignity), he turned Mr. Kyparissis' coffee-cup upside down on the saucer, then set it right again, raised it to his nostrils, scrutinised the interior of the cup with a profoundly wise expression, directly mimicking the "kyparissian" look, and in the hoarse-but-shrill voice of a gipsy-woman, he chanted: "Me tell you fortune: baby doll, you gotta grand door before you, and you out the door, always outside door; good luck; I don't see nothing else, nothing." And he set the cup down, raised Mr. Kyparissis' half-drained glass of water, drank a bit and slowly poured the rest of the water over Mr. Kyparissis' head; the crowd roared with laughter, they were in stitches; other people gathered near the doors, and it really was Carnival; here came other masqueraders as well, with masks and toy trumpets. "Let's go dress up too," said Anna. "Let's exchange our clothes with the boys," said Maria; volleys of laughter; whereupon Kyparissis arose, soaking wet, as though he'd just been dragged out of the sea; and he proceeded all alone towards the doorway; and Petros arose too, approached and held him around the waist; both of them proceeded along the road of the Thymarákia neighbourhood in the evening; our laughter ceased; the other people stepped aside; and all of a sudden, we all felt so sad, as if a general misunderstanding held sway throughout the whole wide world.

Athens, March 9th, 1983

Faultlessness

Eh, what can we do? We're only human. And often, in the late afternoons, I am inundated with a calm, comforting, melancholic pardon for everyone and everything, even for myself; and I catch a cold, and my nose starts running, like some poverty-stricken, snivelling child at the corner of Ayii Asómati and Psaromilíngou, near the Planetarium, down below the Jewish quarter, where the synagogue is, down towards Piraeus Street, where an old-fashioned street-organ, but without a tambourine, used to play right out of tune: *"My plaintive little waif / what's ailing you, what makes you weep? / why don't you tell me your sad tale / so I can help you go to sleep?*; and the sun bleeding in the west and the muddy patches on the road sparkling in the old days; and I say to myself with precocious childish wisdom and am pleasantly aware deep down, and now again, I tell myself in secret – not saying anything to anyone else – I say: "No one, absolutely no one is at fault for anything." And this *faultlessness* is floating up above the quite muted noises of the evening, up above the busses when the proletarians finish work, up above the motorbikes, the billiard rooms, the cinemas, the garages, the jukeboxes, the glittery jewellery shops, the glassware shops, the elegant wax dummies modelling fur-coats; on Stadíou Street, on Panepistimíou, and even more, on Papanastassíou, that *faultlessness,* which is also plaintive, floats high up on the lamp-posts, in the honey-coloured Christian light, together with a few moths; and I keep saying again and again, so as not to forget it: "No one, absolutely no one is at fault for anything." And I'm so nice and this pleases me; yes, no one – except (as Martha remarked the other day), except for "Capitalism, Fascism, Imperialism", as throngs of demonstrators shout this phrase on the streets, young people, and disabled veterans of World War Two, and old ones from Acronafplía, and old-time members of the Resistance, refugees and former political exiles and prisoners, condemned to death, but set free at the very last moment (along with all the others who were hanged, beheaded, executed, burnt – not only Greeks, but also from other countries), all shouting: "The only enemy is this ism/Im - pe - ri - a - lism." And so many books state this too, very serious books indeed; yes, I can't deny it; but on the other hand, I say to myself: "All right, all right; surely this *is* at fault; however, is there perhaps something false in the very nature of human nature or of fate, as they say (*vide* both Orestes and Oedipus), which makes human beings, the poor wretches, take the wrong and ugly path, and do wrong and ugly things to good and beautiful and righteous people. And both the former and the latter, deep, deep down, are deeply unhappy." This is actually the reason why on a winter twilight, but also on a spring or summer twilight, that doleful *faultlessness* remains afloat in the air, though rather tremulous – (perhaps because it too has its own doubts), floating up as high as the telegraph-wires, where the swallows nestle after madly flying around like arrows all afternoon – black, tiny black notes on a long musical stave of a sad song everybody knows without knowing they know it. This is why I love swallows, as I also love pigeons and seagulls and sparrows dressed-up-in-brown; and it was just then that I saw Mr. Kyparissis soaking-wet (Mr. without quotation marks, this time) and he was Christ himself, naked, pale, soaking wet (and not just pulled out of the sea by the oarsmen), soaking wet from a delicate, silent rain on the Mount of Olives or *"on that pitch-black ridge of Psará"* – I can't quite remember. But Petros also loved swallows and I caught him red-handed on my terrace, gaping at them as they built their nests (I was spying on him though the window – pretending to be asleep in the front room, on my usual couch); and that rascal, Petros kept tiptoeing in and out through the wide-open doors, thinking I was asleep; and the rascal started pulling the straw out of my kitchen-chair in order to provide the swallows with building materials, until I did really fall asleep; and when I woke up, I caught a smile with my left hand on my mouth, that smile which only my mother knew; I caught it and I wanted to offer it to Petros and I called out: "Petros, Petros, Petros," and as though from somewhere far away, I heard the echo: "Peter, Peter, wherefore hast thou forsaken me?" But Petros had gone out without making any noise, while I was asleep and I felt a gentle kind of sadness, though I didn't really believe that Petros had forsaken me; and I went into the kitchen, opened the fridge, gulped down a glass of ice-cold water, and ate a teaspoon of grated bitter-orange preserve Falitsa had sent me from Karlóvassi, just like the preserve they make in Monovásia; and I drank a second glass of water and a sweet, sweet bitter tang was left on my tongue and now, I called out in a laughing voice: "Petros, hey Petros." And here was Petros, right in front of me, freshly bathed, with his black hair freshly washed, full of tangled shiny ringlets; with his chest and his legs bare, wearing my beach-sandals, and my plush yellow bath-towel tied around his waist. "Why are you shouting, Ion?" "I thought you'd gone." "Well I haven't gone." "Why didn't you answer when I called?" "Just so you'd go on calling." "Eh, you're mad as a hatter." That rascal, Petros. While I was asleep, he was leisurely having his bath; he'd also washed his socks; now he went out to the terrace, spread them smoothly over the iron railings, with the painstaking experienced ways of a former political prisoner, all the while casting furtive glances in the direction of the swallows. Now after all this, don't try to tell me that there is no happiness in this world – there is and there is in superabundance, by the Holy Cross, I'm telling you, there *is*; and I began saying out loud this time: *"faultlessness, faultlessness, faultlessness"*; and Petros came back inside from the terrace, wiping the palms of his hands on my towel, tied around his waist. "I think you're a bit of a nutcase," he said. "Not just a bit – very, very much so, a super nutcase," I answered and I truly was. And outside on the terrace, the swallows were chirping, chirping away.

Athens, March 9th, 1983

My bits of string

Call it friendship, call it sympathy, call it love (deep, mystical, inexplicable), whatever ties me to certain things, to certain words. E.g., here we are, the word "string". I say "string" and my mouth waters, or I quite forget myself, gazing far off behind the mountains at a dimly-lit procession of young girls, who are holding a long embroidered veil in their hands (one of them slightly limping as a matter of fact – perhaps her sandal has slipped off and she has to tie it with a piece of string), (*"string"*); so history walks on and on, up and down, and I pass by through a high, rather narrow corridor; to the right and the left, large sculpted cornerstones; imagine some 45,000 odd stones to count, record, align, measure with a piece of *string*, according to their length, width, height, to balance one stone on top of the other, by dangling a *string* with a weight attached to the end, and the "Plumbliner" nearby with a torch – 45 thousand stones to re-arrange, that's a wild goose chase, the Temple of Aton, the Akheaton god, or Ammon of Amenophis – a mass of lines and designs on the stones semi-effaced by the fingernails and the teeth of so many centuries and so many human beings (many of these stones were taken by the people to make their own homes – what did the gods need with so many houses – usually the gods prefer the open air and the sky in its entirety – on the one hand, they're too big to fit anywhere and on the other hand, like airy bodies they can pass through keyholes or buttonholes); and the images engraved there are half eaten away and the colours totally faded (not the Prince of the Lilies), but some figures are half visible, the bodies straight, the head and the legs sideways – ah, how lovely Nefertite is, with all her features and colours and her tightly sealed fleshy smile more imperceptible than the Mona Lisa's – lovely, lovely as Marlene Dietrich, even if she doesn't sing and doesn't wear high heels – so lovely that I slipped a piece of *string* around her swan's neck – and the stones had other designs as well, suns, flowers amassed there, numerous birds and butterflies (let this be a lesson to "Mr." Kyparissis, in quotation marks again, completely dry now); and when I returned to our old home, after 50 odd years, I found under the bed (just like Iphigenia, when she returned to Mycenae with Orestes and Pylades, from the kingdom of Thoa, she too found under her bed her childhood Carnival mask, a deer, which [albeit female] had two miniature trees for horns), I found my old kite-flying strings, with a thousand folds of string, there amidst the dust and cobwebs, and inside it, some half-alive insects stirring about; and I unwound it a little, and the string was strong, not at all rotten; you'd be able to unleash the largest kite, higher than all the other kites, with its paper tail and its flaps flittering high in the sky, its paper colours glowing in the sunshine – gloria, gloria, in excelsis – ah, my kite-flying string, my first pride and joy; the more the string, the higher your kite flies, and the higher you fly; my first flight, the piece of *string*, my first measure of height, my first angel, my very own, (not painted), real, my very own, my wings, and I kept flying, always flying, not only when asleep, but now, also when awake; that's why religious old women and the moonstruck Aryiroula (Saint Nikolaos had actually given her a handful of rice inside a sheet of notebook paper with blue lines – Aryiroula had shown us the paper and the rice – a miracle, real miracle, you see – and then, prayers and vigils), yes, and as I was saying, the old women used to cross themselves and leave votive offerings, lest the comet descend and burn us, and three whole rounds they used to make around the Church of the Chrysaphitissa Virgin, with waxed *string*; and furthermore, the cobblers in the narrow lane (which smelled of old wood consumed by termites) used a piece of waxed *string* to sew the welt to the inner sole, of course, after first using their awls to bore holes in the thick strips of leather; and they also tied their wild hair with string, to keep it from falling into their eyes and hindering their work on their right knee, as they hammered away at some long wide leather-strips resembling the tongue of an ox or a lion or the soles of Polyphemus' feet – And what about old Kyr-Kostas? yes, the one at Parthéni on Leros Island, who used to pick up bits of string from the parcels of the political exiles (all lined up on the long wooden table under the eucalyptus-trees, this side of the barbed wire, and only a step away, the sea reeking of seaness; and the prison guards used to cut the string with a knife, very angry as they tossed it on the ground, tore off the wrapping-paper, searched the contents one by one, eggs, biscuits, a pair of underpants, a sweater, and if there happened to be a jar of marmalade, they would stick in a long rusty nail and stir it up so hard that the marmalade would produce lots of bubbles, as though suddenly it was suffering from an allergy). Well now, old Kyr-Kostas, who never received any packages, used to stoop down picking up other people's useless bits of string off the ground; he used to untie the knots with his fingernails, then knot them together again, winding separate skeins, according to the quality of the string; I recall those skeins, plump, plump like babies, some made of whiteish straw, others of pale-grey cotton, and others of shiny blue-green nylon, most of them white and one red. I really loved old Kyr-Kostas' skeins, lined up there on a shelf next to his camp-bed; they were Kyr-Kostas' children, and not at all sulky, wry-faced children, but smiling ones, yes, by God, perhaps to keep their papa from feeling sad. And all day long and even all night long (by a small oil-lamp on the wall), he used to thread my darling bits of string, in a huge needle with a big eye like that of a cow; and he'd sew and improvise slippers, little slippers open at the back or closed, little purses and bags, and doilies to put your ashtrays on. And if a visitor happened to arrive, once in a blue moon, he'd offer some really beautiful little shoes, "for the children", as he said. "They are soft, won't hurt your feet; wear them and you'll remember me." And we did wear them and we did remember sweet old Kyr-Kostas, poor generous Kyr-Kostas, with his plump straw children, and there were so many and he made gifts of them. As long as they were in good hands. Oh, my bits of string. But there's also Uncle Anaxagoras – unfortunate man, he'd gone quite barmy; he'd scattered his belongings to the wind, and now he had to live on the philanthropy of his younger brother, Uncle Hippocrates, together with Aunt Roxani and their seven children. A real nuisance, Uncle Anaxagoras, wandering around, winter and summer, in his long, faded ash-grey overcoat, wandering from room to room, into the courtyard, onto the balcony, in and out of the hallway, or rather, to and fro, into the kitchen, especially, the kitchen, not uttering a word, he used to stare and listen, sniffing something conjured up by himself and distant, far beyond us. "What on earth are you doing here?" nagged Aunt Roxani. "What on earth are you doing here?" complained the servant girls. "What on earth are you doing here?" asked the children. And Uncle Anaxagoras would just calmly turn his back and, not uttering a word, go off into the hallway, the other rooms, the courtyard, never uttering a word. However, in deepest secret, on tiptoe, Uncle Anaxagoras used to collect every single bit of string, even the tiniest bits, from post-office parcels, from shopping done at the grocer's or the butcher's or the greengrocer's, he'd collect them with feigned indifference and stuff them into the deep pocket of his overcoat. And if someone happened to call out, albeit rarely: "I say, lads, a bit of string so I can tie this little parcel," or "the grapevine," or "so I can mend my broken ruler" – then Uncle Anaxagoras would stick his hand into his deep pocket, take out a handful of strings, choose the strongest and the shiniest one, and offer it. And then, Uncle Anaxagoras would smile to himself, smiling way up above our heads. Anyone who ever saw that smile of Uncle Anaxagoras knows why I love the word *string*.

Athens, March 10th, 1983

The inconspicuous Yotis

"Extremely moving your Kyr-Kostas," remarked Mr. Kyparissis; "as for Uncle Anaxagoras' smile at the finale, that was a genuine old-fashioned, edifying moral." "Hey there, Kyparissis, you've mucked things up again for us," said Telis, ordering another beer. "Oh, Ion," said Anna – nothing else. "I really liked it; my eyes were full of tears," said Maria. "Mine too," said Persephone. "Woe betide us if the word provokes tears or fits of enthusiasm; it turns into a sort of demagogy," Mr. Kyparissis added. (This person could never have been on the Mount of Olives or *"on that pitch-black ridge of Psará"*.) Petros cast a fierce glance his way – ready to strangle him, but didn't say a word. Alekos just smiled. "I liked it too," said Martha, "for this very reason, because it was moving." "So did I," said Goghos clumsily. "Well, so we're holding a plebiscite? All plebiscites – don't you know this? – are spurious," Mr. Kyparissis again. "I liked it very, very much," said Yotis last of all, rather hesitantly and as though sadly. For a while now, Yotis had been in our clan, one of us, a handsome lad, though rather flat, reserved, lacklustre, or rather as though protected by his own intentionally lacklustre manner. A boy from a poor family. After hundreds of difficulties, he'd finished high school at Pírgos, in the province of Elía. He'd come to Athens to study at the Institute of Technology. And he managed to get in. An aunt of his, his father's sister, Missus Euterpe, a widow without any children and with quite a good pension from her late husband, who'd been a military man, looked after Yotis; she could just make ends meet and feed him as well. Only that name of hers – where on earth did she find it? – think of that: Euterpe; it didn't suit her peasant figure and her broad smiling face. She'd been christened (Yotis told me) by an old-fashioned parliamentarian from the provinces, one of those politicians who frequently played the role of godfather in order to make sure of gaining votes. Yotis also had lots of cousins in Athens, some of them workers, others students, and one of them a notorious merrymaker, slick operator, womaniser, practical joker, Mitsos, the everlasting student, Big Mitsos, the expert in brothels, the wag whose laugh could be heard three miles away. One evening when the cops had used their clubs and water-pumps to break up our Workers' May Day demonstration, after we'd been chased all the way from Sýndagma Square on foot, Yotis and I took refuge in a small taverna high up in the Zográphou district. There, Yotis told me everything, little by little; by that time, we'd also drunk five or six rounds of retsina; anyway, we'd had our demonstration and there'd been plenty of people and placards and flags and big red slogans: "Chicago Lives" and "Workers of the World, Unite". Well now, as soon as any country-bumpkin arrived in Athens from his home-town, Big Mitsos would take charge of him and give him a tour of all the brothels. "Gotta stir up your blood and your brains," as he said.

"Hey there, mates with your wopping big dicks, are you still virgins or what? You gonna spend the rest of your days wanking? Here, we gotta big load of women, a big load of meat; just sink your teeth into the meat, gobble it up; get the blinkers off your eyes and let your randy cock and the whole wide world expand." So (as Yotis was saying): "From the very first night I arrived, my cousin Big Mitsos, took charge of me. 'Where are you taking the boy at this time of night?' asked Aunt Euterpe. 'To see a bit of real electricity on Stadíou Street; his eyes are still bleary from all those oil-lamps.' And straight down to the brothel on Proastíou Street. You open a faded wooden front door, without banging the thick iron knocker decorated with a hand and a ball; you walk into a paved courtyard; at the back, a small kitchen with a window facing onto the courtyard; in there, they make lemonades or orange juice with a squeezer and a strainer; they also make coffee and heat water for the girls' wash-basins, each and every time, after each and every client. To the left, the waiting-room; bright lights; laughter; I'm still dizzy from the trip and all the lights and also from something else I don't know, I'm so inexperienced. Women in dressing-gowns, stylish hairdos, feathery little slippers; with half their bosoms sticking out and legs completely bare all the way up; lots of grease-paint; a smell of eau-de-Cologne, powder, hair-oil, along with the stench of rotten wood – perhaps from that old velvet couch, where three women (one of them fat) are sitting with their arms exposed; they are less jocular than the other women who are standing. Men with moustaches and lads already depraved. Big Mitsos, familiar to one and all. Welcoming loud voices. And he went about pinching the odd thigh, laying his hands on a few boobs: 'Take your paws off me, you filthy man', or kissing some girl's neck with a real smacker; 'Where did you find the laddy, mate?'; 'Ah, he's from our village, a good lad'; 'And you've already corrupted him?' 'Yeah, he's that loose, he is'; and me there, struggling to stifle a cough – from my cousin's pack, I was smoking my first cigarette – mustn't make a monkey of the man, coughing 'ghouk ... ghouk ...' – out we went back into the courtyard; men and women chitchatting, spooning and canoodling; and there she was, the famous 'rouser', an old woman, made up with a thousand layers of grease-paint, a really clever old hussy, teasing everybody, catching a phrase here, a phrase there, getting the men ready to go with the other women, but also getting her own share; she made a pass at me too, but no reaction from me; off to the side was the outdoor wooden staircase, which led up to the second floor, where the girls' rooms were; men kept coming downstairs buttoning their trousers; women kept rushing upstairs with wash-basins; other girls came down, with their hair freshly arranged now; a real mystery; I was scared. We went back into the waiting-room. A lot of heavily painted flesh. 'What's up?' Big Mitsos whispered into my ear. 'Aren't you gonna take one of the girls? Get an eyeful of them, tasty bits of stuff. Hey man, what about that chick over there; she's come all the way from Egypt; she's brand-new, name's Leila. Not to worry about the money. This is Big Mitsos here; my old man's just sent me a big wad, the old bugger's still rolling in it. So get a move on, Cousin, don't disgrace me.' And he dumped Leila on me. 'Take good care of the boy; he's my cousin, you know.' So we go up the stairs. I glance upwards, – just sky and stars. We enter a dimly lit corridor. Silence. Someone seems to be groaning nearby. Is he being slaughtered? No, no, it must be something else. We go into the room. A double bed, two lame armchairs, a bedside table with a small red lightbulb. The bed stuck against the wall; and a cheaply embroidered wall-hanging – with a man dressed up in a fustanella and a girl surrounded by hideous flowers. Leila is already undressed. My word. What beautiful breasts. She's naked. And legs like a young girl's. And only a necklace of red beads around her neck, down to the gap between her breasts. 'Come on, don't just sit there. Get undressed.' I took off my clothes (her breasts are really beautiful). 'Your underpants too,' says she. I take them off. 'Come,' says she. 'I'm embarrassed,' say I. 'What do you mean, embarrassed? You've got a hard-on a mile long. Come on now, just put it in.' So saying, she sits down on top of me; up-and-down, up-and-down; I close my eyes; my hands warm up and grab her tits; I can't believe all this light inside my closed eyes, such terribly different feelings in my knees, toes, tongue and my own breasts, ah, ah; and afterwards, while we were dressing, Leila was still beautiful, even more beautiful than before and with a sort of maternal kind of smile, as she put on another pair of turquoise knickers: 'You're a green kid,' said she, 'but you've got it big and strong, peasant style. I really fancy you.' And when we came down the stairs, I no longer felt dizzy, only a bit drunk and light-headed, although I was a man now; as light as an angel, not ascending into the sky, but descending the staircase, slowly stirring its wings now in order to tread gently on the earth. And I fell for Leila once and for all. She taught me so many things. She taught me about my own body and something still more: she taught me about that other body which my own body needed, and in this way, I could come out of my body and *be*. In those days, I was indeed a greenhorn – inexperienced – only some slushy caresses, a bit of smooching, some silly little love-notes in our religion studies textbook, something else with my cousin down by the river, he was also called Panayotis, diddling with my dick and me diddling with his – kid's stuff, half-hearted and remorseful. Ah, that Leila. I had a real crush on her. Maybe she did too, a bit. She didn't take any money from me. Every time she had her day-off, she took me to her own big private room, in the Hotel Splendid, up above the Omega clock-shop. And from early on, I would start washing myself in a tub down in the basement, and Aunt Euterpe would say: 'I don't like the way you keep washing yourself so often.' That's why I never spent all night with Leila. But Big Mitsos caught wind of it and spread the news about town to all our cousins, to all the boys from back home, though not to Aunt Euterpe. 'Yotis is head over heels in love with Leila; search him, he's always sporting newly scrubbed, spick-and-span underpants.' He made a real fool of me. Because in those days, it wasn't at all in fashion to be in love. You could be a fucker, yes, but not in love – and particularly, not with a whore. Though in the movies, Billie Dove carried on with her romances and gladiolas and her tiny hats. And I really fancied her. But not like Leila. And sometimes we used to chat about this with the other neighbourhood lads, at the grocer's when we went there to shop: 'What a tiny mouth that Billie Dove has, the minx'; but who could afford to go to the movies every time Billie was playing; and those who did manage to go would tell us the whole plot: 'Billie Dove this, Billie Dove that, Billie Dove had a little doggy and Billie Dove simply swooned at the sight of a man combing his hair in front of the mirror' – oh my, oh my, and the grocer, Mr. Boyaris eavesdropping. And one evening when Billie Dove was playing again, and I'd gone there to shop, Mr. Boyaris suggested: 'My dear boy, want me to take you to the cinema to see your sweetheart? The tickets are my treat.' So we went. Before three minutes were up, he started pawing me. I was furious and gave him a stinging hard slap and walked out. I'd hardly had time to see three shakes of Billy Dove's hips. Out on the street, a crowd, bright lights, trams, a listless feeling, a sour taste in my mouth and this lout Big Mitsos making a jackass of me. I never wanted to set eyes on him again. I was avoiding him. Well, should I go back to Leila and find comfort in her bosom? What's become of that first woman in the world? – yes, by Our Lady, that very first woman." Yotis told me all this, so many years ago, there in the small taverna in the district of Zográphou, for the first and last time. And tonight, midsummer, here in Thymarákia Square, where we were drinking our beer, everybody, one by one, started leaving, one for home, another for a meeting, someone else for I don't know where; and we were left, only me and Yotis and the empty chairs. We fell silent. And all of a sudden, Yotis said: "Me too – I collect bits of string, like Uncle Anaxagoras. Look here." And out of his pocket, he pulled a handful of strings and showed them to me. And the moon had come out.

Athens, March 11th, 1983

The end of Carnival

I don't know why, they all come to me to confess their troubles, disappointments, frustrations, complaints, fears, failures or even their anger; sometimes, very rarely, their happiness – love-affairs, friendships, illnesses, dreams, anxieties – their professional problems, their family problems and problems with the Party; the house used to fill up with newspapers, brochures, pamphlets, anti-biotics, sleeping-pills, aspirins, yellow, red, brown pills, sedatives, small bottles of surgical spirit, red iodine, peroxide, pills for the heart, for the stomach, for the kidneys, small and large bandages, gauze, nickel-plated forceps, scissors, and above all, thermometers: wall-thermometers for the temperature of the weather, under-arm thermometers for human beings, and just such a thermometer left on the table, next to the big ashtray, an automatic one, perhaps electronic (but invisible), which indicated the temperature successively of the speaker and of me, the listener, with the mercury moving up and down like a silver minute-hand on an internal clock, not round, but an oblong parallelogram; and the minute-hand would not trace circles, but merely move up and down, and the clock would not have only 12 numbers, but also 36, 37, and 39 and 42; also, some numbers below zero were shown, lots of plus-and-minus lines or glass notches, and you couldn't tell where it would all lead; I was always afraid this thermometer might break (just as Jocasta's thermometer broke) and the mercury would spill onto the floor in thick drops from concealed tears or hot sperm and then, the silence would appear in its innermost entirety and we would no longer have anything to say or do and we would both extend our hands to take a cigarette from the same pack, simultaneously. So they all took refuge in me: Anna, Alekos, Goghos, Maria, Persephone, (not Martha), once, even Aristoboulos (yes indeed, Mr. Kyparissis), Lefteris, Yotis, even Petros. Not only our own chums, but even strangers. They used to knock on the door and: "Mr. Ion, may I –?" "Do come in." Young girls and boys, shipwrecked old women and former comrades in exile, restless anarchist students, and graduates of hospitals or of mental asylums who had just come out now and their instability showed in the way they walked, and their own personal misgivings showed in the baggy pockets of their jackets; and a lovely swarthy girl with long flowing black hair and a big square peasant-style bag handwoven out of wool and strung across her shoulder (maybe there was a gawky, one-eyed man woven on her bag with small white-and-black squares against a dark red background), she used to ring my doorbell (she never rang the downstairs bell; she'd slip in only when someone else opened the front entrance); when I opened up, she would stare at me like a sad wild animal, half open her beautiful mouth to say something, but never say a word, then take to her heels at top speed, rushing down the staircase like a flash of lightning (never taking the lift); two or three times, like this, until one day she came in, long hair, handwoven bag and all, and sprawled out full length on the rug, resting her head on the base of the red armchair and pressing her bag to her bosom as if she wanted to hide it, the way women do when you enter the bedroom and find them already naked and they cover their breasts with their hands. I waited. She stared at me fiercely, voraciously. She didn't speak. I stood up and with a perfectly paternal gesture, tried to fix her hair, which had fallen over one eye and half of her cheek. She sprang up. Stood there. Looked at me less fiercely and rushed out again, faster than ever. A few days later, I received a letter: "I'm the girl with the handwoven bag. Thank you for existing. If you didn't exist, what would life and the world be?" And she never appeared again. She vanished, the only person who never confessed anything to me – except for that laconic letter of hers. And I missed her. And I still do. So they all take refuge in me. And I listen, keep listening; I see and observe the formation of their lips, eyes, hair, hands, knees, shoes, clothes, and I can see through their clothes; sometimes I assume their position and I become they themselves and I am the one speaking in their voice; yes, I listen to them with true empathy, interest, even curiosity and with a certain sense of self-interest: *"to enrich my art"* with some elements of all this. But most of the time I listen to them with indescribable perplexity. I too should confess to them something corresponding and equivalent to their own, in order to restore the balance of our friendship. But I wasn't the type prone to confession (and if I wanted to say something of my own, I put it in the mouth of somebody else – as I am doing now, anyway); nor did I enjoy telling lies for the sake of conciliatory analogies. And thenceforth, I had to put on an act with as tender and as simple a natural air as possible (the tenderness I did have), playing the sick person with the sick (approximately the same sickness as his own, from which I'd recovered, therefore he too would recover), playing the moribund with the moribund, the amorous with the amorous – and sometimes, I truly fell in love (as I did in the case of Goghos' confession); and occasionally, I managed to invent a fictional personal story relevant to that of the narrator, and I too started to talk and talk, almost getting carried away by my own words, till I actually began to believe that it was a true personal story of my own; and in my own voice, I could hear a sentiment of generous humility, as I assumed the position of the ailing previous speaker and yielded to him the privileged position of confessor; and I started to speak and speak and I looked at his eyes or hands, and he wasn't there, he wasn't listening; he hadn't heard a word of my beautiful confession, which remained like a closed, unread book on his knees; he could hear nothing but his own words, and he was absent, and he abandoned me alone, all alone, rather tired, but in a way more free, with more white inside myself; he left me utterly alone in Kypséli Square, at the end of Carnival, at daybreak, everybody asleep, houses shut tight, cold weather, parked cars, the busses hadn't begun their scheduled routes yet; day was breaking; little by little the walls of the houses were turning white; in the Square and in the surrounding streets, mounds of leftovers from the last night of Carnival yesterday – plastic cups, bottles of lemonade, Coca Cola, Seven Up, beer, greasy napkins from cheese-pies, trampled flowers, shiny silver paper from chocolates, cellophane wrappings of crisps, confetti, little mounds of streamers, a scarf, a torn handkerchief, small paper flags barely stirring, not in mid-air, but collapsed on their back on the asphalt, and masks, masks, masks (why did they throw them here; why didn't they take them home – strange – to keep for next year or as a souvenir?) small, large, masks, half-size masks covering half the face, the whole face, masks made of velvet, paper, cardboard, with rubber-bands at the side attached to the ears or behind the head, and sometimes down to the nape of the neck and leaving a mark on you; masks, masks (well, does the unmasking ever take place, only for a moment, at the end of an end? – and is that why they've locked themselves up in their own homes now?), masks, masks, and huge snouts, a horse (now it appears sad), an elephant with a broken tusk, a cow, a lion with an open mouth like the Lion of Haironeía; and all of a sudden, a loud noise resounds, as if the tanks are back again; no, it's from the Municipal rubbish-vans, the street-cleaners are collecting the litter, silent, grey, spectral in the misty morning; they leave; silence; a white silence; and I am all alone and free in this Square; my foot kicks something which starts to roll along: an untouched package of biscuits; I pick it up, tear off the stiff paper and begin nibbling the biscuits one by one, here in the deserted Square of Kypséli, in the white morning, alone, all alone, free, without even a glass mask, dawnlike, dawnlike, after the last night of stark raving mad Carnival.

Athens, March 12th, 1983

Goghos, one summer

That summer, we all scattered here and there – one to an island, another to his home-village, another on a short trip inland; Petros disappeared again – perhaps on a mission; Yotis back to Pírgos; Alekos to Naxos, with a beautiful girl, a recent acquaintance of his; some of the girls to Hydra, others to see Monovásia, with or without their boyfriends; Persephone to Olympia; Eurydice to Aráhova, so she could go back and forth to Delphi – she was in love with the Charioteer, so she said, maybe also with Aghias, the pentathlon champion or with the younger Antinoüs – not Alcinoüs of the Phaeacians; Martha went to Thrakomakedónes, in the shadow of Mount Párnitha, with some comrades – she very much liked the pine-trees with their abundant cicadas and resin; Goghos, who worked at the Bank of Greece, set off for Corfu, without his girlfriend; Telis, astride his enormous motorbike, was knocking about the Peloponnese and who knows where else, picking up any young tourist-girl he happened to meet along the way; where could Kyparissis have gone? – he couldn't possibly know how to swim; and what about Lefteris? – not back to Ikaría again – give us a break; I went to Neórion in Poros, together with Koulis – a lad from Ionia, a refugee, with a swarm of sisters, girl-cousins, mothers, aunts, uncles, all of them huddled together helter-skelter in the laundry-shed, in the kitchen, in bed, in the midst of smells and vapours from pan-fried entrails, slices of camel meat, watermelon rinds, Turkish love-songs, together with Menoússis and Birbílis; they used to get all tangled up in your legs, you tripped up on the laundry-lines, the women's hair, their apron sashes. I didn't spend a single second in the house; all day long out in the sun and in the sea; I only went for lunch at noon and dinner, in the courtyard; at night, I slept under a big pine-tree, with just one blanket – it seems I was training for future bouts of political exile; in the morning I made my own coffee, holding the *bríki*-pot on top of fragrant dry sprigs of thyme; and what coffee that was; old Vassilis had taught me how to make it; I too had a few household articles of my own – water-canteen, glass, cup, coffee-pot, pan; I also ate the odd rusk with a tomato and salt; and the day was full of rays, many rays, golden and green, vertical and horizontal, and at the points where they intersected, they sparkled even more; and in the background, sky-blue. Koulis was a good lad – from the time he'd been a kiddy, sometimes an errand-boy, other times a vendor of *kouloúri*-buns, still other times, he had a basket of combs and night-school; he'd succeeded in opening a little shop where he sold iceboxes – he also repaired them all by himself – he made quite a bit of lucre, was able to assist his family, and also build the house in Neórion, which was always in the process of being built and never finished; I met him at Trade Union meetings; he was broad-chested and pot-bellied, with a bald patch already, but his laugh, my God, what a laugh, with a smile from one ear to the other, so sugar-sweet it made you forget about his bald spot; actually, he also wrote proletarian poems, but let's not talk about those; I never said a thing about them to him. There, we also met Nena and her brother Iosiph; they read books and did a lot of difficult gymnastics; they both swam like dolphins, especially Nena; they did dangerous trapeze-stunts from a rope they tied to a thick branch of a pine-tree; they rowed like Argonauts; and when it was boys only, Iosiph used to swim in his birthday suit, that's how we realised he was Jewish; but Nena was a true-blue Greek girl, Amazon, Artemis (I called her Artemis – and she liked it) – long chestnut-coloured hair, with lots of waves, large greyish-green eyes, she had the shoulders, breasts, thighs of an ancient javelin-thrower; such nights – boat rides by moonlight, guitars, gramophones, the two of us in a boat, Nena pulling the right oar, me the left one – who'd manage to turn the boat their way? I had a hard time managing; her mouth, her soft lips; in secret, we became engaged. When we returned to Athens, the clan gradually reassembled; we met up again. I continued seeing Nena twice a week. But didn't say anything about it to the chums. Everything was as before. Except that Goghos seemed to have changed after Corfu. He was distracted. Didn't participate much in our conversation. He also broke up with his girlfriend. He always had a Greek-French and French-Greek dictionary in his hands. He'd set his mind on learning French – he halfway recalled a bit from his high school days. "What's gotten into you, Goghos old boy, with all this French?" "Learn another language and come to know another nation – isn't that what they say?" was his answer. He'd grown a moustache. It suited him splendidly. He was more handsome now, but he seemed to have something terribly hot and secret and remote between his shirt and his sun-tanned face. One day, quite unexpectedly, Goghos said to me: "Since you know French, don't you think the words mirage, miracle, the name Mireille, muraille, mouráyio and our own Moira, have the same root?" I laughed. "How did you come to this conclusion?" I asked him and repeated: "Mirage, miracle, Mireille, muraille, Moira." And I started to translate: "Reflection, miracle, Mireille." I paused. Then repeated: "Mireille; lovely name." "Yes," said Goghos, "really lovely." The name Mireille stuck in my mind, and all at once, everything became clear as daylight to me. "Lovely name," I said, without looking at Goghos. And Goghos: "Recently I was reading a little poem: '*All night long / your name / sings in my mouth / drinking my spittle / drinking me.*' That's how I spent all night: Mireille, Mireille, Mireille, all night long." "The name?" I asked with amiable slyness. "The girl," he answered. "French girl from the South; in Paris now; at the Beaux-Arts. Mireille." Evening was falling. My room had grown rather dark. I didn't turn on the light. A train-whistle echoed. Among the shadows, boats, a guitar, the beating of oars on the water, Nena, Mireille (what would she be like, actually?), mouráyio-wharf, muraille, the wet ropes of the ships coiled up on the jetty, where we used to sit at night, in the starlight, smoking, mirage, miracle – "She called me Coco. 'Not Coco,' I kept telling her. 'Goghos.' Little by little, she half-learned it, something like Grô-gro, and later on, almost Goo-ogo; I didn't really like it that way; no, it was better before: Coco; she laughed, we both laughed, how lovely my name *Coco* sounded in her mouth. Say it again: 'Coco', Mireille, 'Coco', a thousand times over when we made love. She arrived the second afternoon after I'd gone to Corfu, when I was sitting alone on the rocks, flushed by a six-hour morning swim; I wanted to watch the sunset at leisure. She approached. 'Mee seet 'ere wiz you?' 'Do sit,' I answered her. She sat down and laid her hand on my bare knee; and immediately, our bodies were ready, like two eternal expectations meeting as an integral whole, in the absolute. She twisted the hairs on my leg into little rings and worked her way upwards. We gazed at the sunset. Seeing nothing. That same evening we made love, right there on the rocks, and there was a sound of music from the park and the sea. Afterwards, we continued in my third-class hotel. She moved into my room with her few bits of baggage and her sleeping-bag, which remained tied up in the corner. Twenty days of sheer lovemaking. Every moment, anywhere at all, even in the sea. We didn't even think about eating. In the evenings, we bought some sandwiches or cheese-pies from the shops and we'd eat them in bed, in the nude; the crumbs fell on our bodies and we picked them up one by one with our tongue, those delicate glassy morsels from the cheese-pie pastry-sheets, delicious, delicious, with our tongues; and on certain parts, we'd linger, even if there weren't any crumbs – especially on our breasts, both mine and hers; the first times I got quite angry: 'What? my nipples? am I supposed to be a woman?' I repelled her hands and her mouth; but she insisted: 'Coco, Coco, mee désire zcos'; and I allowed her to and I enjoyed it; when we made love, my fingers and her fingers played with each other's nipples; such lovemaking; and such words, terrifying and incomparable – for the very first time – I'd never uttered them before, never even heard them before:

sheer lovemaking, until the point of exhaustion, despite the exhaustion. 'Coco, Coco, mee fatiguée, you fatigué, but me désire, désire, désire and you désires mee too, Coco.' And I really did desire: 22 days and I didn't even open a newspaper once. Only sometimes, around noon, after our swim, back in our room, she used to read me some poems from her small, linen-bound album, in her own French, all of which I could understand, without understanding a single word; and while she read, her salt-stained thumb (we never rinsed off after swimming; we left the sea-salt on us), her thumb inside my mouth, toyed with my tongue and cheek from the inside. And they were really lovely poems and they all said: 'Mee désire, désire, désire'; and I attempted to translate for her sake some verses I'd recalled: *'Your body is infinite / your body indescribable, but I desire to describe it / to hold it more tightly to my own body, to fit it and to make it fit me.'* And Mireille said: 'Non déscription: me désire eat you bodie.' And whenever we bought some fruit and went back to our room, I used to ask her: 'What do you want? A peach or melon?' Mireille would answer: 'Boz ze pèche et ze melon, et mon Coco.' And as we ate, she rubbed each piece of melon here on my thingummybob, which was ready (because we ate in the nude), then put it in her mouth, saying 'délicious, délicious, délicious'. And when we lay down in bed: 'mee désire eat, mee désire drink Coco. Entre more een mee; non solely preeck – all ze bodie, Coco, all ze bodie.' And in the afternoon when we went out for a walk, she would take my underpants and put them on; 'For mee,' she would say. 'What about me?' I'd ask her. 'You poot ma panteez.' 'No,' I'd say. 22 days, 22 centuries, so endless and so brief. She's gone. Now, only her letters come, every day, in French. I can't understand much of them. Maybe I'll bring them to you some day, to translate for me. Now you know everything. What can I hide from you? That's why I broke up with Lisa. I couldn't go on. 22 days of Mireille." He fell silent. By now, night was here to stay. From time to time, for a moment, a headlight from a passing car lit up the room through the window. Goghos had his elbow resting on the table and his forehead on the palm of his hand. Perhaps Mireille was sitting opposite him on the couch. I made bold to ask: "Don't you have a photograph of her?" "I do, right here," and out of the inner left-hand pocket of his jacket, he pulled a bunch of photographs. "Only don't turn on the light yet," he pleaded. I didn't turn on the light. I left the photographs on top of the table and I noticed, although it was dark, that Goghos was still wearing his white linen summer shoes. With that automatic mechanism of identification (perhaps also because of these linen shoes), I felt that I was Goghos, and I felt like weeping for Mireille, who had left us; I longed to weep copiously in this Corfiot evening, Coco, my Coco.

Athens, March 13th, 1983

Mireille's photographs and letters

We fell silent. Noise from the street below. And a piano. Chopin's third Waltz. A-minor, again. Not that piano in the reception-hall with the screens and the mess-tin rations set before the red armchair – that empty piano without strings or keys, and inside it, those cigarette-cartons filled with hair-curlers and leftover lipsticks; no, there were not any cigarette-cartons; I rummaged inside with my hands: they were photographs – photographs of Mireille. I got up and turned on the light. Goghos said nothing. Sitting like this, with his forehead on his palm. He was missing. Back at the Corfu hotel, with the crumbs of cheese-pie? Back on the rocks, that sunset? And a ship was passing by with all its lights lit up. I went back to the table. The photographs. Here, just in a petticoat; or here, with a small linen hat; there, with a discus-thrower's ribbon in her short curly black hair; she comes up – "mee seez 'ere wiz you?" "Do sit"; here in a swimming-suit – the size of three postage-stamps; behind her the sea and a minuscule cloud to the right, oh Coco; here, lying on her stomach in the sand – her head raised, her chin cupped in the palms of both hands, her bra unfastened, the little cords, right and left, two sly little snakes about to bite her tits – a white horizontal line along her tanned back – a soft slit for you to enter her back here; and here? together with Goghos, both of them stark-naked; never had Goghos been so handsome, naked except for his moustache, even when we knew him at the beach, but then, always in a bathing-suit and without Mireille; Mireille, ah Mireille – what a bosom, more beautiful than Leila's and Lena's, erect, taut, ample, with a very fine line underneath, a mark left by the exquisite weight of her flesh and her taut nipples, expectantly ready for somebody's mouth and fingers to clench them; and what about those white triangles on both their bodies? On Goghos, the triangle was bigger, covering half his hips and half his belly, and at the end of the white triangle, the heavy penis after the erection, in a toned-down state awaiting a new erection, and the satisfied testicles – penis and testicles gripped by the thick black hooks of hair; Mireille's triangle much smaller, minuscule, and at the base, the pubic mound swollen, all swollen, all excited, a tiny swallow with its head dipping into the spring to drink a few drops of water; ah, Mireille; and those two tiny white triangles on her breasts, the kind which have the acute angle pointed upwards. The couple standing in their hotel room; window open; the lower corner of the bed showing; the sheet down on the floor; the sleeping-bag in the corner; she looking not at Goghos, but towards the window, yet she can see him and she knows she can be seen as well; a ray of light shines on the underside of her feet, the bridge, the toes, the toenails, a sparkling light on her toenails; on the littlest toe of her right foot, a minuscule callous, a tiny white dot, the beak of a bird which is laughing; I'll tweek its nose, the little minx; I'm thrilled to see it; Goghos hasn't seen it, even if he's the one who licks her toes; but *I* have seen the tiny callous –

it has become mine, has grown on my own toe: I told you, my shoe's too tight for me. And look here, two letters. I open them. Goghos isn't looking; he doesn't say a word. I translate them, not for Goghos; I translate them to myself in Mireille's patois and with her own pronunciation, and I can hear her saying the words to me: "Coco, Coco, mon Coco, black leetle roc (not little rock), black leeteel rock (mistake), bleek leetle roc in ze sea, beeg roc in mee, sea-urzeen, me leetle feesh, mon leetle leo, bleu seagool, mon beeg beeg preeck, mee désire you, mee désire you, mee désire you, encore eenside mee, moi, toujours eenside mee, in mouz, nose, 'air, boobz, 'ands, stomac, birdee, eyes, k'neez, feengres, feengrenials, sperme, spittle, mee lov, mee lov you, moi, mon Coco, your leetle Mireille, o Coco." I look at the photograph again, with the discus-thrower's ribbon around the forehead. Ah, Mireille. Not just beautiful. Unique. Eyes slightly slanting, large, stunned, totally open, and yet as though half-shut, with the slyest innocence, without a grain of distrust; soft, suckling, sucking mouth; limpid, laughterful chin; crazy hair, merry black ringlets; smooth neck (I could slip a string around it), smooth, melting away till it fuses with her receptive shoulders; and further down, downwards, naked, Mireille; unique, unique, unique. And the second letter. I quite forgot: "Coco, mon Coco. Mee bleu et red, mee blanc and blac, et on ze top a leetle verdant, mon leetle birdee, mon aigle, ze sea et ze mountagne weez trois fir-treez et une fountaigne; et zere ees un spaireau et une appl et boz we eat, one piece mee, one piece you, et encore mee eat your piece, me eat your dents, pecause mee lov Coco so mooch, et mee am une leetle leezard-samiamídi (zees you name eet zat day we voyeur eet in ze foret, non?), une leetle teeney leezard entre ze beeg toe et ze seconde toe de your feet, mee your leetle teeney teddy-bare (say eet again, mon leetle teeney teddy-bare, mon Misha, Misha de ze Moscou Olympique; toujours mee lov mon leetle Misha you offer mee, eenside mon soutien et Misha eetch ma gauche boob), mee ta leetle Mireille, she lov her Coco, oh so mooch – mon Coco, me lov you, so so mooch; je t'aime, *mon Ion.*" Ion? I turn round and look at Goghos. He's looking at me too. Has he been looking at me quite a while? He collects the photographs and letters; I glance at his hand (he's being nasty); he stuffs them into his pocket. "Well now?" he says, sarcastically, yes. I feel lost. "Lovely, lovely," say I, with an inane smile. "Don't you want some lemonade?" I ask. "No," says he. "Some orange-juice?" "No." "Some beer?" "No." (Ah, how nasty of him: always "no", "no", "no".) "Coffee?" "Coffee, yes." I go into my kitchen by myself. Put some water in the *bríki*-pot. He drinks it medium-sweet. I know. Two spoonfuls of coffee, half of sugar. I light the smaller gas-ring. I hold the half-burnt match between my teeth. A soft frou-ou-ou sound. From that spurt of fire? No. I turn round. Mireille. Nude. Three small white triangles. I turn back towards the *bríki*. A chair knocks against the cupboard. Luckily, without making any noise. She comes up behind me. Caresses me. Taking hold of it. "Slow down there, you'll make me spill the coffee. And Goghos is in there." She vanishes. I pour the coffee. Set the cup and a glass of water on the small silver tray. Go back to the other room. Goghos has gone. I leave the tray on the table, where the photographs had been just now. The cup is steaming-hot. The coffee is black. I'll have to go find Petros.

Athens, March 14th, 1983

When I finally reached Petros' place

Just under the ground-floor of our apartment building is a stationer's shop and old Kyr-Stephanos' flower shop, filled with all sorts of flowers, branches of almond-blossoms, flower-pots both large and small, earthenware platters, small cages, big ones, empty ones, or with birds inside, canaries, goldfinches, robin redbreasts, motley multi-coloured parakeets – terribly serious for their age – and quite grown-up parrots who take speech-training lessons, don't succeed in them, and get angry, to boot. But there's also a depraved, crafty parrot, who is supposed to be their teacher; but his highness never consents to address the schoolchildren of his own race: he talks exclusively with human beings, and even in their case, rather condescendingly. "My name is Yoryis," says he with flawless diction. "What's your name?" He doesn't expect any answer from the customers in the flower shop, who are waiting for their roses or carnations or gladiolas to be wrapped in silver tinfoil and then in a big piece of squeaky cellophane; nor any answer from the neighbourhood housewives, who gather there to exchange recipes with Kyr-Stephanos' wife, for cooking and pastry-making or to discuss their fears (God forbid) of some new war with those huge poisoned mushrooms, or of dictatorships again with those nasty-looking, blackish tanks on the streets and those falsified pseudo-"demotic" songs always on the radio; again Yoryis asks the children from the school across the way, who rush to gape at him during recess: "What's your name?" and all the children in unison cry out: "My name's Kostas." "Mine's Yannis." "Mine's Yoryis too." "Mine's Katerina." "Mine's Annoula." "Mine's Veniamin." "Mine's Kollitiri." "Mine's Babouras." However, in a lofty manner, high up in his cage, handsome and imposing, Yoryis just shrugs his shoulders, fluffing out his feathers, twisting his head slightly with his wise-looking, aloof eyes, smirking underneath his sharply pointed nose and never answering. He repeats, up above the turned-up noses of the children, which are almost as pointed as his own beak and full of jolly impertinence (at least that's how the parrot sees them), he repeats: "My name is Yoryis. What's your name?" He doesn't expect an answer; and in a deliriously crazy state, all the children in unison cry out: "Yoryis, Yoryis, Yoryis"; the goldfinches start to screech in their cages; the canaries get flustered and start shaking their hempseed and vitamins into the children's hair and drops of water onto their cheeks; and with smiling severity, old Kyr-Stephanos says: "Come now, children, leave Yoryis in peace." After a momentary hesitation, Yoryis plucks out one of his gold-and-sky-blue feathers with his beak and tosses it at Annoula's hair (in particular), for it is very blond and very curly and Yoryis prefers blonds, even old blonds like Kyr-Stephanos' wife, who continues embroidering behind the cash-register; anyway, the school-bell has just rung, the children have rushed off, Yoryis has shut up; and at whatsoever hour and in whatsoever weather, in rain and in wind, in cloudiness and in muddiness, or even in the snow, with overcoat lapels raised high and wet shoes, Kyr-Stephanos' display-case is the impartial indicator of all seasons – and all seasons (in the opinion of the display-case) are in full bloom. (I believe it too and proclaim this to my friends); or rather, maybe because of Yoryis, old Kyr-Stephanos' display-case is the permanent railway station of Springtime, where Spring itself observes the passenger trains with all their lights, or the thick commercial rail-vehicles with their grimey engineers and the workmen carrying pickaxes and shovels, or the farmers of Kilelér with hoes, and Marinos Andipas surrounded by old-time gendarmes, or immigrants returning from Australia, or plastic yachts for next summer and huge fridges for fisheries; night and day, the trains pass by, the springtime always here, it never leaves, remaining stationed or stationmaster, here on Mihail Kóraka Street, behind old Kyr-Stephanos' display-case; and Kyr-Stephanos himself does not at all remind you of the "crown of thorns", but of a flowered May Day wreath, like the wreathes we hang on the lintel of our door, since his son is a revolutionary and is studying in East Germany now; and the springtime never departs, perhaps for me as well, because it knows I view it correctly and really appreciate it and at any given moment, am capable of juxtaposing it most convincingly with the surliness of "Mister" Kyparissis; and I thought of saying all this to Petros now that I was on my way there; no, better to Alekos; not to Goghos or Yotis. And I reached Petros' and the whole clan was gathered there, except for Goghos (Kyparissis never visited our homes) and they were discussing something connected with "nuclear weapons" and I felt quite uncomfortable about my not paying attention and their not paying any attention to me either; but we were out of cigarettes and Martha said: "I'll dash to the kiosk and bring some back." And there was a break and then, they did pay attention to me: "Welcome back, Ion, you've quite forgotten us." And I felt it was really me in Petros' room and I could speak in simple terms, not only to Alekos, but in front of everyone, about "My name is Yoryis. What's your name?" And cordially, comrade-like, I could say: "My name is Ion"; and this time, Petros would be the first to laugh and he'd say: "There's something we didn't know; anything else, Ion?" And I told them about the parrots, and also about Judas-tree blossoms and japonica-flowers and roses and carnations (I made a pause at the carnations, in particular, – you know), about Yoryis, about old Kyr-Stephanos and his blond wife embroidering, about the permanent railway station of Springtime (indeed, I even added a basket of eggs and a signalman holding a lantern), about the cries of the schoolchildren; for (I also told them this) it's easy and pleasant for you yourself (and also, for other people too, I think) to talk about birds and flowers and children rushing off as soon as they hear the school-bell, with their hair still full of the canaries' hempseed; it's very easy (and maybe even charming) to talk about small things, without pretensions and conceit, things which do not know what they are and you can ascribe anything at all to them (as also happens in dreams) and even the pompous manner (of the birds, the flowers, the children) is a genuine, jolly seriousness, free of anything highbrow – when birds make love; when boys wear their blue school-caps askew on an early afternoon; when young girls try on their mother's dress, while she's away on a trip, and they hold her parasol and as they come down the stairs, they get all tangled up in the frills-and-furbelows and they tumble down without getting the least bit hurt – How can you talk about the other things, the large and hard and stupendous things – Makrónissos, Yiáros, Acronafplía, Kolokotronis in the dark dungeon of Palamídi, the Occupation, the December events, the Civil War, April 21st, the tanks, the Military Prison of Avlóna – Tatakis, Yemelos, Beloyannis, Ploumbides, Aris, Lambrakis and our own Electra (not Sophocles' – they say some poet dealt with her again in the *Dead House*, in *Under the Shadow of the Mountain*, and in *Chrysothemis*, as well as in other works, or Antigone and Ismene; no); I mean our own Electra, with the burnt body, the burnt hair – martyrs and heroes – they themselves said all these things, all by themselves once and for all, without words; and when you talk about them, it's as though you're sticking your nose into it, and your tone of voice takes on an element of misappropriation and boastfulness (particularly in the case of those who've never been in prison and never been executed), something incongruously didactic (and who are you mate? – You wouldn't want to say who you are, because then, you'd appear still more boastful), in the last analysis, something like self-seeking propaganda; whereas the birds and the – "Yes, the birds, but also the other things," Alekos interrupted suddenly. "First and foremost – not your little canaries now," said Petros. "Impossible," I answered in a low voice, involuntarily. "But in that case, what are –" asked Petros, quite indignantly, "what are your *Neighbourhoods of the World*, the *Letter to Joliot-Curie*, the *Time of Stone*, the *Soot-stained Pot*, the *Circumstantial Verses*, the *Comradely*

Songs, tell us what they are?" "I don't know," said I; and truly, at that moment, I didn't know – perhaps because in the meantime, the three tiny triangles of Mireille had intervened and the parrot Yoryis and the children with the hempseed in their hair – "But of course, and also the *Fourth Dimension* and *Becoming*, by all means," Alekos added unexpectedly – and I felt something akin to shame in the presence of the lads, and terribly alone and terribly sad, but at the same time, as though privileged and just; and to myself now, I continued: the children with the hempseed in their hair, the railway station of Springtime, Coco, my Coco, the girl with the discus-thrower's ribbon around her forehead, all of it, all of it, all of it, the light, old Kyr-Stephanos, the crown of thorns and that other crown of flowers for May Day – *the May Day wreath around Lambrakis' neck at Marathon*. And I exclaimed in a loud voice: "That's it, yes, that's it." And pandemonium broke loose and in unison, they all called out: "Yes, yes, yes,"; and they hugged and kissed me and I was very young and my socks had no elastic and had fallen down; and "Yes, yes, yes," it was as if they'd all heard what I was saying to myself: *"The May Day wreath around Lambrakis' neck, at Marathon."* And Goghos was also present, strange to say, and he started kissing me. And I kissed him too, more than any other time in comradely style, together with Petros. And I raised my feet to the chair, one at a time, and in an absolutely natural way, I pulled up my socks.

Athens, March 15th, 1983

The compulsory end

Well now, I had the right (acknowledged by the others, indeed) to say this, that and the other, the most secret and eternal things, and insoluble and inevitable and unalterable and incommunicable and unattainable – how many, many, infinitely many things to say and keep on saying and never end: endless, I tell you, my boy. And it had started raining. Petros gave me his raincoat, holding it up for me to put on, near the door. And I went away, totally reconciled with the lads and with the whole wide world. The rain was strong, but very pleasant; it didn't get me at all wet – maybe because I was wearing Petros' raincoat and a hat – anyway, personally, it didn't even sprinkle me, though I could hear the big drops beating down on the raincoat – a really beautiful sound, and I told myself I must remember it, "I mustn't leave it out," and also the rain on Telis' helmet atop his motorbike, and the rain in Yotis' open courtyard down on Proastíou Street, or on Mireille's sleeping-bag on the deck of a ship sailing off; or on the eucalyptus-trees of Parthéni with their leaves dripping onto the long table, where the prison guards opened the parcels and old Kyr-Kostas collected the wet strings, and how could he ever dry them afterwards?

But I forgot there's a stove in the middle of the munitions storeroom left by the Italian army, which explains the rails, right and left, for the wagons with heavy loads; and the rain on the tents of Aï-Stráti and inside the wooden washtubs of the political exiles; and the rain on old kites caught on the telegraph wires or in the trees on Mount Pendéli, on Shrove Monday after the Carnival festivities, still full of toy-trumpets and masks, and the masks got soaked and the dyes trickled down our faces and we went into the tiny kitchen of Missus Despoina, who'd also been a prisoner, to wash ourselves; and the rain inside the deep pockets of Uncle Anaxagoras' overcoat – his bits of string all soaking wet – endless things, my boy, I'm telling you, the things before, the now, the after, the inside, the outside, the everywhere, the nowhere, everything; and how can you put a full stop? not even a semi-colon or a comma; – better a dash; and not even that, because every end of any book is a mistake, a lie, a violation, a barrier; it's a "Let's just finish up any old way and pull ourselves together." This is the reason why we are so careful about the end; of course, it should be a compact and apparently necessary end, and it should not appear to be an end, but have a continuation in the midst of human beings and time, for life itself is continued, despite all its contradictions (and also, because of them) and every true book, every genuine work must be never-ending, infinite. But in our mortal state, how can we express the infinite as a whole? In our own individual mortality? The vital analogies are missing – not of depth, but length; not qualitative, but quantitative – in a word, of measureable time. Furthermore, there lurks the danger of infinite *verbosity*. And then again, what will the critics and the uncritical brains say (and quite correctly so): "Gosh, what a polygraphic, poly-persona, a-persona, anti-persona person this is; old boy, this person doesn't write words, he pisses words." But even the most kindly-disposed critics say: "Golly, such a forest, jungle, tam, tam, bam, bam, boum, pritch." And even our chums: "Such strange things these are: shameless, pornographic, cocographic, Cocographic. Who ever heard of such Leila, Mireille, Kavouras creatures; phew, wash his mouth out with soap; the bloke must have gone off his rocker; we'll have to give him a piece of our mind; we've been pampering him, you see; we'll just have to box his ears. But Petros is in on it and so is Martha. We mustn't forget this. Sure, but what about his former works? Ah, those, yes indeed. Let's not distress him, that's what I say. He's one of us. He's sure to recover." But I love my chums and I know that they (not all of them, of course) love me. And I never get angry, whatever they say. And I know that some day, they'll remember me (as they do remember me and honour me) and some day, my comrades, those of today (and even more, of tomorrow) will sense that precisely in these "strange things", I have given them the most and best and freest, whatever is most crystal-clear that I have and they have and we have and they will ever have, of white, of red, of deep and secret and of blue, of wing and of eternity. However, I may possibly be cut down by one-eyed (I didn't say cock-eyed), but always vigilant censorship and subjected to a trial, like Lousias and like de Sade. Oh, I must at all costs find an end. To end up once and for all and to cease being a brain-teaser. Yes, let me just end and take off my wet socks and lie down with my eyes open, watching the drops of rain glint like fake sparks on Petros' raincoat, which I've hung on the coat-rack. I've come to an end. The end.

Athens, March 15th, 1983

BOOK THREE

With a Nudge of the Elbow

Starting

When you start writing, you don't know what will come out, where it will take you. Inside yourself, you hear a "crik", something breaking – hesitation? Fear? Decision? Obstinacy? This break is like a crack in a glass. But you can throw away a glass. Take another. And if you have enough lucre, you can buy a dozen and better ones, at that. Because, so to speak, in the crack of the glass, germs collect – perhaps because precisely at this point, the glass or the crystal shines brighter. It seems the brightness attracts germs just as honey attracts flies. But flies are big. You can see them. You unstick them with a toothpick or better still, with a little spoon, in order to remove them along with the contaminated honey. Afterwards, you can eat it without fear. But germs are very small; your eye can't even discern them. They swarm like ants inside the crack and you drink them down just fine along with the water, in one gulp. And after that, you go tagging along with doctors, taking pills and some day, they tear your vitals apart and seek to find where the devil these bat-blind (more likely, invisible) insects nested and the doctors pull them out with big tweezers and lancets utterly disproportionate to the size of the germs. And this disproportion is always annoying and I may say, in bad aesthetic taste. Because it's a well-known fact that the law of aesthetics is founded on the clear proportions between the what, the how, the why, as well as space, time, lighting, memory, dream and reality, feeling, intellect and intuition, etc. Except that, of course, these proportions are invisible, like the germs – indefinable and weightless – nor can you count them and weight them; not even the best critic-microbiologist, with the most perfect microscope (I wonder if there are microscopes for those who are eyeless?) can locate them, record them, *document* them. So each of them says whatever pops into his mind, but with ornate and above all, *crabbed* expressions, till they reach the common denominator: that nobody understands anything. Nevertheless, there's no lack of excuses, since – as they say: "Literature and especially, literary criticism are the recording of the non-comprehensible." (And perhaps of the nonsensical?) But this isn't our topic now. We were talking about that "crik" which can be heard inside us. Not about the crack in the glass. About that other crack. Oh, that's something else. A real fissure on dry land or up on a high rocky mountain. Perhaps also on the lips of this fissure, myriads of germs are stuck – big germs, though they too are invisible. All of them are silent in a tremulous motionlessness. On all sides, the terrifying lightning-bright whiteness of the paper – terrifying in its ignorance and in its lurking exuberance. And suddenly, through this fissure, there begin to explode winds, straws, clouds of smoke, boards, clock fixtures, burning bank notes, peasants' boots with flaming shoe-laces which look like golden cross-stitches, a purple umbrella, large withered leaves from a plane-tree, faces, hands, feet, not chopped up, whole bodies solid and aethereal, until all things become fluid, swept away in a flowing mass, something like what we call lava, rolling, rolling with huge speed, waves, waves, black, gold, green, red, statues made of melted metal, laid on their side, rolling along – there are no longer any details, features, shapes – all the beauty lies in this everlasting rolling, in the current, in the impetus and tone – because a bit later on, you notice the existence (and maybe it existed from the very start) of a deep musical tone and an inward rhythm, which does not accompany the flow or originate from it, but is contained within the flow, is its physiognomy, its very heartbeat and movement. Ah, the profoundly resounding beauty of the unsolved, untraceable, unnaturalised and absolute proportions, of the simultaneous and synonymous movement, colour, sound – intoxication, realisation of the unknown, uncontrolled and unlimited freedom. But suddenly you are overpowered by fear of the impersonal and anonymous, fear for the extermination of comparative limits, road-signs, communication, and the even greater fear lest this beautiful flowing fiery mass burn down the picturesque little villages further on, the orchards, animals and human beings, the rope-ladders leaning against the trees, that black cow who had bent down to the brook (I'd seen her at twilight; looking her in the eye, I asked her: "Are you related to Our Lady?" "Yes," said she; and she bent still lower and with a sort of sorrow, she rested her lips on the water; and then, down in the brook, I dimly discerned Our Lady offering water to the black cow in her own two hands; and her hands glowed in the water like two moons). My God, what fear lest this brook be burnt and the icon of the twin Virgin, and the canary with its cage hanging on the small window of Kyra-Leni and the little green bench in the garden where the other day, early in the evening, we sat (my friend Vanghelis and I) and Vanghelis was wearing open sandals without any socks, because the day-before-yesterday it was summer (but it's also summer now) and I said to Vanghelis: "Hey there Vanghelis, gosh, what big feet you have." And Vanghelis said in a smiling sly way: "Big and beautiful. Don't you like them? The bigger your feet are, the stronger you are for standing on the earth." And he was quite right. Big and beautiful. Strong toes. Broad curved toenails. His curly black hairs came all the way down to his ankles, pouring out from the sleeves and collar of his shirt, smothering his neck, climbing up his cheeks, just under his eyes. A real ape. A beautiful ape. He was quite right. But I felt rather sad and as though rather angry – I don't know why – and I hid my feet under the little bench, although I wasn't wearing sandals, I was wearing socks and shoes. And when I arrived home later on, by the light of the white new moon, I sat at my table, opened my papers and this time, I wasn't frightened by the whiteness of the paper and I said: "You'll see, oh you rascal Vanghelis; you'll see, I'll write now and we'll see who has bigger feet; and not only feet, but also two big paper wings. Come on, now let's compete in flying as well as jumping." That's how I spoke and as I started writing, *other things* came out and I stared at the letters, the words, the lines, all pitch-black on the white paper, like very small bridges above two shores which were very far apart – better say, above two non-existent shores. How could you make the bridges firm? To bridge what? And this time, I was truly angry, not with Vanghelis, but myself. And I started erasing whatever I'd written, absent-mindedly tracing spirals, cylinders, contiguous circles, scratching out each word, syllable by syllable, letter by letter, breathing marks, accents, as though in order to leave no trace; and when I reached the last word, I saw that in the course of erasing, I'd sketched Vanghelis life-size, with his thick curly coat of hair. At this point, I smiled in a sly rogueish way like Vanghelis, and on the lower part of the page, which was still blank, in a conscious way now, I sketched Vanghelis' feet, but without sandals. (Sandals and shoes in general, were always difficult for me.) And I was glad. It was really a very beautiful drawing. And I said to myself: "I think painting seems to say things better and more correctly." And the next day, I showed my drawing to Manthos. "Fine," said he. "One of your best. But why did you draw Vanghelis without his sandals? They suit him very well. And you know, he made them all by himself." "By himself?" I acted lost. "How?" "Quite simply," said Manthos; "with a razor, he cut up a pair of his old brown shoes, leaving only one strap on the *coup de pied*. No cobbler ever made more perfect sandals." I was speechless. Maybe I even turned pale. How did Manthos know all this? Why hadn't Vanghelis told me too? And what was that Frenchified "coo-de-piay", so incongruous with Vanghelis' feet? You see, Manthos had completed a painting and sculpture course at the School of Fine Arts and had also spent a brief time in Paris. He always painted nudes - men, women, boys, girls, black men, white men, even old men and old women. Never landscapes and still lifes. "Ah, the human body," he used to say. "It says everything. It needs no comments and explanations. I've also made a sketch of Vanghelis, in political exile, there by the edge of the sea in Aï-Stráti, where they let us swim. I drew him wearing his swimsuit and his sandals. In fact, I told him to take off his swimsuit. But he didn't. How did you get him to pose nude?" "He didn't pose for me. I drew him from memory." (I didn't tell him the drawing had made itself, while I was erasing my written text.) "Maybe that's why it's so successful," he remarked, pensively and a bit sadly. "You avoided the occasionally negative quest for anatomical precision and you gained a more essential precision. Perhaps memory and the first feeling see better than our eyes and guide our hand better." We both fell silent. But in a little while, for no reason at all, Manthos burst into loud laughter. "How foolish people are," said he. And he continued laughing in a strange way, as though he wanted to dissociate his position from mine. And after a few seconds of silence, he said, in an acquiescing manner (and I couldn't understand for whom the acquiescense was – for me? for himself? for Art?): "Vanghelis' handsomeness and manliness are not appropriate for painting. They demand marble, white marble. He must be absolutely upright and absolutely nude with his beautiful sandals. White marble." "And must his hairs be white too?" I asked and my voice sounded to me full of childish naiveté. "No," he answered. "Ancient statues all had a layer of paint on top. I would paint Vanghelis' statue brick-red and on top, with thick black semi-circular brush-strokes, I would paint his hairy coat as though he were enclosed inside the net of his destiny, like a new Agamemnon, but much more handsome than Agamemnon." I grabbed my drawing, rolled it up and rushed off in haste, leaving Manthos alone (and perhaps bewildered) at the "cafeneíon", without paying for my coffee. When I arrived home, I unrolled the drawing on top of my table, glanced at it one last time and said: "Nonsense, nonsense; neither painting; nothing." And I tore it up into tiny, tiny pieces, threw it into the toilet-bowl and pulled the chain. I could hear the water flowing noisily. "Thus –," I said. "Thus", without knowing the meaning of this *thus* of mine.

Karlóvassi, July 17th, 1983

A listless day

Yesterday my whole day was wasted. I did nothing. Listless, listless. I kept searching for something to please me, something beautiful, so I could feel happy and be able to say to myself "thank you" (as happens to me now and then) and want to live, and afterward say "thank you" out loud and the echo would repeat this to me in its own voice, I mean would say "thank you" to me. Yes, I always really yearned for something beautiful, especially in the evenings, before sleep, when I was lying down, I searched to think, remember, dream, presuppose, predict something beautiful, making sure that it exists, even in some uncharted and undefined region, so that I could sleep without contracting my eyebrows, and with the muscles of my face relaxed in a mild smile, without that foolish counting backward from 100 to 19, and all over again. Likewise, in the mornings, as soon as I woke up, while I was making my coffee on the small gas-stove, I searched with my eyes, ears, nostrils, skin, tongue, searching for the square of sun on the floor, the shadow of a passing bird in precisely this brightly-lit square like an exclamatory "aaah" (both visible and audible), the trickling of water in the sink, the scent of jasmine from the little garden, mingling with the smell of coffee, the taste of the coffee and cigarette, the touch of the tablecloth or sheet or your own hand – I used to search for something beautiful, which would be like saying a ticket *paid for* with my own attention, permitting me fearlessly and rightfully to enter the day, freshly washed, with my hair neatly combed, with my cigarette on my lips in a dignified style (even with a sort of brashness or insolence), and not like some grimey stowaway in a baggage-compartment littered with cigarette-butts, coal soot, sloppy bundles and two rotten fish. Well now, with this ticket, I can sit comfortably in the right place and look through the window at a tree, a balcony, a rakeish white little cloud responding to me in a smiling way, as well as at the itinerant knife-grinder, the ice-vendor, the donkey of the greengrocer, Old Uncle Thomas, laden with apples, pears, peaches, cantaloupe-melons, and like this I can travel the whole world, and the world can come to me, become mine, and I can offer it to everybody in a more beautiful and more serene form (though rather intoxicated, not by alcohol and such things, but by its beauty, and yes, also by my own beauty). For beauty, old boy, is something which compels you (or rather, prompts you) to preserve it and be preserved along with it – something like a full moon in summer, with many crickets and fragrant scents of pine-trees, grass and brightly-lit, erotic open windows. And still more – something you can't stand by yourself alone and you want to share it with everybody, so that without a single exception they can all see it and enjoy it, and the more you share it, the more it multiplies and the more it becomes your own and names you. As you take a stroll some afternoon with a friend of yours along the avenue lined with oleanders, outside the big patisseries with their glass windows and a beautiful woman passes by – such a gait, such legs, knees, breasts, hair – and with your elbow you nudge your friend's elbow, so he can see as well and you can rejoice together, and so the woman becomes still more beautiful; and now, I recalled one noon, years ago, we were passing by the Arsákion Arcade, Chryssa, Nikiphoros and I; Chryssa was two steps out in front (or rather, Nikiphoros intentionally slowed down his pace a bit and I along with him, to let Chryssa move ahead); she was wearing a white jersey dress with loosely spaced blue stripes and a small gold chain for a belt, which emphasized the delicate grace and elegance of her waist; the lovely shoulder-blades, the shapely buttocks, her unaffected sway were delineated with such natural nobility, that Chryssa seemed not to be at all aware of the beauty of her body; and just then, Nikiphoros nudged me with his elbow, turned and glanced at me, pointing to Chryssa with his eyes (though I'd seen her long before) and I said to Nikiphoros: "Thank you; now I understand how much you love her" and both of us almost burst into tears like fools, but exactly for this reason, we started laughing, and Chryssa turned round and said: "What are the two of you guffawing about?" and simultaneously, Nikiphoros and I answered: "About this." "What's this?" asked Chryssa. "Eh, *this*," we repeated and all three of us burst out laughing in front of the tailor's display-window, where two dummies stood staring at us – the one dressed in sports clothes and the other in a tail-coat, top hat and a slender black cane with a silver handle in his right hand, and you felt like grabbing his charming little cane away from him and in a funny, soft way you wanted to tap the bottoms of all the people passing by the Arsákion Arcade and momentarily, they would be startled and get slightly annoyed, but when they realised you're a good-hearted lunatic, they'd begin to laugh too and we'd laugh together, just the way a singer in the Záppion Garden sings a well-known song and when he reaches the refrain, he says: "Everybody together"; and everybody together, we start singing, regardless of sex, age, colour, ideology, and on the little tables, the glasses, tiny nickel-plated spoons, bottles of beer and orange-juice sparkle without a bit of bigotry, even the customers' shoes and the trays and the chairs. So is beauty perhaps a happy contagious mass form of laughter? Or like a glorious sunset in Karlóvassi, Samos, where you're sitting on your cement "throne" alongside the sea and you don't have anybody near you: Falitsa, Eri, Nana, Nicola, Antoine, Fereydoun, Vanghelis, Rubini, to share with them the gold and rose colours, their reflections in the sea and on the window-panes of the fishermen's houses, the whistling of the boat, the swift broad-winged oblique smooth flight of two seagulls, just then you nudge the stone with your elbow and the stone becomes a friend who can see and together, you both see the sunset, and with the double or triple or multiple gaze, the sunset becomes doubly, triply, multi-fold beautiful, and the whole world becomes your friend, and you say: life is worthwhile, and we are worthwhile, and you feel an infinite, equitable, unknown gratitude flooding you to the very tip of your hair and fingernails. But yesterday, all day long, there was nothing doing. No excitement, no tremour. I kept searching for childhood memories, past love-affairs, books, magazines, newspapers, my own papers. Nothing doing. There was something at fault. Maybe I myself. Maybe Vanghelis. Why? I even invoked Ariostos – that generally speaking, ironical and ironical-against-himself (and perhaps, basically, desperate) good humour of his, his skill in making comparisons, his polite smile, which had the power of abolishing or synthesizing contradictions and transforming the negative into the positive – with convincing virtuosity – allowing the elation of the attainable to hover over it. But Ariostos could do nothing either. I thought of going out at noon to have a bite to eat at the neighbourhood eating-house of Kyr-Nikos, who was an ex-railway-worker, maybe I'd encounter somebody, exchange a few words, and unwind a little. I changed my mind. Boiled two eggs and swallowed them, shoving them in without any appetite, lonely, estranged and cranky. The only good thing I found was this word "cranky". I said it to myself several times and felt like puking, as though I'd eaten something rancid. I started breaking the eggshells into tiny, tiny pieces, in order to do something, to find some occupation, some serious occupation, as though out of these white eggshells, I was building a tower with balconies, flags, guards, buglers and four long-legged tall thoroughbred dogs, which were arrogant and rather sad, as though a handsome twelve-year-old boy had died and the masters of the house were away on some distant journey. Because these small familiar (fraternal I used to call them) details moved me and in actual fact, with these details I could sometimes build towers and temples and statues and airports and theatres with three-thousand seats, red velvet curtains and exquisite cardboard forests full of genuine golden apples, like those of the Hesperides or of Paradise. But now the shells refused me my kind of metamorphosis – they remained merely eggshells. Goddam it. The entire afternoon I tormented myself like this. In the early evening, I went over to Kyr-Nikos' eating-house – it was almost a cellar, you had to go down five stairs to enter. He also had one of the very few telephones in the neighbourhood. My own phone had been cut during the Civil War, in 1948, when they arrested me and sent me into political exile. In 1952, when I came back, I made efforts to have the phone re-connected, but time passed and I hadn't any results. So now and then, I used to go to Kyr-Nikos to make a phone-call and on rare occasions I gave his number to a friend to call me in case of urgent need. And poor Kyr-Nikos used to send one of his three sons to call me, for my home was only a few steps away. And now, I thought of making a phone-call to Piraeus, to ask Vanghelis to get on his motorcycle and drop by to keep me company. But I don't know why, I was too bored. Leave it for tomorrow, said I. I wasn't hungry and ordered plain fish-soup. There was hardly anyone in the little taverna. Only two little tables further on, five workers from the Machine-shed across the way, where they repaired freight-cars – young men, sturdily built, sunburnt, wearing smudged athletic shirts, which showed their broad chests and strong muscular arms. I ate my fish-soup without any appetite and glanced at them furtively. They were gulping down their fish-soup in high spirits, with big pieces of soaking wet bread; right in the middle, they had the platter with a large boiled fish, served with olive-oil and lemon, where they all stuck their forks in company; they also had a deep bowl of cucumber and tomato salad with plenty of olive-oil and vinegar, onion, peppers, *féta* cheese and small black olives. They didn't talk. As though the most important thing in the world was the food. And what a coincidence: they each had a boiled egg and all at once, as though by agreement, all five cracked the eggs on their foreheads, shelled them and cut them into the salad (do you suppose they might be celebrating their own proletarian Easter with white eggs? – because that simultaneous movement of theirs had something ritualistic about it, something like a heretical initiation-rite). And just at that moment, all five laughed loudly, neutralising my own morbid hallucinations. They tossed the eggshells under the table and crushed them with their army-boots. (What could they do with the useless shells? – those are for white-collar workers.) I envied them. The future is for them. Workmen – frank, robust, innocent, erotic. What can they do with eggshells? These men make strong useful things, which are shared in common. And I told myself to give up writings and books and to go ask for a job at the Machine-shed, in order to have simple colleagues and collaborators, flourishing and beneficial human beings worthy of the revolution, without metaphysical ideas and hot air and frills. But do you think they'd accept me? And what did I know about iron parts and machines and wheels and greasey oils and smudges? And what about my arms? In a bitter mood, I looked at my long slender fingers. At that very moment, the swarthiest of the five, the one with the thick black moustache and long eyelashes, which cast a prickly shadow on his cheeks in the light falling from above, called out: "Hey, Mastro-Nikos, won't you put a record on the gramophone, to add a bit of flavour to our retsina, which I think you've started watering down." And Mastro-Nikos turned on the gramophone (one of those beautiful old ones with the pink funnel-shaped loudspeaker opening up like a huge lily) and he put on "Moonless Night has Fallen". I was getting ready to leave. But I stopped short. I imagined they'd get up, move the tables and chairs aside and start dancing the *zeibékiko*. Because these people don't know only how to make useful things, they also know how to sing and dance with bravado. But they didn't dance. They just went on eating and drinking. I paid for my half-finished soup and went out. Up above the Machine-shed, a slim new moon was poised. My foot stumbled against a broken dry branch. I stared at it in a friendly way. And started pushing the withered branch with my right foot every two steps. I'd found company. But Kyr-Andreas (my next-door neighbour, who was a watchmaker with bronchial asthma, and had had to stop working) was coming along behind me, without my being aware of him and he called to me: "Watch out, Mr. Ion, there's a branch tangled up in your feet; be careful not to fall. Good evening to you." "Ah yes," said I. "Good evening." And I picked the branch up in my hands. Kyr-Andreas passed me by, coughing away. I delayed. Raised the branch to my face and saw the new moon sitting on it like a single silver-flower. "Aï-aï," said I. And the withered branch with the silvery flower was mine. I too had something. I unlocked my door, turned on a light, laid the branch on my table on top of my papers, opened the window and tried to smile, like Ariostos, towards a piece of sky. Did I perhaps want to deceive myself? "Just think," said I, "you love the world so much and you're so alone in the world." To whom could I say "good night"? I grabbed the withered branch and threw it out the window. The moon remained in its own place, an alien, far-away silver-flower.

Karlóvassi, July 18th-19th, 1983

The same evening

I sat on my chair. Threw my hands on my knees. To relax. Not to keep searching inside, outside, for purposes, supporting documents, justifications, affable receptions – where, when, who? To touch the empty, the blind, the limpid, the alleviating, the invigourating. Sleep. There's nothing to be done. I rest my elbows on the table, thrust my face into the palms of my hands. Better like this. A dark sinking. But I can hear high, high up, above me: *"I'm waiting."* What the devil are you waiting for? What do you want? At long last, say it, define it. Let me know too. Again, nothing. Nothing. I open my eyes, uncover my face, and decide – what? Suddenly I remember a verse from a poem entitled "The unknown rival of Phidias". I liked it then and underlined it. Now, I repeat it to myself: *"The unfinished is the hall-mark of masterpieces."* A correct verse, a true one. I still like it. Even tonight, here's something I like. You're telling lies. Hey there, damn it all, are you checking up on me now? Lies, yes. In those days, I used to leave my poems half-finished in order for them to become masterpieces. However, the voluntary stop was clearly apparent. And this conscious pre-decision and pre-meditation created something like a tail-piece of conclusion – viz., an end. Whereas the real "unfinished" is never intentional. So it was vital to get rid of the intentions of there being or not being an end. I became more cunning with other people, with myself and with words. I changed my manner of writing. I said: "I'll allow the poem to end or not to end, whenever and wherever *it* wants and not when I want. I won't interfere. I won't plan beginning, middle, end, theme, manners, synthesis. I'll let it move along on its own, as it pleases. I'll lie in ambush for it, without being seen, (and perhaps without participating, yes?) and just where it appears to be rounding off and heading towards an end, I'll go 'kratsch' and stop it. Well, isn't this genuinely unfinished?" "No," says the poem; "I didn't stop on my own, from doubt or indifference or fatigue; you cut me. I'm not of my own accord unfinished; I'm cut by your own pseudo-aesthetic censorship." So it's a wild goose chase. Try and make heads or tails of it – intentions, counter-intentions, conscious, unconscious, technique, counter-technique, art, anti-art. Warily I re-read those works of mine. A blank. Neither unfinished, nor finished, nor anything at all. I also re-read that poem, the stumbling-block, the main reason responsible for all my misfortunes:

THE UNKNOWN RIVAL OF PHIDIAS

He knew it: the work they were expecting from him, he
  would never give,
despite the material he'd carefully collected through the
  years,
despite all his technical experience – superior to everybody's
  – a work, e.g.
such as the enormous, extremely ornate Zeus of Olympia

*beneath whose feet was an inscription: 'I am a work
by the son of Charmides, Phidias, Athenian citizen.' Oh, such things
with such emphasis, such extravagance – he knew – he'd never achieve;
he lacked the simplicity, the lovely naiveté of easy faith
which by flattery, coquettish vanity, exaggeration,
and sometimes by cunning condescension, creates magnificent works
accepted by the throngs – who stand around on all sides, gazing for hours,
shoving one another, talking, chewing sunflower-seeds, admiring them
(actually, more for the weight of the gold and for the precious stones)
calculating their value in talents; without the ignorant fools even suspecting
that these are just plain coloured bits of glass, – and the genuine diamonds
the genuine Artisan keeps well concealed in his wooden trunk,
deep down in the big basement, where he descends alone at night,
with a guilty, trembling candle in his hand, testing his own death,
and hewing only his own statue – knowing that even this he'll never finish.
A doubtful consolation for him: 'The unfinished is the hallmark of masterpieces.'
(And perhaps this statue was not only of him, but also of the others,
who were not gods, but who go on for ever, never stopping, never.)*

But this poem, darling, is finished and all too finished, without gaps, deficiencies, abstractions, concealments. Consequently, it isn't a masterpiece at all. However, this was not written by Phidias' rival, another man wrote it about him. So he himself is not responsible. Probably his own statue is in actual fact *unfinished* and a masterpiece. But now I pay attention particularly to another verse: *"A doubtful consolation for him"*. To hell, a thousand times to hell with all doubtful or sure consolations. I can't accept them. I'm proud, even if I don't have Vanghelis' big feet and his splendid improvised sandals cut with a razor out of his old shoes. Ah yes, these are in actual fact *"unfinished sandals"*, therefore also masterpieces (more beautiful, said Manthos, than the winged ones of Hermes). I've found it. So this is the way I'll do it too. Here's the ideal method. I'll take that unsuccessful poem written two months ago, with the persistent attempt to make it "unfinished"; with a pen (not with Vanghelis' razor), I'll cut the front part, the heel, the iron holes for the shoelaces (above all, the shoelaces themselves, which plug up the holes and cover the tying knots with two funny coquettish bows) and I'll leave only one strip (better two or three strips – sandals with three strips are more beautiful) so I'll leave only three strips on the *coup de pied* of the poem (as Manthos also says). I seize the clearly written manuscript of my long poem. And prepare myself for the surgical interventions. But I change my mind. (It is so calligraphically written with my neo-Byzantine letters and the orange rubrics at the beginning of each chapter.) Anyway, the cut will be intentional and will be obvious from a thousand metres away. Aside from the fact that I'll be the first to see the smudges and erasures, and I'll know. So then, intentional, everything intentional, and worst of all, coquettish. But aren't Vanghelis' sandals also intentional? Yes, yes, intentional? But sandals are forgiven, because they have an immediate, specific, practical expediency: during hot spells, they allow the feet to be aired, not to perspire and not to get pricked by thorns. But what about the poem? What is its expediency? To please? Ah, whatever seeks to please always becomes repulsive. And what if, by erasing the verses, once again a hairy sketch of Vanghelis emerges? I'd better tear up the final manuscript in tiny bits and pieces and throw them into the toilet-bowl too and pull the chain, like yesterday. And when I hear the noisy guttural water running, I'd better say again *"thus, thus"* and return to the very first disconnected, invertebrate, chance, blind notes of the poem, which didn't even know if they'd become a poem, and which were never actually used in the poem. These are not intentionally processed, censored, selected. Of their own accord, they are unfinished, incomplete, scattered. Here they are:

1. – *How bitter for you to abandon your nights to the teeth of the absolute*
2. – *Maybe the same aqueous thread moves from the wolf to the cicada and from the cicada to the star*
3. – *Oh, we've always loved desire in e x c e s s*
4. – *The girl's circular dance around the stark-naked statue of Apollo*
5. – *How many storeys in the sky on an autumn evening*
6. – *Big ricks of moonlight remain afloat gliding slowly in the river*
7. – *Grieving woman with lifeless hair on dark thresholds*

8. – *One third of your body grows dark*
   the rest glows in the twilight
9. – *I can hear the deep breathing of the night*
10. – *Tonight the moon is a burning house.*
    On the mountain opposite, chairs in flames are falling
11. – *We're hidden inside each other.*
    No one will find us. Only the moon
    on your expectant lips
12. – *Oh, Greek hills, you gaze at us in such a friendly way*
13. – *Such a sad happiness that you exist*
14. – *Many secrets lying in bed between the pages of books*
15. – *I traversed the pink darkness with fresh tobacco-leaves*
    in my trousers pocket
16. – *The miracle and immortality of our mortality*
    small blueish fires on the hills
    and down below, the desolation of the great waters
17. – *Exquisite, penniless night –*
    the scents of grass, strawberry and public urinals
18. – *Jolts and roars of steam-engines; railway stations and*
    a sad girl selling pistachios
19. – *The sense of the unknown and general ignorance*
    condense, crystallising into a brilliant ALWAYS
20. – *And at this moment, I felt I was a big sewing-machine*
    abandoned in the desert
    and attached to its needle, a half-finished 18th century
    calico nightgown, by full moon
21. – *Alexander in front of magnifying mirrors*
    recites excerpts from the epic of the night
22. – *Deep orange shadow above the night-blackened city*
    and around the closed well scents of fresh green corn
23. – *He shouts in broad imperatives: kiss, fuck, get pregnant*
    strip others and yourselves naked, raise flags, bite,
    push forward –

*oh, great rivers full of floating oak-trees, and love-
    struck motor-vessels,
smoke, fumes, windblown dresses, knees, words,
prosperous star light and succulent little moon
    with a stolen cigarette dangling on its lips*

24. – *At Avlákia, down on the seashore, big octopuses
    clutch the legs of the little swimming girls*
25. – *Filled with sorrow, the wanderer stares at the infinite
    where only a single star is pinned*
26. – *I saw women deer and men who were wild boars and
    one man who was a unicorn
    on his curved horn a daisy-chain dangled*
27. – *From their curly black hair fell fragments of rebétika
    songs*
28. – *A good-looking woman in the elevator is holding five
    roses and a smoked herring*
29. – *Always from the bottom you climb the highest mount*
30. – *In this man I discerned a solitary mildness
    like trampled sawdust in a closed cabaret at 3 o'clock
        after midnight
    and maybe, it was already daybreak on the fringes of
        the city*
31. – *Fine lust of satiated lust, of noble insatiability,
    idle gentleness after lovemaking and you aren't even
        wearing your wristwatch*
32. – *I slept at noon under the plane-trees of Aï-Demétres
    small birds, most of them sparrows, peered at my sleep
        – they didn't find me a stranger
    and this deep affinity filled my bosom with cool clover*
33. – *The dark sky glimmers above the earth with a gentle
    blue*
34. – *From the girls' laughter flowers fall on the freshly
    washed sidewalk*

multitude of flowers – roses, chrysanthemums, violets, jasmine, pansies

and one lone orange; it rolled as far as my feet; I picked it up,

I scrape it with my fingernails and smell it – how fragrant the world

35. – *The night is full of stars, leaves and shirts*

36. – *How I eyed you with my whole body*

37. – *Not with a calm sea. With tufted waves I want to struggle*

38. – *Cold wintery evening. The frugal little house reeks of scorched sheepskin*

39. – *I don't know what to do tonight. I'm filling in the gaps between the stars*

40. – *A blind lion in the wild forest*
   who doesn't even know where he is, where he's going, what he is

41. – *Let me sit like this for hours, thinking about the roundness of the potato in the ground*

42. – *The recollection of our silent love swells again*
   just as testicles swell from the heat on an August noon

43. – *I'd tossed a golden coin into the big earthenware urn,*
   its sound accompanied me for years along the river
   at the hour when all things were disappearing further beyond the clouds
   and the labourers, returning from work at the carpenter's, glanced hastily at the Evening-star up above the chimneys
   without suspecting that it was really my coin, the only coin I ever had

44. – *A delayed raindrop dripping from leaf to leaf*
   until it falls on the back of my hand

45. – *The innocent murderer with the long shirt*

46. – *The bugler in the golden sunset high up on the ramparts*
   lowers the bugle from his mouth and pisses.
   How many warriors killed, how many horses killed.
   Last post.
47. – *Dancing, dancing, dancing – bare feet,*
   second, third leap in mid-air, the air becoming seized,
   the women's breasts shake up and down,
   the men's phalluses beat first their thighs, then their bellies,
   country-churches come out-of-doors and survey the world,
   clouds with double yolks grow hot under the sun,
   old women sit on the stones with their spittle congealed in the hollow of their one-and-only tooth,
   the amber-coloured medlars on the ground are crushed under the heels of Glory
48. – *Many things I've said for many people; it's time to keep quiet.*

I cast one last glance. No, no. Neither *this*, nor *thus*. I stand up. Get undressed. Look through the window. Sky. Crystal-clear sky, indifferent. The moon has come closer. I go outside, barefoot, in my pants. Not a soul on the street. I find the withered branch I'd thrown out. And go back in. Put it in a vase without any water, on the table. I turn off the light and lie down. Let me sleep, my God. I get along better with dreams – even if they're nightmares. Better.

Karlóvassi, July 20th-21st, 1983

The dream with the lilies

I'm asleep. Even in my sleep I know easily that I'm asleep. Gentle penumbra, a little after sunset, without colours. I'm in Samos, on a hill of Ambélou. The place is altered, yet familiar. What's become of the pine-trees and the fir-trees? Nakedness, rocks, big rocks. And how did I get up here? On foot? No. My shoes aren't at all dusty. By the one-and-only bus? Neither. In my hand I'm holding a blue plastic flight-bag. Inside, I have my raincoat carefully folded like a book. I've hidden something inside the book – I can't remember what now. I also have a thick ash-grey pullover and a terra cotta statuette of Artemis – the one Alekos gave me when I was sick and he sat next to my bed and put one hand on my forehead and with his other hand gave me the statuette, and just by holding it and looking at it, I got well immediately – maybe because Artemis was wearing a short pleated chiton, which left one breast sticking out; maybe because Alekos had his hand on my forehead; and surely, from inside, the chess-set has black and white regular squares like the little tiles in the kitchen of our ancestral home, and when you opened the door, the smoke emerged bearded with a tiny ancient lyre, which is why I too pressed my blue bag tight to my chest, when the women's wailing cries were heard behind the rocks: "Spring-well, Spring-well, Spring-well" and I couldn't make out if they were crying "Spring-well" or "Springtime"; and for me they were both equally pleasant, both Spring-well and Springtime, so the tragic wail was neutralised and a gurgling song was created in the *"solitude of the great waters"*; and the Seven Women of the Chorus (do you suppose they were Libation Bearers? Suppliant Women or Bacchic Women?) now appeared, now disappeared, naked from the waist up, and down below they had a short chiton made of newspapers, and as the wind blew, the newspapers rose and, fleetingly, the one woman's thing appeared shaved, the other's thing, not shaved – you didn't have time to see – oh Spring-well, oh Springtime, oh, oh, Spr-r-ringtime – the wind was blowing again, bringing down the newspapers; the women disappeared behind the rocks, but their breasts pulsated, up and down in the dance, white, swarthy, broad, pointed, erect, the nipples taut, many tits, and they kept multiplying, the evening became full of breasts dangling like bunches of grapes, one of them had flowing milk, which became a white line, reaching as far as the thumb of my right hand; I wanted to lick it, but I was holding my plastic flight-bag, and what did I want with that raincoat? – oh Springtime, Springtime – I'm going to miss the bus, "Phemonoë" was heard clearly now; so the one with the broad, taut, white bosom was called Phemonoë, and the other one must be called Nausicaa, because as she ran backwards, her soles looked like white birds, doves or seagulls; but what did the Seven Men want (there aren't any men at all in the *Libation Bearers* or in the *Suppliant Women* – perhaps in the *Bacchae*? – I can't remember), and they too had bare chests and newspapers around their waist, not all of them, the Five, the other Two were dressed, the One in a labourer's blue overalls, the Other in a white sailor-suit and sandals, and as the wind started blowing again, the newspapers were raised, the thingummybobs of these Five also showed, and the broad white trousers of the sailor-suit undulated; but then, lightning began, hasty long white flashes-of-lightning; now and then their faces were lit up, I began to recognize – here's Telis, Goghos, Yotis, Alekos, Iosiph (yes, it's he – the Jewish boy from Poros), this one in the overalls is Petros, that one in the sailor-suit is Vanghelis (because Vanghelis had done his military service in the Navy and from there, they'd sent him to Makrónissos and afterwards to Aï-Stráti, with his white trousers fitted at the hips, bell-bottomed down below – he also had another very short pair of shorts, also white and – once when he was sitting opposite us on a stool, chewing a peach with the peel on, a testicle was hanging out on his left thigh – Lefteris was also with us – we pretended not to see, but Vanghelis realised from the way we avoided looking in that direction, and he said: "Hey there, the rascal just popped out for some fresh air," and with his fingers he pushed it back inside his underpants; but then, he was dressed in army-boots and thick khaki socks, which were fixed like two thick anklets above his boots – because he didn't yet have his Hermes' sandals), oh Springtime, Springtime; but Vanghelis' parenthesis dragged on long in the dream and there was a fear I might miss other words too from the declamations, which the women with the newspapers were making collectively now; although also earlier on, when I'd been paying attention, I couldn't make out a single word, except for those two or the one, unless they meant the breasts of Phemonoë (yes, surely), because they were cool and springlike; until somebody shouted: "We'll miss the last bus." And we all started rushing in that direction, leaping over the rocks; the newspapers got torn, the posteriors shone in circles and more circles; with my blue bag I was actually flying and from the speed, my transparent nylon raincoat unfolded and became two large transparent beige wings with small square creases (apparently since I had it wrapped in the shape of a book) and it kept opening and closing, flapping its wings like the pages of a book being leafed through by a secret wind, and until I could collect my winged raincoat, wrap it up again and put it back in my flight-bag, I delayed quite a while and by the time I arrived, all the seats were taken and I was left standing up, shoved into the corridor way at the very back, and we all lurched back and forth, as soon as the bus started, as though we were making love collectively, because there weren't any grips up above to catch hold of, to keep your balance; and in front of me I felt the slit of a bottom stuck there in a perfect fit, and I began to get into a flap and I tried to move slightly backwards in order to come unstuck: "You infernal sluts, to make it the talk of the town that I'm starving for it and catch fire at the very first touch." I keep trying and I can feel Phemonoë's breasts stuck to my back like two big cupping-glasses sucking my blood. "Goddam it, two women are going to jump me now, but as far as I know, a trio means two men and one woman, and not the reverse." I reach the climax, the liquids start flowing, and what's curious is that in all this crowding, I can't discern anybody, there isn't anybody, only the density of the closed air, and the bus is an empty beer-garden on

wheels with spectral shapes of big glasses and white
patches of foam on the tables, and through the glass
partition, in the driver's seat is Telis and I recognize
him although he's naked and wearing only a motorcyclist's helmet, but this helmet is neither like Agamemnon's nor like Kolokotronis', that's why I feel alone in
the corridor of the beer-garden, cut off from Greek
history, ancient and recent; nevertheless my flight-bag is
blue, therefore Greek, and inside my bag is the terra
cotta Artemis, and I open my bag to make sure it wasn't
lost at the moment my raincoat escaped; yes, here it is,
with my fingers I fondle the sculpted folds of the little
statue and a gland of my cock is moist, and Telis' voice
can be heard: "We've arrived." And I proceed into the
corridor alone with my flight-bag; but on the steps of the
bus, Vanghelis is standing in his white sailor-suit, holding a flower-pot with five big red lilies (and although my
whole dream is black and white, I can see that the lilies
are red, absolutely red, only I don't know why there are
five of them and with my eyes I count them again and
find them correct and this brings me a special calculating satisfaction). "You scamp," Vanghelis says to me and
offers me the flower-pot with an exquisite smile; and in
order to free my hands, I put my flight-bag between my
legs and take the flower-pot; "My heavens, thank you," I
say; but Vangelis has disappeared and doesn't hear me,
and Telis in his helmet has disappeared, and I'm alone
in the empty bus – no, I'm not in the bus now; I'm in my
own room, holding the flower-pot with both my hands
and my bag is open on the chair; I bow my face over the
five lilies, no longer asking why they are five, since I can
see that they're red, absolutely red, and this is the
answer, and the walls of my room become porphry-red,

and also the table and the raincoat and Artemis and that unsuccessful poem become porphry-red (no, not at all unsuccessful); and one lily touches my cheek and caresses my chin with velvety fingers; but I am alone, I can't endure so much beauty, I want to show the red lilies, to share their delight, to shout: "Look, look all of you." I try to nudge the world with my elbow, even the elbow of the air; "springtime, springtime, springtime," I shout, nudging with my elbow, bam, the flower-pot falls out of my hands, bam, it breaks and I wake up. I'm in my bed in my own room. Springtime, springtime. Saliva flows from my mouth, moistening my pillow. A chunk of plaster has fallen from the ceiling onto my right hand. I rub the plaster with my fingers. Is the soil perhaps from that flower-pot? The sun enters aslant through the window. The wall becomes rosy-hued. And yesterday's withered branch also becomes rosy-hued in the vase on the table. How beautiful everything is. I must get up, wash myself quickly, go out on the street, to shout "springtime, springtime, springtime", because by my faith, I love you all and whatever you say, I'm going to give the five red lilies to you, a hundred lilies, a thousand lilies, myriads and myriads, oh springtime, springtime, springtime.

Karlóvassi, July 22nd, 1983

Broúma, broúma, broúmatzá

I love bears very much and also little bears, who are so playful despite their plumpness. I saw my first bear when I was a child in Monovásia with a skinny gipsy who was banging on a tambourine. Later on, I saw another on the waterfront of Gýthion, next to the park with the jujube-trees – and maybe with the bear, it was the same gipsy, in bare feet, with black curly hair and a rope tied around his waist. I've also seen many bears in books and in Athens, in the neighbourhood of Thymarákia, on certain meagre afternoons, there in Atlas Square, and there was also a neighbourhood soccer team, which had the same name, and all the small fry used to gather round and toss ha'pennies and pennies into the gipsy's tambourine, and the housewives and hundred-year-old old women used to stare from the doorsteps and low windows of their shabby homes – "Ah, what an unfortunate creature," the old women used to say: "The bear's not in good spirits tonight; what a tormented creature, more tormented than the cows in our village." And in the sunset, from high up there, the Parthenon, in a very sad mood, also used to watch, because in those days, all the houses were low and all Athens could be seen spread out like a centre-dish with her little hills, chimneys, swallows (and there were many swallows from May until September) and down here, there were wild mallows and dandelion-greens, so if you went out with a basket and a knife, you could pick quite a lot of greens free-of-charge and prepare your evening meal, along with a fried egg, sunny side up, a real egg, from a genuine hen, which cackled for hours and the whole neighbourhood celebrated, and there were many songs about the "poor people's neighbourhood" and the "poor lad of the neighbourhood" and the "light rain in the neighbourhood", beautiful songs of Spelios Mendis, not to mention the morning and evening chants of the itinerant professions – vendors of milk, yoghurt, umbrellas, quilts, menders of chairs, knife-grinders, fishmongers, women selling vegetable greens, women selling eggs, tinkers, second-hand vendors, greengrocers whose donkeys were laden with golden and rose-coloured fruits and whitewashed chapels and old fairy-tales, and now and then on a moonlit night on the wall of the brick-works, you could see the shadow of Papadiamandis with his beard and his cane, or the shadow from the grocer's hand weighing a few sardines from a barrel in the scale, in Karyotakis' "Préveza", and you could hear the thick salt crunching as they were wrapped in rough paper, because at that time, folklore-morality and twilight melancholy were not at all old-fashioned, and the tram reached only the middle of Acharnón Street and you had to make a whole trek in order to reach your home and take off your shoes – beautiful days; each house had a slanted iron-scraper in front of the door to clean the mud off your footwear before you entered, and inside there was a small mirror, and an oil-lamp, and a food-press dangling with a delicate wire net, where you could put leftover food to give it fresh air and keep flies from settling on it, and often on summer nights, they used to lower these food-presses and jugs with ropes, half-way down into the well to keep them cool (because each house also had its own well); later on, of course, iceboxes came in, and icemen and ice cream-vendors, with their carts full of ice cream cones, vanilla, chocolate, strawberry, pistachio, banana, and all the neighbourhood children with a cone in their hand, some of their cheeks were red, some green, some brown, according to which kind of ice cream they were licking; they all used to gape at the unfortunate bear, and one of them indeed, Kolyas with the curly hair (not Kolyas from the *Brothers Karamazov*) tried to give his ice cream to the bear and the bear flashed her teeth, but he was a fearless little lad, and he didn't budge a step backwards – yes my dear, he, like his namesake, would be capable of lying down between the railway tracks and letting the train pass by over him; but during those Carnivals with the cardboard horses, the men in fustanella-kilts, the daoúli-drums, the clarinettes, the tall strapping fellow with the moustaches, dressed up as a bride, with a very, very long veil dragging in the dirt and gathering dry thorns, the bear really was not in good spirits, the gipsy kept tugging the rings, her lips kept rising, her white teeth showed, not threateningly but sadly, like the keys of a small piano belonging to a girl who'd died in the other neighbourhood, a schoolmate of Loula; and the bear lay down on the ground on her back, revealing her broad slack belly, at which point a brave old lady from Roúmeli shouted at the gipsy, who was flogging the bear with a leather whip: "Leave the animal in peace, you jinx of a man, or I'll crack your head with this rock." And in truth she was holding a big stone, and the children scattered, having changed their minds, and Kolyas tossed his ice cream cone into the dust and trampled it, twisting the sole of his foot on it, and the gipsy with the bear went away all alone, raising a cloud of dust in the twilight; and ever since then, I believe the *Moonlight Sonata* was getting ready, because up above our neighbourhood there was actually a large full moon, which made the pieces of glass sparkle on the coping of the lumber-yard wall, where the red letters "Freedom or Death" had not yet completely faded away.

At certain times, at the hour when evening falls,
I have the feeling that just outside our windows
the man with the bear is passing by with his heavy old-lady bear,
with her hair all thorns and thistles
raising dust on the neighbourhood road
a solitary cloud of dust sending incense up to the twilight
and the children have come back home for supper and aren't allowed to go out any more
although in back of the walls they guess that the old-lady bear is walking along –
and the bear wends her way, weary in the wisdom of her solitude, not knowing about where and why –
she's grown so heavy she can no longer dance on her hind legs
cannot don her little lace cap to entertain the children, or idle people, people hard to please,
and the only thing she wants is to lie down in the dirt
letting them step on her belly, in this way playing her last game,

revealing her tremendous power for resignation,
her disobedience to the interests of others, to the rings on her lips, to the needs of her teeth,
her disobedience to pain and to life
with the certain alliance of death – albeit a slow death –
her final disobedience to death by continuing and knowing life
which moves upwards through knowledge and action surmounting her slavery.
But who is able to play this game up to the very end?
And the bear stands up once again and wends her way
obeying her leash and the rings on her lips and the needs of her teeth,
smiling with her lacerated lips at the ha'penny coins tossed her way by the beautiful credulous children
(beautiful precisely because they are credulous)
and she keeps saying thank you. Because with bears who've grown old
the only thing they've learned to say is: thank you, thank you.

Eh, well, Vanghelis looks like a bear and not an ape. And of course, not like this bear. Because Vanghelis would never want to lie down on the ground and let people trample on his belly, for Vanghelis had learned to play the violin all by himself, at the age of 15, when he was still a little bastard, and then he gave up the violin and learned to play the accordion splendidly (indeed, on my name day, on Aï-Stráti, we called for him and he came to our tent and played the accordion all night long and we sang and danced, and Lefteris along with us, until the police guards rushed in and shouted "shut up" and broke the glass frames on three oil-lamps we'd used to cast a festive light on our tattered tent with its thousand patches, exactly at the hour when Lefteris was dancing *tsámiko*, as lead dancer, and he made certain leaps, by God, which kicked the khaki-coloured tarpaulin way high up, so high, you thought he'd knock down the tent and cover us all up, along with our songs and our coffee-*bríkis*); after this, Vanghelis gave up the accordion as well and now, he says, he's gone all out for the bouzouki, and the other day, he told me: "I'll come with my bouzouki some evening and play for you and sing for you, and you'll see what true-blue *rebétiko* means," – so what connection can Vanghelis have with this bear, except of course for the hairy part, but then again, Vanghelis was curly-haired; then perhaps was I the bear? But I too would never let people trample on my belly; however, I did feel some relationship to her – maybe for this "thank you" of hers; because ever since I was a child, I've enjoyed saying "thank you", always "thank you", even to Azor for wagging his tail at me, even to Asproula for purring on my knees, even to the sparrows for their falsetto-warbling, even to the chickens for cackling, and to the sea for being blue, and to the stars for their tiny lanterns and to Mother for her sweetest silence as she sat over her exquisite embroidery, and to Nina for her new lace dress when she danced the mazurka all alone in front of the drawing-room mirror and in Nereid style her loose silky blond hair blew in the wind, to Loula for her long black Christian braids, to Mimis for that naval cadet's little sword, and later on, to the waiters each time they brought me bread, a glass, a plate, each time one or two "thank you's"; and when Uncle Leonidas returned from Liverpool, a fabulously rich merchant, bred on English manners, a "Sir" with diplomatic contacts high up, he invited me to dinner at a luxurious restaurant, the "Alexandra", and he said to me: "Aren't you ashamed of yourself, Ion? What's all this? We must never say thank you to the waiters or address them when we order our *menu*." And I started sulking and didn't eat anything, and when he left for England again, I no longer wrote to him, though he was the one who'd sent me the first coveted case of oil-paints, with which I painted my first burgundy-coloured and golden chrysanthemums on satin; and ever since then, for my revenge, I used to say "thank you" more often and more correctly, even when I made love, above all then (and I didn't even remember Uncle Leonidas with his English bits of advice), I would say with all my heart – exactly after lovemaking – "thank you", "thank you", and not only now that I was grown up and knew the meaning, but even then when I was a seventeen-year-old boy, I used to say "thank you" to Rubini as soon as we'd finished and one night Rubini asked me: "Why do you say thank you to me? It's *my* pleasure." And then I told her: "Eh, now, I'll say thank you twice." And as we lay there on our backs, Rubini rested her head of copper-coloured, perspiring hair on my chest and said: "I thank you, I thank you very, very much; now I understand how much I thank you." And we made love again; and at some point, I read a verse: *"I asked nothing else in life except to reach a state of thankfulness,"* as though I'd written it myself (maybe it was really mine?); and once, again in a book (this I think was a novel), I read: "Whoever hasn't learned to say thank you has not yet become a human being." Blessings on that voice; furthermore, in her silence the bear had a thankful voice of her own: *"broúma, broúma, broúmatzá"* (as Attila

Jozsef says so correctly in his poem "The Bears' Dance") yes, *broúma, broúma, broúmatzá*, which I say to myself or out loud (omitting my own "thank you"), whenever I happen to find myself with certain persons like Uncle Leonidas (except, of course, for the Leonidas of the Three-Hundred – with him, we exchange plenty of "thank you's" and in a loud voice indeed) and let's not forget that there was also the other bear of Alexis Tolstoy, whose footsteps, *broúma, broúma, broúmatzá* (because her one leg was wooden) could be heard thunderingly in the night of *Graganda*:

and when I climbed the rope-ladder leaning against
    the wall
to change the burnt-out light-bulb up at the highest point
I knew I'm alone
and in the world without divisions
on my soles a calm wind was blowing
before going up I'd removed my shoes
and down below, the two jesters to whom I'd lent my colour-
    ful clothes
and my two cardboard noses tied behind the ears with
    strings
shouted on purpose: "He'll fall, he'll fall; his feet are off the
    ladder, and the ladder's off the ground,"
and they lit matches in front of the lions' teeth
while the big bear with the wooden leg went on walking all
    night long around the tent –

and then, I could have added "*broúma, broúma, broúmatzá*", i.e. the bear's "thank you", but I hadn't learned it yet, and I liked it because it was a fierce "thank you", an almost angry "thank you"; and once in a Zoo in a foreign country, when I saw four little bears playfully giggling, I called out "thank you"; only the one turned round, stared at me and gave me a smile, whereas when I remembered to say it to them in their own language: "*broúma, broúma, broúmatzá*," all four turned round and smiled at me; and I saw many other bears later on, in zoology books, in the movies, on television, but I considered it a grievance that I'd never seen the God-Bear on a full-moon evening climbing up the great mountain, breaking the trees of the perennial forest under the soles of his feet, in order to reach the highest peak and be closer to the moon and stick out his broad damp tongue to lick an edge of the full moon like a honey-cake, and I was sure that if I made love with Goghos' Mireille, we would both say "thank you" simultaneously and afterwards we would laugh a lot and be inexplicably joyful, like the white bear in Petros' dream, for surely Mireille loved bears, this sylvan heavily-treading silent everlastingness fragrant with fir-tree resin, since Mireille swam nude at night, since she spoke such a nude language and had the discus-thrower's ribbon around her forehead, anyway that's why Goghos had given her a tiny little bear in Corfu, the grandchild of Misha of the Olympic Games in Moscow and Mireille always kept it over her heart inside her bra, and we all knew that Misha is the beautiful Russian diminutive of Mihalis (or perhaps the first word of Beethoven's "Missa Solemnis"?) – and what else was the French form of URSS than the French word for Bear: OURS? (Ehrenburg mentioned this to me once when he came to Athens, pronouncing both words with the same French accent, without making any distinction between the "u" and the "ou"; but since I looked at him rather stupidly, he wrote it on my packet of cigarettes, and then, we laughed together in a resounding Russian style, though Ehrenburg's blue eyes remained melancholy, or at least, pensive) – ah, the great, good-hearted, long-haired Soviet Bear with the snow on her snout and in her ears, more beautiful even than Petros' bear; and in those days, Moscow was full of Mishas in all sizes – enormous electric Mishas up above the boulevards, badges, dolls, stamps, matches, balloons, lighters – omnipresent the smiling little Misha; and what about the bear on the east side of the Stadium, huge, enchanting, made entirely of human bodies, and the other equally huge bear flying into the sky above the choreographed flower-shaped formations, amidst thousands of doves, hello there, hello there, *broúma, broúma, broúmatzá, broúma tza, broúma tzá*. So by all means, I should make a phone-call to Vanghelis to say "thank you" to him for that flower-pot with the five red lilies he gave me in my dream yesterday evening. But no. Vanghelis didn't like such things. He'd burst out laughing and make fun of me. However, I went to Kyr-Nikos' eating-house and rang him up. "Hey there, Vanghelis," I said to him, "won't you zoom up here on your donkey, bring your bouzouki as you promised and drop by for a bit of company?" "I'm too bored," Vanghelis answered, slothfully and in a rather hoarse and crafty tone. "All right," said I. "What's all right?" he asked me, changing his tone. "That's not your style." "Eh, then, *broúma, broúma, broúma tzá*," I answered; "that's my style." And I rang off. To give you a lesson, Mr. Vanghelis. Yes indeed. *Broúma, broúma, tzá, tzá, tzá*. Well what do you think, you smart alec, if I may say it in your own language. Got the message? I paid a drachma to Kyr-Nikos, glanced at the young workers from the Machine-shed, having their lunch at the little tables; a bit of sun grazed the stone steps of the basement and this was something which made me want once again to say "thank you" to somebody – but to whom? – and I could feel this "thank you" all dried up under my tongue, in my own congealed spittle, like a hard chick-pea.

Karlóvassi, July 23rd, 24th, 1983

Expectation

You're sitting in your room, leafing through books, reading and re-reading, you put a bookmark to come back again another time, you take notes, write whole big pages, dig up memories, head further than what you're writing, you get perplexed, sometimes you feel you're smiling above your papers all alone, as though you're free and self-sufficient, and your papers glow happily, and you are happy as though you're looking at yourself in your own private mirror and you find you are handsome, more handsome than any time before, worthy of being loved a great deal and still more worthy of loving; however, even at these hours, you are aware of your ear straining *outwards* (above what's *inside* you) listening for a footstep on the sidewalk, a knock on the door, waiting for a re-assurance of yourself, from *outside things,* from *outside people.* And you know: together with your ear, you too are waiting with your entire body – waiting for the milkman, the postman, some former schoolmate or fellow-political prisoner, even someone who's knocked on your door by mistake and you stand at the threshold and tell him very politely: "Missus Merope doesn't live here; is she perhaps a lady with blond hair in a bun? Yes? Then, you'll have to turn the first street to the right, third door, just next to the bakery." The gentleman, who is an attractive thirty-year-old with a small moustache says: "Thank you, sir"; and involuntarily you too say "thank you" and go back to your writing to wait again, to wait for anything at all, but not for any former girlfriend of yours – they bring you bitterness and embarrassment; in their face you can see the passing of your own time; stale desire, like that time when Magda arrived in a freshly pressed dress, with her hair dyed pitch-black and her lips slightly painted (in the old days, she didn't use make-up), and she embraced me and kissed me, all ready for us to make love after twelve years; and she said: "Yesterday I read in the newspaper that you'd come back from political exile, and I wanted to rush here right away, but I controlled myself; all day I fasted so my belly would shrink, and today, I haven't put even a morsel in my mouth." And I didn't know what to say or do; my heavens, how fat she'd grown; those superb breasts of hers bulged out now, squeezed into her bra, two ugly bloated white balls strapped together up at the aperture of her neck; "Let me make you some coffee then," I suggested, "since you're famished." "No," said she, "I'll make it myself, for you too, the way I used to bring it to you at your desk; only show me the way around. Well, well, so you still have that camp-gas? Did you have it in exile? Go in there now; I'll prepare the tray the way you used to like it." And this was Magda, the sweet immaculate little housewife, mistress and sister and my own little mother, when we lived in the Zográphos district, our houses very close by and she knew where I hid the key of my room, and when her two brothers were away at their jobs, they being strict as Cerberus, she used to drop in, take my unwashed underwear and hide it under her mattress. "I want to have something of yours close to me," she said. "At night, in the dark, I take it out and smell it and clasp it to me like your own body." When she found an opportunity, she used to wash the underclothes, press them carefully, take them to my room and when I got back from work or from the Trade Unions, I found them arranged in a very beautiful way; and on other occasions again, I found a small aluminium pot full of artichokes made with tomato and egg-and-lemon sauce (she knew I really loved artichokes cooked in this way) – poor Magda, ten years older than me, my little mother so tender and greedy for lovemaking. But Rubini was another matter. She came too when I returned from Aï-Stráti. She didn't ring the doorbell. She slipped a little card under the door and went away without any noise. And I was writing at my table, with my ear always straining outwards, and I heard the tiny rustling-sound of the paper and I thought the postman must have left a censored postal card from a political prisoner; I got up and it was her little card without an envelope: "I remember you always, I thank you always for those unforgettable inexhaustible double 'thank you's' of ours. *Rubini*." I didn't open the door or rush out to catch up with her. We both knew. Quietly. I didn't see her again. Only once, at the Ayios Nikolaos station, I caught sight of her in a compartment of the Patíssia-Piraeus train, in profile near the window-pane – unbelievable – she was the same, absolutely the same as so many years ago – it couldn't be – her perfect profile, her copper-coloured hair (the lights had turned on in the station and inside the train), her blue eyes – and I said, impossible, it can't be she, so young still, a young girl like then, slightly more serious; she didn't look out towards the station, she was staring straight in front of her, maybe at a toothpaste ad or at the "No Smoking" sign, for often we concentrate on something without seeing it, because we're dreaming; but on her shoulder she'd pinned a little bunch of violets, and by now, surely, it was she (I really loved these flowers, which were my mother's favourites, and it was my meagre gift I always gave Rubini, and she loved them too, and every time violets were in season, the small bunch was never missing from her shoulder); I thought of calling her, of tapping on her window-pane; no; no; I went into another compartment and got off in Omónia; Rubini did not come out; maybe she'd be going on to Monastiráki, more likely to Theseíon, my beautiful beloved girl, the profoundest "thank you" of my youth. When you wait like this, something always comes, at home, in a station, on the road, along the Corfu seashore (like Mireille to Goghos – "Me seet wiz you?"), or on the shore of Poros, in Neórion full of pine-trees, or in Karlóvassi with the August sunset, or even in your sleep, in your dream, because all human beings expect, and all expectations are erotic and one expectation attracts the other; and one evening, in front of my mirror, when I was trying on a lovely white shirt with delicate brown stripes (five or six comrades had chipped in and made me a gift of it on my birthday), somebody was breathlessly knocking on my door, instead of ringing the bell; in a hurry I opened up and a girl burst in: "Save me, Mister," she cried, "save me; there are three men after me." She took off her terribly dusty frayed little shoes and left them in the entrance; I was trying to stuff my new shirt into my trousers without undoing my belt; a beautiful dark-complexioned girl with lots of youthful pimples on her cheeks, curly black hair, a small very insolent nose and a saucy mouth, honey-sweet. "We were at the taverna," she said, "two streets up the way; we ate; I had nothing to drink, I said I had a stomach-ache; and afterwards, all three of them wanted me; they said we should go to the apartment of one of them; but I didn't like any of them; I don't deny it: I do it, but I have to like it; if I don't like it, there's nothing doing; at the age of twelve, I was raped by my father's younger brother; I enjoyed it; in two years, I ran away from home; so I told them: 'Just a moment, I have to go to the loo'; and I escaped through the back door; they caught on and started chasing me; I turned the corner and knocked on your door." (Here, the second person singular started.) "If they knock, don't open up, they'll kill me; if you want, I'll stay with you all night; we can sleep together, real nice, you'll see." As she talked, she wiggled her toes through her cheap stockings; I liked her too with her bold childish little face, especially if I could use my fingers to break that little pimple next to her nose; but I won't say "thank you" to her. "No, no –," I told her; "I'm married; any moment now, my wife will be back." (That's all we needed now, to start such things). "O.k," she said; "no problem; that's a cute shirt you've got on; how much did it cost? – but let me stay a little more till they lose track of me; if your wife comes, I'll explain to her; you've got lots of books; I cut you off from your reading; are you a student? – I'll go put on my shoes; I don't want your wife to find me barefoot and get the wrong idea." She went out to the entrance; I followed her; she put on her shoes, holding her finger back on her heel; as she bent down like this, her plump taut buttocks stood out clearly. "Turn out the hall light," she said. I turned out the light. She opened the door halfway.

Searched the half-dark space. Silence. No running steps could be heard. Nothing. "Bye-bye," she said, "and thanks." And she disappeared, at a run. I remained at the door, gazing at the evening, which hid from me this crazy young girl with the pimples. The stars came out. One, two, five, seven, as when I was a child in Monovásia. I hadn't asked her name. She must be called Anna. Little Annoula. Yes. What a little minx. And I closed the door with a strange, inexplicable sadness. I took off the shirt. Picked up the pins I'd left on the table. Put them in a round iron box together with some buttons, safety-pins, an old tie-pin and other things. Something comes over me like sad high spirits. I shake the iron box close to my ear. A joyful, memory-laden, childish noise, as though there are glass marbles inside. And I look in the mirror, dressed like this in my undershirt and holding the box in my hand. I stare persistently into the mirror *so it can tell me*. And suddenly, there's the noise of a motorcycle outside the house. It stops just under my window. It must be *they*, I say to myself. Catching my breath. Soon, they ring the bell. What can I do? I'm absent. But there's light in the house. They know I'm in here. Again, they ring the bell. I switch on the hall light and open up. Vanghelis. In his left arm, hugging a flower-pot. A flower-pot with *five red lilies*. In his right arm, strung around his forearm, a white linen sack. On his back, the bouzouki. "Hey there Ion, what are you gaping at? Aren't you going to let me in? Are you still pissed off about that phone-call?" "Did you know?" I stammered. "What?" he asked. (I was ready to tell him about the dream with the lilies. But restrained myself. Perhaps because I was annoyed by the phrase "pissed off".) "Did you know," I said, "that I like lilies?" "And who doesn't like red lilies? They're like wide-open cunts." And he laughed broadly through his big mouth under his thick moustache. I took the flower-pot. Not knowing where to set it down. I avoided bringing my cheek close to the lilies. And left it on the window-sill. "See here what I've brought you," he opened the linen sack. "Fresh eggs from my aunt's chicken-coop, straight from the chicken's ass today, not from the fridge. And whole-wheat bread and wine from the barrel, so good you'll lick your chops, and tomatoes sweet as sugar, from a garden with real manure, and oil, which is really olive-oil, with zero acidity. We won't go to the taverna. We can eat here, family style. I'll get it all ready for you, like in the old days on Aï-Stráti. We'll drink our bit of wine and then we'll have a bouzouki spree, you'll see, you'll dance *zeibékiko* for me, not the *tsámiko* and *pendozáli* you used to dance on the island." He unfastened his bouzouki from his back and laid it out on my bed. Then he went to the kitchen. I went along too. "Come on now, you stay in there," he ordered me; "go brood over your papers. I told you, I'll fix everything myself and call you. But hold on a second. What were those 'all rights' of yours and that – how did you call them? – '*toúmba-tzá*', the other day on the phone? Hey now Ion, were you pissed off because I told you 'I'm too bored'? Hey pal, don't you know me? As a matter of fact, I was bored." Now I went into the other room, really "pissed off" this time, and I could hear his laughter from the kitchen, along with the sizzling sputter of the frying pan. I picked up the shirt I'd left folded up on the chair. I arranged the books on the table. Glanced at the bouzouki laid out on my bed. There was a sour taste in my mouth. I picked up the bouzouki and stood it upright on the couch. Not knowing what else to do. I fidgeted around the room till Vanghelis called me. "Come on, Mr. Ion. It's all ready." The table was laid. The food was served – scrambled eggs with tomato sauce. Whole-wheat bread cut in slices. "Nice, eh?" said Vanghelis. "Good for you; it's all just fine," I said with fake enthusiasm to conceal my lack of appetite; and bite by bite, I forced myself to shove it into my mouth. Vanghelis was gulping down huge mouthfuls, slurping with his tongue (till now I hadn't noticed how savagely and greedily he munched). This way of munching emphasized our *difference* and intervened like a wall between him and me, so I wondered: Is it true that we're sitting at the same table, eating the same food, drinking the same wine? When we'd finished eating, he said to me: "You go in, I'll clear the things, wash the dishes and odds-and-ends – I'll fix everything shipshape, niftier than it was before." I was about to go off, mumbling: "Yes indeed, nifty, nifty." But he stopped me. "Listen, as soon as I finish, you'll hear a *zeibékiko* that'll make you blow your stack." As I waited in the inner room, the time seemed endless to me. How good our solitude is and we don't even realise it. He was delaying. What the devil was he doing all this while? Let him just come, so we can get it over with. And he did come. Standing there, he picked up his bouzouki. Plucked it. Whirled round, bent his knee, called out: "oh boy", stopped short, glanced at the table; with his left hand he grabbed one of the many letters piled there. "From your dear old fiancée?" he asked. "Yes," I told him. "So you're still carrying on with Tania. I recall back then, on the island – aren't you bored stiff? always the same dish of food? and what about the wedding-jazz? I just screw them a few times and then beat it. I get cheesed off. Can't get a kick from the same old cunt. You should try to have a ball." (For quite a while now, Tania and I had been separated, on friendly terms. But I didn't tell him this.) He sat down on the couch, leaving the bouzouki next to him, stuck his hand into his pocket and pulled out several envelopes. "Here's how my girlfriends write to me." He took a letter out of an envelope. A paper napkin, with a lot of thick red lipstick-marks. He took out a second letter: the same. He took out a third: the same. Marks from different lipsticks – cherry-red, vermilion, orange, pearly-pink – and from different lips – wide lips, narrow lips, baggy lips, tightly sealed lips – kisses to Vanghelis. "No need for name or address," he said "they're easy to recognize." He burst into coarse laughter with his mouth wide open; his leonine tongue looked red in the middle of his spittle. "Ah, you lousy slut, Life, if only a man could fuck you all over, in front, in back, through the mouth and the ears and the nostrils"; and he grabbed his bouzouki and started off on Vamvakaris' "Franghosyrianí", "Your Eyelashes Shine Bright"; he sang and played one song after the other, without any interruption, beating the rhythm with his foot on the floor (he no longer wore those sandals from political exile) – ah, Vanghelis, where was that natural, devil-may-care gallantry he'd had in the old days? – he'd turned into something like a professional tough-guy, dressed to kill (do you suppose by selling himself as a lover-boy?). And as I stood there, I started backing up very slowly, till I sat down on the very edge of my bed; I looked at him and could not see him, he was far away, so very far away, *elsewhere*; even if I had nautical spyglasses, I still couldn't see him; how upsetting, he was a stranger: *"Your eyelashes are as bright as the flowers of the plain"*, and he finished up.

"Eh?" he was only asking. I forced myself to show enthusiasm. "Fine, fine, just splendid," I said, hearing how dead my voice sounded. "Splendid," I repeated in a louder tone. He realised I didn't like it. "O.k.," he said. "Let's get going. I guess I've made your head spin. Come on, bouzouki darling, it's night now, let's beat it." He loaded the bouzouki onto his back and picked up his linen sack; I accompanied him out and stood there at the door; he got onto his Vespa, still handsome but a stranger; he started the engine, then for a second, limply waved his left hand at me, by way of farewell (maybe the last?); I also waved my hand towards him, sadly; I wanted to call out to him: "Thank you for everything, for the flower-pot, for the eggs, for the songs, for the *sandals*." But I wasn't able to; I could only say "good-bye" (this time in my true voice); I watched him going off along the dirt road raising the dust in the little bit of moonlight; a voice inside me said: "Vanghelis is no longer one of us." I was still standing there in my doorway, rigid as marble, till he disappeared at the turn of the road. I closed the door noiselessly in order not to hear it closing. I went into the other room feeling sad with myself, for not being in the mood tonight to say my well-loved "thank you" to anything, or to nudge another elbow with my own elbow. I took the flower-pot from the window-sill and carried it to the kitchen; the kitchen was desperately tidy; I went back to the other room, not knowing what to do; I got undressed and put on my comrades' shirt; "good night," I said vaguely (not "thank you"), "good night"; I turned out the light and lay down in my new shirt, white with the slender brown stripes. However, I fell asleep.

Karlóvassi, July 25th 26th 27th 1983

Sounds and memories from smells

Here it is again, the affable morning (I bid you welcome) – erasing with a tawny, dew-moistened sponge, it erases from the blackboard of the night strange anxious exercises of some nightmarish algebra or trigonometry, pentagrams or heptagrams, with empty containers from rancid yoghurt left down on the cement; morning turns the blackboard upside down on its trestle, and on its backside, the blackboard is smoothly planed, white wood and glows like a window opposite another window of a room looking out on a little garden (someone expressed it well, that art is a matter of inversion) and from the little garden comes a smell of mint and neighbourly coffee (and at the same time, this smell can be heard); and of course, at this hour, Petros must be buttoning his clean shirt in front of the glass-pane of his small bookshelf, and Telis must be cleaning the glass partition of his motorcyclist's helmet; because you don't only catch the scent of smells, but you also hear them (and the People express this beautifully: "Can you hear that smell of the acacias?" "Do you hear the smell of the pine-forest?" or "Can you hear a smell of fried liver from Baroufas' taverna?" or "I hear a smell of gunpowder – something's brewing"); and now I become aware, though I always

knew, that there are visual scents and acoustic scents, in
other words for images and for sounds, or also simultaneous, audio-visual scents – as e.g., the other day, when
Polyxeni placed one leg on top of her other leg and her
knee rustled almost imperceptibly and along with this
rustling sound, the smell of her stocking could be heard
and of what was inside her dress, and the smell was a
long way, because Polyxeni's legs were long and beautiful, though she never wore high heels; and perhaps,
indeed, there are also smells connected with touch and
taste (this I haven't yet investigated – I'll think about
it), but when we eat a peach, don't we say: "What an
aroma it has" and not "What a flavour it has"? – and
when we were high school lads in Gýthion and used to
take twilight strolls in springtime along the quay,
outside the Garden with the jujube-trees whose fragrance mingled with the brine of the sea and the other
smells of seaweed, crawfish, crabs, sea-urchins, lobsters
and also the laughter of the girls, all this filled our lungs
with unbearable bliss and fear, and then, didn't we used
to say: "This smell seizes me by the throat"? And again,
one evening when we were sitting in my little garden,
Alekos told me, as though ashamed of it: "I believe the
smell of jasmine feels my pulse with three slim white fingers, here on my left wrist under my watch, and when I
wind my watch before I go to sleep and bring it up to my
ear to see if it's working, I don't know if the tick-tock
sound is from the jasmine, from my pulse, or from my
wristwatch." "You must write this," I told him. And
Alekos answered: "I feel embarrassed," just as Yotis had
told Leila back then. And now, I recalled a story Yotis
told me connected with smells. "One day," he said,
"when Leila had her day off from the brothel, we took

an excursion off to old-time Patíssia, one hot noon in springtime; the patches of grass were thick with camomile buds, daisies, and most of all, poppies; we spread a small cover over the poppies and sat down to nibble some improvised snacks we'd brought along; (I could just see the poppies of Patíssia pulsating with aggressive blood); well, when we sat down on the ground, the poppies were crushed and an acrid smell struck our nostrils, and Leila said: 'This smell rubs my hips and I'm starting to feel horny.' (Yotis spoke this last word, blushing like a poppy himself, and added hesitantly: "She was quite right; I got into the same fix too"). Then Leila cut two or three poppies, rubbed them with her fingers and stuck them in my nose so I could smell them. She laughed and laughed, rubbing the poppies on my cheeks; laughing still more, she took her little mirror out of her purse and handed it to me so I could see myself. There were two funny splotches, like bruises, on my cheeks. And now we both laughed and she shouted: 'You're my sweet little clown in the Poppy Circus and your birdy (she didn't call it like in the old days) has a big poppy on its tip.' And we kept laughing, and on her fingers, there were also bruise-coloured marks, and when we lifted the cover before leaving, around twilight, it too was full of violet-coloured splotches." And when you reflect and remember, you discover there are thousands and thousands of smells, some melancholy (such as violets, osiers, odourless pansies), others cheerful (such as poppies, medlar-trees, brambles), and there are also other scents from things which have no smell (such as the scent of sleepiness, of premonition, of daydreaming), scents of human beings (not from their body, but from what is inside them).

E.g., Petros smells of a ship in the middle of the ocean. Telis smells of sperm, in spite of his cleanliness. Alekos smells of untrodden grass down below the hill of Ayia Marína. Goghos smells of salt from Mireille's hair and sometimes, on his neck, under his right ear, you can actually see the grains of salt sparkling. Yotis smells of the outstretched branch of a plane-tree in a sunset near the sea. What does Vanghelis smell like? Lots of things. I don't know. Martha smells of carefully printed leaflets. Anna smells of Petros' armpit. Polyxeni smells of silk material with a broad cotton bag. Tania smells of household birds, particularly swallows at twilight. And don't birds have their own characteristic smell, each one of them – the eagle, the hawk, the thrush, the sparrow, the blackbird, the partridge, the turtledove, the jackdaw. But what about that warbling of the lark at dawn, high up at the zenith, whirling the dim-blue particles of the air – what a fragrance. And what about the nightingales? Bridal rosewater and white sugared almonds on a silver tray. But also a sob from shadows on a crumbling wall. And what about insects? Mosquitoes, grasshoppers, the praying-mantis, dragon-flies, butterflies? As I glanced through the window a moment, I saw a white butterfly passing by near the small olive-grove, below the church. I caught the scent of something. But didn't have time to understand what. And I continued staring at the same point. And the butterfly returned for a fleeting second, to let me ascertain. It smelled of a white rose shedding its petals after a lovely woman has passed by, without even touching it with her shoulder. And the cicadas with their noontime and afternoon loud voices also have their own smell. Yes, the smell of elongated leaves of eucalyptus seared by the great blaze-of-the-sun, even if the river flows by below. Everybody and everything have a smell. And their smells – breaths, images, musical phrases, memories – jostle inside me, whirling around, whirling me around, sometimes uplifting me, other times anesthetizing me (as in the hospital, back at the time of my operation, with the general anesthesia, when I didn't know where I was, what I was, and the window was a large square empty eye, but calm and utterly unresentful); scents which are garrulous or silent, dancing or motionless, statuesque, and furthermore, they all ask me *to be heard*. And it isn't only the flowers, the fruits, the earth, the sea, the human beings, the animals (lions, tigers, elephants – small blood-stained eyes so hard to read enclose a sleepy eternity – wolves in the snowstorm before Grevená, crafty foxes who are poultry-thieves, lambs, goats, cows, billy-goats with their Bacchic beard, beetles, weasels, hares standing up on their hind-legs and tensing their ears like little devils in disguise, dazed by the headlights of the car, there, bolt upright in the middle of the dirt road in the midst of the pine-forest, or the white rabbits in the basement of Papanastassíou Street burrowing under the built-in laundry-boiler and coming out black as the coal miners of Ostrava, or the frogs in the murky waters of the Karlóvassi tanneries and behind their calls, soldiers were concealed with rifles throughout the years of the dictatorship, and the muzzles gleamed in the moonlight and betrayed them, although the frogs appeared not to participate and continued croaking in exclusively erotic tones, as in the great lake of Bucharest, Herestrau). How many, many things, each with its own smell and image and confused origin. And now I recalled that long-ago excursion of the Worker's Cultural Society to

Megálo Péfko and Comrade Katina recited the threnody from the *Erophile* really beautifully; but the cicadas were clamouring so madly that the heat kept growing and many words were lost, without the rhythm of the fifteen-syllable verse's being lost, and Martha leaned towards my ear and whispered: "Don't you think that cicadas are the consciousness and expression of Greek summer?"; and abruptly, for no reason, I answered her: "No," perhaps because I found the cicadas' intrusion into Erophile's lament unfitting and I'd have preferred this heavy solar silence or the nocturnal crickets; and I believe that thenceforth, unawares, the lament of my own *Epitáphios* was my inner response to the lament of Erophile, because you never know how many things. images, memories, fragrances, compose a verse, a poem, along with a bit of thyme, a bit of crushed origan, some pine-needles, a mother's sweat-stained black scarf, and words, words from myriads of sighs, blood-shed, fir-tree roots, mutilated statues, flags, large thorns from tares. Because books also have their own smell, not merely the smell of paper and antimonium, their own personal smell. Here now, the other day I was reading a book and when I closed it, I was left with the smell of an uncorked phial of ether on a marble bedside-table in a hospital. Years ago, another book left me with the aroma of an ethereal woman wearing an ethereal dress, as she passed by the wall leaving an orifice like a glass closet, inside which you could discern two hunters' sacks hanging – the one with a partridge, which had been killed, and the other sack with a golden-red bee-eater, which Botis had killed at Tálanda, with a double-barreled shotgun up in the beech-trees above the river. But the stars also have their own particular scents – Orion, Lyra, Sirius, Arcturus, the Hyades, Berenice, Altair, the Bear, both Big and Little, especially the Little Bear smelled of black raisins spread out on the terrace in Veliés, where all night long the drinking fountain could be heard flowing, a large fount where every evening they offered water to the horses, mules, livestock of the peasants; and the peasant-women filled their jugs or little barrels loaded on their back. What beautiful smells of fortitude, limpidity, seclusion, bewilderment, infinitude, when the shadow of a human being on a seaside road stops every four steps, as though he's invalidating a decision of his own, or when a sinful woman rivets her gaze on that part of the dark mountain whence she expects the delayed verdict of the moon. And very often, things become mixed up in your haste to catch up with them, phonemes, waters, leafey-branches, meteorites, goblets, vapours, baskets, apples – saw-mill, pork-meat shop, greengrocer's shop, fishmonger's shop, bakery, musktree, shipyard, rosemary, mint, a well, a slug, noise of sunshine, rain on window-panes, on tin, on bricks, there's a smell of a rain-soaked horse in front of the Cart-Drivers' Inn between Levétsova and Sparta, there's a smell of a wet pigeon in the hands of the twelve-year-old orphan on his way from Monovásia towards the high school of Gýthion, in an open cart full of rainwater and mud; ah, what a smell from a dog sound asleep in the corridor of an uninhabited hotel; and an open suitcase on the floor after a sea voyage, and there were many lemons floating in the harbour at night, as well as citrons, acetylene-lights, and another suitcase from a voyage by train or lorry or bus or horse-and-buggy or barge; rust-stained latches of Venetian fortresses; life-size trees chopped down and floating on the river along

with dry peels of moonlight; big sunflowers in old Uncle
Thanassis' little garden and they're like working-class
alarm-clocks which have stopped during the summer
holidays; manure, a rubber hose for the late afternoon
watering of the rose-arbour; Ourania's three little pairs
of shoes under the bed: white, aquamarine, and yellow,
at the hour when the moon – like a baby turtle was
strolling along the terrace of the apartment building
among the half-withered flower-pots; the forest-ranger's
boots in the doorway of the wooden shack; the straw
mat of the grape-picker shining in the sun; the straw
mat of little Anthoula with the pink ribbons blowing in
the breeze of Hatzálaga; a bell ringing in a house abandoned as far up as the staircase; the clothes of sick people; the cloth pads from the first period of a dark-haired
peasant-girl, who washes them in an earthenware basin
atop a whitewashed ledge in the courtyard; the kitchen
of Aunt Photini, spick-and-span, with the polished little
coffee-pots hanging in a row on the wall and the loom in
the corner, which has flowers intermingled with birds
and fish and the snow-white wash basin in front of the
window; old clocks with musical alarm clocks (like the
one we found in the old trunk among Carnival costumes
and small gauze sachets of dried lavender); the big black
pendulum of Ismene which had stopped centuries ago;
refugees' bundles; prisoners' bundles, and an old man
who'd been released from prison was sitting on his
bundle on the sidewalk, as though he had amnesia and
didn't know where to go, and Vanghelis was nervous,
with his hands in his pockets; and sad stags and keys
from houses which had collapsed, and rust-stained large
keys which have nothing to open or close (and then,
there's a stronger smell of rust and more abstract); blan-

kets, rafters, mirrors, glasses, chinaware, crystal (again a smell of transparency), beds, copper utensils, bronze, iron-smithy, bellows, weaving-mill, brick-yard, pottery workshop, cement-mixer, tools, jack-knife, sickle, hammer, pliers, saw, screwdriver, side-board, chairs, shutters, cistern with rotten leaves, bookshelf, money-safe, chandlers, wax, iron spoon, and the other wooden spoon, wire, string, a dusty hatbox on top of the closet with the x-rays of the three consumptive persons (two of them died, the one is still alive), ancient coins, bus tickets, cigarette-packets with nocturnal notes or sketches drawn from memory, small spiders in the ear of the terra cotta statue, lace or velvet curtains, wilted chrysanthemums on the bathhouse tiles, wet towels, a piano which has been shut for years, the hollow of a violin or guitar (where I used to hide my childhood drawings to keep my Cousin Babis from finding them and ripping them up – there on Psaromilíngou Street and the street-organ used to play on the road: *"I'm here to sell you herbs / and other magic cures / and for the nice young girls / I know secret potions"*); lamp-posts, kerosene-lamps, Cavafis' lamp going out at daybreak (a perspicacious smell), an oil-lamp, a deserter's torch, a lampion in the evening iconostasis emitting sparks and trembling, as though the grandmother in the black dress was about to die (and she truly did die); medallions, bracelets, rings in blue velvet jewellery-cases (which were sent back when Nina broke off her engagement, because Yanghos was slightly bald); crates of beer, hay for the horses, bran for the hens, church-bells, whistle of a train or a boat, fish-soup, lettuce salad, oil-and-vinegar, oil-and-lemon, a night-time bar, a sailor's taverna for dancing, tables wet with retsina-wine and *zeibékiko* dances, eau de Cologne from a neighbourhood barbershop, on the floor hair which has just been cut, brushes full of lather and another mirror; a football player's undershirt; underpants full of wet-dream sperm; an empty winter theatre after the performance of the *Persians*; the tragic red curtain and the feet of the electrician, who is turning out the lights in the entrance; Nausicaa's harp in the junk-room; sheets which have been ironed; a swallow's nest; the dead woman's gloves and umbrella; tent, stanchion-pole, Bible, Communion chalice, the hand of the vicar full of incense on All Soul's Day in the provinces, and the great invisible hand of Him-Who-Holds-the-Keys; the hat and twopence of the blind man; and above all, the ambivalent smell of eternity transgressed. My head is humming, congestion, miracle upon miracle, whirlwind, the infinite, the inexhaustible, I am enchanted, in a dizzy spell to write an *Iliad* concerning smells, images, sounds, trains-of-thought and their adventures. Oh my God, I've quite forgotten myself. I glance at my wristwatch – 6:00 p.m. And we'd agreed I'll go by Petros' and we'll take the evening bus to Marathon together. We're going to spend the night there. And at daybreak we'll set out on the Peace March with all the throng. Luckily, I have time. On my way to Petros', continuously inside my head, I could hear splashes from smells, landscapes, sounds, small marvellous familiar details constantly multiplying and proselytising the infinite for us, offering specific fragments of the indefinite, the unknown, the inexplicable, in forms of perpetual magic. Almost intoxicated, I staggered and kept saying: "Yes, I'll write my Iliad, and I'll tell Alekos about it (not Petros) for relief." But when I reached Petros' and he opened the door, limping because he was wearing only his right shoe, and then he sat on the edge of his bed to put on his other shoe, and maybe because his broad shoulder-blades had stooped so far to put on his left shoe and the sock on that foot was so clean, and maybe because his room smelled of a freshly-swabbed deck on a ship, I felt in the mood to tell him about my *Iliad of Smells*. At first he listened to me smilingly, then condescendingly and later on, with silent disapproval. "All this is fine and lovely," he said, "but can't you smell the blood being shed throughout the world? And instead of writing an Iliad of Smells, though of course it's beautiful, shouldn't you better write another poem about peace? As you know, I'm not on very good terms with verses, but I know almost all of that poem of yours by heart:

> *when the dead can rest on their sides and sleep without sorrow*
> *knowing they have not shed their blood in vain,*
> *that's peace.*

Or that other part:

> *when the prisons are repaired and changed into libraries,*
> *when a day just past is not a day lost,*
> *when death doesn't take up much room in our hearts,*
> *when poet and proletarian man alike can catch the scent of the vast carnation of eventide,*
> *that's peace.*"

Petros spoke these verses in such a simple, beautiful, modest and clear-cut way, and his face had such a sweet pensive severity that I enjoyed them too. "You're quite right," I told him and asked him for paper and pencil. And began writing. Noiselessly, as inside a church,

Petros went to the kitchen, made coffee, for me too, set the cup and a glass of water on the table next to me, lit a cigarette and after lighting it, put it in my mouth (without a drop of saliva on it); then he lit himself a cigarette, sat off to one side, on the very edge of his bed and drank his coffee without breathing a word. I felt his gaze enveloping me with that deep comradely trust, and my eyes blurred with tears and my entire body was encompassed by that just and well-loved "thank you" of mine. And so, in less than half an hour, I wrote the poem "Peace March" about the *"multitudinous solitude of the martyrs"*. I read it to him, involuntarily copying his voice. He stood up, gave me a hardy hug, kissed me, and by my faith, for the first time, I saw tears in Petros' eyes. The next morning, at the peace ceremony, I recited the poem at the Marathon Týmbos, and the comrades, young and old alike, wept and clapped their hands. And a big sun had come out, and in its bright light, I could see Lambrakis assassinated last year, with his arms wide open in the shape of a cross, holding the banner "GREECE" stretched across his broad chest and he entered now at the head of the March. And we set out, calling PEACE, PEACE, PEACE. And somebody laid his hand on my back. I turned round. Vanghelis. Yes, Vanghelis (just as he is), still one of us. We caught hold of one another's shoulders. And walked on, all together, singing:

> *In the midst of peace,*
> *the whole wide world*
> *with all its dreams*
> *can breathe in a wide-open way.*
> *PEACE, PEACE, PEACE.*

Karlóvassi, July 28th, 29th, 30th, 31st, 1983

Goghos, Mireille and I

That summer we lost Goghos again. I thought he must have gone to Corfu – he must have a rendez-vous with Mireille. He left without saying anything to us, without a single word of farewell. And then one evening, early in September, there was a knock on my door. And it was Goghos, more handsome and more serious, and he seemed thoughtful now. We hugged. "You skirt-chasing rascal," I teased him, "you've sneaked off again for Corfu on the sly." He smiled sadly. "Not to Corfu," he said. "To Paris. Yes, for Mireille." Goghos. Yes. Something's changed. Maybe his Parisian style of dressing. Maybe he's let his blond moustache grow. Anyway, I knew that this time, his pockets weren't full of photographs and letters from Mireille. There was something empty rising from his pockets to his lips. I pretended not to understand. I bombarded him with the news of our clan, just to pass the time any old way, till the moment he'd decide to tell his own news. Because I could see he wasn't listening; he wanted to talk and to talk in a sincere, simple way, as though about a stranger's story and this is exactly what was so difficult for him. And suddenly, just as I was telling him about Kyparissis ... "Listen, Ion," he told me, "I'm not interested in all this.

I went and found her. She invited me. She couldn't come to Greece, she said. 'When we meet, I'll explain to you,' she wrote. And her letters were few and far between. Once, a whole month went by without a word from her. I sent her a telegramme. The answer: 'Don't worry; I'm well; I love you; I'll explain to you.' Explain what to me? Does she love someone else? Does she want us to separate? All right – her job, her studies – I know about them. So? I hadn't seen her for thirteen months. She was waiting for me at Orly Airport. By her side, a child's carriage. She leapt up. Embraced me. And holding her arms around my neck she turned her head and with her eyes, pointed out a little pram. I took a look. An infant. A child three or four months old, beautiful, plump, blue-eyed. Curly blond hair. 'Our child,' she said. My knees were trembling. I wanted to kneel down and weep. Nothing else. Nothing else. But I only said: 'That's the reason; yes, that's it.'" Here, Goghos stopped. His eyes were misted. And mine too. My God, how foolish we are. How beautiful we are. Is it possible not to love the world? From this point onwards, whatever Goghos says, I'm with him too. The child is the spitting image of Goghos. There, in Corfu, eating cheese-pies in bed, or swimming. We must find a taxi. Mireille lifts the child in her arms. It doesn't cry. Just stares in a pure blue way. Everything is blue, even Mireille's chestnut-brown eyes. Goghos' hair is golden. I'm not at all jealous. The child is also mine. It belongs to the three of us. We put the pram in the boot. The two of them, with the child, are sitting in back. I'm next to the driver. It's hot. August. And strangely enough, whereas usually the car's speed makes the breeze blow from the front towards the back, I can feel it blowing from the back towards the front, from where they're both sitting with the child. Indeed, the breeze messes up my hair, tossing my forelocks into my eyes and I'm obliged to push them away with both hands, as though I have a headache and am clutching my temples. This amuses me. I prefer that they think I have a headache, rather than that I'm absurdly moved by the breeze blowing from their direction. We arrive. An old, three-storey house, near the Luxembourg Gardens. We leave the pram at the concièrge's desk. There's no lift. We climb the wooden staircase, which creaks with a meaning of its own, though I at least, also feel it as my own from our old family home. Mireille is holding the child and goes upstairs very easily. Goghos has two suitcases. I have nothing. I'm free. I don't look at Mireille's legs, she's out in front. An attic. A large, low-ceilinged room. A tiny bathroom. The kitchen separated by a green screen. A bed, a cradle, a table, a bookshelf, three framed pictures. The windows look out on grass-covered rooftops and water-spouts. Not a sound can be heard. Not even noise from the street. Maybe the attic is high up. The child must have gone to sleep in its cradle. In the tiny kitchen, behind the green screen, Mireille is preparing something for the evening-meal. Goghos is staring at the baby. He twists his fingers, embarrassed and impatient, profoundly sad with an unknown happiness. If only the food were missing. Now I'm missing, maybe out of tact or the eavesdropper's secret curiosity, since I'm no longer in love and my relationship with Mireille-the mother has changed and become almost paternal. Through my absence, I can hear their forks tapping the plates and their comments, sometimes full of interruptions, sometimes breathless, friendly or antagonistic, (not erotic), with signs of a conciliatory encounter or a controlled dissension. Goghos seems to feel that everything he'd been prepared for has not come true. He wants them to get married. So the child can have his name. He wants them to live in Greece. "No," Mireille answers. "I can't. Whatever I could give you, I've already given you. Whatever I could take from you, I've already taken. I don't want to take or give anything less than that great thing we lived once and for all. And this can never be repeated. And only by saying the word *less*, my mouth becomes bitter. In Corfu, each time we made love, I didn't want to pee afterwards, so as not to lose a drop of your sperm. Even two or three hours afterwards, when I went to the bathroom, I didn't sit down on the toilet-bowl. I peed almost standing up, so I could see my urine hazy with your sperm, and I got excited and said: 'My pearls are gone.' And I'd come back to bed and I wanted to make love again, make love again, make love again. And you, my dear, were always ready." (At this moment as well, Goghos was "ready" and underneath the table he held his penis and with his fingers lifted it inside his trousers up to his belt, because it hurt him from the tense excitement, and this was the first time Mireille didn't want to see him.) "Do you remember once when I asked you to masturbate alone? I watched the broad palm of your hand moving up and down and I trembled through all my body and melted with the deepest primitive fire and I could feel the perpetual element of the sea stirring around a tall-pole where boats are moored. And when your fountain spouted on your belly and your chest, all the way up to your jawbone, do you remember, I called out to you: 'The fountain of creation' and began licking you from your jaw all the way down. And during the first month in Corfu, when my period stopped, I was overcome by an unprecedented emotion and I wanted you still more, thousands of times more. But I was afraid it might be just a delay. However, the second month in France, when I didn't have my period, I was sure. I don't know if any other human being has ever lived such happiness. And I loved you and I wrote to you, and kept writing to you, and I wanted you and hour by hour, I was becoming *cosmos*. I didn't write you a word about my pregnancy, so you wouldn't think me *biassed*. I don't know why. Yes, *biassed*. I felt your sperm swelling inside me, becoming flesh, and it was as though I had you inside me with all your body, just as I used to dream when we made love and I told you about this in Corfu. In the sixth and seventh months, I was crazy with joy and pride, a strange pride all my own, rather cut off from you. I won't hide this from you. I was proud of my belly. If you'd seen me then, you wouldn't have liked me at all. And for the first time, I felt this wouldn't bother me. At night, I put both my hands on my belly and listened to it stirring inside me, smiling to me inside me, my own, my own, and I said: 'My God, my God, I'm not only a creature, I'm also a creator, I too am God and *mother*.' And thousands and thousands of times, I kept saying 'thank you,' 'thank you,' 'thank you,' like Ion's bear, 'thank you, Goghos,' 'thank you, Corfu,' 'thank you, Mireille,' 'thank you, Ion,' 'thank you, life,' 'thank you, world.' I didn't write to you even then. I was afraid that what was fulfillment for me would be a failing for you." Goghos said nothing. He just listened. He was no longer holding his penis. He no longer had a hard-on. And little Misha, the tiny bear he'd given her in Corfu, was no longer inside Mireille's bra, but on the bedside-table – he'd noticed this at a glance, from the very first moment he came into the room. And Goghos felt alone, somewhere else. Neither in Corfu. Nor in Athens. Still less in Paris. Maybe he was all alone in some large unfamiliar airport, among thousands of extremely busy, hurried foreigners, with curious luggage and squeaky noises of push-carts, and indeed one man was holding a cage with a green parrot and another was holding a big bouquet upside down and the flowers were dragging on the floor, sweeping away cigarette-butts, plastic cups and a big shoe from a huge foot belonging to some primitive race; and Goghos was standing up between his two suitcases and he no longer knew what was inside them and he didn't know where he wanted to go and he didn't want to go anywhere and then he remembered that in one suitcase, at the last moment, he'd put a pair of unwashed briefs, which must have soiled his freshly pressed shirts, and he felt an abominable disgust for his suitcases, for the airport, for this abominable hubbub of foolish airplanes and still more foolish travellers, a profound disgust for the whole world and above all, for his own genitals withdrawn into their own independent, but noisy silence, because the distance between him and that woman who was talking had grown so much and this was clearly evident from the distance existing between her former words (those words in Corfu and those in her letters) and her present words now, because now, she said "sperm" and not "preeck-joos" and she said "inside me" and not "een moi woum", and she said "intercourse" and not "fouckin", "penis" and not "balles" (these words she learned in Corfu and she always wanted the most clear-cut, the most popular, the most unequivocal words – and how she said them in those days, as though inside her mouth, she held the shape of each organ named by each word); and she didn't mention those evenings when she'd been insane, childish, on the rampage, and had made love with his toes and at the same time, also wanted his two big toes inside her and both his feet in their entirety, and fortunately, she didn't say anything about these, because then, the unwashed briefs in Goghos' suitcase would have become still more unwashed, and would have soiled all his clothes, even his electric razor and his shaving-brush and then, how could he make lather for his face with such a brush, better leave a beard, even if it's blond and curly; (and then I remembered that coloured photograph from Corfu, where the hairy part under his belly appeared black – perhaps was it really black there? or was it perhaps, merely a question of lighting?). However, the child was asleep in its cradle. Mireille hadn't cleared the table. The food was left half-finished on the plates. The salad untouched. Only the bottle of wine was empty. And it was a dark green colour like bottles of olive-oil. And the glasses didn't shine at all, as they usually shine both before and after dinner. But maybe the low lighting was to blame, dim so as not to bother the child. Maybe the smoke from Goghos' cigarette was to blame (because from the time of her pregnancy, Mireille had actually given up smoking, and with her left hand she kept pushing the smoke away from her nose, and this movement of her hand increased the distance between her and Goghos, and she got up and opened the window, and remained there a moment inhaling her own night, with her back turned to the room, and by now it *was sure*). But maybe the green screen in the kitchen was more to blame and Goghos' two suitcases, which were still

closed. But more than everything else, that cloud which
fell vertically like a curtain and was also green, must
have been to blame, increasing the distance between
words and *things*. Goghos refused to look in the direction of the cradle. This child who looked so much like
him, his own child (no, not his own) had intervened
definitively and irrevocably between him and the
mother. All in all, Goghos stayed five days. The suitcases
remained always closed. Two or three times they did
make love (Mireille was more or less obeying his desire,
which anyway had also really waned). They got too hot
in the same bed. The third evening, Goghos took a cover
and went to sleep (if he did actually sleep) alone, on the
floor. Only on the fifth day, in the late afternoon, when
he was about to leave, he opened the one suitcase (not
the one with the unwashed briefs) and took out the gifts
he'd brought for her – a blue bathing suit, a flowered
dress, and a picture frame to set on the table, with a
little watercolour of Pontikonísi, Corfu. Mireille held
them to her bosom and her eyes started to flow, without
a single sob. She went and laid his gifts on the table,
opened a drawer and took out two photographs of the
child and a small French book and put them in the left
pocket of his jacket. She slipped both her arms around
his neck and for a moment, rested her damp cheek on
his neck. Maybe Goghos also wanted to weep. Tenderly,
he removed both her arms from his shoulders, bent over
the cradle and for the first time, kissed the child. The
child burst out crying. Mireille rushed to pick it up in
her arms. The child quieted down. Embraced like this,
mother and infant, they took him out as far as the door.
There, in the doorway, Goghos bent down and kissed her
on the forehead. Her cheeks were still moist. He also

kissed the child on the hair. They didn't accompany him
to the airport. He walked down the staircase alone, with
his two suitcases. Returned to Greece. But didn't go to
Corfu. Without notifying any of us, he headed for Poros.
He wanted to remain alone, far away from acquain-
tances, to look after himself, to see who he was, what he
was, what he could do. He had a brief affair with a girl.
But it wasn't *like then*. Now, nothing was *like then*.
Neither the girls, nor the boat rides, nor the sea, nor the
moonlight. There was only one night, when he was
sleeping under the pine-trees and he heard guitars and
songs from inside a boat and he said almost in his sleep:
"Yes, yes; like then." He got up and plunged into the sea,
naked. And he swam. And when he came out, all
refreshed, he saw his body in the moonlight and once
again, he could feel his *whole body*. He touched his soaking wet paps and got a good-humoured hard-on. That's
just how he said it: "good-humoured," and he laughed
(maybe *like then*). Here, Goghos stopped. I was listening
to him, as though I were lost, with a strange, very tender, almost happy sadness. I didn't look at him. I kept
staring at the table. As though reading a beautiful book,
a novel (without a question mark in brackets). After a
while, he said to me: "You know, Ion, I believe I'm not a
good comrade. I'm too pre-occupied with my own affairs.
Once when I read a short poem which said:

> *your own tooth hurts you*
> *more*
> *than thirty men who've been killed*

I had the impression it was written for me." He grew
silent again. Suddenly he laid his hand on my shoulder

and in a voice which seemed to be guilty and repentant, he added: "I'm neither a good comrade nor a good human being. Yes, Ion. I concealed many things from you when I came back from Corfu. I was jealous of you. I thought Mireille was in love with you. Because along with those other poems, she'd also brought the *Moonlight Sonata* in French. She read all of it to me one night and afterwards, we made love. Our craziest night. And the next day, when I told her that you and I were friends, she wanted to meet you. Then I told her that you were at a conference in England. 'What a pity,' she said. 'For years now, I've been wanting to meet him. I've seen photos of him in the French newspapers. I like him.' And she insisted that I read the *Sonata* to her in Greek. I didn't have the book with me. But she insisted. I found it in a bookshop – the first edition, it was faded. That same night I read the whole poem to her and she kept saying: 'Oh là là, oh là là – moi no compréhend, but plus belle in Grec zan in France-language.' And we made love all night long – lovemaking which was desperate for me, as though I wanted to detach her from you. And when I showed you the photographs and letters, I wanted to test you. And I felt sure that you were in love with her too. And I was jealous and I hated you. That's why, when you went to the kitchen to make me a coffee, I ran away. I didn't want to see you. Forgive me, Ion. That's why I'm telling you I'm not a good comrade or a good human being. Now I'm no longer in love, or at least, not the way I was then, and maybe that's why I'm no longer jealous of you. On the contrary, since I feel guilty towards you, now I love you still more. You're my only friend. To you I can say everything. You understand everything, both your own problems and those of us all. We don't understand you. And you know this. And you never talk about your own problems – or else, very rarely, like that time about the May Day wreath. But even when you do talk about yourself occasionally, it's as though you keep something silent and in the end, you remain alone in your worldwide tenderness. 'Worldwide tenderness', that's how Mireille spoke about your poetry. And do you know what she told me recently in Paris? – 'Our child was conceived in the moonlight of Ion's sonata.' And do you know how she calls the child? 'Goghos-Ion.' Now you may turn on the light." I turned it on. He put his hand in his jacket-pocket and took out a small book and two photographs. He laid them on the table. Picked out the one photograph and stuck it in his inner pocket. The book: *The Moonlight Sonata*. The photograph: the child's. "What a beautiful child," I exclaimed. "The spitting image of you. Little Goghos." "Mireille has sent them for you – both the book and the photograph. Read what she's written on the back of the photo." I read: "*A Ion, avec toute notre amitié – Mireille et Gogo-Ion.*" (My eyes become blurred. And I say to myself: "The child of us three.") "What a beautiful child," I repeat and with my elbow I nudge Goghos' elbow and we both bow our heads very, very close, fraternally, above the photo of the blond child. We smile. Goghos' smile is rather sad. Mine is joyful. For now I know that poems not only give birth to other poems, they also give birth to real children, thousands and thousands of peace-loving children born to make the world beautiful. That's just how it is: behind the words and inside the words, something incorporeal breathes, intangible, desolate, something big and invisible which makes all the unfinished things, all the secretmost wishes we've whispered clandestinely, secret even from our own self, in our most unknown sleep, which we've already forgotten, and this has remained deep within us and functions beyond our own will, like an unuttered "ach", like a musical sound which can be heard from all sides and always and acquiesces.

Karlóvassi, August 1st, 2nd, 3rd, 1983

The golden hour

My God, what a glorious sunset. The sun is sinking red, cherry-red into the sea. The colours flare up in the west, the mountains grow dark in the east. You remain between the light and the dark, holding your breath as though you yourself are the point of their separation and their union and you tremble lest an unknown balance be disturbed. Little by little the bright colours grow dim. The shadow falls lightly, turning the air blue. It seems the twilight assumes the secret synthesis which, briefly, had been entrusted to you. And suddenly a widespread flash, like an explosion of silence, leaps up and is crystallised in a deeper silence and immobility. The ecstasy of itself. Sea and sky all-golden. The golden hour. At a standstill. Illustrious hour of windless lull. The absolute of oblivion till the ultimate memory. Further on, in the dark harbour, the lamp-posts light up. The green lights quiver in another world all their own, even yesterday also our own world, of familiar household preparation for a home-made meal, in an ancestral dining-room, where the three servants light the hanging lamps one by one, and the Forefather, tight-lipped, alone, before the family gathers round the table, smokes his pipe, yes, alone, on the carved wooden settee, and from the way he refuses to look at the servants, you sense that his mind retains incontestably the clear though indefinite knowledge of the roundness of bread and of the world. And perhaps from the sparks sent up by his pipe, the first evening-star becomes riveted two inches up above the mountain. At that very moment, as though by some secret understanding and agreement, the golden hour gives way to the rose-coloured hour. This too at a standstill. Rose-coloured, rose-coloured, rose-coloured, until equally noiselessly, the ashen-blue darkness falls like *"someone sitting sleepily astride his horse"*. Just then, a big ship (merchant-marine or war-ship?), brightly-lit, full of healthy mechanical noises and fine youthful nautical voices, sailed into the harbour, pinpointing time in a definite present, it did not anchor at the pier, it cast anchor in the very middle of the harbour, glang-glang, chains, mooring-lines, little boats, porters, curse words, laughs, sailors leaping out onto the mainland, fine young Greeks, handsome gallant lads, with a little moustache and the white cap tilted, the darkness becomes white, there are more and more lights on, popping sounds from fizzy drinks, and the girls, where did they catch wind of all this? When did they manage to rush down to the waterfront in their best clothes and hair-styles, and with their best hip-swaying, their best laughter, their best voice? One of the girls had stuck a rose in her wide-open bodice (supposedly, for a joke); the other girl (also for a joke) had put a few jasmine-buds in her hair; another girl was holding a sprig of basil and she kept smelling it and smelling it in order to conceal one of her front teeth, which she'd broken, cracking almonds. And then, I recalled Maria telling Petros' Anna – because Maria is a good comrade with a good mind and heart; she's eager, energetic and thoughtful, all at the same time; she never leaves anything half-finished, never postpones or loads things on to other people; whatever she does she does correctly; she speaks in a lovely, simple, rational way, with a kind of controlled emotion (which seems very rich and that's why she doesn't let it flood and smother her meanings); yes, Maria speaks just fine when she's in a small friendly group; but at large sessions, with lots of people, she falters, loses the train of her thoughts, repeats the same things, twists her fingers with embarrassed anxiety, scratches her neck discreetly in the same spot, just under her right ear, as if a fly keeps settling there every so often, and Maria's afraid the fly might fall into the child's milk and contaminate it. Well now, Maria had been telling Anna: she must have been seven or eight years old, and one August twilight (seems it must have been a little after the golden and after the rose-coloured hour), a big, big ship arrived on their island, with many, many lights and many little flags on the masts and a big flag right out in front, and when the breeze blew, the whole flag unfolded and took up half the harbour, hiding the light-house, and the crowd rushed out to the breakwater to ogle and admire, boys and girls, gallant little lads and schoolchildren (the schools hadn't opened yet), as well as level-headed men and respectable old men, only the old women were left behind to tend to the homes, and the mothers to get dinner ready, but now and then, they too glanced through the kitchen-window at the big brightly-lit boat – a glance which seemed terribly sad and also angry. Well now, Maria told her mother: "I want you to dress me up in my turquoise velvet dress, the one my nice Uncle Meletis brought me from Athens, so I can go down to the harbour like everybody else"; and her mother answered: "Goodness, how can you wear velvet in summer? You'll perspire and soil your best dress, and what's more, you'll get a heat-rash like measles." "I want that dress," said Maria, "even if I do get a rash." "Can't be done," said the mother. "Then let me wear my Sunday dress, the one with the flowers." "I think you're barmy, daughter; it's not Sunday or a holiday; just go as you are, or else mind your own business and help me save on your shoes, which you've almost worn out, shoes we bought last year." I thought of not going and not eating a single bite that evening to make her bust a gut with worry. But I couldn't stand it and I went. All the girls were beautifully decked out in their best clothes. Only I was in my old clothes, with my hair uncombed, I felt dirty and abused. And there were some sailors, handsome as the ones in Tsarouhis' paintings, only these sailors were dressed. I hid behind a lantern-post, so nobody would see me and I watched. My girlfriends from school noticed me there and called to me. I got flustered. When I tried to speak, I started stuttering. I didn't know what I was saying or how to say it. I got tongue-tied. Ever since, I've been left with a lump in my throat, whenever I'm in front of a lot of people; and that's why, lately, whatever I have to say, I write and then, read it out from my handwriting. I've found a solution. You know, Anna, from that evening when Mother didn't let me wear the clothes I wanted, I've had the impression I'm no longer capable of handling my clothes, my shoes, or my words; I feel I don't know how to use my own abilities or any powers I may have. That's why my brain started working a lot and at the same time I started to work a lot, every possible kind of work, as though by action, I could steer clear of my problems and set my thinking on an even keel. That evening, you know, I thought everything had turned to glass and if I moved my hand like this, everything would break; and I thought I too was made of glass and if anyone touched me with his little finger, I'd break like the glass-panes on the windows of the mad girl, where one evening, the children of the noble Kyr-Basista threw stones. Now, I no longer feel that things are made of glass and are about to break, or that I myself am made of glass and if people touch me, I'll break. Coming close to all of you helped me in this. To tell the truth, Anna, from the time I've been near our comrades, near you, Petros, Yotis, Vanghelis, Andreas, Ion, Alekos (Alekos she mentioned last and from this very fact, it was obvious that she liked him more than everybody else), when I find myself elbow to elbow in a demonstration, I feel the world is steady and I myself am steady and I don't want to hide behind a lamp-post. Without fear I can look at human beings and I am sure that all of us together can fix many things. Only when I'm up on a platform for the purpose of speaking, as you know, I start to feel that lump again. Maybe because I'm standing three feet above the other people (and I find this unfitting for me), maybe because they can see me more than I can see them (and this too is unfitting), maybe because I feel rather *alone*, cut off from other people like then, by the difference in the height of our seats. It bothers me (now that I'm talking to you, I realise this), it bothers me to see our comrades from up above, looking downwards; I prefer to see them from down below, looking upwards; and better still, all from the same position, at the same height of our eyes, as is the case with paintings in order for us to see them correctly. This gives me the feeling (therefore, also the comfort) of an *equality which has become reality*, which is what we all dream of and this is what we are all struggling for." This is more or less what Maria said to Anna and she was, so she said, very moved and Anna was also moved and kissed her, particularly when the last words about equality were spoken ("this is what we all dream of and this is what we are all struggling for") and she burst into tears and as an antidote to her being so moved, she added: "Forgive me for my ridiculous sermon." And all at once, she stopped weeping. And Anna told all this to Petros and Petros found it perfectly correct and fine and liked Maria still more. And one day Maria made a mess of things again and she kept stuttering and stopping and repeating again and again: "Well now, comrades; well now, comrades"; and when she'd finished up and was drenched in sweat, and most people had gone, and just we the clan, were left, we made game of her a bit: "Hey comrade, what's wrong with you again and you've mucked up, muddling your words as if you've got lupine prickles under your tongue; you've really given us a rough time with your 'Comrades and Comrades'." Maria turned all the way pale and grabbed her purse: "Forgive me, I've got work," she said and went off. And when Maria had gone, Petros gave us a real dressing-down (first time for him), red as a lobster with anger; but after a while, he calmed down and told us Maria's story, at first severely, but later on, almost tenderly, emphasizing that phrase of hers: "I didn't know how to use my own abilities." And Petros ended up by saying: "Our comrade knows better than all of us how to use her abilities and she has more abilities than all of us." And we felt ashamed, guilty, guilty, guilty; indeed,

Yotis commented: "Are we comrades or boors?"; and we all wanted to rush out and find Maria and kiss her hands; and Petros sensed this and he looked at us again in a comradely way and in his sweetest, admonishing tone of voice, he said: "Onwards, comrades; we've quite forgotten ourselves; let's get back to work." And tonight, here in Karlóvassi, on these rocks along the seashore, how I'd love to have Maria and Alekos near me, very, very near, all three of us, sitting at the same height and at the "same height of our eyes" watching the big brightly-lit ship, and with my right elbow I'd nudge Maria's elbow and with my left elbow I'd nudge Alekos'; how I wish we could share in that deep fond "universal equality" and in equal quantity that we could share the golden hour, the rose-coloured hour, the ashen-blue darkness slowly falling like *"someone sitting sleepily astride his horse"*, in equal quantity and equal value, in a comradely way with all people, multiplying the beautiful and the good unto the infinity of Time. Because the girls are beautiful, the sailors are laughing in a kind-hearted way, the balconies are full of pots of basil and geraniums, and an accordion is playing in the taverna, two old women who are co-mother-in-laws are sitting on their doorstep with folded hands (they aren't sad), the sea quiets down and water can be heard irrigating the garden, and the white horse can be heard in the field munching dry weeds and a scent spreads through the world, my God, origan, marjoram, cinnamon, manure, burnt sugar, burnt bulrushes, fills your lungs, and you can't endure it, simply cannot endure it unless you sing. And this, I say, is the starting-point of song. And Maria was never so beautiful, so comradely, as on that early evening in the all-golden hour, and her face all misted with shadow and light, like the face of that other Maria of our childhood; and I long to hear the noise of Telis' motorcycle, and see the glow of the sunset on his helmet, so that things can solidify into a sort of certainty and so that I can know that it's me in this *now,* because I sense I've forgotten something and I'm trying to remember what I've forgotten – (perhaps that I'm out of cigarettes and my fingers of their own accord search the inner corners in my empty cigarette-packet), because this is what you can't stand and you have to sing, but you lack the voice for it, and at least, you must smoke, to make something come out of your mouth, something you can see. I get up from my rock, start walking quickly (simultaneously aware that my quick pace is in total antithesis to another beautiful internal slowness, an ecstatic slowness); I reach the first kiosk near the sea to buy some cigarettes. In front of the little window, a tall old man is standing. I can see him from behind and slightly from the side. Long thick grey hair. Grey beard. Broad robust shoulder-blades under the hemp shirt. Ancient man-of-the-fields? Shepherd? *The Creator* in Michelangelo's painting? *The Thinker* of Rodin? I can't see his face. Only his hand as it takes the packet of cigarettes (same brand as mine) and pays for them – an enormous, hirsute hand with broad worn-away fingernails. He turns in the other direction (not towards me) and walks off, slowly, majestically, in the direction where I'd been sitting just a moment ago. I still can't see his face. Hurriedly I pay for my cigarettes, don't bother to take the change, and run to catch up with him. He has stopped to light his cigarette. He lights it. I find a pretext of not having any matches. "Please, can you give me a light?" He turns round. His face is faintly lit by the light-bulb in the kiosk. What a magnificent face, round, clear, stern, free of wrinkles, framed by the grey hair, grey moustache and grey beard. Golden eyes, but motionless, like those of statues. (Maybe can he be the old-time God of my childhood? But no. God didn't smoke.) He doesn't want me to light my cigarette from his. Out of his huge pocket he takes a shepherd's old tinder-box with a long wick. With the edge of his wide palm he strikes the little wheel of the tinder-box three times, lights the wick and hands it to me to light up. As I bend over the tinder-box, just above his enormous hands, my nostrils are struck by the smell of burnt cotton and I sense his massive shape towering over my head like Mount Ararat. "Thank you," I say to him. "Thank you. Thank you." (And I have never so deeply felt the meaning of this "thank you" as at this moment.) He doesn't look at me. Just smiles a stern, distant smile beyond. "Are you from these parts?" I ask. He raises his index-finger up to his lips (I imagine he wants to impose silence on me; no), he opens his mouth and with his finger shows me his truncated tongue. He is mute.

Karlóvassi, August 7th, 8th, 1983

Our relationships with dreams

How many thousands of dreams I've seen – countless dreams. And I still see. Some I enjoy and want them to last all night, all my life. Others constrict my heart and I want to wake up and escape from them. And when I do wake up, I'm afraid to go back to sleep in case they snatch me up in their claws again in the same way and worse. However, when I see good dreams, I don't want to wake up, so they can continue; and in my sleep I keep saying: "How lovely, how lovely"; and I say I'll remember them when I wake up, so they won't slip away from me and so I can tell them to someone else who'll also rejoice in them, or so I can write about them. But when I wake up, often I remember absolutely nothing and I'm left with the sense of a great loss, terribly sad, bewildered, silent, and afterwards, I feel insulted and I find fault with the pillow, with the sheet, with my own right hand, with one of my shoes, which I didn't know was in the middle of the room, or with the alarm-clock on the bedside-table whose minute-hand moves much more slowly than my brain and I can't manage to coordinate them in order to think my thought with continuity. At other times again, I can remember bits-and-pieces of a dream and I tremble lest they elude me and I try to re-create and re-articulate them, but other adulterated parts interfere and get mixed up, changing positions and altering themselves, and I'm left outside, and I actually begin to make a selection: "This part I'll keep." "This I'll throw out"; and I'm very annoyed by this involvement of mine, which I know and characterize as *forgery*, because the insubstantial substance of the dream hardens unbearably and actually starts to be transformed into logic and symbol and to be recommended for psychological or sociological interpretations or even ethical, pedagogical conclusions. Eh, then everything goes to the devil. And I torture myself all over again to remove the clumsy additions and to try and preserve at least a few fragments from the first ethereal essence. Again, nothing worthwhile emerges. However, sometimes, rarely of course, I can recall a *whole* dream, and I circulate inside it, and am part of it, as in the "Shadowy Space" or "The Dream with the Lilies", and I too am ethereal – a suspended smile, an uncreated creator, who poses no questions and has no questions posed to him, who owes no answer to other people or to himself, and who is free within the dazzling, *inexplicable* element, which is (perhaps) the awed wonder, beauty, ignorance, magic, erotic love, all of eros and death together, eternity, (both visible and metaphysical), purity, sanctity. I live a few hours in this intoxicated state and all of a sudden, shake myself and slap my thighs to make sure that I've woken up, that I am I, that I'm here, not an angel or cloud or aerostat balloon, I'm a human being alongside other human beings, here on earth, in the motherland of human beings, in my fine mortal body, and I slap my thighs again, like Odysseus when the people of Phaeacia brought him out of the ship sound asleep and set him

down on his ancestral land, and then they went away,
and when he woke up at dawn in Ithaca, he didn't know
where he was, and he started counting the brass utensils, perhaps in order to re-locate himself, with the aid of
profitable practical occupations:

RETURN I

*They brought him out of the ship sound asleep, along with
   his blankets;*
they left him gently on dry land, a little way above the harbour of Phórkina,
*in front of the cave, under the olive-tree; next to him they
   laid*
the gifts of the Phaeacians – tripods, brass utensils, cauldrons –
and then they went away again. When he woke up
*he could not imagine that the hospitable boat, which had
   brought him,*
had turned to stone at the entrance of Schería,
in the harbour across the way; nor could he recognize
his ancestral land at all. Divine mist enveloped him
after his twenty-year tribulation. Nevertheless,
*he counted the brass utensils, one by one, in case anything
   had been stolen from him.*
And not even at this moment, did he lack cunning,
when he asked the beautiful shepherd, to learn
*about this place where he stood now, its customs. And the
   Goddess*
not only tolerated this, she demanded it, and was proud of it.
A way had to be found in order that nothing would be lost
*from the memories of the great voyage, from the gifts he
   had received and would leave behind.*

RETURN II

Well then, when he awoke, he looked all around –
trees, rocky paths, spacious
harbours down below, in the south, a cloud; –
nothing, he knew nothing. (Would he find them
greater or smaller?) That which he most
dreamed of, now that he'd arrived, seemed
most alien and unknown. Wasn't this the fault
of the long interval of time or the fault of knowledge
outside time? With the palms of both his hands
he slapped his thighs to make sure he was awake.
"Where am I?" was all he said. And then,
like a dog going out through a big door, at daybreak,
there, at the root of the good olive-tree, he relieved himself.

So I shake myself from my bed. I too go to the loo to relieve myself. I listen to my urine in the toilet-bowl. And *I am,* and I'm *here.* I return from the divine mist to things and events. Pour plenty of water on my face and my hair. Boil my coffee, light my cigarette. Blow the smoke through my nostrils and my mouth, externalising my previous fear that I might turn into vapour in the dream. Inside myself, the words take form, utterly alive. In a friendly mood I name the objects which determine us and re-assure us of our position and our course: bed, table, window, chair, glass, cup. And it really is a cup. I pick it up by its likeable handle, raise it to my lips and sip my coffee. Whereas in the dream, when I tried to lift the cup, it fell apart and the coffee remained in the shape of the cup, but there was no handle for me to hold it and bring it to my mouth and I was obliged to bow my head every so often to drink my coffee, sip by sip, precisely as chickens do when they drink water in the courtyard trough. In just the same way, we move our heads up and down. But to tell the truth, I actually enjoyed it – eating and drinking like a bird – not, of course, like a chicken, but a pigeon, or even a sparrow. So now, I sit at my table, drinking my coffee, smoking, searching my papers, making my acknowledgments, scribbling some notes (in order not to forget); and I too count my brass utensils one by one, the oracular tripods, the cauldrons for cooking and laundry, because Homer was the first who taught me to find ways not to lose anything from the memories of the *great voyage*, from the gifts I've received and would leave behind – so that nothing would be lost from the dream, from myth and from history. And isn't the dream itself also a grand voyage in the previous, in the now, in the afterwards, in our own unknown and the unknown of the world, in the eternal? As long as you find the time and the way to say it and do it, it's as though you achieve the unattainable. That's why I struggle night and day to record the beautiful and good things of this world, so that life can become better (insofar as possible) for me and for all people. And just now, I recalled another dream and I want to narrate both parts of it, because it was actually divided into two parts or two acts. Well, I was somewhere near the sea (I don't know if it was on the seashore or inside the sea or above the sea) and inside the sea there was an upside-down cone made of unfired clay – not a cone which floats and bobs up-and-down like a half-sunken boat, but a cone constructed down in the sea, with its peak resting on the bottom of the sea, and its rims two inches above the sea, forming a circle of serene water full of light, while on all sides around it, the tempest thrashed. And I was puzzled that the waves didn't make the clay crumble, since when I laid my hands on it only for a moment, they got all full of potter's clay. And then, (even now, I don't know how), about twenty-five little children, boys and girls stark-naked, appeared at the mouth of the cone, holding hands, all the way around, forming a big beautiful daisy. They bowed their heads towards the water full of light and their beautiful faces were reflected there, forming another circle in the water full of liquid and all of a sudden, myriads of goldfish filled the inner circle like the daisy's gold-dust. After this, some miners arrived in huge lorries; they removed their clothes, dressed up as frogmen, raised the clay cone and headed I know not where. They just disappeared. Only the water could be heard gushing out on the road further on, as the cone went on draining, but I'm not sure if the noise of the water could be heard in the dream. Then, I found myself alone on dry land and perhaps it was raining and it was all black. Hundreds of black umbrellas were walking on their own, half-a-metre above the earth – apparently, hands of underground people were holding them and strange to say, I wasn't at all puzzled by the fact that the umbrellas, although their handles were held by people under the earth, could move through the earth unimpeded as though it were air. I found this very natural. And it was. But while I was staring at the umbrellas and about to pick up a friendship with them, my eye spied something shiny on the road – a pair of eyeglasses. I picked them up. Wiped them off with the left corner of my jacket. Put them on. What's this, good heavens? What light? White light, white, absolutely white. It isn't raining. No. It's snowing. No, not snowing either. This white isn't speckled with snowflakes. The snow has already fallen. The mountain-slope's like cotton. The person tottering down the mountain looks like Nijinsky. Yes, that's who it is. He's aged. He staggers. He, whose feet used to be like birds. He's run away from home. He's angry with his wife, because she insists on feeding him meat. And he doesn't want meat. He doesn't want to see her eating meat either. And he's run away. But where is he going? His feet sink into the snow. He'll collapse. The murderer is concealed somewhere. This pile of snow is a grave. Two dry poles are stuck on top of it. They must have buried him here. Nijinsky knows this well. He moves on. But after all, where is he heading? He arrives at the rim of the precipice. He'll fall and be dashed to bits. But just here at the very edge, there's a tiny tree. He embraces it. Catches a firm hold and steps back. I approach. "Did you see that?" he asks me. "I saw it," I answer. "God caught me by the waist with both His hands. He held me. And didn't let me fall." "Yes," I said. "This means I must return home." "Yes," I said. "I too am God," he tells me. "You used to be," I answer him, but immediately correct myself: "You *are*," I tell him. He tries to take my eyeglasses from me. I push his hand away. He vanishes. I fit the glasses firmly on my nose, because I can't make them fit well behind my ears. The lighting changes. Crystal-clear night. Far down the avenue, which is beautifully lit by tall lamp-posts, I catch sight of Telis astride his motorcycle. At top speed he comes straight at me. He stops there without turning off the motor. "What about a ride on my donkey?" he asks. "Let's go," I answer. I climb on in back of him. Off we go, fast as lightning. What an ungodly rogue. He darts in between two busses, racing now to the right, now to the left, passing the cars, not stopping at the red traffic-light, racing past both lorries belonging to the miners. "Slow down," I shout at him, "we'll be smashed to bits." No reaction from him. I tighten my grip on his strong ribs. The racing speed of the wind tosses my hair to and fro. I take shelter behind his sturdy shoulder-blades and helmet, as though hiding behind some gigantic warrior clad in bronze. No. I don the whole body of Telis, I arm my whole body with an invulnerable steel panoply. And I don't even have an Achilles' heel. I grip his rugged ribs still tighter and cling to him. "Don't," he shouts. "You're tickling me." I start laughing. Bringing my hands down to his waist. This is equally well-knit and robust. We are racing along. About to depart. Flying. It's no longer a road, cars, traffic-lights. Only sky. We are flying along the line of the Milky Way with terrifying speed. "Want some peanuts?" he shouts to me. "Stick your hand in the right pocket of my puff-jacket and take some." I stick my hand in his pocket. And take out a fistful of peanuts. They're warm from his body. I nibble them one at a time, gripping his waist tighter with my left hand. I can hear the gnashing of my teeth. From the gnashing sound I wake up. It's daybreak. Before opening my eyes all the way, I rush to my bookshelf, and find *Nijinsky's Diary*. Start leafing through it. Read the part I'd just seen in my sleep. I also glance at other pages of his magnificent madness. And isn't it true that our dreams are our own madness, which we live in our sleep in order not to be insane by day, to remember the madness, and yet remain controlled, and by avoiding its exaggerated elements (though we have lived these in full) to go about our work correctly, in a measured way. And I think some wise person said: "Wisdom is no more than the awareness and naturalisation of insanity." But I myself don't know about such things. Further on in *Nijinsky's Diary*, I read some lines I liked and back then, I underlined them: "Only today, at lunch, I was able to observe my mother-in-law. She asked for a tangerine and I offered her the one they'd been saving for me; I told her I wouldn't mind eating an orange. Without opening her mouth, she took it. I didn't conceal the fact that I didn't like this at all, not at all. My father-in-law, Oscar, immediately took her side. I took back the tangerine. Gave half of it to Oscar, the other half to my wife. But she didn't want to take it, because she thought I wanted to eat it. So I put it back on my mother-in-law's plate. She refused to eat it and didn't utter a word." Hey there, the old cow. (Nijinsky didn't write this, it's me who said it.) They're quite right to say that anyone who hasn't learned to say "thank you" has not yet become a human being. When I step outside, I'll go to the greengrocer next door and buy lots of tangerines. Not oranges. And I won't give even half a tangerine to the old cow, even if she is a splendid actress. The two of us will eat them all, peeling them with our fingers, the two of us, face to face, in our bare feet (so that I can see his feet, which are still winged), me and Nijinsky. The pips and the peels we'll throw on the floor and they'll glow golden in the sunlight streaming in through the open window and they'll be fragrant. The five remaining ones I'll give to Petros.

Karlóvassi, August 9th, 1983

People, dreams, things

I'll have to be on my guard to see that nothing escapes me about dreams in front of Kyparissis – especially that dream with the "sea daisy"; he'd find it romantic in a terribly outmoded style (this person who is himself so very outmoded in his clothes, shoes, hair-style, cuff-links, but who pretends to be so very, very modern in his "aesthetic principles"); he'd also find it figuratively descriptive and insufferably grandiloquent. But of course, I also shouldn't talk about the "Shadowy Space" or "The Dream with the Lilies" or "Petros' Bear" or the "Umbrellas Walking by Themselves". But no; this one he'd probably have rather liked, because he himself, all winter, and even in springtime, goes around in his rust-stained raincoat with a big black pre-War umbrella – to be ready for any contingency, as he says – (and perhaps this has stuck to him ever since that masquerade dousing; but no – as far as I recall, he used to cart his umbrella around with him before, long before, and indeed, perhaps he'd had it with him that evening when the Male-Rosa splashed him all over with water – but at the time, why didn't he open it to protect himself from the dousing? – a big black umbrella open in the evening coffee-house would have suited the Carnival atmosphere, he'd have appeared as a masquerader himself, participating in the company, and not as a masked blackguard with his spurious, passive seriousness). Well then, surely he'd have liked the dream with the umbrellas (by eclectic affinity), and he'd have ascribed it to me honourably as an interesting surrealistic invention, but rather pretentiously (and not spontaneously) original. And there you are, completely unexpectedly, one evening in Kostikou's beer-garden (as a matter of fact, Petros was there too, even if he wasn't drinking beer), Kyparissis himself told us about a dream of his own: He was in a large, luxurious palace, he said, among many unfamiliar personnages of High Society, all of them dressed in something like tail-coats, and he too was in a tail-coat; whereupon, behind a heavy curtain, a child dressed in a sailor's-suit emerged very cautiously – he looked like a rich boy, but rather sickly – and in a low tone, he asked for a five-pound bank note; Kyparissis searched his pockets, but found nothing; his wallet had been stolen – a beautiful wallet made of soft leather with gold initials: A.K. (which sounded like "akou": listen). "Then, I gave him my wristwatch, which was also gold, along with the chain, also gold; precisely at that moment, a spotlight was aimed at me and all the guests began to clap for me; however, the spotlight also lit up the child, who was holding my wristwatch and trying to hide behind the curtain again; my gold chain dangled from his hands, it was very glittery and betrayed him; then three servants, who apparently had been hunting for the child, caught him and searched him; they found my wallet in his bosom; the tallest servant caught him by the ear and dragged him along to take him to the Public Prosecutor; the Public Prosecutor was sitting on a throne inside the mirror; until then, I hadn't seen him; 'No, no'; I shouted, 'he didn't steal these from me, I gave them to him; indeed, I also gave him my tie-pin, because he seemed so very sad to me, but he didn't want to take it'; (this stood out a mile – stolen from Jean Valjean); I removed my diamond tie-pin and pinned it right in front, on his sailor-suit collar; then the child turned into a black dog, stood up on its hind legs and bit my arm; and I woke up. Isn't it beautiful?" Kyparissis asked. "Beautiful, beautiful," we answered, looking at him in a puzzled way, not knowing how to explain this dream of his (there we were now, seeking interpretations, we who scorn those scholastic, thorough, whimsical interpreters, who produce the most arbitrary nonsensical conclusions; we couldn't understand in which points this dream applies to "Mr." Kyparissis and represents him; and do you suppose it really is his dream? or perhaps did he just concoct it in order to show off his own "poetic" imagination? "Ever since then," he added, "I've had the impression the mark from that bite has remained indelible on my arm, and at night, even now, I search for it with my fingers." Kyparissian balderdash, I said to myself. However much you search this dream, you won't find even the slightest sensual allusion – perhaps only the pulling of the ear – this too is doubtful. So then, what sort of poet (because now, he also writes poems), what sort of critic can Akyparissoglou possibly be – a person devoid of erotic sensations, premonitions, hallucinations, with a big black pre-War umbrella, winter and summer, for eternal malignantly-sickly precaution, lest his forelocks get wet and my dandy Morphonios of Zakynthos looks ugly. Eh, well now, I'll also concoct a fake dream for him and I'll make him bust a gut and be obliged to say "beautiful, beautiful, very beautiful"; and this he will say, as though he has no reservations, to keep us from realising that his own dream was fake too. But no. I'm too bored. Bored to have quixotic competitions with persons like Kyparissis in every sector. I'm too bored with "Mr." Kyparissis as a whole, and still more so now, with his tail-coat and his *Les Misérables*. He was better with his umbrella – more in keeping with his own self. However, among ourselves, we who belonged to the clan, used to tell each other our dreams, now and then, as well as our troubles and personal problems; indeed all of them used to tell me their problems and from time to time, I felt ashamed that I was the one who confessed the least. Petros of course, and Martha very rarely confessed; they seemed not to have any private life, other than that of the organisation. But the one who never said a word about himself was Telis. He disliked the endless comments about psychological complexes, existentialist problems and such things. He was bored stiff with effusiveness, with confessions, with those (how do they call them?) aesthetic "diachronic recurrences", and in general, theoretical discussions, even if they were sociological. He would yawn in an obvious way or start joking. Give him practical work, he was a past master at running so fast nobody could reach him. And all in the twinkling of an eye and to perfection – leaflets, banners, notifications, meetings, demonstrations; he had a strong, stimulating brain, good at organising – almost like Petros, but Petros studied, actually stealing hours from his sleep, from his meals, and certainly, also from his love-life. Telis had no books, no, only quick wits and hard work. Except one evening, when we were alone at my home, I don't know why, he told me just like that, as though having no connection with our conversation: "Between our legs, we have a piece of meat, and *it* rules us, we don't rule it. As soon as a female approaches, it springs up and then, just try and bridle it. Weaknesses. Great weaknesses. And you can't tell if it's by nature, or our own – I believe, rather *my own*." And this very small thing he said revealed Telis in his entirety, with all his beauty, frank bluntness, manly pluck. This is why we all loved him and were proud of him, but we never told him so, because this gangling big fellow seemed to be ashamed and he made a wry face. And once, when the organisation recommended a position for him, Telis said: "No, comrades, I'm not for such things. I don't deserve it. I know what I'm telling you. Leave me down here. I'll be able to do more." And then I remembered his words that evening: "Great weaknesses *of my own*." And I understood why he didn't accept: He didn't want the organisation to be accused for "his own weaknesses". Because he respected the organisation above everything else in this world, with a very deep respect, which was almost religious, I might say. And I wonder why *weaknesses?* Because he was handsome, erotic, swift-as-a-winged-creature and strong? When he gripped a stone in his fist, he could crush it. Why weaknesses? Because he loved and delighted in women and they were crazy about him? However, he would never give trouble to a woman-comrade, even if she looked tenderly at him. Telis, like Vanghelis – no, no; they were different from each other – Telis wasn't a smart-aleck, he was a man. And just when I was thinking about all these things, bowed over my papers, there you are, someone knocking on the door, not the doorbell, someone banging with his fist. I open up. Telis: "Hey, Ion, won't you leave your clutter of papers, and we'll go for a ride on my donkey?" (Exactly as in the dream.) "Let's go," I answer. The motorcycle is parked on its two iron legs, the motor hasn't been turned off. "But go easy," I tell him; "let's not break our noggin on some Electricity Company pole." "Agreed," says he. I climb on behind him, behind his robust shoulder-blades, behind his warlike helmet (exactly as in the dream – and the same feeling). Actually, he is going at an easy pace. There's no need for me to cling to him. "Which way shall we head?" he asks. "Wherever you want," I answer. "You're an islander. You'll want to be near the sea. I love the sea too. Women and sea." He laughs loudly. I can hear his laughter booming inside his helmet. The warrior with the bronze breast-plate. The comrade. We pass by Liosíon Street, Attikí Square, Lárissa Railway Station. The lamp-posts light up all at once. The day grows cool. And here's a small rose-coloured cloud next to that black chimney. We turn into Metaxouryío. Go up Ayíon Asomáton Avenue. Pass through Theseíon. Green, red. A crowd. Under the Acropolis. The Parthenon also rose-coloured in the sunset. The Heródeion Theatre pensive in the shadow. We come out at Syngroú Boulevard. Traffic congestion. We delay. I notice a shop-window with women's clothes, a brightly-lit sweet-shop, a sheet-metal door, a lorry-driver, a little girl – she's wearing an airy white dress and is holding a fluffy brown teddy bear. When we reach the coast of Palaió Pháliron, Telis steps up the speed. The sea-breeze shakes my hair to and fro. (Just as in the dream.) I tighten my grip on Telis' strong ribs. "Hey, Ion, stop tickling me," he tells me. (Eh, now that's just too much. Absolutely as in the dream.) I lower my hands to his well-knit waist. Won't it be funny if he mentions roasted peanuts now. I wait. He doesn't mention them. Nor do I say anything to him. I'm just enjoying this *great journey* with him. We arrive in Glyfáda. And cast anchor in an open-air restaurant. Fine. Flower beds full of blossoms. Greenery. A grapevine. Few people. We order beers and titbits. The sea can be heard, phsiu, phsiu, phsiu, nearby, further on, as far as into the depths of memory. Telis' helmet is resting on a chair next to him. The archaic warrior. No. The modern fighter. His thick black hair, which had been tamped down by the helmet, begins to breathe and grow bushy again. The broad palm of his hand around the big glass of beer. He refreshes himself. Unbuttons his shirt all the way down. Myths, images, campaigns, triremes, oarsmen, statues, rituals. A distant, very distant song. The low sounds of a record-player and the sea. We eat and drink with appetite. Talking about trivial, joyful things. I don't know what. Beautiful things. A young couple passes by next to us. Telis' eyes begin to play. His whole face, his body, his voice and movement exude eros. They sit down at a small table a little way beyond us. I glance at them stealthily. The girl is staring at Telis. His magnet. And I don't know why, I recall a doll I'd been given on New Year's Day, when I was an eight-year-old child. When you wound it up, it started lurching as though drunk, at the same time waving its arms and playing a very small harmonica – a joyful and yet sad little waltz, very simple, in C-major. Sol fa mi, mi re do, re mi re, do re mi. Sol fa mi, mi re do, re mi re, do o o. I can hear this little waltz inside me vibrantly alive, I learned it immediately and could play it on the piano. I can hear it along with the sea of Monovásia, and suddenly, I'm overpowered by the desire to tell Telis my dream, not the first act with the umbrellas and the eyeglasses and Nijinsky; but only the second act which I've lived with him. I tell him everything, with all the trimmings. When I reach the point of: "Stop tickling me," he starts laughing so hard that he sprays me with the beer in his mouth. Laughter, laughter, laughter. Beautiful laughter, stentorian and carefree. The girl is staring at him and restrains her laughter. Everybody turns round and stares at him, men and women alike, from all the tables. He goes on laughing – he doesn't give a damn about their staring at him. He doesn't even see them. He sees only me and our dream. And when I reach the "roasted peanuts", there, real pandemonium breaks loose. He pours his beer into his helmet, exclaiming: "Hey, Ion, do you make poems even in your sleep?" And what a coincidence: at that very moment, a peanut-vendor passes by with his basket. "Do you have any roasted peanuts?" Telis asks him. "I do have." He buys two little cone-shaped packets of roasted peanuts and empties them onto the table. "Just so our dream can come true, absolutely all the way." We both start crunching the peanuts. We can hear the sea and the gnashing of our teeth. But this time, *we do not wake up.* We are *awake,* in our comradely dream, inside the whole, wide world.

Karlóvassi, August 10th, 1983

Closing the interminable with a smile

Great journeys every night, every day, every hour, every moment. Very great. I return from the unknown to the known – and this is enveloped with the mist of the unknown. I wipe it with the palm of my hand, as we wipe window-panes from the inside, in order to bring it closer to me, so I can see it better. I dilate my eyes, close my eyes halfway, concentrate, observe, look at it. It always has something serious to tell us and never tells us the whole of it – not with the intent of hushing it up or hiding it from us, but probably because it becomes absent-minded, forgets itself in the midst of so many memories, so we too become absent-minded, forget ourselves, remember ourselves, interrelate, go astray, forget to remember. I look and I concentrate: the lighter, a fine metal lighter, a gift from Alekos last year on my birthday, the hands which hold lighters, a "tsak" sound and you light a cigarette, the flame, the smoke, two erotic palpitating nostrils lit from below, a phrase from the record, Halkias playing the clarinette, a glass breaks, two legs in a *tsámiko*-leap, the word "thoughtlessness" and the word "providence" and the double word "recollection-regeneration", and still more, the word "krrrouououou", but the matches sounded different, not "tsak", but "tsououf", the smell of phosphorus and the smell from the burning little stick, a tiny firecracker at night at Easter in childhood, in a Venetian lookout-tower of Monovásia, and down below, the fisherman Vegleris' house pitch-dark, his old wife had died the other day, and the grandmother lighting the lampion near the iconostasis with a match and the way the grandmother's hand is lit, pale, absolutely pale, you don't know which is the grandmother's hand and which is the Holy Virgin's; the match burns at its tip and becomes pointed, you can also make it into a toothpick, and pick your teeth and think, and perhaps a little smudge is left between your two front teeth, look at yourself in the mirror, you're too bored, Vanghelis had also said: "I'm too bored"; but thoughts spread beyond, and further still; behind the mountains, there's a country chapel on the peak and a woodcutter, and instead of cutting trees in the fir-tree forest with his hatchet, the woodcutter uses his pocket-knife to carve an idol of Artemis on a log, but he doesn't know this, he believes these are the features of Vassiloe; and still further on, as far as Aï-Demétres, in the village-house of Kyra-Kostandou, who had two sons: Botis, who was tall and thin and had blood in his urine all the time, and Stathis, who was rather fat; and she also had a daughter, Zoe the lame girl   her left leg was an inch shorter than her other leg, and later on, Zoe married Stamatis, who at the age of 22 became Stamatis, because Stamatis was born without genitals and had been christened Stamatia, and grew up wearing dresses and always kept company with the girls, during the vintage and the harvest, at the village pump with her jug, near the river washing her rough woollens with green soap and a pestle and lye, well at a certain point, Stamatia started to grow whiskers and a moustache, and in secret the poor thing shaved with her father's razor, and her folks took her to Athens for 43 whole days (the village was counting the days, one by one, on its fingers), and there you are, on the 44th day, on the feast-day of Saint Elias, Stamatia returned with her long black braids cut, her hair nicely parted with brilliantine hair-oil, a nice little moustache, my heavens, Stamatia wearing trousers and a shirt and a bow-tie into the bargain, a regular dandy – my word, such shameful deeds – and Stamatia had a cock, so they said, and a big cock at that, and all the girls lowered their eyes now, the former girlfriends of Stamatia, because it was the talk of the whole village that Stamatia had laid them all during those nights among the plane-trees; and the old women made the sign of the cross: "Saint Symeon has laid his mark on her." So then, Stamatia (now Stamatis) got married to Zoe-the-limper (as she was called) and just at the end of their first year, she gave birth to Stamatis' child, and in the second year, another child of Stamatis, (both boys), and they spent a blissful life, so blissful indeed that she started limping much less; but her mother, the widow Kyra-Kostandou, always put the matches on top of the fireplace, and this woman with the golden fingers was so thrifty that with a single match, she hastened to light both the candle-wick and the oil-lamp as well as the fire, and she kept the half-burnt matches on a small earthenware dish on top of the fireplace and she used to take one of these, light it again in the fire and re-light the oil-lamp, which a gust of wind had blown out; and once, when Botis, her elder son, lit his cigarette with a match, instead of from the oil-lamp, and then threw away the half-burnt match,

Kyra-Kostandou started hollering: "You ill-starred, good-for-nothing brute, let's just see what luck you'll have in your life; it's bad enough you don't use the oil-lamp for your lighter, you also burn up my match and throw away a whole half of it." And Kyra-Kostandou rummaged through the rubbish, found it and put it on the earthenware dish atop the fireplace. However, aside from lighters and matches, there were also the tinder-boxes (even now), belonging to the shepherds, the forest-ranger, the rural-guard, and that tinder-box with the long wick which belonged to the grand Old Man, the Mute, who gave me a light one beautiful twilight after the golden hour. But I really love the lighter Alekos gave me, both in the morning and at noon, as well as in the late afternoon and in the evening and on moonlit nights or without a moon. And tonight, here on my island terrace, 8:30 in the evening, I light my cigarette with this lighter, and as I smoke, gazing at the sunset, I hold it in the palm of my other hand and its metal cools me and I think of Alekos, Petros, Telis, the whole clan, Martha, Anna, Maria,... But this month, what gets into these swallows, always at this hour? Dozens and dozens of swallows whirling around up there, twittering madly, tracing semi-circles, broad circles and reverse circles, closing them above the ceramic-tile roof across the way on the handsome neo-classical house, and then the swallows begin their whirling movements again in the clear sky, shrieking fiendishly, more loudly than the cicadas, as though they want to raise trees, animals, people, into the air, back and forth, some going, some coming, endlessly, inscribing extremely small mobile black crosses on the blue crystal and these suspended black crosses are so contrary to their own cheerfulness and their shrill twitters, until it begins to grow dim and dark, and they all disappear without your knowing where they've gone and where they've taken roost. Another lighter was given to me by Lefteris on Aï-Stráti, when my own lighter broke. He also gave me a little bottle of kerosene and a few flints for the lighter, in a matchbox, "by way of supplies", as he said. A crude lighter, made of tin, round, strong, it was sure to light up, even with the first attempt, even in the strongest wind. Yes, strong like Lefteris. "All good things," he used to say, "are useful. This is their beauty. Their shape and material aren't so important, as long as they do their job well." And this is what Lefteris said, he with the raving mad dreams, the prolific erotic visions, the glorious schizophrenic nightmares with women and water-canteens and barbed wire and penises and soles of feet and upside-down trees and rivers with sharks and a female camel with two humps and she was being jumped by two male camels together, and the camel-driver was masturbating and a heap of camel-hairs was left on the sand, like sawdust on the tiles of a popular taverna after *kalamatianós* and *tsámiko* dances had trampled the sawdust, at the hour when the taverna closes after 4 a.m., in the middle of the night. But maybe he was actually saying this, first and foremost, for himself. From Lefteris I learned to want to make "simple and useful things", like the *Soot-stained Pot*, which I'd written in Kontopoúli, Lémnos, before I met Lefteris, there in the barbed-wire camp for political prisoners, as well as the *Diaries of Exile*; and we didn't have water, and we had to carry water in jugs from the village spring (always with a police escort), and one evening the police guards came in and broke all the glass fixtures of our oil-lamps, and the uncovered wicks started smoking, the place got thick with smoke, we blew out the wicks, several of us blowing at the same time, darkness spread, the police guards were howling and cursing, they were terribly angry because Yorghos Hatzopoulos, I, and one other man were teaching the political prisoners how to read and write, the ones who'd never gone to school: Mihalis, the rebel with the brave body and the broad chest and the constant smile; Phanis the building-worker, a handsome lad who used to sing "A Mother Waits" in a heart-breaking way; old Barba-Nionios from Cephallonia – he caught on to the reading and writing very quickly and on top of that, wrote entertaining compositions – and in the evenings we all used to sit at the long wooden table, under our tiny light-bulbs, like well-behaved diligent little students, bent over two battered school-primers; and a while later, Mihalis wrote his first card in his own hand to his betrothed: Irini, and he went wild with joy and kept waving the card and shouting: "I wrote it all by myself." And he put it on top of the table for us to see with our own eyes, so we could believe in this miracle: "Here it is." And he read it out loud to us, but also showed it to us pointing with his finger, there on the table; and Mihalis' letter wrote: "My Reenoula, o I-love yoo with omikron, o I-love yoo with omega, I-don-knoe how and hoow-mooch I-love you – yous-Mihali"; and we all reacted enthusiastically, hugging and kissing Mihalis for his progress and "fine expressions" (these were the words of Hatzopoulos, who'd been a secretary at the University of Athens – in the old days, of course – and he wore carefully-wiped eyeglasses with a gold frame – and what a thrashing he got later on, in Makrónissos, and they broke his glasses and he couldn't see to read or even to walk); indeed, Yannos the young shepherd from Roúmeli, who'd finished primary school and also wrote little verses (he'd even read some poems of Lorca – and very much liked the verses: *"The tail of the song / goes out the window at night / trailing along down below / along the star-studded seacoast"* – something like this, he knew by heart and used to recite for us, but Hatzopoulos had objections and smirked); well now, Yannos said: "Ah, oh my good Michalió, what's this thing you've created. I'm going to steal it from you. And make it my own poem," he shouted and sat down and wrote it on a big sheet of paper, with correct spelling and fine handwriting (because Yannos was also a calligraphist):

> *"Renoula dear*
> *O, I love you with omikron*
> *O, I love you with omega*
> *I don't know how and how much*
> *I love you*
>
> *Your Mihalis"*

And on Mihalis' name day, Yannos pinned this up with drawing-pins above Mihalis' mattress, and underneath it placed a nosegay of wild flowers picked from the campsite, some little yellow lilies and dry tufted weeds found in November, tied with red string and a scrap of paper pinned to it, which said: "To Michalió and Renoula, with love, Yannos and the whole camp." And when Mihalis returned from the pump with two big jugs, he felt very moved, the jugs almost fell out of his hands; he hugged Yannos: "Ah, oh my good Yannos, what a fine frank lad you are." And he lifted the jugs again, stood like this for

a moment, gaping at the piece of paper and the wild
flowers above his mattress, and after this, he went and
set the jugs down in their place as though a great weight
was gone from his heart, a weight which he wanted.
However, after several days, it was learned that the only
son of Panoussis had been killed in the Republican Army
and Panoussis doubled up on his straw mattress,
covered himself up with his goat's hair shepherd's cape,
keeping his head inside it, without a single bite of bread
in his mouth, or a single swig of water to drink, for
God's sake Panoussis, we could only see his shoulder-
blades shaking, without a single sob being heard, and he
never breathed a word. We didn't know what to do any
more. We stopped our evening lessons of reading and
writing. Mihalis cut his thunderous laughter. Panoussis
got up only to pass water, without speaking and as
though bereft of his eyes. He returned, still more bereft
of his eyes and wrapped himself up again in his cape,
although in the course of those days, a heat wave had
started, which made the very stones explode. The next
day after the bad news, Manthos the painter, plucked up
courage and asked Panoussis for his son's photograph,
which he had in the inner pocket of his duffle-coat;
Manthos said he'd make him another much bigger one.
And strangely enough, Panoussis – this was his first
movement since then – took out his son's photograph
(many times he'd shown it to us with pride) from his
huge pocket, gave it to Manthos and wrapped himself up
again. In three or four hours, noontime by now, the
drawing was ready, on a big piece of thick paper. The
spitting image of Panoussis' son, even more handsome,
with a laurel wreath on his head, and underneath, written in capital letters: THE SON OF PANOUSSIS, THE BRAVE

LAD OF GREEK ROMIOSYNI. He brought it to Panoussis and nudged him: "Here's your son, the brave lad," he said. Panoussis stuck his head out, opened his bleary eyes, gazed at the drawing of his son, opened his mouth as if he wanted to say something, but didn't utter a word, made the sign of the cross, embraced the drawing, placed it next to him on the wall, covered himself up again, maybe leaving his nose and his eyes out, in order to look at it, since he was turned towards the wall. That same evening, when we'd all lain down, Panoussis' bowl full of broad-bean-soup from the mess, was still untouched, all by itself, alone, on top of the table. In a little while, a stray cat crept in through the low window and started gobbling down the bean-soup, phlatsch-phlatsch. We thought that at long last, Panoussis' sobs had broken loose. And it was true, along with the phlatsch-phlatsch sounds of the cat, his sobs could be heard, thank God. The cat went away. Soon, in the light of the small night-lamp, we could see Panoussis get up without making any noise, sit down on the bench, and with big mouthfuls of bread eat the bean-soup left by the cat. We turned carefully on our other side, towards the wall, and started weeping. And tonight, on my cool terrace in Karlóvassi, I light another cigarette with Alekos' lighter, and I dream and remember, and what don't I remember, and a moon tiny as a fingernail is about to sink behind the tobacco-lofts, behind the date-trees of Ayía-Pelayía, behind the old breakwater. And Lefteris' lighter – done for, also broken – I keep safe in the drawer of my desk in Athens, together with a very few reminders from the old days of exile, some seashells, two or three coloured pebbles, a cigarette-case carved out of wood and a very beautiful paper-knife, also carved out of wood, a swordfish, delicately wrought, scale by scale, "simple and useful things," as Lefteris used to say – ah, what a beautiful paper-knife, gift of a fellow-prisoner, the folk-artist, old Barba-Vlassis – how many, many pages of books I've cut since then; and Lefteris is quite right about the "useful things", because he too, despite his tangled and insatiable visions, was an indefatigable hard worker and always first – in the workshop making stools and little tables for the political prisoners, in the book-bindery (we'd also made something like that) to bind some French and English grammar-books badly damaged from so many hands using them, as well as some books of political economy (mysterious how they'd reached this far), even some collections of poetry (Solomos, Sikelianos, Hikmet, Neruda); in the kitchen he was first to peel the potatoes and clean the lentils and rice, stirring the mess-hall cauldron with the big ladle; again, when the days for cleaning the camp came, he was first in the team to sweep the corners and troughs fastidiously with a big broom, collecting the cigarette-butts, boxes, dry leaves – but about Lefteris and the other comrades, we'll talk again some other time, because now, my wife Falitsa is calling me from indoors: "Come, your food will get cold; everything's ready on the table." I leave my little terrace with the flower-pots watered and the half-finished, interminable recollections. An appetizing healthy smell of roasting meat strikes my nostrils from the hallway. I go into the dining-room. An impeccable white tablecloth. On the plates, grilled meatballs – not cooked in an electric broiler, but on the old ancestral brazier, on the charcoals which Falitsa's sweet patient mouth has blown on. Tomato salad full of finely chopped onions, green peppers and plenty of pure olive-oil from our own olive-trees. Honeydew melon, cut slice after slice, already served on the plates, so that Falitsa won't have to keep going back and forth to the kitchen. Muscat-scented Samos grapes from our grapevine. Peaches from our garden. Without saying a word, we both eat. Eri hasn't come yet. The third plate has not been served yet. It's waiting. We're waiting. "My good Falitsa," I can hear inside me, "our old impassioned love has burnt out. Thirty whole years, you see. But this deep fraternal tenderness goes on growing year by year, more infinite than infinity. I wonder, will we live a few more years to enjoy our fine, calm, prudent, wise old age while we can still work hard?" For a moment, we both raise our eyes, looking at one another with love and perfect understanding, and together we smile a twin smile above the plates of grilled meatballs cooked on the ancestral brazier with charcoals blown on by her persevering lips. Outside, on the courtyard tiles, the swift step of Eri. With my elbow I nudge Falitsa's elbow. Listen, listen. We both fasten our eyes on the dining-room door. My God, how beautiful life is. How beautiful we can make it. How beautiful it can become. Welcome to our child.

Karlóvassi, August 11th, 1983

NOTES

BOOK ONE

p. 13 *Kesarianí* – working-class neighbourhood of Athens, where many refugees from Asia Minor settled after the 1922 uprooting.

p. 15 *Mazourka in the Rhythm of the Rain* is Ritsos' poem.

p. 40 *Antinoüs* – a handsome ephebe from Bithynia and a favourite of the Emperor Hadrian.

p. 40 *Aghias* – a famous athlete in the ancient Greek tradition.

p. 71 *Kanaris* – an illustrious figure in the Greek War of Independence.

p. 71 *Vouliagméni* – a suburb of Athens, on the seacoast towards Sunion.

p. 81 *Aï-Yoryis* – St. George, whose name day is celebrated on April 23rd, according to the Orthodox Greek calendar.

p. 87 *Monovásia* – Ritsos' way of writing the name of his birthplace, which is usually spelled Monemvasía.

p. 88 *Karaghiozis* – the crafty, hungry, barefoot hero of traditional Greek shadow theatre.

p. 90 *mastícha* – grown mainly on the island of Chios, it is the fragrant substance from which a sticky sweet is made, usually served on a teaspoon in a glass of cold water.

p. 108 *Agra-Oudh* – names of two provinces in what used to be British India.

BOOK TWO

p. 115 *Demetres* (Papageorghíou) – a Greek artist living in Spain. He illustrated Ritsos' *Moonlight Sonata* and the *Eighteen Short Songs of the Bitter Motherland.*

p. 116 *Kollitiri* – the mischievous son of Karaghiozis – see note on p. 88.

p. 116 *Barba-Yorghos* – another character in Greek shadow theatre, who is a kind of loud-voiced, country "bumpkin".

p. 125 These verses are from Ritsos' collection of poems, entitled *Distant* (in Greek, *To Makrinó*; the specific poem is "Re-Building".)

p. 135 *Ostrava* – an industrial city of Slovakia, referred to several times by Ritsos, in connection with the coal-miners.

p. 137 This verse is by Ritsos himself; but as in several other instances, he playfully refers to "some other poet".

p. 138 *Saint Sebastian*, a life-size oil-painting by Yannis Tsarouhis, Greece's most celebrated painter, who was also a good friend of Ritsos. The immediately following titles are also references to actual paintings made by other famous Greek artists.

p. 138 *Apartis* – a well-known Greek sculptor.

p. 141 *Rebétiko* – a kind of popular Greek music, which grew out of the downtrodden "fringe" and used to flourish in such out-of-the way places as opium dens. After World War Two, rebétiko music came into its own in more respectable milieus.

p. 143 *Zánte* – The island of Zákynthos, like the other Ionian islands, was strongly influenced by European – and particularly, Italian – finesse.

p. 146 *Póros* – a nearby island in the Argosaronic Gulf.

p. 150 *Mikrí Dápia* – like Portélo, seaside locations in Monemvasía, where people used to swim.

NOTES 357

p. 152 *tsámiko* – a traditional Greek folk dance, with extraordinary leaps in mid-air.

p. 155 *Rangavis* and *Paraschos* – 19th century Greek poets.

p. 158 *Lárissa* – a city in the plain of Thessaly.

p. 161 *zeibékiko* – a traditional Greek dance performed by one man alone.

p. 162 *Elkómenos* – an epithet referring to an icon which depicts Christ being "dragged", with his hands in shackles. This church, like all the others mentioned in this passage, is inside the old walled town of Monemvasía.

p. 166 *Saint Sophia* – the church at the very top of the rock Fortress of Monemvasía.

p. 166-167 A host of names of illustrious figures from Greek history, starting with the 6th century Byzantine emperor Justinian and ending with Licinius Andreas, a Corfiot philosopher hung by the Turks in 1715 and considered a martyr by the Greek Orthodox Church. Other figures, such as the Patriarch of Constantinople Jeremias the Second (1536-1595) also appear; but as this is the section where Ritsos "demythifies" dates, let this suffice!

p. 168 *Makrónissos* – the most infamous of the detention-islands for political prisoners with left-wing beliefs.

p. 168 *Aï-Stráti* – another island for political prisoners and frequently referred to in the *Iconostasis*.

p. 175 *Tassos* and *Miranda* (Filiakos) – two particularly close friends of the poet.

p. 176 *Kálamos* – a seaside place near Athens, where Ritsos often spent his weekends, in the home of the Filiakos couple.

p. 179 *Veliés, Aï-Demétres, Hatzálaga* – large family estates of exceptional natural beauty in the vicinity of Monemvasía. As a child, Ritsos used to spend his summers there.

p. 179 *Falitsa* – the name of Ritsos' wife.

p. 179 *Thymarákia* – the neighbourhood near the Ayios Nikólaos train station, where Ritsos lived.

p. 182 *Megáli Dápia* – another seaside area inside the old walled town of Monemvasía.

p. 182 *On the Foothills of Silence* – a 1000-page roman fleuve written in 1942, in the midst of the German Occupation. The manuscript was burned, along with Ritsos' other papers, in the course of the December events of 1944.

p. 184 *Omónia, Sýndagma, Ambelókipi* – central areas of modern Athens.

p. 184 Names of actual friends, colleagues, publishers, translators, fellow-poets, etc.

p. 188 *ELAS* – the Greek Liberation Army, established in 1941, to combat the Nazi Occupation. ELAS became the symbol of Partisan Resistance in Greece.

p. 188 *Sarafis* – the Leader of ELAS; he was killed in 1957.

p. 192 *Benissovolent* – Ritsos' puns involving Kyparissis' other names, Aristóboulos and Cacóboulos, are approximately captured by the Latin roots in Benissovolent and Malevolissent.

p. 194 *Coffee-cup* – in Greece, coffee-dregs (instead of tea-leaves) are commonly used for "reading" somebody's future.

p. 196 *Ayii Asómati* and *Psaromilíngou Street* – in the old days, an elegant neighbourhood of Athens near the Theseíon and Keramikós.

p. 197 *Papanastassíou Street* – Ritsos lived there all his adult life, until he moved next door in 1971, to a small apartment on Mihaíl Kóraka Street.

p. 197 *Acronafplía* – one of the most oppressive prisons for political prisoners, located near Nauplion.

p. 198 *Psará* – the tiny island near Chios mentioned in Dionysios Solomos' famous verse. Symbol of resistance to Turkish Rule.

NOTES

p. 198 *Karlóvassi* – the seaside town on the island of Samos, where Ritsos spent most of his summers, at his wife's family home.

p. 202 *Parthéni, Léros* – the site of another exile-island for political prisoners, during the Colonels' Junta (1967-1974). Ritsos was there between 1967 and 1968.

p. 206 *Zográphou* – an outlying district of Athens, where Ritsos lived for a short time after leaving the "Sotiría" T.B. Sanatorium, in 1930.

p. 217 *Thrakomakedónes* – place near *Mount Párnitha*, on the outskirts of Athens.

p. 217 *Ikaría* – an island near Samos, which was also used for political prisoners.

p. 217 *Neórion* – a place on the island of Póros, where Ritsos went for occasional excursions.

p. 218 *Menoússis* and *Birbílis* – two characters in a Greek folk song.

p. 220 *Moíra* in Greek means destiny.

p. 230 *Marinos Andipas* (1873-1907) – Socialist leader of the Greek peasants of Thessaly. He was assassinated during a rebellion against the landowners, near the village of Kilelér.

p. 232 Among the many names of heroes connected with Greek Resistance against oppression, from the time of Kolokotronis in the 1820's to Lambrakis in the 1960's, the following names are of freedom-fighters who met their death on behalf on their political beliefs: Deloyannis, Ploumbides, Aris Velouhiotis, Electra Apostolou. The December events mentioned in this passage led to the disarmament of ELAS – see note on p. 188.

p. 232 *The Dead House, Under the Shadow of the Mountain,* and *Chrysothemis* – long poems of Yannis Ritsos included in *Fourth Dimension.*

p. 233 *"May Day wreath ... at Marathon"* – here, Ritsos refers to the famous Peace March of 1963, which was the prologue to the assassination of the left-wing Greek M.P., Grigoris Lambrakis, late in May of 1963.

p. 235 *Mount Pendéli* – an impressive mountain-range near Athens, site of the ancient marble quarry.

p. 236 *Lousias* – hero of a novel by Nikos Houliaras, Greek writer and painter.

BOOK THREE

p. 250 *Chryssa Prokopaki* and *Nikiphoros Papandreou*, close friends of Ritsos. Prokopaki has written several essays on Ritsos and translated many of his works into French.

p. 251 Names of other close friends, as well as Ritsos' wife Falitsa and daughter, Eri.

p. 257-258 This poem is from Ritsos' *Stones, Repetitions, Grating*.

p. 260-264 These 48 fragments are verses discarded from Ritsos' *Victory Odes*.

p. 271 *Gýthion* – the seaside town about an hour away from Monemvasía, where Ritsos attended high school.

p. 272 *Spelios Mendis* – musician who set a few of Ritsos' verses to music.

p. 272 *Papadiamandis* (1851-1911) – the celebrated and saintly author from the island of Skiathos.

p. 272 *Karyotakis' "Préveza"* – characteristic poem by the Greek poet, Kostas Karyotakis (1896-1928).

p. 274-275 *Moonlight Sonata* – excerpt from perhaps the best-known of all of Ritsos' poems.

p. 278 *Gragánda* – small excerpt from Ritsos' long poem *Gragánda*.

p. 284-285	*Patíssia - Piraéus - Monastiráki, Theseíon* – on the railway-line linking Piraeus with Kifissia, stations on the way.
p. 288	*pendozáli* – a traditional Greek dance from Crete, in a very rapid tempo.
p. 290	*Vamvakaris*, Markos – probably the most well loved of the old-time bouzouki-musicians, who composed many songs of his own, including the favourite "Franghosyrianí" mentioned in this passage.
p. 294	*Patíssia* – a section of Athens, now heavily modernised, though it used to have handsome old houses and gardens and even meadows.
p. 295	*Ayía Marína* – from the context, this may refer to the hill topped by the Church of Saint Marina, near the Theseíon.
p. 296	*Grevená* – town in Western Macedonia.
p. 296	*Megálo Péfko* – a seaside area near Mégara.
p. 297	*Erophile* – a masterpiece of 17th century Cretan literature.
p. 297	The *Epitáphios* – Ritsos' long poem in rhyme and in the traditional 15-syllable metre. It was an immediate response to the bloodshed in Salonica following the general strike of the workers there in 1936. Various stanzas of the poem were set to music by Mikis Theodorakis and along with *Romiosýni*, are sung widely.
p. 297	*Túlunda* – small village very near Monemvasía.
p. 298	*Levétsova* – a town midway between Monemvasía and Sparta.
p. 299	*Hatzálaga* – see note on p. 179.
p. 301	*Persians* – Aeschylus' tragedy.
p. 302-303	The verses quoted here are from Ritsos' poem *"Peace"*, in his collection of poems, entitled *Vigil*. The single verse is from his so-called *Comradely Songs*.

p. 311 *Pontikonísi* – a tiny island near the old port of Corfu.
p. 317, This verse is from a poem by Anghelos Sikelianos.
322
p. 327- The verses quoted here are from Ritsos' *Testimonies II*.
328
p. 340 *Glyfáda* – a seaside suburb close to Athens.
p. 346 *kalamatianós* – another traditional Greek folk dance, so named from its place of origin: Kalamáta in Messenía.
p. 346 *Kontopoúli*, Lémnos – site of yet another exile-island for political prisoners.

CONTENTS

Book One: *Ariostos the Observant Recounts Moments of His Life and Sleep*   7

Book Two: *Such Strange Things*   111

Book Three: *With a Nudge of the Elbow*   239

NOTES   353

YANNIS RITSOS

Yannis Ritsos (1909-1990) was born in the old walled town of Monemvasia. He was the last child in a rich family of landowners. His birthplace was laden with historical memories, which left their indelible mark on the poet and his work. As did the memories of his own family, which was destined to financial disaster, sealed by death and insanity.

In 1925, in Athens, he became ill with tuberculosis. At intervals, up until 1940, he was under treatment in various T.B. sanatoriums, although – whenever possible – he continued to work hard for a living. His dedication to poetry and his belief in Socialist ideals (at a young age, he had joined the Greek Communist Party) fortified him and gave him courage. From 1927 on, he began publishing in magazines and in 1934, he brought out his first collection, entitled *Tractors*.

During the period after World War Two, he was imprisoned repeatedly for his political beliefs: 1948-1952, on the exile-islands of Lémnos, Makrónissos, Aï-Stráti; 1967-1968, on the islands of Yáros and Léros; and 1968-1971, under house arrest in Karlóvassi, Samos. Throughout the periods of detainment, his work was banned, though he himself went on with his creative activity, undaunted.

Until the period of his full maturity in *Fourth Dimension*, Ritsos' work ranged from intense lyricism, as in his early works – *Song of My Sister* (1937) and *Spring Symphony* (1938) – to works of epic magnitude, such as *Romiosýni* (1945-1947) and *Neighbourhoods of the World* (1949-1951).

In *Fourth Dimension*, various monologues in poetic form have been collected, including: *Orestes, Philoctetes, Chrysothemis, The Eleni*. Through myth and history, as well as through contemporary social conflicts, the poet develops his poetic meditations on human destiny. Together with numerous collections of small poems written during the same period – 1956-1975 – (e.g. *Testimonies; Stones, Repetitions, Grating; Gestures*, etc.), the *Fourth Dimension* is the distillation of his human and poetic experience. The visionary compositions collected in the volumes *Becoming* (1970-1977) and *Victory Odes* (1977-1983) complete Ritsos' poetic testimony.

A large part of Ritsos' work is still unpublished. Up to the present, 108 books of his poetry have appeared, four books of his plays and nine prose-works under the general title *Iconostasis of Anonymous Saints*. There are also 12 books of his translations of foreign poets, including Hikmet, Neruda, Ehrenburg, Mayakovsky, Yesenin. Approximately 280 foreign editions of his work have appeared, in 40 different languages.

AMY MIMS

With a B.A. in ancient Greek Literature and History from Harvard and another degree in Byzantine and Modern Greek from Oxford, Amy Mims has made her permanent home in Greece since the 1960's. She has translated two of Kazantzakis' travel books and almost 400 pages of his letters to Eleni Kazantzaki contained in her *Biography*. She has also translated various works of Ritsos and her five creative books include her prose-poem *Eleven Seastones for Yannis Ritsos*. Between 1980 and 1990 she translated approximately 20 plays by modern Greek playwrights and for the past many years has been working on the English translation of Ritsos' largely autobiographical book entitled *Iconostasis of the Anonymous Sainto* and her own autobiography covering these past four decades in Greece, entitled *The Minotaur and Me* (33 years in the neo-Greek Labyrinth).

LIST OF TITLES IN THE "MODERN GREEK WRITERS" SERIES

PETROS ABATZOGLOU *What does Mrs. Freeman want*
  Novel. Translated by Kay Cicellis

ARIS ALEXANDROU *Mission Box*
  Novel. Translated by Robert Crist

SOTIRIS DIMITRIOU *Woof, Woof, Dear Lord*
  Short Stories. Translated by Leo Marshall

MARO DOUKA *Fool's Gold*
  Novel. Translated by Roderick Beaton

EUGENIA FAKINOU *Astradeni*
  Novel. Translated by H. E. Criton

ANDREAS FRANGHIAS *The Courtyard*
  Novel. Translated by Martin McKinsey

COSTIS GIMOSOULIS *Her Night on Red*
  Novel. Translated by Philip Ramp

MARIOS HAKKAS *Kaisariani and the Elegant Toilet*
  Short Stories. Translated by Amy Mims

GIORGOS HEIMONAS *The Builders*
   Novel.   Translated by Robert Crist

YORGOS IOANNOU *Good Friday Vigil*
   Short Stories.   Translated by Peter Mackridge and Jackie Willcox

IAKOVOS KAMBANELLIS *Mauthausen*
   Chronicle.   Translated by Gail Holst-Warhaft

ALEXANDROS KOTZIAS *Jaguar*
   Novel.   Translated by H.E. Criton

MENIS KOUMANDAREAS *Koula*
   Novel.   Translated by Kay Cicellis

MARGARITA LIBERAKI *Three Summers*
   Novel.   Translated by Karen Van Dyck

GIORGOS MANIOTIS *Two Thrillers*
   Translated by Nicholas Kostis

CHRISTOFOROS MILIONIS *Kalamás and Achéron*
   Short Stories.   Translated by Marjorie Chambers

COSTOULA MITROPOULOU *The Old Curiosity Shop on Tsimiski Street*
   Novel.   Translated by Elly Petrides

KOSTAS MOURSELAS *Red Dyed Hair*
   Novel.   Translated by Fred A. Reed

ARISTOTELIS NIKOLAIDIS *Vanishing-point*
   Novel.   Translated by John Leatham

ALEXIS PANSELINOS *Betsy Lost*
   Novel.   Translated by Caroline Harbouri

SPYROS PLASKOVITIS   *The Façade Lady of Corfu*
    Novel.   Translated by Amy Mims

VANGELIS RAPTOPOULOS   *The Cicadas*
    Novel.   Translated by Fred A. Reed

YANNIS RITSOS   *Iconostasis of Anonymous Saints*
    Novel (?)   Translated by Amy Mims

ARIS SFAKIANAKIS   *The Emptiness Beyond*
    Novel.   Translated by Caroline Harbouri

DIDO SOTIRIOU   *Farewell Anatolia*
    Novel.   Translated by Fred A. Reed

STRATIS TSIRKAS   *Drifting Cities*
    A Trilogy.   Translated by Kay Cicellis

ALKI ZEI   *Achilles' fiancée*
    Novel.   Translated by Gail Holst-Warhaft